Table of Contents

I0614208

Crunchy with Ketchup

Edited by
Carol Hightshoe

WolfSinger Publications ⌇ Security, Colorado

Acknowledgements

Dragons on the Bayou © 2021 by Robert Lupton
The 5102 World Championships © 2021 by Sonia Focke
A Dwindling Supply of Goats © 2021 by Marti Aamus
Dancing With Thunder © 2021 by Dana Bell
Dragonfire © 2021 by Susan diRende
Felt in Her Bones © 2021 by Nancy Kay Clark
Thea and the Dragon © 2021 by Emma Melville
Witches in a Dragon © 2020 by Christopher Fielden
Originally Published by the *British Fantasy Society* – August 2020
In a Time of Revelation © 2021 by Kay Hanifen
Knight-Time in Adelaide © 2021 by Steven Streeter
She, Being Born in the Body of a Maid © 2021 by Taria Karillion
The Dragon's Curse © 2021 by Ted Pennella
Nukes for Breakfast © 2021 Emily Martha Sorensen
The Dragon Sword of Valenharel © 2021 by Takayuki Ino
Ophedities and the Dragon © 2019 by JF Capps
Originally Published in *Serial Magazine #8* – April 2019
Of Stolen Crowns and Fricasseed Sheep © 2021 by John Lance
Something the Cat Dragged In © 2021 by Robert Wenson
The Dragon Lord © 2021 A.K. Stuntz
The Dragon's Eye © 2021 Geoff Hart
The Seventh Trap © 2013 by Adam Knight
Originally published in *The Big Bad* – Dark Oak Press
Hoarders © 2021 by Xauri'EL Zwaan
The Bala Worm © 2008 by James Dorr
Originally published in *Black Dragon, White Dragon* – Ricasso Press
Unmasking the Dragon © 2021 by Matt Bille
Wormslayer © 2021 by DJ Tyrer
Don't Mess With Dragons © 2021 by Criag Crawford
Do Not Disturb © 2017 by Gregg Chamberlain
Originally published in SciPhi Journal – June 2017

Copyright © 2021 by WolfSinger Publications
All stories copyrighted to their individual authors

Cover Art copyright 2021 © Lee Ann Barlow

ISBN 978-1-944637-03-3
Printed and bound in the United States of America

Dragons on the Bayou

Robert Allen Lupton

"Child, what's that song you listening to."

"Grandma, it's called the Battle of New Orleans. My favorite part is when General Jackson's cannons melt and they use alligators for cannons."

"Alligators for cannons? Can you play it again, Henri?"

"Sure, Grandma. I downloaded it on to my phone and gave the song its own icon. I just press and play."

"Henri, your Grandma don't understand a word you said. Play the song."

The British finished running through the briars and brambles. Grandma Fonteneaux filled her pipe and poured chicory coffee into a mug stained brown inside from years of use. "Henri, that's a fine song, sure enough, but it ain't quite right. Your grandpa, six or seven times removed, on your momma's side, Andre Broussard, fought in that battle alongside of General Jackson, Jean Lafitte, Captain Dubuclay, General Garrique de Fllanjac, and a host of other folks who lived hereabouts. The battle took place less than ten miles from here. Just outside of Chalmette."

"Was my grandpa a general? Did he chase the British after the fight?"

"Hush, Henri. Fetch yourself a cream soda from the icebox and be quiet. I need a full pipe to get my thoughts in order before I tell you what really happened. One thing I know for certain is they wasn't no alligators involved."

Henri retrieved a cold cream soda from the refrigerator. He decided he deserved a handful of grandma's pecan cookies as a reward. Grandma could tell a fine story, but she took a long time to do it. He glanced out the kitchen window. Clouds were building over the Mississippi. It would be raining in the French Quarter in a few minutes and in his Algiers, Louisiana backyard soon after. He mumbled under his breath. "Can't play outside. Might as well listen to Grandma. Too bad there aren't alligators in the story. I like alligators."

Grandma pounded out her pipe and refilled it with Prince Albert tobacco. "I hope you brought enough cookies to share."

Henri smiled. "Of course, grandma. Three apiece."

Grandma relit her pipe. "You be quiet and listen up. I gonna tell you the real story of the Battle of New Orleans. They don't sing it right in that song and they don't tell it right in the history books. I have the story from my momma who had it from her grandma. Folks in our family passed it down since old Andre Broussard came home from the battle. I'm gonna tell it the way it was told to me."

~ * ~

General Andrew Jackson and his men camped near New Orleans on December 1, 1814. The British had been in the area for a while already. They might would have left, but their ships were blocked by American boats. Jackson was a smart man. He knew his arrival trapped the British between his army and the American Navy waiting offshore.

The British commander, General Pakenham, wasn't a fool. His forces outnumbered Jackson considerably. The British would have to fight their way out and it looked a whole lot easier to whip Jackson on land than to fight the Navy on the sea.

One of the first things Jackson did was to recruit help. Local militias came to his aid. Jean Lafitte, a notorious pirate joined him. There were lots of volunteers. Andre Broussard volunteered, and he commanded a group of men that had relocated from Arcadia up in northeast Canada. Being from Arcadia is the main reason folks call us Cajuns.

But Jackson didn't get enough volunteers and he declared martial law and ordered every able-bodied man to join him. He set up his battle line near the Rodriguez Canal. He planned where everyone was supposed to be for the fight. He put twenty cannons on the West Bank of the river and positioned the rest of his artillery carefully. He was outnumbered, but he had built an earthwork barricade to protect his men. He was ready. Andre was positioned on the end of the battle line nearest the canal. He thought Andy Jackson had a good plan.

The day before the battle, Jackson inspected his fortifications. He stopped where Andre and his men were knee deep in the muck and mire wrestling with the cannons."

He yelled at Broussard. "What the hell is going on? Why are you moving those cannons?" He pointed with his sword. "The British are that way."

Andre yelled back. "We aren't moving no cannons. The swamp's moving them. They're too heavy and they're sinking. We're trying to save at least one of them."

Jackson dismounted and helped, but the cannon stayed bogged down in the mud. "General," said Andre. "If we had a couple of weeks, we could pull these free with teams of horses, clean them up, and make them usable again, at least until we put 'em back in the swamp. They'll just sink again."

Andre pointed at the British encampment. "The English will have the same problem. They'll come, but they'll be slow. It's hard to drag cannons through a swamp."

Jackson mounted his horse and looked across the swamp through his telescope. "They may be slow, but they won't stop. We're badly outnumbered. Without artillery, we haven't a chance."

Your Grandpa Broussard said, "You just need a way to shoot cannonballs at the English, am I right?"

General Jackson took the telescope from his eye. "The fog's thick this morning. I can barely make out our cannon emplacement on the West Bank of the river. It looks like those cannons are sinking. I expect the British to attack tomorrow at dawn and we can't stop them with small arms fire."

Andre grabbed the General's boot. "Sir, I think I can bring help. I gotta get to the swamps over to Meraux."

"Man, you can't carry any artillery back here by yourself."

"Sir, the artillery in Meraux can carry itself."

"I don't understand. Explain yourself."

"General, this is one explanation that has to be seen, not told."

"If I have to see it to understand, I'm going with you. Get a horse and let's ride."

Broussard knew the swamps and bayous like the back of his hand. He guided General Jackson along a meandering path of dry land for eight miles to a cypress grove near the crossroads of Meraux, Louisiana. The Spanish moss hung almost to the ground and the early evening air smelled of rotting fish. The horses shied and whinnied in fear. Broussard and Jackson dismounted and tethered their horses to a cypress stump. Broussard called out, "Remy. Remy, it's Andre Broussard. I expect I need your help."

The cypress forest was deathly quiet for a moment. It wasn't a good silence. It was the kind of silence that makes a man want to go home and hide under his bed. A soft slithering sound like a snake crawling through wet leaves grew louder. The horses strained at their ropes. Broussard patted both horses to calm them. He took an oil lamp from a saddlebag and lit it. "Remy, don't be this way. Come out and talk to me."

A long reptilian head on a long reptilian neck extended from the forest. Soft light from the setting sun found its way through the cypress leaves and dappled the gray green skin of the creature. General Jackson pulled his pistol. "Mr. Broussard. There's smoke curing from its nostrils. Is it a demon? Have you brought me to the gates of hell?"

"Relax, General. This is just a little cypress grove where Remy and his family live. They're not demons. They're dragons. Put away your pistol. If you shoot him, it will only make him angry."

Remy, the dragon, snorted. "Broussard, mon chéri, so good to see you. I see you've brought two horses. One would have been enough. We've eaten well this week."

Broussard caught Jackson's arm before the General could aim his pistol. "Remy, these horses are for riding. They ain't for eating. This is General Andy Jackson. There's a big fight brewing down by Chalmette and we need your help. The General's cannons are too heavy to use in the swamps. They sink."

The dragon came into full view and lifted his head. Jackson said, "My God, Broussard. A dragon, a real dragon. Imagine that. How big is this thing?"

"If you measured him like a horse, Remy stands about thirty hands at the shoulder. From nose to tail. he'd go about thirty feet."

Remy spread his wings, large and leathery, and the horses shied away from the shadow. Broussard laughed. "And his wings. He's got really big wings."

Jackson put his pistol away. "I didn't know dragons could fly. No, that's not right. I didn't know dragons were real, but if they were real, I didn't know they could fly. Does he breathe fire?"

Remy pointed his head upward, opened his mouth, and fired a column of flame into the air. He circled twice like a cat, sat on the ground, and rested his head on his forearms. "I can't imagine why I care about a fight between humans. I don't see any reason to be involved. We might stop by the battlefield after the fight and have lunch."

General Jackson shook his head. "Dragons in the Louisiana swamps. Are they from here?"

"No," Broussard said. "Dragons are like Cajuns. We both kept moving until we could find someplace where folks would leave us be. Cajuns left France and we went to eastern Canada and northern Maine, but folks thereabouts didn't like us and we moved down here. Mostly, we live in the swamps and bayous. If folks can't find you, they leave you alone. Remy and his European dragons are the same. They moved to America almost three hundred years ago."

"And they can talk," Jackson said. "Why did they leave Europe?"

The dragon answered for himself. Little sparks and puffs of smoke accompanied his words. "We were smart enough to know things were changing. Humans kept inventing things. Swords, arrows, and knives were bad enough, but guns and cannon are frightening. To make things worse, men, especially knights in particular, felt obligated to hunt us down and kill us."

"Yes, I read about dragons kidnapping princesses and fair maidens," Jackson said.

"Hardly. For what purpose. Horses and cattle taste better than human women. More importantly, horses and cattle don't talk, complain, or whine. There were two years back in the fifteenth century where I never got a good night's sleep, what with all the villagers, soldiers, and knights traipsing all over the English countryside hoping to kill a dragon. That Saint George was relentless."

"Dragons live a long time if they don't get killed," Broussard interrupted. "Remy's over four hundred years old. If you don't mind, the two of you can tell each other war stories later. Here's what I have in mind. Our cannons are no good to us, but the dragons can move easily through the swamps and take the place of our artillery."

Jackson shook his head. "You want them to throw cannonballs."

"No, sir, I do not. I want them to spit cannonballs. You saw him breathe fire. The dragons will put a cannonball in their mouth, let the pressure build up, and then with a gout of fire, spit it out."

Remy moved one forearm and slid his hand through the swamp grass. He trapped a large rat with one talon. He lifted it by its tail, blasted it with a slow steady flame, and popped it into his mouth. "Medium rare. Excellent. Gentlemen, thanks, but no thanks. I can't think of a single reason why we should help humans fight each other. Best of luck. I suggest you leave before the rest of my family smells your horses. We do like horsemeat."

Jackson backed toward his horse. He never took his eyes off the dragon. He untied his horse and called to Broussard. "We should go. There isn't much time. I'll have to find another way to defeat the

British."

Remy coughed and set the swamp grass on fire. The dragon waded into the bayou and splashed water on the fire. "Excuse me. Did you say you're fighting the British? Dragons don't like the British. You know about that whole Saint George thing, right? We'll help you fight the British. Do our young ones a world of good. When's the fight?"

Jackson said, "Maybe tomorrow. Maybe the next day. I'm not sure."

Remy unfurled his wings and fanned the air. Broussard and Jackson shielded their eyes from the onslaught of leaves and twigs. "We can fly and check the British positions by air. We'll report back and tell you what they're doing. You'll know their every move."

Jackson fought to keep his expression neutral and forced himself to walk toward Remy. The General stopped less than a foot from the dragon's mouth. He brushed the dust and leaves from his face. "Remy, I mean, Mr. Dragon, sir. I'd be honored to fight alongside of you and your fellow dragons, but I want it understood, I'm in charge. I'll expect you to follow my orders."

Remy stood and towered over the men. He reached one claw toward Jackson. The talons on the clawed hand were as long as a bull's horn and colored like old ivory. "General, we always follow orders, until we don't. Ride back to your camp. Place an 'X' made from cloth on the ground outside your tent. I'll gather my folks and we'll join you before sunrise. I suggest you tell your men about us before we get there."

Jackson nodded and took Remy's claw. "Shake on it."

Remy nodded back and pumped the General's hand. "Shake on it."

~ * ~

Just after moonrise, fifty dragons skimmed above the bayous and between the cypress trees. They came out of the northwest and were invisible in the dim moonlight. They landed and Remy met Jackson and his officers at the General's command tent.

Jackson said, "Gentlemen, let me introduce Major Remy. No doubt you've noticed he's a dragon, but I've given him a battlefield commission. He's in charge of artillery and reconnaissance. His troops will overfly the British and report their positions. Major Remy, let me introduce Commodore Daniel Patterson, my second in command. The Commodore will show you where to position your artillery. He will provide men to support your dragons. The soldiers will furnish small arms fire protection and so forth."

"Certainly, mon chéri. As we flew here, I noticed the British are dividing their forces." Major Remy placed one slightly cracked and discolored talon on the map. "It appears one group will attack your gun emplacement on the West Bank of the river and another group is massing to march up the river. The British are also digging a new canal. They have thirty or forty boats ready to move up the canal and into position to fire on your lines. The boats will support the ground assault with cannon fire."

"Thank you, Major. We will expect the British for breakfast tomorrow. Remy, can you do anything about the canal?"

Remy snorted and set fire to the map. Jackson quickly snuffed it out. Remy shot three short bursts of fire into the air and a second dragon joined them. "Yes, General. This is my son, Beauregard. He'll take Andre and three more men and destroy the canal before sunrise. They'll think of something."

"Excellent. Gentlemen. I suggest Major Remy and Commodore Patterson distribute our fire breathing cannons along our battle line as soon as possible. I'd like the men and the dragons to become accustomed to each other before the battle."

"Sir, begging your pardon, but I have one question for the Major," Adjutant-General Robert Butler said. "It concerns their diet. I've never met a dragon; indeed, I must confess I never believed they existed. My men are concerned about whether or not the dragons might decide to eat us. No offense, Major Remy. They also want to know if the dragons can tell the difference between us and the British."

Remy took a long sniff of Adjutant-General Butler. "None taken. No offense, but what we eat usually smells better than you do. We never eat our comrades, well, until we do. As for telling the difference between you and the British, our eyesight and sense of smell are excellent. The British will be wearing red, shooting at us, and they smell like tea. I expect we'll figure it out."

Major Remy ordered his dragons to assume positions along the line of defensive fortifications. Commodore Patterson ensured each dragon had an adequate supply of cannonballs. At the West Bank emplacement, Sergeant Peltre, who was in command, blanched when the dragons arrived. His face lost its color and he stared wide-eyed at the four dragons assigned to his area.

"At ease, Sergeant," Patterson ordered. "The dragons are on

our side. They won't be eating you or your men. They'll be belching cannon balls at the British. I expect you to do your duty and support the beasts, same as you'd support your cannons."

Peltre stepped back. "Begging your pardon, Commodore, but does support mean we're expected to load the dragons? By that I mean, are we to put the cannonballs directly into their mouths?"

Patterson looked at the largest dragon of the four and asked, "Well, dragon. How is this doing to work?"

"I have a name. Call me Josette. We can bend over and pick up the cannonballs with our mouths, re-aim, and then spit the cannonballs out in a gout of fire, but it will be faster if the men will put the cannonballs in our mouths. That way we don't have to take our eyes off the targets."

Peltre almost cried. "My sweet Lord. Not only does they have teeths as big as my arm, but they talk too. Did the beast say that he breathes fire?"

Josette glared at the Sergeant. "My name is Josette and I'm female, thank you very much. I can talk and I can breathe fire. I dance a pretty mean fais do-do when the fiddle's hot, the accordion's fast, and the rum is sweet, but that doesn't matter right now. We're here to help you fight the British, but you have to help us help you and that means putting the cannonballs into our mouths."

"Not sure that I can do that."

The Commodore slapped his thigh. "Sergeant, time to get sure. There's no powder to blow up if the barrel's too hot when you reload. I'm told dragons don't misfire. This is safer than our regular cannons. Am I clear, Peltre? Do I need to put someone else in charge?"

"But Sir, what if the dragon decides to bite?"

Smoke curled from Josette's nostrils. "Sergeant, if I decide to bite, it won't matter where your arm is, but we're comrades. Rest assured dragons consider it poor form to eat our comrades."

Sergeant Peltre shook his head. "I'll talk to the men, but this reminds me of a story my sweet mama used to tell me about a spider and a fly."

The Commodore pulled up his shirt sleeve and held his bare forearm in front of Josette's mouth. "Madam, with your permission."

Josette nodded and opened her mouth. Patterson put his arm inside as far as he could reach. Josette gently closed her mouth around his arm. Patterson flinched, but he didn't try to remove his arm. Josette held her mouth closed for effect before she released him.

Patterson stepped away from the dragon, held his arm overhead, and turned his hand from side to side to display his uninjured fingers. "I trust this demonstration resolves your concerns. If there are no more questions, I've five other gun emplacements to visit."

Josette smiled a dragon smile. "If it isn't too much trouble, we'd appreciate it if the men would wash their hands before they start sticking them in our mouths."

Patterson laughed. "If you like, but I doubt the taste of swamp water will be much of an improvement."

~ * ~

An hour before sunrise, Beauregard, Broussard, and three other men approached the earthen dam at one end of the trench the British were digging to create a canal to use to move their boats into position to fire on the American defensive line.

"You men, help me smear more mud on Beauregard," Broussard said. "Once the sun comes up, he'll shine like a beacon in a lighthouse and give away our position."

Beauregard stoically submitted to the coating of slime and mud. "How do you want to do this?" He looked at Broussard.

"There's fifty or sixty men digging in the trench, but only four guarding the dam holding back the water. The British plan to open the dam slowly, let the trench fill, and then sail their boats into the battle. We'll take out the guards and you tear the dam apart. The rush of water will collapse the walls of the trench and it will never become a navigable canal for the British. Try to rip it apart with your claws. No fire. We don't want to warn the British."

Beauregard snorted a puff of smoke. "You really think it's going to be that simple?"

"Well, no plan survives contact with the enemy, but it's always best to have a plan."

"It's not always best to have a bad plan. I've got a different plan," the dragon said. "Stay behind me. I'll attack and kill everyone that isn't us and blast the dam into little pieces. Stay out of my way."

"The British will hear you and know that we're here."

"Don't be stupid. The British are lined up ready to do battle with us. Trust me, they already know you're here. There's heavy fog this morning. They'll never see me coming and they'll never know what hit them."

Broussard took off his hat and scratched his head. "Well, when you put it like that, I suppose you've got a point. Try to stay in the fog."

"Try to stay behind me. Fire isn't very selective and while I can hear almost as well as a bat, people in the fog all look the same to me."

"Okay, but General Jackson said to not let them see you. Kill the guards, destroy the dam, and collapse the canal."

"Right. That's what I said. Do humans always take so long to say yes or no? Never mind, don't answer me. Try to keep up."

Beauregard spread his wings for balance and streaked through the marsh. He kept himself low to the ground and flew in the cold fog through the cattails and cypress saplings like a ghost. The dragon caught the predawn breeze at the base of the dam, tilted his wings, and rode the slight updraft up the slope only inches above the surface. He lifted his feet to avoid making a sound. He crested the earthen embankment and backstroked his wings to halt his progress.

The dragon dislodged small rocks when he landed, and the stones bounced down the dam into the trench. The guards turned at the noise. On man held up a flickering lantern, but the light reflected off the thick fog. "Who goes there? Is it time to start letting water into the trench?"

Beauregard started to answer, but after a moment's thought, he didn't. It seemed pointless to start a conversation with dead men. He wondered what a British soldier would taste like, maybe chicken or alligator, but probably salted beef. He glanced quickly to the east and the fog had a grayish pink tint. He turned his head toward the men struggling to follow him up the dam. They were barely visible in the mist. He didn't bother to whisper. "Boys, you might want to cover your ears. It's time to wake everyone up."

The dragon turned toward the guards, inhaled deeply, and then lit up the gray mist. The stream of flame roasted the guards instantly. Beauregard took flight and made the first of what could only be called strafing runs at the dam, blasting huge chunks of earth and stones into the air. The branches and underbrush packed into the mud and rocks smoldered and smoked. The wood was wet, but dragon flame is hot enough to melt steel, and the organic material in the dam burst into flame.

The fog was a ground fog and Beauregard launched himself above it. The tops of several ships' masts emerged from the wisps like ghostly towers along a castle wall. The dam was hidden in the mist, but he could tell where it was by echolocation. He rotated his ears to target the dam and made another pass. He heard water eroding the fire damaged dam. First a trickle, then a stream, and finally a torrent ripped the structure apart. Beauregard flew along the trench. He roasted workmen with gouts of fire and blasted the cypress timbers shoring up the trench banks into burning rubble.

The trickle became a flood, tore the dam to pieces, and carried the debris into the trench. The flotsam and collapsing walls filled the trench.

The fog began to thin, and the dragon surveyed his work. No ships would pass this way today, maybe they never would. He circled above the remains of the dam. Broussard and his men waved at him. The dragon wiggled his wings and flew barely above their heads in a victory pass.

Beauregard targeted the British ships that were lined up waiting to enter the canal. He didn't have orders concerning the ships, but they were so close and he'd never burned a ship. There was no point in being quiet, his attack on the dam had awakened everyone in five parishes, and there was enough fog for him to be mostly invisible in the gray light of dawn. He flapped quickly to gain height, smiled to himself, dipped one wing, rolled over, and screamed down at the last ship in the row. The front ship couldn't go forward because of the collapsed dam and if he sank the last ship, then all the ships in between them would have nowhere to go.

The guns on a British ship are mounted to shoot at other ships or targets on land. They aren't positioned to shoot straight up, and Beauregard came directly from the overhead fog. Wooden ships with linen sails aren't designed to withstand dragon fire. Beauregard tilted his wings, leveled out, and held a blast long enough to sweep the ship from stem to stern. He was like a wraith flickering in and out of the low-lying clouds, weaving around a mizzen mast, rising just above the stern of the next ship in line, and burning its sails as he flew past.

He pounded toward the sky to make another pass, but in a matter of seconds, the ship exploded beneath him. *Gunpowder,* he thought. *The ships are packed with gunpowder.*

He coasted upward on the rising heat from the fire. He was going to target the third ship, but it was already on fire, and so were the next two. The explosion had flung burning timbers into the air. Most of the flaming wood had fallen harmlessly in the swamp, but pieces had fallen onto other ships and set them ablaze. A second British ship exploded.

The British are marching. I hear them moving through the swamps, the dragon thought. *Time to get back to the American fortifications before the fog clears enough for the British to see me. It's time to spit some cannonballs at the limey bastards.*

~ * ~

Beauregard joined your grandpa and the other men. They hurried back to the American lines. The British drummers pounded the advance cadence behind them. Andre peered through the mist. "There's thousands of them. They're marching like they're on parade."

"It's easy to be brave when no one is shooting at you," the dragon said. "There's a cannon emplacement just ahead. The big guns are useless, as you know, but four dragons are there. There's not room for one more. Hurry to safety. I'm going to make one more pass at the ships and then go find my father.

Beauregard made a slow circle and spotted a group of British Officers. One man was obviously in charge. *That must be the British leader,* the dragon thought. *What was his name? Packingham? Brackington? No, it was Pakenham. Doesn't matter, I'll swoop down, grab him, and have him behind the American lines before the rest of those officers know what's happened.*

Beauregard dropped to just above the swamp and skimmed above the scummy water like a dragonfly looking for tadpoles on the surface. He barely moved his wings. He tilted the front edges upward and burst through the top branches of a buttonbush grove. He grabbed General Pakenham by his shoulders, pounded the air as he fought for elevation, and sped toward the American lines.

Pakenham was terrified, but to his credit, he didn't just give up. He pulled his sword and did the best he could to attack the raptorial claws that gripped his shoulder. He was terrified and couldn't get any leverage, but he kept swinging. He hit the base of dragon's left hand middle talon three times and almost severed it at the third joint.

Beauregard didn't scream. He flew directly to General Jackson and released the British officer at the American's feet. "Compliments of my father," he said and took to the air.

Beauregard circled once and turned away from the West Bank and searched for Broussard and his men. They were busy at a cannon emplacement.

~ * ~

Jackson ordered three orderlies to restrain Pakenham. "General, order your men to surrender."

Pakenham's face turned as the blood dripping from his shoulders. "I think not. I'll not surrender to a man who consorts with devils and demons. I didn't get a good look at the fiend who captured me, but it was no doubt some minion from the depths of hell. Your deal with Satan will not help you. My men will make short work of you rebels."

Jackson considered the General's words, smiled, and responded. "This is not the work of the devil. You were captured by a rare creature, a flying bayou alligator."

"Preposterous. There's no such thing."

"Believe what you like, General. I expect the blood dripping from your shoulders may have a different opinion." Jackson nodded to an orderly. "Fetch the doctor and see Pakenham's wounds are treated. Make the General comfortable in my tent until the battle is over or until I have need of him. Keep him inside."

The British advance was controlled and relentless. Their lines were straight and unbroken. Twenty drummers or more sounded the pace in perfect rhythm. The marching British matched the drumbeats with their footsteps and the noise and vibrations shook the swamp. The water bounced in harmony to the drumbeat and cypress leaves and Spanish moss rained down on the American soldiers.

The British line faltered briefly at especially muddy spots, but was disciplined enough to quickly recover. Commodore Patterson whispered to Jackson. "For the love of God, General, give the command to fire. They'll be on us in moments."

"Hold your water and your fire, Patterson. As Bill Prescott said at the battle of Bunker Hill, 'Don't fire until you see the whites of their eyes.' We're outnumbered and outgunned. Every shot must count. Hold for my command. Without Pakenham to lead them, the British will run like rabbits soon enough."

"Dragons, General, we've got dragons."

Jackson shook his head. "Indeed we do, but I never saw dragons before last night, so I've never seen them fight. The British ran the species out of Europe, didn't they? The beasts look formidable, but they're an unknown. For all I know, they'll fly away once the shooting starts. Signal the men to be ready. See that lone cypress stump with the white shirt nailed to it? When the British reach the stump, we'll open fire."

Beauregard, his claw dripping blood, landed at the emplacement where Andre Broussard and his men were prepared to load cannonballs into dragons' mouths. "You're hurt. Let me help." Broussard ripped off his shirt and wrapped the dragon's claw.

Beauregard forced his way between two other dragons. "Time for that later. I can still spit cannonballs." He glared at the other dragons. "Aim well and remember Saint George."

The Americans passed the order to prepare to fire up and down the line. It reached Remy on the West Bank and Beauregard at the opposite end of the American fortifications at about the same time. Almost a half mile apart, Sergeant Peltre and your grandpa hefted cannonballs into air simultaneously and prepared to drop them into different dragons' mouths.

Jackson held his spyglass with one hand. His other fist clenched the bugler's shoulder. "Wait for it, man. Wait for it. Counting to ten. Take a deep breath. Five, six, seven, eight, and nine, and now."

"The bugle sounded the call to open fire. Clear crisp notes rang above the cadence of the British drummers. The American sharp-shooters aimed, shot, and fifty men dropped fifty cannonballs into the mouths of fifty dragons. The dragons burped fire and launched the cannonballs at the British before the bugler played the last note.

The effect was devastating. The dragons' aim was almost as good as the American riflemen's. The British line fell like cornstalks in a hailstorm under the first withering fusillade. The Americans used a three-row firing technique. The first row of men fired and stepped back to reload. The second line of riflemen stepped up and fired. They too dropped back, and the third line took their place. This rotation technique allowed for an almost continuous stream of fire.

The dragons and their helpers used a similar technique. A man loaded the dragon and moved away to fetch another cannonball. A second man dropped another cannonball in the dragon's mouth, while a third man waited his turn. Beauregard spit a cannonball at the British every few seconds.

On the West Bank, at the other end of the American line, Remy took a short break. "Hold, Peltre. The British line is melting faster than icicles on a warm day. They're about to break."

Sergeant Peltre wiped his face with a dirty rag. "Agreed. Let's take our time and pick our shots."

Remy pointed. "An officer on horseback."

Peltre dropped a cannonball into Remy's mouth. "Take him down."

Remy fired and took the man's head off without touching the horse. The riderless mount turned and ran. Peltre looked at the dragon questioningly. Remy said, "I got no fight with horses. Some of my best meals were horses."

Peltre indicated a second mounted officer, but before the pair could spit a cannonball at him, the British line fell apart faster than a dandelion in the wind. The mud-splattered red garbed warriors dropped their weapons, abandoned their dead and dying, and ran. They staggered through the mud and mire, ripped their clothes and their flesh on the blackberry brambles, and tripped over cypress roots in their mad rush to escape death at the hands of the American forces.

Jackson's bugler played charge and the American soldiers, militia, volunteers, and conscripted citizens erupted from the American lines and chased the invaders. Remy and Beauregard kept the dragons behind. Remy passed the word. "The British are routed, but we mustn't chase them. We can't let them expect that we exist."

Two days later, Remy met with General Jackson. Andre Broussard, your ancestor, was there. So was Jean Lafitte, the pirate, and Jackson's officers. Beauregard, who the other dragons were calling Badfoot, was with Broussard."

"Thank you," Jackson said. "This is a great victory. What's left of the British have surrendered. I've sent word to President Madison. I'm releasing the conscripted citizens and the local militia. There's the matter of what to do with the dragons and the pirates. I don't want to seem ungrateful, indeed, we couldn't have won without you, but I don't know that the country is ready for pardoned pirates. I'm sure it isn't ready for talking dragons."

Remy snuffled and smoke drifted in the clearing outside of Jackson's tent. "Don't worry about it, General. I knew it was about time for us to move on anyway. Louisiana is getting too crowded. Humans are building a church and a school near Meraux. Churches and dragons don't get along well. We seem too much like hellfire incarnate to a good deacon."

"General, it don't seem right to make the dragons leave," Commodore Patterson grumbled. "We'd of likely been killed if they hadn't helped us."

Lafitte coughed and Patterson added, "And the pirates. We needed the pirates too."

"Gentlemen, my men and I appreciate your praise, but we'll be moving on," Jean said. "Thanks are nice, but a thank you doesn't buy rum or salt pork. Kind words make thin soup. My men spent the last two days recovering British guns, swords, and knives. There's talk of a revolution brewing in Mexico. We should sell them for a nice profit. I've been a sailor, a pirate, a shopkeeper, and patriot, but now I'm going to be a pirate king. I'll set up my own kingdom on a little island southwest of here."

Remy coughed a short gout of fire and ignited a clump of Spanish moss. He quickly stomped out the flames. "Like I said, it's too crowded here. We'll accompany Captain Lafitte. His plan to start his own kingdom sounds like a good one."

Two days later the last barrel of water was loaded onto the only pirate ship still at anchor. The crew climbed aloft and unfurled the mainsail. The black sail billowed in the freshening breeze and the ship sailed south.

Andre Broussard saluted the men standing on its stern and turned to Remy and Beauregard. "Wish you weren't going with them."

"Thank you, Broussard. You and yours have been good neighbors. We'll miss you."

"You'll just miss the free food."

"Well, there's that. Thanks for doctoring my boy."

"Welcome. Sorry I had to remove his talon before I could stitch up his toe."

"Nothing else to be done. Besides, our talons are like your fingernails. It'll grow back in a hundred years or so. Looks like the pirates are almost out of sight. We'd best be on our way."

~ * ~

"Grandma, did my great grandfather Broussard go with them?"

"Of course not, honey. If he had, we'd be living in a pirate kingdom somewhere. He said he watched for three hours until the last dragon flew out of sight."

"Did the pirates and dragons set up their own country?"

"They tried, dear. It worked for a little while. Lafitte called his country, Campeche. Today, the island is called Galveston. Lafitte lived on the island for almost ten years before the Marines made him leave."

"But Grandma, that's no way to treat a hero."

"Indeed, but he was a pirate at heart and America had no place for pirates. He sailed off into the Caribbean Sea. No one knows what happened to him."

"And Remy and Beauregard?"

"The dragons? Their involvement in the Battle of New Orleans is a secret. We don't tell anyone—except family. As for the dragons, they disappeared, just like Jean Lafitte. My daddy thinks they're living somewhere in the Amazon rain forest. Remember, they don't like to be around people."

"Grandma," Henri said. "That was a nice story, but I think you made the whole thing up, leastwise the parts about dragons. There's really no such thing as dragons."

"Child, don't you be calling liar on your grandma. Fetch me that cypress wood box from the bookcase."

Henri pushed a chair close to the bookcase so he could reach the third shelf. The cypress box was gray with age. The brass hinges were tarnished, and the hasp was locked with a rusted padlock.

Grandma pulled a necklace from under her blouse and fumbled for an old-style key. She fiddled with the lock until it screeched open. She lifted a long yellow brown cylinder from the box, blew the dust from it, and polished it on her skirt. It was about a foot long and looked like a gently curved cow's horn. It was chipped in several places. "Look at this. This is Beauregard's talon. The one that was injured when he captured General Pakenham. Pakenham cut it halfway off with his sword and your great, great grandpa cut it the rest of the way off and patched up Beauregard's claw."

Henri turned the talon in his hands. It felt like a giant fingernail. It was similar to a bird's talon, but much larger. He touched the point and a bead of blood welled up on his fingertip. Over two hundred years old and it was still razor sharp. "Grandma, is it really the one from the story?"

"Yes, it is. Remember, you can't tell anyone except your children and grandchildren. Your ancestor, Broussard, promised the dragons."

"I'll never tell anyone, but I have one more question. How old do I have to be before I can go to South America?"

~ * ~ * ~

Robert Allen Lupton is retired and lives in New Mexico where he is a commercial hot air balloon pilot. Robert runs and writes every day, but not necessarily in that order. More than a hundred and seventy of his short stories have been published in several anthologies including the New York Times best seller, "Chicken Soup For the

Soul – Running For Good". His novel, "Foxborn," was published in April 2017 and the sequel, "Dragonborn," in June 2018. His first collection, "Running Into Trouble," was published in October 2017. His next collection, "Through a Wine Glass Darkly," was released in June 2019. His newest collection, "Strong Spirits," was released on June 1, 2020.

His third novel, "Dejanna of the Double Star," was published in December 2020.

His edited anthology, "Feral: It Takes a Forest to Raise a Child," was published September 1, 2020.

Robert has been an active Edgar Rice Burroughs historian, researcher, and writer since the 1970s. His contributor page includes several of his articles, stories, and over 1000 drabbles, on the ERBzine website is: https://www.erbzine.com/lupton/, and includes several of his articles and stories.

Follow Robert on Facebook and see over 1000 drabbles, his 100-word short stories based on Edgar Rice Burroughs, at https://www.facebook.com/profile.php?id=100022680383572.

The 5102 World Championships

Sonia Focke (with music by Jonathan Guss)

"Welcome back, hens, cocks and gentledragons, to the bian-nual Torching World Championships. Up now for the Singles Open Village is Razorback, two-time silver medal winner and Swedish Nationals champion, for those of you just tuning in. He's started out with two simple Incendiary Banks, taking out a large swathe of the perimeter, followed by a Swooping Billow to torch the church. Carol, what do you think of this unusual tactic?"

"You know, Bob, he's had a lot of success with this tactic in the past. If done well, it's an excellent way to gain points, as the vil-lagers are now trapped inside."

"Still, standard tactics are to flame the church first, causing people to flock together to put it out. Remember, folks, it's Open Villages this round: a river, one bridge, a church, 2,000 villagers and no walls or other fortifications."

"That's a wonderfully executed Catherine's Wheel Barrel Roll, cutting a swathe through the villagers, followed by a Swooping Billow, very nice, but his wings could have been a bit more sharply angled on the backstroke. What do you think, Bob, will that cost him points?"

"With the Danish judge maybe, but I haven't seen anyone with better execution today except for Perry on his Port Fortifications round."

"Now you see the strengths and weaknesses of his tactic. The villagers are all in one place, with only a few trying for the river. How-ever, he might be a bit tight on time. By not torching the church first, there's no guarantee the roof will collapse in time for him to get the treasure."

"He might be counting on making up the points elsewhere, Carol."

"He could pull it off, but it's quite a gamble. He'd need to beat Dreamscale and Pyrokratos on technique and get at least ninety-five percent on the villager count."

"Oh! Look at that dive!"

"He's going for the treasure! The roof beams on the church are still intact, do you think he can make it?"

"I don't know, Carol, but it's magnificent to watch. He's broken through the beams like they're matchsticks. Time is running out, folks. Let's see if he—yes! He's got the treasure!"

"Oh, but that wound on his wing looks nasty. The judges are going to take points off for that."

"Yes, they're leading him to the mud baths now. Wow, gentle-dragons, this was one hell of a performance!"

"It certainly was, Bob. The ground-dragons are out there now, counting villagers, and we're waiting for the score from the judges."

"That's right, Carol. While the judges deliberate, a word from our sponsors:"

~ * ~

An - ti - Rot, An - ti - Rot! When those scales start to itch, and you claw and scratch and scritch; when they peel and fall a-way, An-ti-Rot will make them stay! An-ti-Rot, An-ti-Rot! When your coat los-es its sheen, and you can-not scrub it clean; when that oth-er oint-ment fails, spread An - ti - Rot on those dull scales! An - ti - Rot!

~ * ~

"Hello folks and welcome back to the biannual Torching World Championships. We're on the wing to the site of the next competition, and the points are trickling in for Swedish contestant Razorback's Open Village round. First up are the prerequisites: villager count, treasure and the total destruction bonus."

"Thank you, Bob. Here are the first results:
- Villager count: nine point three
- Treasure: nine point two
- Total destruction bonus: zero."

"Only ninety-three percent on the villager count?"

"One moment, Bob, there's someone from the cleanup crew right here. Hello, gentledragon, what's your name?"

"Er, Crooktooth, ma'am."

"Well now, Crooktooth, you were just down in the village doing the count. Care to give us the rundown on the villagers?"

"Uh, sure, I guess. Um, two of 'em escaped through the river, see, and one from between the burning houses, but we also found several live 'uns in some undamaged houses."

"Thank you, Crooktooth. Perhaps you can tell us what happens with the villagers now? I'm sure our listeners want to know."

"Oh, none of it goes to waste, ma'am, you can be sure of that. There's this organization, see, for them hatchlings as got no home to speak of. They come and pick it all up."

"That's right, Crooktooth, thank you! There you have it, listeners. All the meat left over at the end of a round gets donated to Happy Hatchlings, dedicated to finding orphaned and disadvantaged hatchlings a new home."

"Disadvantaged, Carol?"

"Bob, there are little ones listening. You do know what happens to weaker hatchlings in a large clutch?"

"Oh, right you are Carol. Happy Hatchlings, folks, you can donate by calling our operators here at Sports Radio Europe. Any word from the judges?"

"Just coming in now, Bob. Remember, for this round the judges were asking for one Barrel Roll, one Dive and some form of continuous flame."

"The points are coming in:
Holy Roman Empire: nine point seven
England: nine point six
Finland: nine point two
Sweden: nine point eight
Denmark: eight point seven
France: nine point seven
Serbia: nine point eight
Castille: nine point seven
Sicily: nine point seven
Total, including the village and treasure points: nine point four"

"And there you have it, folks. This brings Razorback down to third place, with Whiptail moving up to second and Diamondscale still set to bring in the gold."

"That's right, Bob, but there's still one competition to go. My favorite: Freestyle!"

"This is Singles Freestyle for those of you just joining us now. Each competitor can choose their own fort, with a few preset criteria from the judges. What are they this year, Carol?"

"Stone curtain wall and artillery for the fort, one Snap Roll, one Reverse Eight or variation and a Sustained Flame."

"There you have it, folks, and we're just coming up on the first contestant's choice. With each fort completely different in both execution and defenses, Freestyle is tough to judge."

"That's right, Bob. Villagers are counted by percentile of the total, but there is a bonus for upwards of five hundred and another if the armed contingent exceeds fifty percent. There is also a bonus for each added difficulty—location, curtain walls…"

"Absolutely! It's a hard decision: go for an easier target and forgo the bonuses or risk a heavily defended castle. The trick is to find a fort that plays to your strengths."

"And it's certainly one of Whiptail's best disciplines."

"Maybe so, but I don't think we should discount Rumblewing yet. Freestyle is his turf; he could grab a medal yet."

"Now, this year contestants were encouraged to find forts along the Rhine to shorten travel time, but if I were you I'd make sure your eggs are covered and toasty and the hatchlings are asleep, because this could be a long night."

"That's right! So grab yourself a bowl of crunchy pigs and settle down. But don't you worry, folks, we have captured a human minnesänger and two jesters to keep you entertained through long flights between contestants."

"You do think of everything, Bob."

"But first, a word from our sponsors:"

~ * ~

When your fangs are yel-low and brit-tle; nev-er so dull have they looked! And time their sharp-ness has whit-tled, and you can on-ly eat your meat cooked:

Try Kettlefang's Kit for Fang Polishing and Care:
For that sharp, white smile that sends enemies running!

~ * ~

"All right folks, you heard it. Keep those teeth strong and white! Here for the Torching World Championships, we're coming up on our first fort in the Singles Freestyle. First up is Whiptail, one-time bronze medal winner, flying for Gwynedd and currently in second place. He's chosen a nice little hillside fort overlooking the Rhine, hasn't he, Carol?"

"It's not much for size, Bob, but location is everything. I think we can expect a lot of bonuses here."

"We're almost there, Carol, and it's a doozy. Just one curtain wall, but we're at the top of a hillside with a cliff leading straight down to the Rhine; there isn't any space for the soldiers to run."

"That's right, Bob. He is somehow going to have to lure them all into a very small courtyard if he wants to nab his villager count. This is going to require a lot of precision flying and the judicious use of flame."

"Very true, Carol. I wonder how the humans ever managed to get up there on those stubby little limbs?"

"Human locomotion is a mystery, but don't forget, they can be very clever with their hands. Whiptail will be starting from a position of—whoa, Bob, what is going on?"

"This—gentledragons, if I weren't seeing it with my own eyes, I would not believe it. There is not one, but three armies at the fort! What are the judges going to do?"

"For those of you at home, the army camped at the foot of the hill has brought three trebuchets, and on the Rhine we have four ships with—yes, their sailors all have brand-new Burleigh & Stronginthearm crossbows."

"Good eyesight, Carol. It's their newest model, too, the CB-4w4, with four-gear cranking and fast-action release. Those tear through wings like brittle leaves. The trebuchets are an older model, Festungsbrecher KA-77s, I believe. Good load capacity but slow pendulum action."

"Bob, that's—quite detailed information on human weaponry."

"Uh, I keep up to date, Carol. I'm sure our listeners want to know exactly what the contestants are up against!"

"Oh, I'm sure they want to know all about the CB-4w4's fast-action release and improved steel springs."

"It's a hobby, all right? And, er—cough—for the folks at home interested in hearing more, tune in Fridays at vespers on 142.3 FM for Bob's Artillery Hour."

"Right. Good for you. So, listeners, let's not forget artillery was a prerequisite for this Freestyle round, so let's see if we can have a look at the fort. Bob, are those *cannons*?"

"I do believe so, Carol. Five of them!"

"That's it? Certain they're not Kaiserliche Gußwerke Pfeilbüchsen with a 250m range? No?"

"Now, Carol, no need for—how did you know that?"

"As you can see, listeners, it's quite the party, and a bit much for one dragon to handle. The judges are still deliberating on whether to move on to the next contestant and let Whiptail choose another venue, or forfeit—oh, Bob, look! It's Whiptail!"

"So it is! Folks, this dragon has just decided he wasn't going to wait for the judges and swooped in on the fort. Amazing! That's a neat Backstroke and—is he clinging to that wall?"

"Yes, Bob he is. Someone just shot an arrow at him but he's flaming right into one of the arrow slits. What *is* he doing?"

"I don't know, Carol, but he's just taken off again, well executed Swoop Dive, those wings tucked in nice and tight and a lovely upsweep and, look, he's just incinerated the load of one of the trebuchets. That was an awkward twist, I don't know what the judges will —oh, he's knocked it out of alignment. What is he—"

"Hah! He cut the rope and the load just torched one of the ships. Oh, good show! But Whiptail's under heavy fire, if he gets hit on a wing, he will be down and vulnerable."

"He can't risk flying over the ships and their crossbows and there is no way he can replicate that stunt with the trebuchet. Wait, is that the Sicilian judge?"

"Yes, Bob, it is. He's come to help Whiptail. That was an impressive Double Roll Firefunnel, a little wobbly on the yaw but remember, they've never practiced it together. They've done for two of the trebuchets, but the archers have rallied around the third. They're under fire from the canons—ah, those are still only ranging shots. Oh, and here's Razorback coming into the fray, he's throwing firebombs at the archers, while the French candidate, Jean-Marie, is heading towards the canons. I—what was THAT?!"

"Whoa, that was—Carol, did you see that? The whole fort just blew! Tumbled Jean-Marie head over tail in the backdraft."

"But how—cannons! Bob, if they have cannons, they use

black powder. It's highly flammable, my sister's hatchlings use it to practice their flame—Fireheart's Potassium Nitrate Flame Training Cordial, for those of you back home. Works wonders for late flamers. Whiptail must have found out where they were storing it during his scouting run. He must have been igniting it when he poured fire through that arrow slit."

"You really think that could have done it? You won't believe this, hens and cocks and gentledragons, but a whole wall of the fort has crumpled in upon itself and the rest is not looking too good either. There seem to be a few survivors, but they're just stumbling around in confusion. Well, will you look at that! The shockwave destroyed the masts on two of the ships and threw another ship entirely on its side!"

"Yes, Bob, and look, the humans are panicking. Some of the ship people are hurling themselves into the water! Oh, not all of them can swim. They do look a bit pitiful, just flailing around like that, don't they? And the fort people are bumbling about like new hatch-lings with their wings still wet."

"You've always had a soft heart, Carol."

"I suppose. But here's Rumblewing from Hungary—and our last Championship gold medal winner—gone fishing. Those are some very impressive dives, perfect execution. Meanwhile, the Castilian judge has started picking through the rubble of the fort."

"Joined by Nigel, the English contestant, settling in with a rather sloppy landing—those were never his forte—and the Serbian judge. Dreamscale is coming in with a very neatly executed barrel roll and swooping landing. And here's the Castilian judge, where did he learn to do such smooth glide landings?"

"He used to be a Torcher himself, Bob. Won two bronze and a silver for Castille in his youth."

"Is that so? And Padraig from Ireland is picking off some sol-diers trying to get down the hill, his hover is a bit sloppy, though, cost him points in the Fortified Town round. Ah, I see someone brought a can opener. They look nicely done—medium-rare."

"Meanwhile, on the plain, the judge from France has found himself a brave little square of pikemen, joined by countryman Jean-Marie. Oh, look, knights *en brochette*! The French certainly are innova-tive with their food."

"And Razorback and the Sicilian judge seem to be exchanging addresses over a little archer roast. Is the Hungarian candidate digging a pit?"

"Indeed he is. Pit barbecue, excellent idea. Litheclaw from Aragon and Iris from Masovia have joined in the fishing. Oh, they're throwing fish in and torching the boats for a little surf n' turf. You have to choose your fish carefully to balance the flavors or the tar from the ships can become a little overwhelming."

"Well, folks, it looks like this is going to be another Undecided Championship. When was the last one, Gwynedd 5085?"

"Novgorod 5092, Bob, if you remember. One of the contestants ate the other on the podium."

"Ah, yes, the Great Mating Disaster of 5092, I remember. So, hens and cocks and gentledragons, tune in again in two years, this will be Almohads' first-time hosting."

"It will be interesting to see the differences in fortifications."

"And of course, we'll be covering the Formation Flying Scandinavian Championships in Denmark in a couple of weeks. Carol, would you care to join me at the barbecue? Grab a couple of knights?"

"Oh, Bob. I'm not really one for pressure-cooking."

"I think I saw some Templars down there. You know you love that holier-than-thou aftertaste. Or maybe a pikeman-brochette or two?"

"Oh, you. You do know how to talk to a girl."

~ * ~

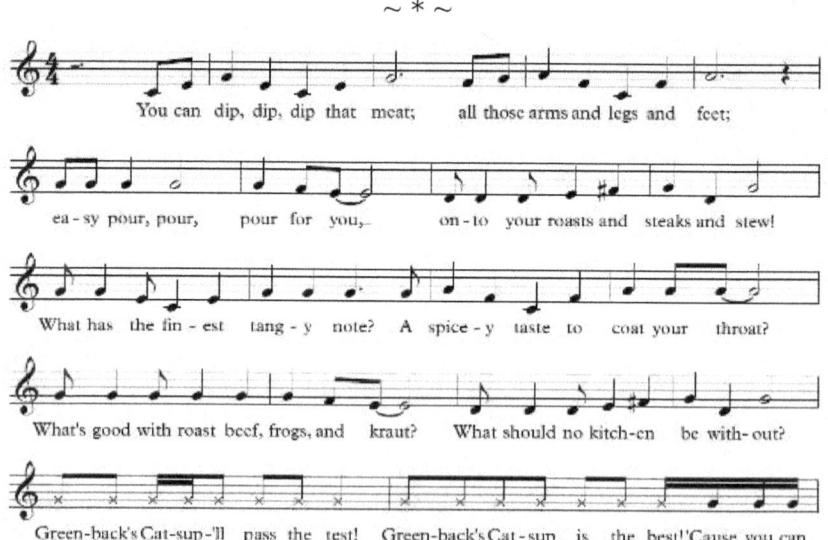

You can dip, dip, dip that meat; all those arms and legs and feet; ea-sy pour, pour, pour for you,_ on-to your roasts and steaks and stew! What has the fin-est tang-y note? A spice-y taste to coat your throat? What's good with roast beef, frogs, and kraut? What should no kitch-en be with-out? Green-back's Cat-sup-'ll pass the test! Green-back's Cat-sup is the best! 'Cause you can

dip, dip, dip that meat; all those arms and legs and feet;

ca-sy pour, pour, pour for you, on-to your roasts and steaks and stew!

Greenbacks' Catsup. In the patented Easy Pour kegs so you can savor every last drop. Everywhere spices are sold.

~ * ~ * ~

Sonia Focke (she/her) is a US-born Egyptologist and dragon enthusiast. She spent most of her childhood living in her head and has recently decided to share her imaginary friends with others.

She has previously published a sapphic Beauty & the Beast retelling (with turtles!) in the Winter Solstice issue of Eternal Haunted Summer and a Lower Decks meets Galaxy Quest sci-fi romp in The WereTraveller's *Women Destroy [Retro-] Science Fiction* issue. She has earned awards for oral storytelling.

Among her many accomplishments are building a Predynastic Egyptian horn bow, showering with a scorpion, writing a Master's thesis in German, defending a hill fort against 1 (one) very angry Viking, baking a Batmobile cake and learning the whole of The Mikado by heart.

She is currently living in Germany with a blacksmith husband and two young padawans and secretly keeps swamp dragons in her basement (and has the scars to prove it.) You can find her on Twitter and occasionally Instagram, or check out her website at www.sonia-focke.wordpress.com.

~ * ~

Jonathan Guss (he/him), who composed the music for the advertisement jingles because he loves his daughter very much, is a New York-born voice actor and singer. He has herded chickens, backpacked across Europe and worked as a singing waiter and New York cab driver. He has sung for New York City Opera and The Phantom of the Opera in Hamburg.

He is also genetically responsible for any and all puns in this story. He lives in Yonkers with his partner.

A Dwindling Supply of Goats

Marti Aamus

For a moment, the farm appeared peaceful and quiet. The sun rose high over the mountain peaks, dotted in old snow, and illuminated the arching blue of the sky.

I watch Keyse meander through the deep pastures and throw pellets out to the pigs. Sometimes, he glanced back and eyed me suspiciously, as if expecting me to swoop in and carry one of those juicy pigs away. I never dared, though. It was not part of my job description.

Besides, it was a small meal. I had larger, more delectable ones waiting just around the corner. I could sense them trembling in their glossy suits of armor. What miserable little creatures they were. I couldn't wait to devour them whole.

Keyse went into the barn, where I heard the sheep, horses, and cows bray back to him. He would be in there for a while, I knew. He often spent the early morning hours inside the barn, as that was where he got milk, wool, and spare hay. He wrapped them all up and tried to sell them at a bargain price whenever a more intelligent human slipped onto the farm for a profit trade.

I sat in a lazy heap right beside the chicken coop, my long, spiked tail curled around it protectively. It became my favored place after I burst from my egg and smelled the crisp, aggressive scent of poultry. I had been tempted to eat one, until Keyse's face appeared moments later, leaning over me with shadowed confusion and evident fear.

He looked so dainty and sad, then—almost like a malnourished beggar—it was decided I needed to stay here to protect the poor boy. As I later learned, he had just turned 23 and gained custody of the farm. I may have been young, too, but I was not so naïve to think the boy could do it all on his own.

In that moment, the boy raised his hands to the sky and called, "Why, God, why!"

To this day, I do not know what that meant. Apart from myself, there was no God in the sky. And right now, I was content to lay on the ground.

But, I suppose, Keyse had not always been the best judge of situations. Who knew what sort of horrible education humans received? Let alone simple farmer boys. This was another reason he needed me by his side. I was an excellent judge of logic and character.

I gnawed on a bone and waited in silent anticipation for the armored fools to try, once again, to invade the farm. It was a wonderful game we played together. I was eager to play it again, but I could be patient. After all, dragons live for thousands of years.

Smoke fumed from my nostrils as I continued to work the bone. Keyse wobbled out of the stables, his hands tight around a full bucket. Milk splashed over the rim as he struggled to carry it. I could have helped him, but it was more entertaining to watch. Humans were truly so weak—and fragile.

But I cared for this one all the same.

Keyse dropped the bucket down beside me with a groan. The liquid lapped at the rim, and a few stray cats and pigs came to lap up the dots of spilled milk trailing behind him.

He wiped his crinkled forehead, the effort jostled his black, graying curls. "This one's for you, Astaa," he said, his voice deep. An abbreviation on the name he'd given me, Astaa'xun. An ancient name born of my ancestors. Like all who never mastered the ancient tongue, he thought it meant "Indomitable Spirit". I didn't have the heart to tell him it actually meant "Bad Omen".

I did not mind Astaa. It was perhaps a touch too *cute* for these same ancestors, but anything was better than the name the knights had dubbed me. They called me, "Flybegone", for whatever ridiculous reason. I could certainly accept Astaa without unnecessary fan-flame.

"I figured you wouldn't want the first batch," Keyse continued and nudged the milk toward me. I swallowed the bone and graciously dipped my long, wide snout into the bucket. It tasted sweet and creamy, just as I liked it.

Yes, sell the first batch to the vile, greedy humans who came to visit—if they survive, I thought. The first batch of milk always tasted sour. Though I didn't actually mind the rotten taste, I certainly appreciated having the best.

Keyse leaned against my knuckle as I drank. He was a fully-grown man now, but even still, he seemed like just a boy to me. He was so small, I could have crushed him with a single claw, but I didn't dare. He sighed and tossed his head back.

"It's exceptionally quiet today. Don't you agree, Astaa? Perhaps we are finally free of scrutiny…" Keyse quietly considered. "Though I suppose, if anyone comes, you will take care of them for me."

I smiled inside my bucket of milk. Indeed—they were all prizes to me.

The farmer slid further down my claw, until he lay completely on his back, with only his head propped up on my knuckle. I gave it a tiny twitch. His neck cracked and he yelled, jumping up and rubbing the spot.

"I suppose that is the price I must pay for such a burden," he said, and sighed. "You know, I never asked for this, Astaa. For you. When my father gave me the farm, I was more than excited for the task. I had hoped the job would be *easy*. I imagined taking care of a farm to be simple, calm work that rewarded me with some coin, security, and comfort." He paused to give me a stern look.

I did not bother correcting him. I had indeed given him all those things and more. He could not be safer than he was with me. But I supposed he would grow to learn that in time.

"Soon after getting the farm, I hoped to find a wife, marry, and have children." His face reddened and he couldn't seem to look at me. "Now, it is too late. I am too old—nearly forty-one—and not fit to raise a family anyhow. All thanks to *you.*"

I fixed my golden eyes on him. He had said the last part scathingly, but it did not offend me. I had very thick skin. Besides, I knew he did not mean it. There was time for him still. He was not as old as he believed.

He, however, failed to see my meaning. Instead, he sighed so loud, it woke the chickens with a sudden *squawk!*

Keyse crossed his arms over his chest, where his heavy muscles rippled. Above them, angry pink ridges and scars tracked across his skin—evidence of when I'd burned him as a hatchling. It had not been my fault, then. I was learning the ways of life, and the world, just as much as him. He could have tried to kill me when I was still small and silly, but instead, he had decided to raise me.

"To this day, I do not know how you came to me from a simple chicken egg. But I do know this: you have guarded me well, and I will always be grateful to you for that."

I nudged him with the flat part of my forehead, careful to apply a minimal amount of pressure. I hoped to show him I was grateful for him, too. Keyse cast me an annoyed look, before his face broke into a small smile.

"Yes, alright. You can be sweet, too. I just wish it was simpler living with a dragon!" he said.

As if on cue, I heard the clanking metal of the approaching creatures. It was the humans, donned in their armor of "honor" and "duty".

Nonsensical notions that serve no end save for filling my belly. A fact I'm thankful for.

They marched over the rolling hills and past the work shed with an unnecessary, dignified air. Most of them trembled as they beheld me, their eyes wide and their bones clacking together. It made my mouth water.

The lead knight stopped just short of us. "You there, boy! You—you are under arrest...for...for dragging a dragon back... from Hell. We will not have demon worshippers in our kingdom!"

Keyse kept his eyes trained to the sky as he said, "I dare not believe in God anymore, nor can I then believe in demons. I am only a poor, broken man with no goals of summoning anything but peace."

I rolled my great, big eyes.

"Okay then...*Dragon!*" The knight turned to me. He did not clack or tremble as much as his comrades, though his voice certainly shook. "Fly! Be gone! And...leave this place...*now!*"

I cocked my head. The action caused half the knights to shiver and quake. The others pathetically stood their ground. The lead knight dared to pull out a scroll, written in fancy letters and dull proclamations.

"By order of the King...!"

My patience, never my greatest virtue, was gone.

In one great movement, I released my wings. The knights gasped. I stood up slowly, allowing the knights time to spring into action. They came at me with their swords out and shields raised high. Keyse tumbled out of the way as I tossed my neck back and roared. Here it was—what I had been waiting for. The game had begun.

I let the knights believe they had me, if only for a moment. One of them slapped my forearm with their sword and it tickled. I pretended it hurt by roaring and stumbling convincingly. Keyse watched from behind the chicken coop, ever the audience for my magnificent theatrics.

I waited for another knight to lunge at me with confidence before falling to my knees. I splayed my wings wide and flapped, begging to fly away...

Until a knight sliced the edge of my wing with his sword. It did not hurt, but it certainly left a wee scratch.

I opened my maw and released a fire so strong, it was like lava bursting from a volcano. Every knight caught flame. Their screams died a second later—along with their bodies. Each and every one of them burned to a crisp.

Just as well—I always liked them crisped. Quickly, I tossed their stiff bodies into my mouth and chewed. I didn't dare swallow them whole. Not when they wore those nasty exoskeletons over their skin. Metal armor did not digest well, let me tell you.

After each one was well-chewed, I stomped behind the chicken coop, where my mound of regurgitated metal, weapons, and armor lay. There were some leftover pieces of charred skin, as well as green-ish-looking bones. I did not bother hiding the evidence of murdered knights *well,* so it was certainly not *my* fault they kept convincing themselves they had a chance against me.

I dry-heaved until all the metal had come up, steaming with green acid under the sun. I sat back down and chewed pleasantly on any stray pieces of meat that had come back up, too.

Some of the other barn animals trembled and cried, still not used to my fire-breathing displays. It had been 17 years—they were sure to learn soon.

Keyse scoffed. "Do you really have to be so dramatic, Astaa? Just kill them as soon as they come! Really, you must start acting more serious. Like me."

I gave him a look fit to ignite, but he did not notice. The knight's declaration scroll had fluttered out of the way just in time. He picked it up and tore it in half.

"Anyway, thank you. I doubt the royal jail would suit me. I suppose I owe you another twelve goats?"

I attempted to grin, but instead, simply spat out a bit of extra acid attached to some charred bone.

Keyse sighed and cracked his back. "Right. I will get on that as soon as I can."

He had hardly spoken when the sounds of different footsteps rounded the corner. A group of weak-looking humans approached in dirty rags, carrying baskets. They trembled as they came closer, though they didn't strike me as wishing to harm me, or him, the way the knights had intended. I gave them a careful side-eye.

"What *now?*" Keyse groaned.

The villagers held up the baskets, which I saw contained a dozen of Keyse's best poultry eggs.

"Sir, we would like to request a refund…"

"Oh, that's right, you lot came just the other day," Keyse said, suddenly cheerful. He was often pleased when people came simply for spoils from the farm. It was the only way he made a profit, after all. But then, his face contorted as he fully registered their words. "Wait, did you say a *refund?*" Keyse quickly peered into one of the baskets. "What's wrong with them?"

"Sir, these eggs…they're just no good!"

I leaned forward and sniffed to make sure. The villagers stiffened, their eyes wide. The eggs certainly smelled fine to me. I released a puff of black smoke and nodded at Keyse. They were wrong; he was right.

I had hardly puffed my last, black ring when all seven of the villagers fell to their knees, their hands to the sky.

Keyse gave them a strange look. "The eggs look fine to me, sirs. Have you tried eating any?"

"Of course not, Lord Keyse!" one of the men practically screamed. His face appeared anguished as he stared straight at me. I cocked my head and snorted. The men practically had an aneurism. They kept mindlessly chanting, shouting, and bowing.

When did Keyse become a lord?

"And why didn't you eat the eggs, may I ask? That is half the reason they are sold."

"We wished to see them hatch into dragons, too!" a small man at the back squeaked. His comrades all shushed him at once.

Keyse gave me a cold look, though I simply flapped my wings. A dragon's form of a shrug.

The villagers began to chant: *"Mountains past and skies below, this creature is a demon to know! With powers vast, and flames so fierce. Fly! Be gone! You are a terrible foe."*

I sighed through my fangs. Would these humans ever learn? You cannot worship something if you do not know its true name. And Flybegone certainly was not *it.* Just like the knights, they did not do their research.

Keyse raised his gnarled hands high—strong and tough from overwork. "Enough chanting! The dragon will not listen to you. He hardly listens to *me.*"

I snorted, a laugh, and dark smoke rings quickly covered the villagers. They began to chant anew, bowing and screaming and coughing as they willingly inhaled the poisonous mist.

"If you continue chanting, I can't be held responsible for what happens next!"

The villagers hesitated, considering. A few of their faces held anxious, daring looks, and I was ready to accept the challenge. Fire built up inside my throat, tasting like acidic bile, or a very hot chili pepper, and I prepared to unleash my wrath once more.

But then, one of them spoke. "Perhaps we are not yet ready to die for our Demon Lord."

"Can—can we still get a refund? We don't eat eggs," another asked.

"Yet you hail me as your Demon Lord?"

"Erm, well, yes?"

"The Dark Tome wishes for us to love everyone unless they harm us first. Animals have never harmed us, so none of us eat animal products," one of the men recited, and grinned.

Keyse breathed in slowly. "Well, good for you, but I only sell animal products."

"And no dragon eggs?"

"*No!* I have no idea how this dragon came to be. I did not summon him, and I certainly did not ask for him to manifest amongst my benign chicken eggs!"

Low blow, I thought, and blew a smoke ring at him. He swatted it away with well-practiced precision.

"So…"

"So, no refunds for you," Keyse snapped. "You will have to figure out a use for the eggs yourself. Now—get off my property!"

The fanatics rose from the ground, brushed themselves off, and collected their baskets, grumbling all the while.

"As our Lord, you must set things right…" one of the more vocal devotees said.

"I'm no more a lord than this creature is a marsh hare!" an exasperated Keyse said.

"Do you think the *dragon* is for sale?" the leader of the group asked.

"Doubt it. I certainly wouldn't part with it. We will have to try sitting the eggs under a snake again, my lads…" replied another.

~ * ~

Just before they disappeared beyond the grassy hill, I decided to give them a show. I stepped forward, spread my wings, and leaped.

Air caught the thin skin underneath and cushioned me toward the sky. My long tail dragged on the ground, and I flapped my wings harder, higher. I soared up toward the mountain peaks and the fluffy, white clouds before making a dive right for the fanatics.

One of them noticed my shadow. He glanced around, confused, before glancing up and pointing. They jumped and screamed, ecstatic. Humans…. They were all such fools.

Inwardly grinning, I dipped my wings toward my body and spun. My huge body spiraled right for them and not a single one of them dared to move. At the last second, I spread my left wing and flipped to the side, skirting the ground and just barely missing these idiots. My tail drove into the grass and knocked a few of the fanatics off their feet. Just before flying away, I opened my jaws.

An inferno sprang from my mouth, as alive as my beating heart. The fire roasted the villagers alive in a number of seconds. It did not even give them time to feel the pain.

A shame, really. I would have enjoyed *that* sorry show. The foolish humans, flailing about and dancing to the rhythm of an eager flame.

Once they were all fried to a crisp, I picked up my tail and changed direction. The wind carried me a few kilometers, until I had enough momentum to flip onto my other side. I flew back at the speed of sound and scooped all their burnt bodies into my maw. The wind carried me down to the ground, where I settled onto my claws and chewed contentedly. I ate them all in one bite.

Once I had my fill, I stomped back to Keyse. He watched with his mouth hanging open. I curled once more beside the chicken coop and rested my head on my scaled arms. They were rough and crimson in color.

I failed to notice the force of my wing's wind had knocked the barn door open. Most of the animals had fled in a blind terror. The poor, tasty things were in a maddened state. Probably dreading the day they'd end up as the latest occupants in my stomach.

Keyse's expression did not change as he slowly turned to me, his mouth somehow hanging open wider.

I gave him a look as if to say: "You're welcome."

Perhaps foolishly so myself, I assumed their warlord would not give us any trouble. Now that I had desecrated the worshipers' bodies, perhaps this *warlord* would think better about coming to kiss my claws. Though I suppose it was flattering, to an extent.

Keyse finally seemed to regain himself. With a long, deep sigh, he dragged his hand down his face. "Might as well change my occupation to cleaner as that's all I ever do these days on this *farm*."

Indeed. Angry, black charred markings had imprinted themselves along the grass and areas of the shed where I had scorched my latest victims.

Keyse gave me a sharp look. "Stay here. I will be back shortly."

I raised my head slightly, as if asking where he intended to go.

Without looking back at me, Keyse called, "I'm going to get you those damn goats!"

~ * ~

As I waited for the farmer to return with my meal, I listened to the wind. It soothed my soul the way it swayed through the trees and brushed over the long grasses. For a second, I thought I heard something familiar, calling me home...

Rumors claimed the mountains beyond echoed with age-old dragon calls. I had never believed them. In all my short life, I had never heard them myself. Though I had often wondered about my real home. The one I left, if only by accident. Keyse, of course, often agonized over it, as he wanted nothing more than for me to return to my true family, wherever they may be, and leave the farm in peace.

Soon, Keyse's form crept over the hills in an elongated shadow. Behind him trailed fourteen goats, all walking single-file. It was almost adorable, the foolish way they followed him. For a second, I felt a spasm of guilt rake my heart. But then, I smelled their sweet, innocent flesh, and it was gone in a flash.

"I cannot imagine how you are still hungry. Make them last, they cost a hefty bargain," Keyse grumbled. "Three gallons of milk, two bundles of wool, and five dozen eggs for these brutes."

He crept up the hill with the goats, his stance bowlegged and low. My human scowled when he saw me. "You best be grateful..."

I hardly gave him time to move before I pounced on the line of goats. They certainly did not have time to tremble, back away, or react. I did not bother with burning them. This time, I yearned for their raw taste.

Keyse winced as I chomped loudly, their bones crunching and their light screams sounding every odd chew.

My human shook his head. "All that work. The milk, the wool, the eggs. Gone, in a matter of seconds. There're not enough goats in the world for you and us."

By us, I assumed he meant other humans. Why would I care about their plight? Besides, there were lots of other delicious animals. They'd make do.

I swallowed and displayed my long-fanged smile. Keyse scoffed and waved a hand. "Make yourself busy, won't you, Astaa? I've still got to clean up here and I doubt any newcomers will be arriving soon."

Keyse sometimes requested this of me. I saw it as an opportunity to patrol the outer edges of the farm. This way, I could check for myself if anyone came or not and smite them where they stood—before they had a chance to escape. After all, I did not believe my human's judgement. It was tainted by human perceptions, which were frankly, quite bad.

Without another word, Keyse turned away. I watched him hobble about the farm—tossing water pails to the shed, sweeping out the barn, and running after the loose animals—before I spread my wings.

I pushed into the air and swept over the farm. My tail practically tore off the barn's roof, but I raised it just in time. I swooped over the shed, where Keyse's form huddled, and swept past the vegetable fields and fruit trees. The season sweltered hot and dry, so not many things grew. Keyse intended to plant some root vegetables soon, I knew, but as it was nothing I could help him with, it did not concern me.

The great, big blue rose closer as the ground below disappeared completely. I soared through the clouds—feeling free, content. It was wonderful being master of the sky. As I flew, the wind brushed against my rough, scaled face and I sensed something new. It called to me in ways that felt familiar. *Astaa'xun...*

The wind spoke my full name—the name of my ancestors. I had no choice but to follow it.

It swept me around the mountain peaks and to the other side, where I had never gone before. Keyse had certainly never shown any interest in the peaks to the West. And as his guardian, I did not bother straying far from the farm.

But today, something was different.

The wind continued to sing my name. *Astaa'xun...Astaa'xun...*

On the other side, there was a cliff that dropped down into a roaring river. I flew under the waterfall, careful not to get my wings wet, and slapped at the rainbow with my spiked tail. It was beautiful over here! The grass was certainly greener, while the air smelled crisp and clean. I would try and suggest to Keyse, in my best words, that he should move his animals over to this side.

Would it be so bad for them to perch the barn on top of a gorgeous cliff? It would still draw cultists and knights, but it would take them longer to find us. Then, I could swipe them off the cliff with a single flick of my tail. I could burn them as they fell. It would be like a sparkling fire-show. Yes, that all sounded wonderful to me.

The more I fantasized about this new place, the more I felt it was right. I needed to be here, so Keyse surely would understand and follow me here, too. Perhaps I could spell out my desires in fire-speak. Surely he could read burning grass just as easily as any other writing. Though with that human education…who knew.

Either way, I knew he was sure to obey me. I flew out of the waterfall on a curling arch and somersaulted backwards through the air. I knew it looked graceful and elegant and longed for a tribe of foolish humans to see.

But then, I heard—*smelled*—someone else. They were not humans at all. They were my kind.

On the other side of the steep cliff hung a thick cloud of smoke. Inside, I heard the lively roars and grumbles of hatchlings—children—whining to their mothers. I heard the airy flap of great, powerful wings and the bubbling up of acidic, fiery breath. I smelled the latter most of all, which is what initially alerted me.

The shock of the discovery practically caused me to tumble right into the rippling river below. Should I reveal myself to them?

Why not—I am Astaa'xun! And as the wind had called me to them, perhaps it was my destiny to reveal my glory to them.

As I beat my mighty wings, I felt suddenly gargantuan in comparison. This was, of course, a usual phenomenon for me. But this time, I had expected to feel *equal*—almost normal.

One of the hatchlings cowered away from me. "It is an aggressor!" he said, in the ancient tongue.

"No," one of the older males said. His golden eyes were sad. "He is merely the dragon we lost."

Lost? I wondered. I may have stumbled into their nest, but I most certainly was not *lost*.

That was when I truly noticed the look of them. They were all red scaled, like me, with specks of green, silver, and blue. Gold flecked their eyes and I wondered if, perhaps, these *were* my ancestors.

No. That couldn't be right. They had cowered from me. They were *afraid*.

"I was just passing by. How long have you nested here?"

"For decades, though we are afraid to move now that the humans have infiltrated most of the lands," the same male said.

I cocked my head. "Afraid? But the humans are nothing. They are simply sacks of meat and bone! I recommend roasting them just before eating, as it will make them warm and crispy."

"We have no intention of *eating* them," the female said, scathingly. "What if they come for us afterward to hunt us in revenge?"

"Hunt? They cannot *hunt* you. They are powerless! Trust me, they have tried to take me many times to no avail."

I assessed these dragons with a new eye. They were not my ancestors. Even if my egg had come from their nest, my blood ran stronger than theirs. It must come from another source.

The male inclined his head. "When we first migrated, we tried to only fly in the middle of the night, to avoid other creatures and humans."

Cowards, I thought again, and almost did not listen to the rest.

"One night, we landed in the middle of a human farm. We knocked over a chicken coop, scattering their eggs and some of our own. In our haste to collect them all, we accidentally scooped up some of their chicken eggs. The acid in our mouths caused a strange...*fusion* to happen to one of them. The others we must have just carried home by mistake. It seems you are the product of that fusion. The poultry egg with a dragon in it. The lost one..."

Relief washed through me. So I was not a direct ancestor of theirs, but a product of my own and still related to dragonkind. Good. These dragons were craven fools. "And my name? Did you give that to me, too?"

"I believe the wind and the sky gave it to you, though we certainly heard it, too, and whispered it against your shell before taking off. It is indeed born from the blood of the first dragons; a name that evokes strength and terror."

"In case you were wondering, we left you because we did not know what to do with you. We were afraid of what you would become...," one of the female dragons added.

"Well, I was not wondering," I said, and opened my wings. "Thank you for this lesson. I suppose now I understand why the wind directed you to me. Travel well, cowardly ones. Try not to fall into another farm."

After enjoying their shocked looks, I took to the sky once more. The force of my retreat nearly knocked their precious rooster right off the cliff. I was not angry so much as I was surprised—what dragon would cower in fear rather than rule the skies with impunity?

But I did not let it bother me. Now, I truly knew where I belonged.

As soon as I landed back on the farm—*my* farm—Keyse greeted me with his usual grumble. He had made great work of the place while I was gone; it looked practically new again.

"Just promise me you will not immediately make a mess of things," he said.

I trudged right past him toward my pile of regurgitated metal, weapons, and bone. Without looking at him, I spit flames onto the heap, melting it down into a malleable, silvery liquid. As carefully as I could, I crafted it into a makeshift sculpture, using my tail for extra support.

When it was done, Keyse stood to examine it with his hands on his old hips. "Why, it looks like me! Sort of…"

In truth, the metal already sagged in the afternoon sun, too supple to stay put. But it looked good enough all the same. The metal pile now resembled a melting version of Keyse holding two milk pails. He walked up to me and patted my scales.

"You're an ill-tempered, violent serpent. But, you are also *my* dragon. I will try to remember that Astaa, thank you," he said with a smile.

And you will always be my human, I thought, as he went about tending to the farm we called home.

~ * ~ * ~

Marti Aamus is a Saudi author of Somali ancestry. Growing up, his parents fostered in him a passion for reading that saw him spend most of his time in the community library where he yearned to explore distant worlds and encounter different cultures.

He has since passed on this passion to his own children from bedtime stories to picture books and middle-grade fare. A lover of football (known infuriatingly as soccer in some places) travel and cooking, he believes these pursuits inform a great deal about the world's distinct cultures and further enrich the learning experience.

Although he holds a Bachelor's degree in Marketing, he's worked exclusively in the Oil & Gas Industry for all of his professional life, something which continues to perplex his co-workers and fellow alumni alike.

Dancing with Thunder

Dana Bell

And humans think us lucky, the serpentine dragon scoffed as she sailed through the heavy gray clouds. Around her lightening flashed, leaving a strong scent, followed by crashing thunder, and frozen pellets fell. No doubt they'd destroy precious crops and shatter fragile roofs.

Such damage should concern her, and not doubt her mother was even now, scurrying about their hut, closing the shutters, and putting down pots and pans to catch the dripping water. Then she'd wrap inside her tattered cloak and sit by the fire warming her thin body.

How much better to be in her dragon form, free to indulge in the winds, diving up or down, above the annoying frozen rain. She felt free!

She whirled delighted how her green and red markings twirled, her scales glittering in the fading light.

Too bad she couldn't stay like this forever. Her mother had often warned her since she'd been a little girl not to stay too long in her splendid form. Some imagined danger of not ever being able to become human again. She knew her mother's words not to be true because she'd stayed out one night playing among the stars and had returned to her frail body at the sun's first light.

The experience had convinced her she should be a dragon all the time.

Flashes zipped around her, like the fireworks the Elder indulged in at the beginning of each New Year. The people crowded the streets of their small village and others snaked through wearing a dragon skin, writhing along, as if they had the right to be such a mighty beast.

She found their arrogance and representation insulting.

Her amazing form came decorated with feathery appendages along her spine and around her almost feline face. Her large golden eyes saw far more than her human form and her sharp teeth sat in perfect rows inside her huge mouth.

While her human arms proved useful for the doing the many chores her mother gave her, she had none and relished having only to turn to go where she wished.

Xia her mother called in her mind. *Enough dragon time. Time to come home.*

No! She never had enough dragon time. If she were a bad daughter she would refuse, yet she could not disobey her mother.

Through the clouds she plummeted, controlling her descent, slowing as the ground approached. At the last possible moment she shifted, rolling across the soft grass and onto her feet. Her clothes still lay on the boulder where she'd left them. Dressing, she smoothed the fabric of the pants and tunic her mother Hu had made for her.

Slipping her sandals upon her feet, she strolled down the winding path to their hut, the hail stopped. Instead a steady rain fell soaking her long black hair and her clothes. Entering their home, she removed her sandals by the door. Her mother had left a towel. Xia dried herself, placing her wet clothes on the line near the fire, before shrugging into her robe.

Her mother had tea ready and gave Xia a warm smile. "You must always be careful," she warned as she always did.

"No one sees me above the clouds."

"That is not what I meant."

She was tempted to roll her almond shaped and colored eyes. Many westerners did so, and she'd had to ask what it meant. "I like being a dragon." Her mother handed her a cup of steaming tea.

"There is a price." Her mother sipped from her cup, before rising to fetch their dinner she had cooking in a pot hanging over the fireplace.

"What are we having?" Xia asked.

"Congee." Her mother's slight frame handled the heavy pot with ease, her gray hair wrapped around her head. She wore pants and a bright top.

"My favorite." Normally the rice contained vegetables and other treats. That her mother would taken the time to prepare this special dish, meant something. She would have to wait and see what surprise awaited.

"I know." Her mother carefully prepared the dish, adding vegetables, spiced beans and meat with a sprig of mint. She offered the dish to her daughter who took it, before preparing another dish for herself.

Her stomach growled in anticipation. Another curse of being a dragon. The chi needed to shift back and forth drained her life force, causing her to age more quickly than a normal human, just as her mother had.

They ate in silence, as they often did, enjoying their meal.

When they finished, her mother did not hurry to wash their dishes. Instead, she sat staring into the fire. Xia knew her mother had an announcement of importance and could only patiently wait.

"Daughter." Her mother sighed as if what she said weighed heavily upon her. "It is time for you to wed."

Xia had sensed her mother had been planning this since the New Year. She'd taken long trips to other villages and farms, on the excuse she wanted to trade.

"You have found me a husband."

"I found you a *suitable* husband."

Considering her mother's words, Xia had hoped to have a few more years of freedom. She'd only turned twenty and normally dragons mated at twenty-five. Why had her mother hurried?

"I considered it best," her mother said as if she'd read her daughter's mind.

"The dragon's curse."

Sadly, Hu nodded.

Not happy, but knowing the matter was settled, she inclined her head. "Is this truly what you think best?" she asked formally.

"It is." Hu gathered up their dishes.

"What's his name?" Xia watched as her mother washed the dishes, taking each and gently putting them in the cupboard when she finished.

"Lei Hong."

Lei meant thunder. A strong name for a man who had the courage to wed a dragon. Vast and yet great. Yes. Quite suitable.

Her mother's smile touched her thin lips. "He is honored to join the House of the Dragon."

Xia doubted he understood what that truly meant. No matter. He'd find out. "When will he come?"

"The next full moon." Hu opened the door and dumped the water upon the soaked ground. The liquid ran in trickles way from their house. When she returned, she looked shrewdly at her daughter, enough to make Xia uneasy. "You will make ready."

Only fourteen short days before her intended arrived. She hoped her mother knew what she was doing. "I'll need a dress."

"I have already completed it."

Bowing to her mother, as was proper, she said, "Thank you."

"You are a good daughter." Her mother hugged her. "I have negotiated the agreements well. We are ready."

With a yawn, Xia gathered their sleeping mats and spread them upon the dirt floor. Her mother had done what she could. She could only be grateful.

Until the ceremony, she would enjoy her dragon form daily and the freedom of the sky, wind and clouds.

~ * ~

Fourteen days passed quickly. Food to feed their wedding guests had been carefully planned and gathered by her mother. A woman from the village helped prepare the spicy and fragrant dishes, before scuttling away, her scent of fear, reflected in her eyes, was unmistakable.

The day before they'd swept clean the guest area above and spread sweet smelling flowers and grasses for them to sleep upon. Xia loved the combined smells.

On the appointed day, her mother helped her into her colorful red and green robes while she carefully braided Xia's hair for her wedding. She waited in the tiny room her parents had briefly shared, as the Hongs arrived.

She could hear their joy and laughter. Their son had been chosen to marry into the House of the Dragon. There could be no greater honor!

Xia smiled, her anticipation growing.

When presented to her future husband, she noted his handsome features with pride. His dark hair had been cut at his shoulders and his eyes were sand colored. "You are Xia." Daringly he looked over her figure and face.

"You are Lei," she returned, looking demurely downward, all the while the banked fire inside her began to burn. Her dragon would enjoy him.

An elder from the village preformed the ceremony and politely refused the invitation to stay for dinner.

The Hong family feasted well and more than once she saw her mother lick her lips. When full, their guests retired above to sleep off their well prepared and tasty meal.

Xia and Lei retreated to the small bedroom. A mat with sweet flowers awaited them.

Outside a bellow sounded shaking the hut.

"What was that?" Lei demanded, backing away from her in fear.

"Did your father not explain?" Xia smiled; her golden eyes glowing. "There is a bride price."

His eyes widened.

"My mother will claim it."

His face paled. "No. She can't."

"She can."

Xia placed her small hand upon his now bare chest. How easy it had been to remove his top. She could feel his heart thudding like thunder. "You are well named."

Realization and fear grew in his eyes and his heart beat even harder. "No," he moaned.

"You will service me well this night."

She silenced his protests with a kiss and kept him awake the entire pleasurable night.

At dawn, he fell into an exhausted slumber. Her fingers tumbled through his hair. Too bad she couldn't keep him, but the dragon roared and she dared not deny that part of her.

"Come," she urged him, forcing him to his feet and not bothering to clothe him.

Outside he shivered in the damp coolness. "My family," he pleaded.

Her smile held no humor. "My mother ate well."

Lifting her arms, she felt the freedom of the wind and her body blurred, ready to dance with the wind.

Lei dropped to his knees and his action made her angry. After all, he'd wanted to join with a Dragon's house.

"Please," he begged.

Despite his behavior, the young she now carried would be well nourished. Opening her mouth, she swallowed him, his body tasting of pleasure, strength and a sweetness she found satisfying.

With joy she accepted the dragon's curse as she danced above the clouds delighting in the lightning and thunder.

~ * ~ * ~

Owned by a demanding cat named Taj, **Dana Bell** used her present and past felines in various tales. She is notorious for mixing genres and tying her various universes together, including her Winter trilogy, Five Systems and Borders Universe and vampire cats. Many of the latter are in *Bast's Chosen Ones & other cat adventures.* Her books include *Winter Awakening* and *God's Gift.* Hobbies include various crafts, doll-houses, and flower arrangements along with collecting dragons, action figures and dolls. Her favorite place to travel is Yellowstone National Park, both oceans and anywhere she can see animals. As an editor she has edited seven anthologies, *Love 'em, Shoot 'em* and *Extinct?* being the most recent. She co-edited another, *Cat Tales-War Zone,* which had a story win an award from the Cat Writers of American. Many of her poems have been published in literary circles or science fiction magazines.

Recently under the pen name Belle Blukat she has begun writing Paranormal Romance with her first novel due out in Fall 2021 plus various short stories and novellas on Amazon. 2021 marks her 10th anniversary as a published author.

Dragonfire

Susan diRende

I don't believe the myth that once upon a time humans were the masters of dragons. That we built the cities and created a great civilization of science and technology. Not only is there no evidence of such a culture, but humans are so fragile and weak, even if we had built our own civilization, it would hardly have been more than a collection of huts. As for the notion of taming the great dragons, anybody who has ever seen a dragon knows what an impossibility that is.

Nevertheless, in their beds at night, people still tell such stories. My parents are the worst offenders. They are freetraders, which means they have permission to travel from town to town, buying and selling goods among human settlements. The workmanship is nothing compared with the products of the dragon-cultivated cities where artisans work under the tutelage of dragon master crafters. Still, people need cloth and pots that they can't make on their own.

Most towns have one local specialty product and trade for everything else they need. It's much more efficient than to try and supply every need themselves. If your town loses its only cooper, you suddenly have no barrels. And because every adult has to be ready to do their servitude season when called, real shortages could arise. So freetraders wander among towns, shifting goods in barter.

Freetraders can usually read and do calculations, which is hugely rare outside the cities. Human schools in the cities are controlled by dragon patronage. All their young charges go to school all day for free for six whole years. That's it. Just school, where they teach not only reading but calculation, dragon social codes, and music for the dragons who write it but cannot perform it on their own.

My parents have a dream they never tell other people about. They dream of finding artifacts from the imaginary human civilization that the dragons failed to destroy. Yes, they actually think dragons have been hiding the evidence for some reason nobody can explain. I love my parents, but that's just crazy for so many reasons.

So we wander off the beaten paths and they put together maps of the land and the vegetation. A couple of times they've been excited, like they thought we going to find some lost city of Atlanta or the Underground Railroad they claim humans built in tunnels and used to travel around the world faster than a dragon can fly. There's no such thing as flying machines or really any machine that can do half of what a dragon can do anyway, so why bother.

The dragons have outlawed unsupervised technology because people kept trying to fly and falling to their deaths. Or they'd try to throw flame and burn themselves and their whole town sometimes. Humans are stupid, let's face it. There's no conspiracy. There's just the adults keeping us children safe the same as any parent who says, "no, you can't jump off the roof."

Still, there's no harm in my parents' looking for imaginary cities of wonder. They're just living a fantasy, and though I think it's a pretty pathetic one, it isn't dangerous and doesn't hurt anybody.

Right now we're following a game trail. My mother sits high, looking around in the half-focused way she does when she's letting her imagination scan the surrounding landscape for oddities. I'm pushing the barrow cart that is usually hitched on the back of the wagon but on narrow trails like these it needs to be wheeled by hand. My dad is walking ahead, daydreaming probably.

My mother calls, "Look over to the right there. What do you see?"

I look and see an open flat area, nothing different from any other break that sometimes happens in the woods. I slap one of the bugs biting my arm and say, "It's a meadow."

My dad cocks his head to the left. Here we go. "Perfectly round. Small enough the nearby trees hide it from overhead view. Nothing growing. No grass. No flowers. Interesting."

"Interesting" means we'll be staying here for a day, eating cold meals so no fire gives away our location to the watchers in the sky.

"Shall I lead the horse over there?"

"Let's not. We don't know why there's nothing growing. Could be poison."

Now there's an ugly possibility I hadn't thought of, and I'm usually the pessimist of the family. "How about back there," I suggest. "That fallen tree has cleared some space plus gives us a log to sit on."

We maneuver the caravan around and soon have trampled enough undergrowth to give us a reasonable area to unload my parents' tools and maps. I set out a cold lunch while my mother does some sketches, and my father goes to take a closer look at the mystery meadow.

He comes back just as the sandwiches are ready and says, "It is very strange. The undergrowth is thick right up to the edge of the circle. And then nothing. Not a stray vine or thistle stalk. I'm thinking we shouldn't go out there at all."

My mother's eyes look past him at the clearing. I know it's hard for her when she nods agreement. I don't want to listen to them spinning ideas.

"I'm going to make a wide circle around the perimeter. This area looks like it might have some woundbind."

"Carry a staff in case you come across any predators."

"Right, wouldn't want to get eaten by a bear," I say sarcastically; bears being another myth right up there with human-built cities.

My father puts on a sour face, but my mother just says, "Don't stray so far you lose your orientation. And make a mark every now and then even so."

I nod and take the opportunity to escape. I break a branch off the fallen tree for a walking stick and duck into the underbrush.

Pretty soon I'm surrounded by the solitary quiet of the woods. There are sounds, soft and sighing, punctuated by the occasional call from a bird or chitter from a squirrel. It's funny that here, where you can't see very far and the sky is closed off, the world seems so big and full of wonders. My mind fills with questions no one knows the answers to. Questions about why leaves are green, why only some change color and drop in winter. How the birds fly and why they sing. Why the sun moves and doesn't just turn off at night.

I see a patch of woundbind off to my right. It will take me out of sight of the clearing, so I mark a tree like an obedient child and walk over to it. Sitting on the ground, I carefully work around the roots. If I can get the plant to survive in a pot, it will be worth a great deal in trade.

I'm totally focused and don't notice the time passing. At some point, however, I hear something crashing through the woods coming toward me. I'm tucked under the base of a large manka bush and I'm covered in dirt so I probably won't be seen if I don't move too much or too quickly.

I glance around and what I see gives me a thrill even as I am frightened more than I have ever been before. A dragon carrying a woman and child has landed not far from where I'm hidden.

The humans are dumped off the dragon's back. The woman

lands on her feet though a little awkwardly. The child, a girl even younger than me, falls down and cries. The woman picks her up, cradling her head against her shoulder, trying to quiet her. I am silently hoping it works because dragons don't like the sound of crying and could just lash out.

The dragon ignores them, though, and walks over to a pile of rocks. Judging by its crest, it is an older male. With his claws, he removes three enormous stones. I can't see what was underneath, but he gestures to the human woman. "Put the child down and bring the food. Now."

The woman complies but the child clings to her. She ignores the arms around her legs as if it is nothing to notice. She opens the carryall on the dragon's shoulders and unloads a heavy basket.

"Take the key."

The dragon hands her a chain with a small rectangular thing hanging from it. She goes over near the rocks, bends down and does something with the key. Suddenly, a big round tube of earth lifts up with a loud hiss of air. The tube is smooth like metal, not stone or wood or earth. There are some grinding noises and it stops when it's a head and a half high. Then a door slides open and a man walks out. He looks tired and haggard and absolutely petrified. Both the woman and the child hug him and he hugs them back, burying his head in the woman's shoulder much as the little girl had done a moment ago. Something is wrong and I am frightened for the family.

The dragon speaks. "Well, shaper? Has the egg hatched successfully?"

The man does not move. The woman sags against him as she realizes he cannot answer.

"Shaper! It is a simple question. Even a human should be able to answer. Yes or no?"

"This happens with eggs. You know as well as I do that only ten percent ever survive to hatch. This one did not. It was developing well and then it was gone. I did everything…"

"You did nothing. You didn't try hard enough. You know the price. A life for a life."

The man crosses to the dragon, his hands held out. "Please. This was my first hatching without Shaper Gray. I told you I suspected he had some secrets he never told us about how to bring the eggs to term. I will figure them out if only you give me the chance."

"Enough of these excuses! How do I know you are not sabotaging the eggs? Blaming a dead man is not the way to gain my confidence. You should be grateful I only require one life, a life that with humans is so easily replaced."

The woman cried out, "No! You can't take her from me! She's all I have!"

"You can have others. A dragonling is rare and precious and your man let it die."

"It's not the same. It's just an egg, not a child, not your child."

"How dare you speak to me like that when I have taken such good care of you. Step away from the child now."

The woman picked her up and held her tight. She kissed the girl on the head and faced the dragon. "Over my dead body."

"So be it." And then the dragon burned them both.

Dragonfire is not flame. It is a spray of the acid from their gut they can spit in a stream or spread in a mist. The acid hits the woman and child and acts so fast there is only time for a short, aborted scream before they dissolve before my eyes. The man leaps for them but the dragon holds him back.

The acid quickly turns to harmless ash in the air. But by that time, there is nothing left of the woman and her child. They are gone.

The man turns and pounds on the dragon's hard shell. The dragon cuffs him and sends him sprawling. "I will choose you another mate. A woman who has a child already. I will bring her next time and let her stay with you while you work. If you do not have another egg quickened by then, I will repeat this day and keep repeating it until you succeed."

"Monster."

"You are to blame for what happened today. No one but you. Remember that as you work. Now back into the elevator and return to your workshop. I will return in a week with more supplies. And a woman." The man throws himself into the tube. "Don't forget these supplies, shaper. You need to eat."

The man doesn't move. "I don't know how someone so stupid got chosen for the honor of shaping our children. You've had the best education and still you cannot be trusted to remember a simple thing like food and water. Get out here and pick it up. Or do I have to bring an overseer to manage you, man? I think a whipping is what you deserve, never mind that Serzhin says whipping is counterproductive in your kind of work."

The man moves like a sleepwalker over to the basket, hauling them into the tube. Then the door shuts and the whole thing recedes back into the ground. The dragon replaces the boulders. I realize it isn't to hide the entrance, but to prevent the tube from rising until he returns.

I hold my breath as the dragon claws its way up a tree and then launches from the upper branches. I wait unmoving for several minutes. Then I walk over to the boulders and push against them just to see. They might as well have been mountains.

Something sparkles, and I see the chain with the key on it sitting in the middle of the pile. When the dragon replaced the stones, he forgot to get the key. Or maybe he couldn't pick it up. Dragons don't have fine control with their claws. That's why they need humans to be hands for them in so many fields. I wiggle my way into the crevasse between the rocks and manage to reach the key.

It is a strange kind of key. It doesn't have knobs or anything. It is a rectangle with a tongue of metal that sticks out one end. The end of the tongue is hollowed out. On the back of the rectangle is a slider, and that pulls the tongue inside the rectangle and pushes it out again. The tongue is what stuck into the lock. I didn't understand even as I knew I was looking at something only humans could use. I put the chain around my neck and race back to my parent's camp by the clearing.

When my parents see me running toward them, they go from looking panicked to relieved. Both of them hug me and then my dad asks, "What happened? We heard a dragon and caught a whiff of dragonfire. We thought…" He didn't have to finish. I know they were worried it had been me.

"I was digging up a woundbind plant when a dragon came into the clearing with a woman and a girl on its back. It moved some stones and…there's an underground laboratory where they hatch dragon eggs."

My parents look at me the way I must've looked at them a thousand times when they started talking about human "civilization."

"An egg died, and the dragon killed a man's wife and child because he'd failed. Then he sent the man back down, covered the entrance with stones, and left. It was horrible. They curled like hair in a flame and turned to ash so fast."

"We have to leave here." My mother starts packing up.

"What about that man? The dragon killed his family and then sent him down there alone. He is locked in, but we can get him out.

Look!" I pull the chain out to show them. "The dragon forgot the key."

My dad looks at the key and slides the tongue in and out. "I've seen a picture of something like this. I can't think where."

My mother looks it, nodding. "A drawing on a forbidden set of cards. The Wildmen of the north use the cards to divine the future."

"We could show this to them, but they're just as likely to kill us for having it as the dragons if it is one of their sacred symbols."

"Flash. That was one of the words." She looks at my father. "Jessor, it could be an artifact. Do we stay or go?"

"We could stay and come back another time when it is safer."

"It's safe now. The dragon is gone and won't be back for a week," Peor said. "Now is the safest time."

We make our way back to the spot. I avoid looking at the pile of ash as we pass it, though I notice my parents glancing over.

"Well, the first problem is the stones. We need a lever and a fulcrum. The three of us couldn't budge these no matter how hard we pushed."

"Why don't we hitch up the horse?"

"Even after a week, a dragon would pick up a horse's scent. It would implicate us."

It takes most of the rest of the day to cut a young tree and strip it. The three of us work together, jigging the lever to get a little rocking started. Then we time a big push as it rocks outward and sure enough it rolls on its side. Not very far but good enough.

We can see a metal circle that must be the top of the tube. The slot for the key is free.

The three of us stand, tired and dirty, looking at the spot on the ground and feeling the immensity of our situation. We have always kept our heads down. That's what humans do.

Sure, my parents have broken a lot of rules, but they were quiet, private actions. Going off the prescribed trade roads. Teaching me to read. Believing in human civilization. Never something as irreversible as moving that stone. So the idea we might enter a place where the eggs are kept would mean unimaginable consequences.

We stand silently and then the air changes. We've decided together without a word being said. My mother steps forward and places the key in the slot. A minute or two later the tube starts to rise. The metal door slides open and the man steps out.

He sees my mother, turns to see my father and me, and sadness seems to just weigh him down. Then he freezes. He looks around darting his head full circle.

He's expecting a dragon, I realize. "There's no dragon. It's just us."

"Who…who are you?"

My father steps forward. "We're freetraders. My son saw what happened. The dragon forgot the key and my son retrieved it. We were worried about you and so decided to see…well, I don't know what we expected. Only that no man should be alone after what happened to you."

The man bows his head and then looks up at my father a completely different creature than the one who had exited the tube. He has fire in his eyes and determination that comes from a plan.

"The secret of the dragons is that they are a human creation, and they cannot breed without human intervention. The eggs are quickened inside machinery only humans can operate. This is why, though they hate us, they must keep humans alive and educate at least enough of us so those capable of understanding the process can continue to generate offspring. I could explain everything now, or you could trust me and help me destroy this facility. It is only one, and there are others, but not many, I think. "

"Are there human inventions we would be destroying in the process? I have spent my life looking…I never hoped to find proof still in working order. I don't know if it is right to destroy it."

"If the dragons are gone, humans will build another civilization. But only if these laboratories are destroyed beyond repair. Will you help me?"

My father nods. My mother is standing so still, not a muscle moving, because she is facing both the proof she has dreamed of all her life and the knowledge she will never be able to share it.

"What if we just destroy the tube. They won't be able to get in…"

"They would dig their way in and get humans to rebuild the tube and then kill them all so no one will know what goes on here."

"Can we salvage some of it? Anything…," my mother asks

"Any artifact showing up would prove the laboratory was sabotaged and I must have been involved. They would immediately set on a killing spree of laboratory workers in the other locations wherever they are. Not immediately, not before having them train new people. But once they had replacements, everyone would be slaughtered."

I chime in, "Won't they know it was sabotage when they dig it out and don't find your body."

The man looked at me. "They will find my body. As long as I am alive, they can force me to work for them with the threat of killing others if I refuse. If I am gone, I rob them of a precious skill.

"The skill I have cannot be learned from reading or watching the talking images the once humans made. That is why for over a hundred years, no dragon egg was hatched. If dragons could reflect on their behavior, which I believe they cannot, they'd have regretted killing all the scientists, burning all the books, and reducing humans to the status of domesticated animals.

"Slowly, humans who were maybe given great privilege or maybe forced as I have been, began to piece together the techniques the books described. We have gotten better and now more than one in ten eggs that quicken will hatch.

"But because the dragons are also so secretive, they only keep one technician at a time, or at most two who know the secret and learn the skill. I have no apprentice yet and when I am gone, all the secrets of my teacher will be lost. Other laboratories may have made progress and have their own successes. But the dragons don't share us. So when I'm gone, every gain here is gone, and this clan of dragons will have no one who knows how to fertilize, tend, and hatch a dragonet. They are long-lived, but sooner or later, if there are no more eggs hatched, they will all die. So yes, I must die, and they must believe it was an accident."

My father steps forward and offers his hand. "My name is Jessor."

My mother steps forward and offers her hand as well. "Alina."

He takes both their hands in his. "Erasuma."

"Pleased to meet you Erasuma."

Erasuma turns to me. "And you. What is your name?"

"Peor."

"Thank you, Peor." He offers his hand and I take it. I don't bend over it like a child is supposed to do when meeting an adult. He is talking to me as an equal.

We all crowd into the tube, or "lift" as Erasuma calls it. "Don't we need someone up here to come back up?" I ask.

"No, I have the code, which you can use above or below to unlock the lift."

"How is this possible? Did humans used to have magic?"

Erasuma laughed and pressed a button. "No. Machines. Like a

windmill or a water pump only much more complex." The doors close and the floor drops. My mother grabs me. I can see through a narrow slit in the door that we are sliding down and then the world is gone. When we stop, the door opens into a small room with a corridor beyond it.

"Would you show us around before we have to destroy it. I would..." My dad looks at my mother, "We both would appreciate it more than you can know. To see it at least...Please."

Erasuma shows us rooms full of things I don't begin to understand. What I do gather is how very advanced humans were before. People who could build this could fight dragons. Then I remember—humans created dragons, and I'm so confused. I can see my father's hands are shaking slightly even as his eyes are as wide as a baby's. And my mother, she is holding herself very still, walking with a minimum of movement and showing absolutely no expression on her face.

Erasuma takes us into a dining hall with half a dozen tables and walls of machines. "Let's sit and talk a bit over some food. You look like you could use a break. I remember how overwhelming it was, and I was prepared."

We sat at a table while he went to the wall and started pushing buttons. One machine spit out cups filled with a hot drink. Coffee he called it. It was bitter and sweet and wonderful. He also gave us some sandwiches that were as good as any I've ever had.

"At least the dragons bring you good food."

"The dragons don't know about this. The basket they bring means I can add fresh produce to the fabricated meals, but the meat and cheeses they bring are so bad I throw then in the recycler to be broken down into chemical components. The machines use the elements to reconstitute whatever I need."

My mother has tears running down her face. "How? How did the dragons destroy this? Why don't we remember? What happened? Do you know?"

"I know some. It seems the creation of dragons changed people. Humans, having overcome their violent natures and achieved centuries of peace, were able to temper the aggressiveness of their dragon creations successfully. At first. But the relationship worked in reverse, too, making humans less in control of their own tempers. Soon wars broke out. Humans betrayed each other, started trusting "their" dragons over other people. When the human population was weakened from the wars, the dragons struck. They didn't plan it, it seems, but rather they erupted in a killing rage after humans used cold iron shrapnel bombs to destroy a large dragon nursery."

"Iron can't hurt a dragon's armor…" We learn that in nursery school.

"Cold iron doesn't actually have any iron in it. It is an enhanced alloy. I read in the archives that the name refers to ancient mythology about magical creatures being unable to touch iron."

"Archives." My father repeats in a wistful voice. "I'd like there to be a way to save the archives if we can."

Erasuma purses his lips. "Maybe we can output the archives into one of the electronic readers. But it won't last without power."

"I'd like to know more about cold iron." I say, thinking about the woman and child and how much I would have liked to be able to protect them.

Erasuma sees the thought behind my words and beckons. "Come with me to the meeting hall and I'll show you something." A large room with a dais at one end opens off the dining room. He points. "There. Do you see that?"

On the wall above the dais is a shield and a sword.

"For all I know, that is the last cold iron in the world. I don't think we have the technology to make it now. It is one of the reasons the dragon's rampage didn't stop until any human who might know how to make it or any machine that could be used to build a weapon against them were all destroyed."

I looked at him. "You can't destroy those."

"I explained why we have to protect…"

"The dragons don't know they're here. They could have come from anyplace. And we could disguise them. The sword becomes a walking staff. The shield the base of a cart."

Erasuma looks uncertain. "I don't like it, but I will agree if you promise me you will make sure this place is completely destroyed before you go. I will show you how to trigger a second wave of destruction after I am gone. If you promise me you will do it…"

My mother nods. "For the weapons and the archive."

He looks at the three of us, all so intent and earnest. His eyes are bright with tears. "It has been so long since I spoke with anyone not living every moment in fear of being killed. Alright. And thank you."

We follow him to a large circular room. Along the walls are a series of clear chambers. Three of them have dragon eggs in them.

The eggs are perfectly round, perfectly gray, and look leathery in texture. Their surfaces glow like they're hot. A shiny black rectangle hangs beside each one with moving lines and numbers constantly running across like a stream.

My mother sees the eggs. "Three more dragons." She says it quietly and calmly, but I see she is determined now. Nothing will save this room.

I looked around, gauging its perfectly round shape. "We're under the dead zone, aren't we?"

"Dead zone?"

My father explains, "The there's a circle up there where nothing grows. We thought it might be poison…"

"Dragonfire fumes leaking out, I suppose. We introduce it into the eggs at a certain point to grow the skin that can withstand it. It has to be monitored closely, because each one responds slightly differently, and too much or too little will kill the developing egg."

"You make dragonfire here?"

"The machines do it all automatically. There are instructions on how to repair them, but we don't understand half of the information and figure things out by trial and error. Human technology was very durable, so there hasn't been a need. However, if we destroy these machines, there is no way to rebuild them."

"What do we do?" Again my mother. My father looks a bit helpless. He wants to find a way to save it all. He won't be able to, not now, now that my mother has decided.

"The best destruction is the crudest." He goes to a cabinet by the wall that says, "In case of fire." He pulls out an ax and hands it to my father along with something that looks like a clear hat. "Put this over your eyes and smash the glass, then smash the eggs."

My dad steps back. "I can't do it."

"It's okay, Dad. I'll do it." I turn to Erasuma. "Give it to me."

"Put these on first." He slips the thing I thought was a hat over my eyes. It was made out of glass, and I could actually see better with it on. Clearer. Like every detail. "These have some technology my teacher never understood. You can see like a god, everything far and near in focus. Writing sometimes appears but we never figured out how to trigger it. Don't be concerned if it does. This is just to protect your eyes. And here." He pulls out a pair of gloves. "These will resist dragonfire. Not completely like the shield. But if any splatters on your hands. you won't get burned."

I put them on.

"Start on an empty one, Peor, for practice. They all have to go."

I step up and start swinging the ax against the glass. I see bright lines appear inside the glasses overlaid on the surface. I realize I'm seeing the effect of my hit. I hit again, and the overlay brightens and the lines spread out. I hit twice more before I hear the glass break. The lines fade. I step inside, smash the circle of lights on the bottom, and smack the black glass rectangle beside it.

The empty cases go quickly after that.

I step up to the first one with an egg. Through the eye covering, I see a red ball at the center of the egg pulsing with light. I smash open the case and stand in front of the egg that would be a dragon. I hit it with the ax. The familiar bright lines appear and the red ball flashes wildly. I imagine I'm seeing the scream of the dragon inside. I hit it once, twice as hard as I can. The shell splits. A half-formed dragonet spills out. My stomach heaves and I turn away trying not to throw up.

The black display has gone still. No numbers. No lines. I hit it over and over anyway, until the light is gone from it.

Then I take care of the other two eggs.

When I'm done, I notice the machines around the room have all been opened up and had their insides torn apart. My mother has a hammer and she's jamming it inside one over and over.

My father is working quietly at a desk. He's fiddling with the surface and then pulling out a small disc. He puts the disc in a box of some sort and repeats the process. He is so focused he doesn't seem aware of the smashing happening around him. It is clear he is saving something and not destroying.

Erasuma is working at another desk. He picks up a tool that looks like the key only larger with buttons on it. He walks over to my mother and gives it to her.

"This is the detonator you will use to set off the explosion. I'm going to take you up and then come back to the main computer one floor below. It was built with a destruction code so the place could be kept out of dragon hands. Unfortunately, the code needs two people in different locations to set it. I will begin the sequence and then you will finish it. You have to press these numbers in the right sequence. 10010000111."

"10010000111."

"Once I leave you up top, count to fifty for me to reach the computer room. Then walk to the dead zone which should put you far enough away to escape but still close enough to trigger the device. Then, to be certain I've been able to do my part, count to fifty again. Don't wait too long or it will reset. Punch in the numbers and then run away as fast as you can. If nothing happens, I will come up and we will try again. Alright?"

"Yes. 10010000111."

"Good."

Erasuma helps my father put the collection of discs in a small metal box with two flat black glass tablets. They looked like the ones on the wall only smaller. "You slip the disc in here and you can page through like this." He demonstrates for all of us. I am shocked to see writing appear bright and clear where it had once been blank. "Once this place is gone, the reader will run out of power and there will be no way to recharge it. Without power, it is blank. You must keep your promise to put this away somewhere and never open it while the dragons are still in control. When it is opened, you will need people to copy every page onto paper. Find people who can write quickly without mistakes. You will not get through everything before the power fades. Someday, if humans figure out how to replace the power, then the rest will become readable once again." He closes the metal box and presses a button. A hissing sound comes from the box. "I've taken the air out of the box. It will keep forever until it is opened. Save it against that day."

My father's eyes are fervent and I can see he will not open the box. He will make an altar out of it against that "someday." The job of caring for its hiding place will fall to me and my children, and their children. Dragons live a long time, and we have nothing to fight them with.

Erasuma looks at me. "Let's get your sword and shield off the wall and we'll go up above."

And we do.

I confess I have slipped the gloves off and stuck them in my pocket. I will return them if he asks. Likewise, I have pulled the glass head cover down and it is hanging backward down my back. The straps are still visible from the front. But if Erasuma doesn't notice them, maybe I will keep them too.

We pack into the lift tube. When we reach the top and stop, a roar freezes our guts. We look out the slit and see the dragon has come back.

"He came back for the key," Erasuma says.

The dragon roars, "Come out you filthy traitor. And whoever moved these stones. I will roast him one limb at a time!"

"Listen. He cannot kill me. They need me to hatch their offspring. I will go out with this behind my back." He takes the sword. You must all stay close together and when you see him prepare the dragonfire, crouch behind the shield. He won't know it is possible. Try to stand away from the lift or any stones that might splash it on your backs. I will try to get close to him and stab his heart from under his armpit while his attention is on you."

He presses the button to open the door. My mother and father move out of the lift to the right. I shadow Erasuma, slipping on the gloves and eye glass. Some part of me, I think, did not want that sword to be out of reach.

The dragon notices my mother and is pleased. "Ah, so you have found your own woman and have saved me the trouble. Excellent."

"O Great One. I was just sending them away. They found the stones and were curious. They didn't know..."

"You took them down below. For that alone they must die. You know this. You are the cause of their death, not I. This is your doing, and I will consider how to punish you."

Looking at the dragon through the glass, I can see his purple heart beating, the green glow that must be dragonfire, and several bright red circles: one in each armpit, one on his chest right under the heart, and a couple more up on the neck and head. Each of these has a gold circle around it. Targets.

The dragon is looking at my father and mother. "Step away from her, man, and I will make your death quick." My father, the shield held low by his side, steps between the dragon and my mother. The dragon roars. "You cannot protect her from me, fool. I can burn your feet off where you stand."

I see surprise on my father's face. I don't think he considered shielding his feet. He will now. Good.

The dragon gives a theatrical sigh. "Oh very well." He gathers himself to spit and I can see a green line of dragonfire threading up his jawline. I call out, "Dad! Now!"

I glance back and see he and my mother have crouched down behind the shield, their bodies behind it from head to foot.

Erasuma leaps. The dragon, without thinking cuffs, him aside like a toy. Flecks of dragonfire fall on him and a few specks on me.

They burn but I don't have time to feel it. Erasuma tumbles, dropping the sword. I tumble as if hit, too, but I tumble to the sword.

The sword's handle is bright green with dragonfire, but I don't hesitate. I grab it, hoping the gloves will give me enough time.

The dragon is almost incoherent with rage. "Shaper! What have you done? They didn't burn. Burn! You will all burn for this!" The dragon's head is waving back and forth between my parents and Erasuma. I see a wave of green pulse upward and I know a shower of dragonfire is about to coat the whole area. I leap from where I'm curled and stab the glowing spot on the dragon's chest with all my might. The sword sinks in like it's hitting water and not flesh. The dragon screams and gargles on its own dragonfire. I roll aside as the dragon crumples, still screaming with rage. I see a glowing spot by the side of his eye and jam the blade into it.

The screams stop. The dragon's eyes dull. He sags and lies still.

Erasuma is badly burned from the dragonfire that spilled on his back. He gets up and waves away help. "I can make it to the mainframe. I can survive long enough to do that, I think. If I can't, let me show you how to call the elevator from above. "

Hobbling and gasping with pain, he shows my parents, then he gets in and says, "Well done youngster. The world has a dragonslayer once more. But keep the secret. If the explosion doesn't destroy the dragon, you will have to carve him up and drag the bits off.'

My mother says drily, "Let's hope that isn't necessary." She leans in and, taking Erasuma's hands, does a deep loving reverence to him. My father and I follow suit.

"Start counting. And let's hope the first try succeeds."

The lift closes and sinks. We walk back slowly to the dead zone, my mother counting to 50 in a steady cadence. When we reach the dead zone, she pulls out the detonator and counts to 50 once more, gesturing for my father and me to move off. When she finishes counting, she presses the numbers and comes running toward us.

We hear a rumble as the earth trembles. Hand in hand, we crash unsteadily away a few more steps before an eruption of air and gas flies up from the ground.

"Get under the shield!" My father cries as he holds it over his head, and we grab onto each other tightly. Rocks and metal debris fall around us. The trees absorb a lot of the power, but things still pummel down on us. We hear hissing that indicates dragonfire is also falling, so we wait until it stops.

The dead zone is gone, caved in and there are fragments, remnants of machinery visible. I look at my dad expecting him to want to go salvage things, but he shakes his head. "Let someone else discover it."

The entire forest between the dead zone and the lift has caved in. The dragon is no longer visible, having been swallowed by the crater and buried in the debris. The laboratory is gone.

My mother hugs me. My father pulls us both into his arms. For all the destruction of the day, I feel safer than I've ever felt. Not because I killed a dragon. I don't want to think about that part of the day for a long time. And I certainly don't expect to have to ever do that again. No, I feel safer because humankind is safer. There is hope for us in the future, even if the present is violent and horribly cruel. We'll disguise the weapons. We'll find a safe place to hide the discs. And then we'll start planning for the future.

~ * ~ * ~

Susan diRende has always been a fan of the empty-handed leap into the unknown: running away to join the circus at 20, decamping to France to study mime at 25, relocating to Seattle to write for the theater at 30, braving Hollywood to make movies at 40, and then selling everything at 60 to travel the world with no fixed abode. Her published works range from serious academic to sci-fi space farce. Her art and videos have been shown in exhibitions and film festivals in the US, Mexico, Belgium and New Zealand. She has won numerous awards and grants, including the 2017 Philip K Dick Awards Special Citation of Excellence.

Felt in Her Bones

Nancy Kay Clark

Just after her 551st birthday, the Grandmother Dragon's hind left knee began to creak. It was the morning the rampaging delinquents were brought before the Dragon Council, gathered in the great stone nest by the southern sea. As the council chair, the Grandmother sat on the highest podium, and used that height to perfect effect— raising and bristling her neck frill and turning her green spots an angry red, she stared down at the five hapless younglings, their lawyers and their parents. Making her voice as stern as possible, she declared: "You've been convicted of cruelty to animals in the first degree."

Brother councilor Hadrian, a diminutive golden, half the size of all the rest, spoke up: "I object. Humans are not animals. They are folk."

Brother Trajan, a large silverback, interrupted: "The Jury is still out on the question of their intelligence."

"It's been out for seventy-five years."

"Brother Hadrian," the Grandmother said. "I am well aware the wording is not quite appropriate, but until the jury reports back, it is the law that most applies here."

"I object."

"Yes, Brother Trajan?"

"Surely, they should not have been charged in the first degree? There was no forethought or planning. These younglings did not mean to set fire to that human town. Surely, it is but a misdemeanor?"

"A misdemeanor, Brother Trajan? More than two hundred humanfolk lost?" Sister Amina said, pulling her head out of the sea and shedding water as she shook her blue neck scales at Trajan.

"Stop calling them folk," Trajan said. "At worse they are an irritating pestilence, at best a semi-amusing pet."

"In some nests, they are considered an afternoon snack," Sister Boudica piped in, her bronze tale spikes shimmering in the afternoon sun.

"I am surprised at you Boudica," Hadrian said. "It is against Dragon Code to eat folk."

"I'm…I'm not saying I eat them myself."

"You progressives are all the same," Trajan said. "So self-righteous. You know what would happen if we never culled their numbers from time to time? We'd be overrun by humans! It would be an infestation!"

"What a dreadful thought!" Brother Attila wrapped himself in his black wings as if to ward off a human swarm.

"Sisters and brothers! Sisters and brothers!" the Grandmother said. "This is not the time or place for such a debate. The conviction stands as stated." There were grumblings, but the Grandmother ignored them. "The facts of the case are not in question. Neither is the younglings' guilt."

The five younglings before her hung their heads.

"What remains now is to decide on punishment."

"I have a suggestion, Grandmother," Sister Amina said. "Perhaps the younglings should do community service among the Humans. Perhaps they should help rebuild their town."

"Absurd!" Trajan shouted, and the parents and lawyers agreed. They shouted and roared their disapproval.

"Why? It's a logical consequence, isn't it? How else are we going to teach our children that reckless flaming will not be tolerated?" Hadrian said.

"Dragons shouldn't be taking orders from animals. I object!"

"And I object to your arrogance, Trajan!" Amina said.

"Well, I object to your stupidity, Amina!"

Then everyone started to object to everyone else. The Grandmother had to roar red flame to call them all to order. "We will put it to a vote."

The tally was close. The Grandmother cast the deciding vote; she voted yeah. "The motion is carried," she declared to the assembled crowd. "These five will help rebuild the town under the direction of the Humans."

Up flapped one of the mothers of the delinquents. Spitting and sputtering, the mother said: "I will never allow my child to submit to such humiliation! Imagine serving the likes of humans!"

Within minutes, the stone nest was full of black smoke and furious wing flapping. The outraged parents tried to take their younglings and leave; the council guards would not let them. The lawyers roared objections. Sister and brother council members argued their positions. And as the Grandmother reared up on her hind legs to call for order, she felt a sharp grinding and creaking in her knee that sent a shiver up her spine.

The creaking persisted for weeks afterwards, but the Grand-mother was so busy with appeal hearings, dealing with citizen com-plaints and an upset ambassador from the Human Lands she hardly noticed the discomfort. Nevertheless, it hovered in the back of her mind, coming to the fore every time she shifted or bent her knee. Two years later, by the time the parents and their lawyers had exhausted all legal means and failed to reverse the community service verdict, the creak had turned into an ache. There were protests almost every week now—groups of dragons who disagreed with the ruling, spurred on by council members who had voted against it. Brother Trajan had even resigned his council seat over it. With every raised voice, the Grandmother could feel the ache in her knee deepen.

In her off hours, which were few, she took to the sky, flying to the northern sea to soak her inflamed joint in the freezing water. She would spend a blissful hour in the quiet of the arctic, resting on an iceberg and listening to the narwhals' singing. But it only relieved the ache temporarily; it always came back when she flew south again.

The day they were to deliver the five younglings to the Humans was overcast. Rain was coming—the Grandmother could feel it in her knee. The grey sky was filled with dragons from every nest within a day's flight distance and even beyond. Arrayed on one side were members of the newly formed Dragon Pride group, led by Trajan, who believed dragons should never serve humans. On the other side were members of the Society of Ethical Human Husbandry, who supported the Grandmother and her Council. Members from each group mingled on the wing, throwing vitriolic flames to singe each other's tails.

Out came the five delinquents, small and pale, forced to wear the leather harnesses with which the humans would control their actions. A dozen council guards surrounded them. Out came the Grandmother and two of her more loyal council members.

From the jeering, jostling crowd, Trajan flapped forward. "This is an abomination. I appeal to you Grandmother, where is your dragon pride? Do not do this!"

"I am following Dragon Law, Trajan. Let us pass please."

"If you do this Grandmother, I cannot guarantee your safety or the safety of the Humans you so dearly love. I will not stay to watch this disaster happen." With a huff, he turned his back on the Grandmother and flew away.

The Grandmother forced her spots to remain a sunny yellow as pain shot through her knee. She addressed the crowd. "Disperse all of you. Go home."

"The sky is free!" came shouts from all around. "We're not going anywhere."

The grandmother continued to keep her spots yellow. "Fine, but remember the land is not free. The land we are going to belongs to the Humans. You cannot touch ground, nor can you flame. Now let us pass."

The protesters parted and the group led by the Grandmother flew in formation south. The crowd followed them.

What a terrifying sight we will be to the Humans, the Grandmother thought, but she could do little to stop the protesters flying with them.

It took an hour to reach the outskirts of the Human town. All the while the Grandmother's knee pulsed with pain. When it was time, the Grandmother gave the signal and the formation descended through the clouds still heavy with rain. Below, in a green rectangle, she saw a small group of humans, their carts, carriages and horses, waiting for them. Beyond them, she saw clusters of human burrows made of wood, and here and there pockets of burnt space, abandoned since the flaming two years ago. As they descended lower and lower, she saw the Humans' upturned faces—some blank, others in awe, others clearly terrified. She wondered, not for the first time, at how tiny they really were.

The protesters descended lower than the clouds, but remained in the sky circling, while the Grandmother, her council members, the younglings and the guards landed. As the Grandmother touched down, her knee buckled. She regained her footing quickly and stepped forward to meet the Human ambassador. His name escaped her—Rickkentory or Rickleton or Rickleberry? Such silly names they had. No matter, she knew from past experience he would do most of the talking anyway.

He did. Bowing low, he launched into a long speech about their two great folk working together and a new era of peace descending. Distracted by the scent of the nervous horses and her rumbling stomach, she barely listened. *Best to speed things up*, she thought, *and take everyone home.* "Quite, quite, I certainly agree, Mr. Ambassador," she said in Humanspeak.

He jumped when she spoke. *I must remember to speak more softly to these creatures*, she thought. He was looking flustered and glancing up in the sky. "We were not expecting, Ma'am, so many of you to grace us with your presence today."

She tempered her voice. "They will not land, nor will they flame, you have my assurance of that, Mr. Ambassador. Are all the arrangements made to house and feed our younglings?"

The Ambassador nodded his head. "We have converted a very large barn here on the outskirts, for their comfort..."

In the sky, the protesters began to hiss. The sky above was a whirlwind of flapping. "Barn? Barn? Did he say barn? Are we cattle?"

The Grandmother looked up at the protesters in annoyance. She looked down again. "Please continue, Mr. Ambassador."

He did not get a chance to—from the sky a dragon yelled, "I do this for the pride of dragons everywhere!"

The Grandmother saw a streak of red flame envelop the Human ambassador and then in the next instant a pile of smoking black ash where he had stood.

"Who did that? Who did that?" She roared, pushing down hard on her bad knee to launch herself up into the sky to find the culprit. It was chaos above.

As the Humans screamed and scattered, and the horses bolted, the opposing factions of dragons, who had merely singed each other's tails that morning, attacked each other in earnest. Soon the farmer's field they had stood on was aflame and the Human town burning once again.

When late in the afternoon, the grey clouds finally broke and rain came to douse the flames, the entire town was in smolders. When the rain came, both sides in the battle dispersed and the Grandmother led her weary troops back to the Dragon Lands. With every flap of her wings, as the hard rain pelted her scales, the pain from her knee began to move up her leg and into her hip.

~ * ~

Ten years after the "Liberation of the Five"—as the Dragon Pride faction called the skirmish in that farmer's field, the Grandmother sat on her favorite iceberg in the northern sea, wrapped in her ragged wings. It was a clear, bitterly cold night and the stars crowded the sky. On the southern horizon were flashes of eerie green and red light.

Close by, a barnacle-encrusted humpback whale breached the water, and sang to the Grandmother. "Is it you, Madame Dragon, back again?"

"Yes, Friend, it's me. How is your tail? Is it healing well?"

The humpback snorted steam through her spout. "As well as can be expected at my age. And your knee and hip?"

"About the same as your tail."

A flash of greenish white lit up the southern sky.

"Funny," the Humpback said. "Our Northern Lights seem to be coming from the south tonight."

"It's not your Northern Lights. What you see is the reflection of dragon flame."

Just then the southern sky burst into red and orange.

"So much flaming! Another battle in your civil war, Madame? But why aren't you there to lead your army?"

The Grandmother coughed blue sparks and phlegm into the sea. "It was suggested to me by my Generals that I remain behind the lines this time—seems I am too slow these days, I'm getting in their way."

In the south, the sky continued to burst into colors.

The companions turned silent, straining to hear, perhaps, the sounds of that far-away battle.

Time ticked by, as the water lapped against the ice and the old humpback dove and came up to spout again. Then the Grandmother asked the question she had been thinking about since the dragon civil war started: "Is it better, do you think Friend, to forget or to remember?"

"Forget or remember what?"

The Grandmother took her time answering, as if recalling a great memorized list. "Scorched wheat fields and blackened stubs of trees, dead humans and dragons both, no food left, water contaminated with carcasses, whole human villages and dragon nests obliterated—I've seen it all these last ten years. The Human Lands are a shambles because of us—our Borderlands not much better. The Dragon Council split in two. But what I fear most are the bitter, angry words uttered on all sides. When the fighting ends, will remembering the war and the mistakes that caused it lead to a lasting peace? Or do you think it is better to forget? And how long does it take to forget enough to forgive your enemies?"

The old humpback clicked and clacked, and finally sang mournfully. "About war, I cannot comment, for other than a few skirmishes among the males at mating time, we whales do not go to war.

But decades ago, a child of mine was taken by a toothed whale, and I have never forgotten. To this day, I cannot hear the songs of those toothed monsters without feeling great waves of rage and grief. I fear, Madame, it will take generations to forget such destruction as you have described."

~ * ~

The last battle of the dragon's civil war took place four years later, in the lush forest of the Dragon Lands' southern reaches. Finally the Grandmother's troops had cornered the last of the Dragon Pride rebels in the Three Sisters Mesa. Rebel red mole dragons had dug deep caverns into the sides of the flat-top mountain. For months, the Grandmother's troops had tried to flush the rebels out into the open, but had failed.

One rain-filled evening, under an overhang on top of the neighboring Three Brothers Mesa, the Grandmother's generals gathered a nest to discuss the situation. They had barely started blaming each other for their failures, when out of the downpour arrived the Grandmother.

Now walking with a dreadful limp, she hoisted herself into the middle of their nest.

"Yes, yes, I know you were not expecting me—that you wanted me stay away." Puffing white smoke and fury into the air, she gave them no chance to reply. "But you have all failed me and you must be held accountable."

"But Grandmother…" Then came the excuses. "Their red moles have created a maze of caverns and tunnels throughout the Three Sisters. Trajan and his rebels do not stay in anyone spot for long," one said.

"Their spotted arboreals emerge like devils to harass us, striking under cover of darkness and stealing back into the forest," another said.

"They leave countless numbers of our troops dead, and eat our livestock, so we cannot feed our remaining troops," a third said.

And the fourth joined in. "They are too well camouflaged, too quick in their movements. And when our scouts do find a cache of them, by the time our troops arrive they are gone. We cannot hit a target we cannot find."

"How is this so?" the Grandmother asked.

"They have better scouts—mostly local blue fishers—who

swim the Channel River and all its tributaries as they please, it seems, without us lifting a talon to stop them."

"It is not my fault," the red mole General Claude said, in a huff. "They are far too small to see."

"Buffoons! Buffoons!" the Grandmother bellowed. "The criminal Trajan and his followers must be stopped. Can none of you accomplish this for me?"

"There is one way," Hadrian said, once on the Dragon Council and now one of the Grandmother's generals. What he lacked in size, he made up for in boldness. "But it goes against the directive you gave us years ago."

The Grandmother bent her head to look at him. "What directive?" she demanded.

"You bade us to treat our enemies with respect and not savagery, so that when the war is over no bitterness will prevail among us. You reminded us to treat the innocent—the ones who have no part in the war—with kindness and there are many such folk, dragon and non-dragon, who live in the forest below us. You wished us to tread gently on the land. We have tried to follow your word, Grandmother, but it has hampered our efforts to bring the criminal Trajan to justice."

A murmur of agreement rose among the other generals.

The Grandmother cocked her head sideways, listening to all the murmurings. "How would you do it then, Hadrian? What is this way you speak of?"

"Bury the rivers so the fishers cannot use them. Burn the forest so they have no place to hide. Boulder through the maze of tunnels until their last refuge is exposed. In other words, be savage."

"And if we do not do this?"

"Then Trajan and his rebels will hide themselves here for many years more. The war will drag on and on."

The Grandmother let out a long breath, as the ache from her leg climbed higher up her spine. There was a pause. No one spoke, except the rain. Finally, she looked at Hadrian and nodded. "Do it."

~ * ~

Three months after that last battle, the Grandmother held a Nest to decide what to do with the remnants of the captured Dragon Pride rebels—those who had not chosen to die with the Criminal Trajan in the rubble of the Three Sisters Mesa. Leaders of the rebellion, including the legendary Dragon Pride warrior Gustus Tyranicus —one of the original five delinquents—were escorted to the center of the Nest and interrogated.

General Claude led the questioning: "Gustus, do you deny taking part in the wanton flaming of the eastern arboreal nests and the murder of three thousand innocent arboreal younglings five years ago?" he asked.

Gustus shrugged. "No, I do not deny it. They were collateral damage in a war zone, sir, and I was a Major in the Dragon Pride army."

"You are a criminal, and it was a war crime," Claude bellowed, stamping his talons on the ground.

"I was a soldier carrying out my orders," Gustus insisted, clicking his tail spikes.

"You gave the orders, Gustus and helped carry out the flaming yourself. And that is just one flaming you perpetrated—there are many others. We have accounts from eyewitnesses you personally led the night raid on the Humanfolk town of Crossover."

"Witnesses? What witnesses?"

"Surviving townsfolk—the ones who barely got out, who had to watch while the rest of their folk, their families, their homes, their property and their livestock burned to the ground."

"Bah! You cannot believe the words of Humans! They have no real understanding of the world. You have no credible witnesses, Claude."

"I can bring to this Nest a half dozen Crossover and Eastern Arboreal survivors."

Gustus snorted green smoke. "Humans and younglings! I object to the legitimacy of this Nest—you have no right to put me on trial, I am a soldier."

The arguments went on for 150 days, defendant after defendant, witness after witness. Throughout, the Grandmother perched stoically on a large slab of stone, which overlooked the circle. She said nothing, kept her neck frill and spots neutral, and tried to ease the trembling in her leg and spine.

On the 151st day, the Grandmother brought the Nest to a close. "Pride and arrogance nested at the center of this war of ours. Too proud we are of our greatness, too proud we are to bend, to admit to our mistakes, to ask forgiveness and to forgive. Too proud we are to see other folk as equals. We are set on argument—even now.

"Tomorrow, I fly to the Human Lands to sign a treaty with the Human King. In that treaty I will pledge to reimburse the Humans for their many losses as a result of our little war."

Murmurs rose from the audience, and someone yelled out: "How? How are we to reimburse them?"

The answer came from the Grandmother in a bellow of black smoke: "Through our minds and bodies. We will rebuild their towns and villages, we will help plant and harvest their food, we will be their advisors, their beasts of burden, and their engines of industry. From this day forward I am implementing mandatory Humanfolk service for all dragons, regardless of race or which side their families were on in the war. Upon reaching adulthood each and every young dragon will serve the Humans for thirty years. Each generation of dragons will serve the Humans until the debt has been paid, and all is forgotten and forgiven."

"How long will that be?" another shouted.

The Grandmother shrugged her massive shoulders. "It will be as long as it will be."

But still the dragons around her were not satisfied and had many questions. "What does that mean? How will you know when enough time has passed?"

The Grandmother's spots turned a bright yellow, and she shifted her weight trying to ease the ache in her spine. "When the time is right," she told her people. "I will feel it in my bones."

~ * ~ * ~

Nancy Kay Clark is an award-winning writer and editor based in Toronto, Canada. She has worked with both non-fiction (magazine) and fiction writers in a career that spans thirty years and has edited and published the online literary zine *CommuterLit.com* for over a decade. Her speculative short fiction has appeared in *Neo Opsis* and *Utopia Science Fiction* magazines, as well as the online zine *Polar Borealis*. Her middle-grade adventure novel, *Prince of Sudland: Escape from the Palace*, is available from Lulu.com. You can also find her stories on Wattpad.com.

Thea and the Dragon

Emma Melville

Thea hated sewing. Each stitch was another wasted moment, seconds she couldn't get back. It wasn't a new feeling but seemed heavier today with death less than twenty-four hours away.

She could see her brothers playing in the courtyard below. They didn't have to sew, wasting their time creating useless tapestries to hang on walls. They learned how to fight, to kill, to meet a dragon face to face without fleeing in terror.

When it was her, staring the beast in the eye tomorrow, what use would a needle be, or a brightly colored thread? They should have taught her how to fight.

She could hear Nancy sniffling again, bent over her own stitching. The maid was driving Thea to distraction. How was she supposed to concentrate on the moves her brothers were making? How was she to learn anything of fighting with that noise going on?

"Nancy, go away," she snapped.

"But—" Nancy's face was all white and blotchy red, blue eyes brimming with unshed tears.

"I want to be alone, to think."

"My mum says it helps to talk at times like this."

Thea laughed, such crass stupidity. "Yes, of course. I'll talk the dragon to death. Why didn't I think of that?"

"I didn't mean—"

"Go away."

The maid went, dropping her cloth in her haste.

In the courtyard below, fighting had been suspended to tend to a bruised knee and a wounded ego. Thea considered going down, but honesty made her admit she would just shout at her brothers as well and she wanted their last memory of her to be better than that. Her father, thankfully, had agreed to keep them away tomorrow so she would say her last farewells at the feast tonight.

Tossing the abandoned sewing to the floor she went in search of a dress. The green silk gown for the feast which complemented her fiery hair and emerald eyes had been delivered earlier. She intended to leave it to Nancy in the morning. She'd be damned if she was going to let something so nice be ripped to pieces. So now she needed to find the pink, fluffy creation her grandmother had sent her for her last naming day. The dragon was welcome to it.

The monstrosity took some finding amongst the jumble of equally loathsome dresses a princess was expected to wear.

The search did little to improve Thea's temper.

"Let me rescind." Her father's entrance had gone unnoticed amidst the crashing and banging.

"No."

"Thea, I—"

"Never. Girls die every month. Why should I be different?"

"You're my only daughter."

"How often do they say that?" They screamed it at her father in the great hall while soldiers dragged their children away to feed a monster.

"I make the rules. I could save you."

"Every girl of sixteen." Thea kicked the wardrobe door shut. "Every. One. It'll be Nancy's turn next year. How could I look her in the eye every day knowing she has twelve chances to die, and I walked away?"

"You'll never look her in the eye again after tomorrow."

Thea dug her nails into her palm, the anguish in his voice almost more than she could bear. "I'm sorry, father, but you taught me to do the right thing however hard." It had sometimes taken a sharp slap and she still complained bitterly about sewing but she had learned to do it.

"I thought I taught you to obey your father."

"I'm sorry." She truly was. Sorry for adding her name to the lottery list against his will. Sorry for misbegotten pride. Sorry for his loss. But, at the end of the day, she was who she was because he'd made her so.

"Yes," he said, understanding, "me too."

They stood, uncertainly, for a long moment and then he smiled a little shakily. "I knew you'd find a use for that present of your grandma's."

"I'm going to scare the dragon away," she said, and he even managed a brief laugh before hugging her hard and leaving.

She waited for the sound of his footsteps on the stairs before bending and pulling a stolen treasure from under the bed. The sword was bright and new, her eldest brother's favorite possession. She waved it in furiously practiced clumsy strokes before the mirror.

At least if she couldn't bring it back stained with dragon blood, she would never hear the fuss when Anton discovered it gone.

~ * ~

The sun shone brightly on the crowds of people gathering to see her go. Thea watched them streaming in through the main gates. She recognized many—faces last seen wailing in anguish as loved ones were marched away.

"They've all come to wish you well," Nancy said, watching over her shoulder.

"They've come to make sure I go through with it. I bet every last one expects father to save me."

"I'm sure he will, miss," Nancy said, slow as ever.

Thea gripped the sword hilt digging into her ribs under the too-tight bodice. "No one will save me but me."

"I don't know. Cook was saying last night about how there's a—"

"No," Thea said firmly. Cook's fairy stories were anything but amusing this morning.

The sword poked another rib and Thea swore in an unladylike manner. She hefted her skirts up to free it. "Sod it, I'll have to wear this outside the dress."

"What will people think?"

"Oh god, what a fashion disaster, the steel clashes with the lace?" She watched the sarcasm sail over Nancy's head. "Just do it or I'll be late."

~ * ~

It felt more comforting to stride towards the great hall with her hand resting firmly on the sword hilt. Her boots rang loudly on the floor, their black leather showing awkwardly beneath the hideous pink.

Thea concentrated hard on the picture she must make; it helped keep her angry and focused. She hated this dress, lovingly stitched by a woman who adored sewing. The hearts and flowers were a masterpiece of pointless brilliance. She hoped the dragon appreciated it. That it could recognize mindless beauty. Her heels struck sparks from the floor as she paced along.

Well-wishers—friends, guards, advisers; people she'd known

all her life—took one look at her face and stepped aside. "Outfit works then," she muttered as she arrived outside the closed doors of the great hall.

She pushed violently. Every expectant face in the throng beyond turned towards her as she threw the doors open. She paused; tried to register them all, to meet every eye. There were so many and few were friendly.

She'd memorized a grand speech, but words failed her. "Time to go then," she said brusquely.

Her father sat slumped on his dais, unable to look up.

"Father!" She strode down the aisle left for that purpose towards the honor guard at the front. They looked cheerful but Thea decided it must make a pleasant change for them not to have to forcibly drag a hysterical girl away from clinging parents.

"Father, it's time."

He raised himself with an effort and stood to look over the throng.

"Will any save this damsel from her fate?" The same futile question every month. No one fought dragons and won. The best you could hope for was a bargain where a maid died each month in return for the survival of the kingdom.

"I will save her." The voice came from the back of the hall. "Let me through."

Thea closed her eyes briefly; what a time for cook to be right with her gossip.

"You want to die too?" She rounded on the approaching man. He was young, barely older than her though his eyes said they had seen too much, and he seemed familiar though it took a moment to place him. "Last year, your sister—"

"Died."

"You didn't offer to save her."

"I didn't know enough. Now I do." His voice was as cold as ice.

"Why me?" She could guess the answer to that one.

"A princess?" He confirmed her suspicions. "I will be well rewarded."

"Of course, of course." Her father was animated; hopeful for the first time in a month.

"Your daughter will be mine."

The silence in the hall deepened.

"Well, if Thea agrees," her father said doubtfully.

"I'm going to die this afternoon," she snapped, her head held high. "If this idiot wants to die with me then that's his choice. If, by some miracle, he kills a dragon then he can do whatever he wants with me. I'm sure such a promise will brighten his remaining hours." She nodded curtly to her father and then turned to the young man. "Come on then, sir." She couldn't remember his name, so many cursing relatives passed through the hall. There would be time enough to learn what he was called if they made it back. "Let's go and die." She led the honour guard from the hall, her fingers white on the sword hilt, the young man matching her step for step.

~ * ~

The path which led down from the sally port to the small beach below had never been well used. It was intended for escape by sea should the king ever find himself besieged. Now it was used once a month to march a maiden to meet a dragon.

The rocks were slippery underfoot despite the sun's brilliance, each step an ankle-twisting risk on the way down. Thea concentrated on watching her feet, trying to ignore the slim dark-haired man beside her. He stared ahead recklessly. The only sign he gave of knowing she was there was when she slipped. His hand shot out and grabbed her arm yanking her upright so sharply she yelped in pain. Without a word, he let her go and continued down the path.

At the bottom, a pillar of stone had been erected bound round with thick chains. Thea glanced briefly at the fire-blackened links and then hurried past.

"Don't worry; I'm hardly going to run. You don't need to chain me." She needed to move about if she was to maintain her anger and keep from yielding to fear.

The captain hesitated. "The rules state you have to be—" His voice died away beneath her stare.

"I will not run," she repeated, enunciating each word clearly and slowly.

"Your highness." He accepted the inevitable, gave a low bow and led his guards away.

No witnesses. The dragon's rules said so. Her father maintained it was a kindness on their tormentor's part; that no one had to see loved ones die. Thea assumed, rather more cynically, the beast simply didn't like being watched while it was eating. She was grateful for the rule today; she didn't believe her anger would sustain her dignity long.

Which left the problem of her 'rescuer'; he hardly featured in the rules.

The young man—she really ought to ask his name—had wondered off down the beach. He seemed to be searching for something. So much for saving her.

Thea glanced skywards to where a speck had appeared on the horizon, growing bigger by the second. She clenched her fists and stared, desperate to make out details. Her stomach tightened, shrinking in on itself; her pulse quickened. Could she make a stand against this creature?

"I will not cry," Thea whispered, "I will not run. I will not cry. I will not—"

"Look!" It was the young man. "Come here, princess. Let me show you something."

She dragged her eyes from what was now definitely a winged shape moving fast above the ocean.

"What?"

"Come here." He emphasized his words by waving.

She strode down the beach, re-capturing her annoyance with the man. "It better be good. In case you hadn't noticed, there's a dragon on its way."

"Look at that." It was a cave hollowed into the hillside.

"You think I should hide?"

"I think you should look inside."

"What the hell for?"

"Just look." He sounded as cross as she was.

Thea sighed loudly, turned away and stomped into the cave.

It was full of corpses. Young girls in various stages of decomposition.

Thea gagged at the smell and stopped. The young man walked into her nearly knocking her over onto the closest one.

"They weren't eaten." She didn't understand. "They weren't burnt."

"No." So cross—as if it was her fault.

"But…I saw the dragon coming, if it doesn't…if…"

"Look closer."

Now her eyes had adjusted to the dimmer light she could make out stomach-churning details. "I don't think I want a closer look."

"Tough, princess." The contempt in his voice was corrosive.

He dragged her forwards and forced her to her knees beside one of the fresher bodies. Wide blue eyes stared emptily at the ceiling; matted hair lay clogged in the sand. Between the eyes a red jewel had been forced into the flesh. Another showed above her heart where the dress had been ripped away.

"They're all the same," the young man said.

"She doesn't look like she's been dead a month." Thea could remember the girl crying, shattering sobs which shook her entire frame as she was carried away.

"A month? She probably went in the past week."

"But—" Icy fingers touched Thea's heart. "What's she...I mean—" She didn't want to think about what sort of death the girl had suffered—the death which awaited her as well.

"She 'fed' the dragon. But not meat. Those jewels are a conduit of some sort."

Thea realized where she'd seen them before. "I saw some. The soldiers brought them in from places that were attacked when the dragon first came."

"And no one ever asked why."

"We did. It sleeps on its hoard, and they dropped from its scales." It sounded uncertain as she said it, nothing like the Chamberlain's proclamation on the subject.

"Children's tales. These are how it steals life and power to survive."

"How can you know?"

"I hid. I watched my sister taken and I've travelled a long distance since."

"That's forbidden."

"Of course it is. If people watched they might learn how to kill it."

"How?" Thea whispered, afraid somewhere outside the dragon was waiting and listening.

"There is a moment," the young man also dropped his voice, "when it inserts the jewels when it must lose itself and become one utterly with the source. That is the moment to strike."

Thea froze, the words circling in her head. She had to submit to this so he could take a chance to strike. And what if he missed or picked the wrong moment? Then she would spend a month dying to give a dragon power. Could she trust this angry young man to get it right? She took a deep, steadying breath. "All right. For my father, I'll do it."

"I wasn't giving you a choice, princess."

Thea stood quickly, annoyed. She'd just agreed to face a dragon so he could be a hero; to risk her life in the hope he could find the right moment. He might at least show a little gratitude.

She pushed past him to the cave mouth and staggered to a halt.

The dragon dominated the small beach its great wings furled across its back; its massive claws dug deep into the sand. Its hide was a multi-colored tapestry of golds and oranges threaded through with scarlet flashes. Its arrogant head tilted towards her, lips curling slightly to reveal a row of needle-sharp teeth.

The hypnotic ruby eyes bored into Thea, burrowing inside her head. She took a step forward without thought.

With an effort, she stopped. "I hope you know what you're doing," she said, her lips barely moving. "It's huge. I'm not sure you'll get your sword through it."

The young man, hidden in the dark behind her, let out a short breath of laughter. "Through *it*? Princess, you don't listen."

"But—" Thea stopped. She had listened, she just hadn't grasped the meaning woven below the surface.

"You said I could do with you as I would to kill the dragon."

She'd meant afterwards but it was too late to argue semantics now.

"It will be a kinder death than my sister suffered. Now, walk."

Stumbling slightly, her fingers fumbling at the useless sword hilt and all anger drained, Thea stepped forwards to join the dragon.

~ * ~ * ~

Emma Melville lives and works in Warwickshire, England. She is a schoolteacher of students with special needs who writes in her spare time, concentrating mainly on poetry and crime and fantasy short stories, often inspired by her involvement with folk dance and song. She has published several poems and short stories in anthologies and won several literary competitions. Her first novel, Journeyman, recently published, was shortlisted by the Crime Writers Association for their Debut Dagger Award.

.

Witches in a Dragon

Christopher Fielden

"I hate dragons," Mildred said. "They're a pain in me nether regions."

Despite feeling annoyed with Mildred for causing their current predicament, Hilda was unable to fault her assessment of large reptiles. Being swallowed was bad enough, but the state of this thing's belly was beyond imagining. All sorts of items protruded from the stomach acid. Animal bones, a cart's wheel, a ship's mast—

"Is that a statue?"

"I think it is, Hild." Mildred was trying to wipe intestinal goo out of her hair, fighting a battle she was unlikely to win. There was more goo than hair. "Looks like the mayor's statue, the one that went missing from Chieftain's Hill last month." Mildred smirked. "Ain't he one of them dragon deniers?"

Hilda nodded. "How ironic."

"Well, at least this proves they exist, eh Hild?"

"Beyond doubt."

Hilda flicked the glowing tip of her wand around their fleshy prison. It was like a blood-filled cauldron; bubbling, brown and full of half-digested bits of lord knows what. Hilda was knee deep in the intestinal quagmire and her irritation was rising.

"It took us weeks to brew that annihilation potion," Hilda said, clambering onto the statue's base. "Why didn't you use it?"

"Only in an emergency, you said, if there was nothing else we could do."

"I think the moments prior to our ingestion, particularly the final few seconds when the dragon drooled on us, could have been classed as an emergency." Hilda unlaced and removed one calf-length boot and poured fluid from it. Her stockings, which Mildred had knitted, were ruined.

"When you annihilate something, Hilda Jane Beauchamp, it's destroyed. Utterly obliterated. There ain't nothing left of it, save for dust. No head, no proof. And we're here for proof." A large blob of goo slid from the brim of Mildred's pointed hat onto her shoulder.

Hilda offered Mildred her hanky. A small one, embroidered

with broomsticks.

"Oh, very funny, Hild." This was a hands-on-hips moment and Mildred didn't fail to take advantage of it. All of her chins wobbled as she spoke. "Hilarious, that is. This is important."

Hilda sighed. Mildred was right. Dragons were posing a threat to humankind, but no one would do anything about it because there was little proof they existed. In the foothills of the mountains, where Hilda lived, farmers were losing crops, livestock and, more recently, farmworkers. This *was* important.

"I apologize, Mildred. The prospect of becoming dragon excrement isn't helping my mood, or judgement."

Mildred's scowl dissipated and she looked around. "How are we going to get out of here?"

Hilda started rummaging through the pockets in her long, soggy dress. Then her shawl. Under her hat. In the folds of her cape.

"What you lookin' for?" Mildred asked.

"You'll see, if I can find it."

"You should use that bag I got you last solstice. Nice lookin'. Spacious. Lots of compartments, so you can find stuff easy."

Hilda tutted. She didn't believe in bags. They always got in the way, especially when casting spells. And one might be liable to forget them; leave them in a tavern or at the alchemists. But pockets...pockets were different. They went everywhere with you and Hilda had a plethora of them. "It's in here somewhere..."

"What's in there somewhere?"

"Be patient, Mildred."

"Me feet's itchin', Hild. Might be me athlete's foot, but I think this stomach soup is starting to digest me toes. Hurry it up, will you?"

Hilda's fingers found what they were looking for. She pulled a small bayonet from a recess in her tunic and connected it to her wand.

Mildred looked at her, eyes so wide there was more white than iris. "Where'd you get *that*?"

"Old Mistress Birdwhistle gave it to me, years ago, when she first deemed me worthy of the title Sorceress."

"She never gave me one."

"Studying was not your forte, Mildred."

"I got the title of Sorceress though, didn't I?"

"Eventually..."

"And when I did, she gave me a hat."

"It's a nice hat."

Mildred glanced upwards. "Yeah, but it ain't no wand-bayonet, is it? I can't believe you've never shown it to me before."

"Shall we discuss this later, Mildred? I think we should probably focus on getting out of here."

"I s'pose we should. You going to use that fancy blade thing of yours—what I ain't got one of because I ain't clever enough—to cut us an exit?"

"Unless you have a better idea, yes."

"Ideas ain't my thing, Hild. I ain't very bright, remember?"

This could continue for days, Hilda thought. *If we live...* "Mildred, do you think a dragon's scales are as tough on the inside as they are on the outside?"

"Funny you should say that," Mildred replied, clambering out of the intestinal juices to stand on the statue's base, "cos I've worn dragon-scale armor."

Hilda raised an eyebrow. "When?"

"At a fancy dress party. I went as a knight. Borrowed it off that chevalier. You know, the one who was blessed when it came to fighting, but not so much in the face department. Had eyes like poached eggs, a nose like an overbaked baguette and a puckered mouth what looked like a cat's butthole. Bought a lot of love potions."

Hilda shuddered, wondering how many lives had been ruined by Mildred's elixirs.

"You know my love potions don't do nothing, right? They're placebos. All they do is make people more confident."

"You can read minds now?"

"No. I ain't that bright, remember? Your face says it all, Hild. Just got to observe. Anyway. As I remember it, the armor was very comfortable."

Hilda was about to ask whether comfort related to strength when a sudden bout of coughing made her stop. The air tasted of acid and her lungs hurt. She looked at Mildred; her chubby face shone with defiance, but her skin was blotchy and her eyes bloodshot. She looked exhausted. A dragon's gut is not a welcoming environment. They had to stop talking and escape.

"Thank you, Mildred, for your insight. I will be sure to take that into account."

Hilda used her wand to shine light around the dragon's stomach, while recalling anatomy classes from her training days. Organs, sinews, cartilage and all the other unpleasant things you find inside bodies are important to witchcraft, so Hilda had dissected many creatures. Of course, she'd never anatomized a dragon, but they were reputed—by those who acknowledged their existence—to share similarities with serpents and reptiles. Essentially, their digestive system was like that of a lizard, just bigger.

Hilda shone the light upwards, illuminating the round, muscular orifice they'd arrived through. "That must be the lower esophageal sphincter."

"I thought sphincters were on the outside. Well, kind of. It's not like they see a lot of daylight between your ass cheeks, but—"

"There are multiple sphincters in the bodies of most creatures, Mildred, not just *that* one."

Mildred folded her arms. "Well, I'll consider myself educated."

Moving her wand slowly, Hilda followed the arc of the stomach lining to the back of the gooey pool the statue was standing in. "Beneath that, is the pyloric sphincter."

"Fascinating, that is. You're *so* clever. But, if I may ask… *so what?*"

"The dragon's midriff should be opposite. The belly is the softest external area and, therefore, the one we have the best chance of cutting through."

"I see." Mildred's scowl softened. She looked at the bayonet. "Do you think that little thing will cut through a dragon?"

"I don't know. But we have to try."

"Well, if anyone can save us, my money's on you." Mildred gave Hilda a hug. "And if it all goes tits up, there ain't no one else I'd rather die with."

Feeling tears welling, Hilda kissed Mildred's cheek, extracted herself from the embrace and jumped down from the statue. She steadied herself in the swamp of gastric detritus and raised her hand. The bayonet shone in the light emanating from the wand's tip.

"Do it, Hild. Gut the bugger."

Hilda lunged forward and swung the weapon. It tore through stomach lining. Their host lurched. Hilda managed to grab the statue's base, but Mildred lost her balance and fell from above her, disappearing with a splash. Hilda plunged her hand into the stomach juices, grabbed an arm and pulled. Mildred came to the surface, gasping.

"Are you alright?"

"Yeah," Mildred said. "He didn't like that much, did he?"

They looked at the wound Hilda had inflicted. The gash was

long, but not deep enough.

Mildred spat, a glower on her face. "I got an idea, Hild. Give us a hand up onto the statue, will you?"

After some rather inelegant shoving, Mildred reached her desired destination and took a hip flask from her belt. She swigged and passed it down to Hilda, who took a sip. The elixir tasted medicinal—it soothed Hilda's throat and cleared her mind.

Mildred then pulled a stoppered vial of powder from her pocket, sprinkled it on her feet and undertook a short dance—the somatic elements of a spell.

Hilda marveled at Mildred's dexterity. A voluminous woman working in a confined space should not be graceful, especially when clad in witches' attire that was both copious and sodden. But the precision of Mildred's footwork was pristine, her balance perfect. When the dance was complete, Mildred floated into the air and drew her wand. Crimson mist poured from her nose, masking her face in blood-shadow. From deep in her throat, the words of the magnify spell resonated. Hilda's wand, and bayonet, enlarged. The blade sparked with tendrils of fire and lightning.

Hilda felt her confidence grow. "Thank you, Mildred. Your witchcraft is impeccable."

Thrusting wand and bayonet forward, Hilda charged. She slashed upward, rending a gaping wound in the dragon's midriff. Fire and lightning sizzled. The stench of burnt flesh filled the air. Through the hole she'd made, Hilda glimpsed the moon and stars.

Before she could celebrate, their host reeled. A tidal wave of stomach acid hit Hilda in the back, knocking her from her feet. She sank, swirling in a whirlpool of abdominal slime. *We've failed*, Hilda thought. *Two witches versus a dragon. What a stupid notion.* Her body was thrown violently back and forth. Something crashed against her head. Pain flashed, extinguished by blackness.

~ * ~

A slap stung Hilda's cheek. She opened her eyes and saw Mildred standing over her, a worried expression on her face.

"Sorry, Hild, did that harder than I meant to. Thought you was dead there for a moment."

Hilda sat up and rubbed the back of her head. "So did I. What happened?"

"You did it, Hild. Cut a hole so big in that thing's gut its stomach exploded outward. Took us with it."

Hilda looked around. They were on a mountain ledge, lit by moonlight. It was spattered with dragon debris. Scales stuck out of the rock face. Flesh and blood decorated everything. A stream of stomach juice was pouring away, over the side of the mountain. And they were in one piece, breathing, *alive*.

"That's one hell of a bayonet," Mildred said, a hint of jealousy in her voice.

Hilda nodded. "Especially when magnified by one of the most powerful witches who ever walked these mountains."

"Oh stop it, Hild, me head'll swell."

The bayonet was still enlarged, glimmering with shreds of fire. "Well, I guess we can use it to cut off the dragon's—"

"Head?" The voice was deep and filled with loathing.

Hilda turned and saw a monstrous shape, looming in the shadows. It limped forward into the moonlight. The dragon was colossal, the carnage that was its midriff exuding a mass of entrails. Everything about it was black: its scales, its eyes, its wings, its claws—even its erupting innards. As it spoke, noxious smoke spiraled from its nostrils. "This time, I'll chew before I swallow."

It raised itself up onto its hind legs, spread its wings and bellowed, revealing a mass of granite-like teeth.

The beast lunged. A blast of rancid breath hit Hilda in the face, but failed to ignite, proving dragons needed an intact digestive system to spew fire.

Claws slashed. Mildred darted left. Jaws snapped. Hilda ducked, but she wasn't fast enough. Her left arm erupted in pain. The dragon swung its head upwards, flinging her into the air.

As she reached the apex of her trajectory, Hilda experienced a moment of weightlessness. Looking down, she saw the dragon rise onto its hind legs and open its mouth. Its black throat glistened in the moonlight, like a doorway to the grave.

As she began to fall, Hilda saw Mildred point her wand. A bolt of energy hit the creature in the back. It roared, turning its head.

Hilda swung the wand-bayonet in a deadly arc. Fizzing through the air, spitting sparks of fire, it sliced through the dragon's exposed neck. As the monstrous head fell with a crash, the dragon's body slid off the mountain ledge, toppling out of sight.

Hilda landed heavily in a mound of intestines. Although disgusting, the guts were soft enough to break her fall. She lay still, fighting for breath. The dragon's head stared at her with lifeless eyes, wisps of vapor rising from dead nostrils.

Hilda felt Mildred take her hand and gently squeeze it. "You okay, Hild?"

There was an ugly gash on her left arm. Tentatively, Hilda moved her fingers. "I think so. Cut and bruised, not broken."

Tearing a strip of cloth from her dress, Mildred bandaged the wound. "That will have to do until we get home." Mildred helped her into a sitting position and they leant against a rock. With shaky hands, they took turns to drink from Mildred's flask.

After a few minutes of quiet, Hilda had regained some semblance of composure. She nodded at the dragon's head. "We have to make sure this is seen."

"We could put it on Chieftain's Hill, where the mayor's statue was. Replace a denier's likeness with what he's in denial of. Kind of poetic, eh?"

"More people will see it in the town square, especially if we take it there on market day."

"True." A somber look clouded Mildred's face. "You think the deniers will say it's fake?"

"Probably."

"Don't see why they don't admit the problem exists. They must know. There's a food shortage because of ruined crops and disappearing cattle. It can't all be down to heatwaves and thieves. People are disappearing too."

"Politics, Mildred. There will be a reason: money, relationships, power, control; something like that."

"Or all of it." Mildred suddenly perked up. "Ooo, Hild, look." She got up, wandered over to the rock face covered in bits of dragon and bent down amidst the debris.

"What is it?"

"More proof." Mildred turned around. In her hands was an egg. It was the size of a watermelon and granite-black. "I guess he was a she."

"They'll have trouble denying the existence of dragons if that hatches. Come on, let's get the cart."

"I hope the horses haven't legged it."

"If they have, we'll find them."

As they hobbled towards the gully they'd used to hide the cart, Hilda removed the bayonet from her wand. It had returned to a normal size.

"It's a lovely bayonet, that is," Mildred said. "Wish I was clever enough to have one."

Hilda looked at the artefact in her hand. It marked a great achievement in her personal history, but Hilda was no fighter—today, she'd been lucky. Mildred was younger, more dexterous. It might be of more use to her.

"You're more than clever enough." Hilda proffered the bayonet. "Happy birthday."

"My birthday ain't for three months."

"Consider this an early gift."

Mildred gave Hilda a hug that hurt. It came from nowhere and crushed the air from her lungs. "You is the most special sister I ever had." Mildred released her and grinned. It was one of those grins that might last a week. Or more. "In return, you can have me hat."

Hilda looked at the misshapen thing on Mildred's head. "I couldn't possibly—"

"I insist."

They swapped items. Hilda removed her own hat and placed Mildred's on her head. It fit perfectly, despite a noticeable disparity in their head sizes. Maybe it was more than just a hat.

Mildred attached the bayonet to her wand and swished it back and forth. "You know, seeing as how this ended up being a swapping of magical artefacts, this bayonet don't really count as a present. You'll have to get me another."

Hilda sighed. "Yes, Mildred."

~ * ~

After loading the dragon's head onto the cart—a process that took a lot of time, rope, horses and swearing—they took their seats and prepared to leave.

As the rising sun appeared to the east, Hilda looked down the mountainside and saw the dragon's body smashed on the rocks below. Out of its midriff, the mayor's statue protruded, surrounded by a giant ribcage. Stomach acid had eaten away at the more intricate parts of the statue, particularly the head, leaving it eyeless.

Hilda nudged Mildred and pointed. "An effigy to the futility of denial. Long may it remind us."

"What you on about, Hild? All I know is I'm gagging for a cuppa. And tea tastes better with cake. You got some cake in the larder, right?"

Hilda smiled. "Always."

"Good. I've had enough of this heroism malarkey. And I need a bath. That thing's innards are still playing havoc with me skin. Can we go home please?"

"Yes, Mildred, we certainly can."

Hilda flicked the whip above the horses' heads. The cart moved forward, and they began their journey home, with a cargo that might just change the future.

~ * ~ * ~

Christopher Fielden is an award-winning and Amazon bestselling author. His work has featured in books published by independent press, established magazines and renowned competition anthologies.

In November 2019, Victorina Press published Chris's short story collection, *Book of the Bloodless Volume 1: Alternative Afterlives*. The book was an Award-Winning Finalist in the 'Fiction: Short Story' category of the International Book Awards, sponsored by American Book Fest.

Chris runs a popular fiction writing blog that attracts over 300,000 visitors each year. He judges the To Hull And Back humorous short story competition and publishes thousands of writers' stories in support of charity via his flash fiction writing challenges.

His book, *How to Write a Short Story, Get Published and Make Money*, has sold thousands of copies. It uses an honest teaching style that has been very well received. In the book, Chris uses his own published short stories as case studies, clearly showing how any advice given has been used in practice to achieve publishing success.

Chris is a member of the ALCS, ASCAP, the British Fantasy Society, Clockhouse London Writers and Stokes Croft Writers in Bristol, UK.

Outside of writing, Chris plays drums in a variety of bands. These include Little Villains—a UK hard-rock band that originally featured the late Phil 'Philthy Animal' Taylor, who is most famous for playing drums in Motörhead—and Airbus—a British rock act that have been recording and touring together since 1988.

You can learn more about Chris on his website: www.christopherfielden.com

In a Time of Revelation

Kay Hanifen

Humans called me the Whore of Babylon who rides the Seven-Headed Beast and drinks the blood of martyrs. Dragons called me On'ria—*small scaleless one*. To anyone who knew me before the awakening, my name was Sofia, but no one has called me that in years.

When I was a little girl, dragons were the stuff of fairytales. They guarded princesses from knights and hoarded gold in caves. I didn't know why the dragons emerged from underground cave systems and the oceans. By the time they might have had an answer, I no longer lived among the humans. What I do remember in visceral detail, though, was the first time I saw a dragon. It was early in their return, back when we thought of them as novelties rather than the end of humanity's dominance over the earth.

I still sat in a booster seat, idly swinging my legs as we passed pastures full of cows, sheep, and horses. Mom and Dad wanted to get to Uncle Barry's compound to wait out the dragon attacks that had been devastating cities and suburbia. He was a doomsday prepper, and, according to Mom, incredibly smug when she asked if we could stay with him.

A Christian rock song played on the radio. We weren't particularly religious, but it was the only station playing something other than static.

"When the trumpets sound,
We'll seize the day,
And Christ will be crowned,
So let us pray!"

A shadow passed over the car. Mom gasped and pointed to the left-hand field where cows groaned and scattered. Dad slammed on the brakes, and we watched in awe as a massive shape descended from the sky, green iridescent scales glinting in the sunlight. It had to be bigger than a house, the flap of its powerful wings shaking the car like the winds of a hurricane. A cow lost its footing in the onslaught, and the dragon plucked it up and bit into the panicking creature without any struggle. Sometimes, when I close my eyes, I still hear the pained cries of the cow, the crunching of bone, and see the viscera dripping from the dragon's blood-stained teeth. I covered my eyes and ears when it snatched another. Dad should have been driving away as fast as the car would go, but instead he put it in park and shushed us. Looking back on it, he probably did it so the dragon wouldn't see us moving and think we were prey, but between the hungry dragon and my first-time witnessing death in such a horrible way, I was too hysterical to listen.

The rest of the day was just fragments. My throat was hoarse by the time we arrived at Uncle Barry's compound, and my head pounded from dehydration. He'd opened the gates and let us in. Mom carried me to a bunk bed where we spent our first night huddled together in the safety of the bunker.

Uncle Barry wasn't the only one living in the compound. The man was convinced the world would end in his lifetime, and God would punish us for our society's turn towards wickedness. He preached to everyone he met that we must repent before it was too late and considered himself a kind of cowboy for the Lord, carrying around a gun and wearing a Stetson hat wherever he went. Over the years, he accumulated a small following in the community, and when the dragons woke, they all hunkered down in the society they'd been building for the past two decades. This was the apocalypse he dreamed of for years.

I was the only child among them, and Uncle Barry saw a potential acolyte in me, a young mind to sculpt in his image. At the age of eight, he began my training with first memorizing Bible verses.

"Exodus 22:18," he said as he sat back in his leather office chair.

"Thou shalt not suffer a witch to live," I replied, standing ramrod straight with my hands clasped behind my back.

He smiled, and I relaxed slightly until he called out a New Testament passage, "John 8:5."

"Let he who is without sin cast the first stone."

He frowned, furrowing his bushy brows. "You sure about that, kiddo?"

My eyes strayed to my feet, studying my dirtied pink tennis shoes. "Yes."

"You don't sound sure. This is the Lord's book, right? He would want you to know it as thoroughly as He knows your soul." He got up from his chair and tilted my chin, forcing me to meet his warm, brown eyes. "Now Sof, do you know why the dragons are here?"

"God promised to never send a flood to cleanse the world

after Noah's Ark, but we got bad again, and Satan sent them to punish sinners with fire and teeth."

"Do you want to be dragon chow?"

Images of that cow torn apart by the massive, green monster flashed before my eyes and I stifled a gag at the thought. "No sir," I replied quickly.

He clasped my shoulders. "Then you'd best get to studying so God will protect you from the monsters."

I scurried off to my usual hiding spot when I wanted to be alone. The storage shed on the outskirts of the compound allowed for privacy and a view of the hole in the electric fence just big enough to wriggle through. We were only allowed to leave the compound to hunt for game, and I used to stare at that hole for hours contemplating if I could escape for just a little while.

The spot was remote and quiet. They rarely patrolled this area, so feasibly, I could slip through for a few hours, and they'd be none the wiser.

It took me two years to build up the courage to escape. In that time, Mom and Dad had both been picked off by dragons while hunting with Uncle Barry, leaving me alone among the residents of his compound. Something intensified in him after their deaths, and he redoubled his efforts to turn me into his little acolyte.

The day I first snuck out of the compound Uncle Barry had been in a mood. Every time I stumbled or misspoke in reciting a Bible passage, he'd force me to start at the beginning. At around hour two, I was ready to cry, but he kept going heedless of my growing exhaustion.

"What sins did Sodom and Gomorrah commit that led to its downfall?" he asked.

"Robbery, pride, and, uh, going after strange flesh, but I don't know what that means." My back ached from standing so straight for so long, terrified to let my muscles relax for even a second. The fluorescents in the dingy room where we held after service meals on folding chairs and plastic tables hummed a grating tune that made my head hurt.

He patted my shoulder. "And hopefully, once the dragons cleanse the earth, you never will."

I blinked, tilting my head. "Uncle Barry, I'm confused. Are the dragons good or evil?" The question had been lingering in my mind for a while, and I had spent our entire two-hour session working up the courage to ask it.

He furrowed his bushy brows and let out a deep belly laugh. "What kind of question is that? Of course, they're evil. Satan sent them as the opening fire of the apocalypse. They kill people."

I studied the grey carpet, ignoring the way the varying shades from near black to white made it look like static to see the plaid-like pattern underneath. "It's just that you don't seem sad about them killing people. They're sinners, but they don't deserve to get eaten or burned alive."

The room dropped in temperature. "Sofia, remind me again of the sixth commandment?"

"Honor thy father and mother," I replied automatically.

He clasped my shoulder, fingers digging in just a bit too tight. "I have no kids of my own, but I like to think of you as the daughter I never had. Which is why it hurts me so much for you to ask me something like that. Of course, I don't want people to die. I'd much rather they find their way back to the light."

"But—"

"You love me, right?"

"I do, Uncle Barry, I do." Tears formed behind my eyes and threatened to spill over.

"Then why would you hurt me by asking something like that?"

"I'm sorry," I said, sniffling. Admittedly, I was a sensitive kid, but something about Uncle Barry's disappointment cut deeper than any yelling by him or my parents.

He patted my shoulder. "I think that's enough for today. Go get some reading done."

I all but fled the room, sobbing as I ran off to my little opening in the fence without even knowing why I was crying—the session, the fingers gripping my shoulder hard enough to bruise, or Uncle Barry's disappointment in my failure as a niece and a student. Sitting against the shed, I stared at the hole in the fence that promised freedom from his and the rest of the compound's judgement.

I was so caught up in my personal misery I didn't hear it at first. A squealing, somewhere between a dog and a pig. It came from in the woods, but not too far away. I'd already disappointed Uncle Barry once that day, but whatever it was sounded like it was in so much pain; I couldn't just let it suffer. No one else seemed to be around, so I crawled through the hole in the fence and wandered in the direction of the noise.

The trees gave me cover as I walked, so I felt safe enough from aerial attacks, but anything could have been lurking in the greenery. Finally, I spotted the source of the noise. A dragon pup about the size of a dog with iridescent blue scales that reminded me of the sky had its leg caught in a steel trap. The poor thing cried out as it tried in vain to fly away from the thing causing it pain.

In spite of myself, I felt bad for it. Dragons may have been sent by the devil and killed my parents, but this was just a baby. I knew I should have left it to die from starvation or blood loss after gnawing off its own leg, but I couldn't turn my back on the suffering creature. Jesus, after all, would've shown mercy.

It snarled as I slowly approached, and every animal instinct told me to run, but instead, I showed it my empty hands and averted my eyes. "You probably don't understand me, but I want to help you."

Abruptly, it stopped struggling, cocking its head as I bent down. When I reached for the wounded leg, it hissed, but I just murmured, "It's okay. I'm just helping you get free." Ten-year-olds aren't strong, but somehow, I managed to wedge my fingers into the sides and pull it apart just long enough for it to free its leg and take off. "You're welcome," I called to the small figure disappearing into the trees.

I never spoke a word of that day to anyone. Uncle Barry rarely laid a hand on me, but helping a dragon escape one of his traps would have led to some of his most creative punishments. Once, I spoke out of turn. I don't remember what it was anymore, but I do remember having to clean all the livestock pens for a week. Another time, he thought I was lying to him about something, so he locked me in a confessional until I made up a confession that the night before, I had stolen some chocolate from the supplies. He had me apologize to everyone at the compound for my selfishness. I shudder to think the kind of punishment he'd concoct for a crime like this.

The guilt alone was enough to swallow me like a dragon's cavernous maw. As the years went on, our population on the compound dwindled as more and more people were taken while on hunts. Peter Stravinsky who baked the best pies and Marge Hollans who taught me to weave clothing on a loom. Alan and Ethan Bartoll, brothers and expert marksmen, and sweet old Laura Daniels who'd comfort me after long sessions with Uncle Barry. Her death was the one that tipped me off.

Two nights before the fatal hunt, I heard them arguing from his office. I'd never heard someone raise their voice like that, loud enough I didn't have to press my ear to the door to overhear.

"Do you have any idea what you're doing to that poor girl? She leaves every one of *your lessons* in tears," Laura said, "She's been through enough without you forcing her to be your acolyte."

Uncle Barry's voice was much softer but held an edge of threat that my heart pound. "Laura, be reasonable I'm just doing my best here."

"Be reasonable," she repeated, her voice a high squawk, "Are you kidding me? Your best is damaging her. She's so scared and withdrawn, like you'd feed her to the dragons the moment she disappointed you."

"Well, maybe she needs the discipline. You know how her parents were. They raised her to be like every other child devoured by the sins of the father. If it wasn't for me, she'd by caught in this great cleansing."

A heavy silence fell between them, and I held my breath in anticipation. "I can't believe I was so wrong about you," she said. Conversation clearly over, I hid around the corner as the door opened and slammed shut.

Two days later, Uncle Barry announced a hunt, and pulled Laura's name from the raffle bowl as his hunting partner. He returned alone sobbing about how a dragon took her, and he was powerless to stop it. It always seemed so miraculous that our leader was holy enough dragons would ignore him in favor of his hunting partner. Obviously, Laura, Peter, Marge, and the Bartoll brothers weren't strong enough believers in the power of the Lord. They had doubt in their hearts and the dragons seized upon it as they seized them. But with Laura's death, another possibility emerged in my mind. What if it wasn't the dragons? What if, because they had dissented, he sent them to die like David did to Uriah? Or worse, what if he'd killed them himself and blamed it on the dragons, and, by extension, their sinful ways?

Thinking back to the way my parents acted around him—their stiff conversations, forced smiles, and insistence dragons weren't the heralds of the apocalypse sent to cleanse the earth like he said they were—it seemed less and less likely they were victims of a dragon attack. Even now, knowing the man who likely killed my parents was the one who raised me makes me queasy.

I wasn't the only one who suspected this. A pall had fallen over the compound. Smiles were few and far between. No one spoke unless necessary. Conversations stopped when I entered the room. They probably assumed I was the little acolyte sent to spy on any dissidents as if my own doubts didn't grow larger by the day.

And then Uncle Barry brought back the corpse of a baby dragon. It was smaller than the one I rescued, with amber scales like the reflection of sunlight on water. He'd already skinned and decapitated it, impaling its head on a spike near the entrance to the compound. He wanted to wear the baby's pelt like Hercules wore the Nemean Lion, but never got the chance.

That night, the forest came alive with a terrible wailing of grief that drove me to tears even in the bunker below. And then the bunker rattled. Somewhere, a fire alarm went off and Uncle Barry slammed open the door. "Sofie, get your gun."

To shocked and frightened to argue, I grabbed my rifle from below my bed—whatever good it would do against bulletproof scales—and followed him and the rest of the surviving members of the compound as the dragons bellowed from above. He led us to an emergency exit that let out near the vehicles he'd use for the occasional supply run.

I was the second to last out, followed only by my cowboy uncle bravely hiding behind a teenage girl. The autumn night should have been cold, but with the heat of the dragons torching our vehicles and harvest, I was sweating in my pajamas. In the firelight, the dragons themselves flickered like flames. There were three. A red one the size of a house, a green one of about the same height, and a much smaller blue one the size of a draft horse. They tore down our buildings and made meals of our livestock, too intent on destruction to see us emerge from our escape hatch.

I stood frozen in awed horror as they destroyed where I'd lived for most of my life. The bleating of terrified animals and smell of cooked flesh haunts me, but there was beauty in its desolation, the flames casting dancing shadows all around me, the embers glowing a soft red that complimented the fiery colors of the autumn leaves, and the dragons themselves shimmering in the moonlight. And something about the smaller blue dragon looked familiar. Before I could place it, though, Uncle Barry pushed past me.

"Sofia, we have to go now."

Shaken out of my stupor, I followed the group as we slipped along the fence skirting the property. I moved slowly, terrified the giant dragons would notice, but it was the smaller one who slipped around and grabbed me from above, one clawed hand wrapped around my middle as it dragged me into the air. "Uncle Barry!" I screamed. He whipped around, taking aim with his gun.

It was too fast, and he didn't have a clear shot, so while the rest of the compound fled the wrath of the fully grown dragons, the smaller absconded with me. I'd never been a fan of heights, and soaring above the treetops, my ribs aching because all my dead weight pressed against its arm, made me like it even less. I screamed until my voice was hoarse and clung to its arm, knowing full well it was the only thing preventing a fall to my death. After what felt like hours but was likely only a few minutes, the beat of its wings slowed, and it glided to the ground.

We landed in a forest clearing near the edge of a cave. The moment it let go, I scrambled back until I hit a tree. But the dragon didn't attack. It tilted its head, reminding me of a curious cat. One of its forelegs—the one that wasn't carrying me—was much shorter than the other as though something had stunted its growth, probably by breaking it at a young age. Something like a bear trap pried apart by the fingers of a ten-year-old so long ago. "You won't eat me, will you?"

Obviously, it didn't reply, instead walking and looking back when it reached the mouth of the cave as though waiting for me to follow. Given the choice between dying of exposure in the woods and following an animal that may or may not eat me, I decided becoming a juvenile dragon's meal was a far quicker death than starvation or dehydration.

A few steps into cave and the darkness enveloped me like a blanket. I glanced back to the entrance illuminated by a sliver of moonlight and wondered if it was too late to die of exposure outside. But, guided only by the sound of the creature ahead, I followed. And then I couldn't hear it anymore. Blindly taking a step forward, I felt nothing underfoot and panicked, crying out as I fell down a cliff whose height I didn't know, but a clawed hand caught me and, digging into my skin hard enough to bleed, carried me down the side of the rocks it clung to. When we reached the bottom, it set me down. There was a faint glow up ahead, and the dragon ambled towards it. I couldn't help my gasp when we reached it.

Glowing mushrooms lined the walls of a giant cavern, illuminating it in blues, greens, and purples. A small river fed into it before disappearing further into the darkness, and dragon pups play-fought in the stream. For almost as long as I could remember, I thought of dragons as these brutal monsters only interested in their next meal, but watching them play, I began to realize just how smart they were. While some were fighting, others played a game similar to Marco Polo where one dragon would vocalize with its eyes closed and the others would respond and swim out of the way.

My kidnapper nudged me forward. Apparently, this wasn't our destination. The exit was on the other side, and I ignored the curious looks the pups gave us as we passed. The next cavern it led us to was full of cells like a beehive. Older dragons flitted about, and, using its wing, it pulled me close and gave me cover as it approached one of the smaller cells near the bottom. It was lined with faux fur and scrap fabric, likely liberated from an abandoned store or the dump. The dragon stepped inside, kneading the fabric as it settled into its nest. It gave me a look that asked, *You coming?*

My throat was parched, but I swallowed anyway as I skirted the edge of the wall and wedged myself into the corner. It raised its head, giving me an odd look before lowering it again and closing its eyes. Despite the damp and the autumn chill, the proximity to the fire breathing creature provided enough warmth my eyelids drooped against my will. I wanted to stay awake and alert, but the adrenaline of the night had run out and I fell into a dreamless sleep.

I woke to the sound of growls and snarls. The two giant dragons had returned, and apparently weren't happy with the blue one taking in a pet. I curled myself into as small a ball as I could, praying they'd ignore me. But then the red dragon met my eyes. It reached in and picked me up. Powerless to do anything but cover my important organs, I felt its steaming breath as it examined me like a thoroughbred horse. It poked and prodded while I cried in small gasping sobs. After an eternity and a few minutes, it stopped, but did not put me down. I cracked open one eye and then another, only to find myself face to face with a monster. I met its lizard-like red eyes, marveling at the way the pupils felt like black holes waiting to suck me in.

With a snort that emitted steam, it set me down. The blue dragon moved between us and flitted upwards, rubbing its chin against the red one and then the green. They reciprocated with a gentle trill and a puff of steam before ambling off for somewhere to rest after a long night of pillaging.

Apparently alive for now, I laid back down in the corner, questions swirling in my mind. Did the dragons kill Uncle Barry and the rest of the compound's inhabitants? Or would he come back with the torches and pitchforks to free his niece from the dragon's clutches? After years of living with a man whose emotional intelligence rivaled that of a cheese sandwich, I'd mastered the art of quiet crying. While the dragon in front of me slept, I let the tears come not just for Uncle Barry and the rest of the people dead at the compound but also for the people like my parents that I believed he'd murdered.

I must have fallen asleep again, because, between one blink and the next, the charred carcass of a rat appeared before me. The blue dragon sat in front of me expectantly and trilled when I picked it up, wincing at the heat that still came from the meat. It smelled of burnt hair and looked as appetizing as the slop I'd feed the pigs, but it was better than nothing. I could only hope the inside was as well done as the outside. It tasted a bit like the wild rabbit Uncle Barry caught sometimes but dried out and charred by fiery breath. "Mmm, thank you," I said, exaggerating my pleasure. If I was to be this dragon's pet, it was probably best to appear grateful for anything it gave me.

It trilled and disappeared, presumably to catch more rats. Joy. Two options warred within me. I could stay in this little cell and wait for the dragon to return, or I could venture out and look for an escape on my own. On the one hand, I had to escape before it got bored of me. On the other, more obvious hand, I was an easy meal for these monsters, and right now the blue dragon was the only thing between me and getting charbroiled alive. So, in the cave I stayed. It was best to bide my time and keep up my strength by eating whatever it gave me.

While I waited, some of the pups poked their head in, their eyes bright and pupils dilated in curiosity. I gave them a weak wave and they stumbled away as though they'd been caught where they shouldn't have been. Eventually, the dragon returned and scared them off before setting down a stick in front of me. It gestured to itself with its smaller arm and let out a growl that sounded something like, "Srrrza." I must have looked completely confused because it gestured to itself again and repeated, "Srrrza."

Finally, it clicked. "Are you saying your same is Serza?"

It nodded emphatically with a lizard-like smile and repeated, "Serza," before pointing to me.

"Uh, Sofia," I replied.

"So-he-uh," it repeated, unable to make the "f" sound without any lips.

It tried a couple more times without success and seemed to be growing frustrated, so I just said, "You could give me a dragon name if that's easier."

The dragon nodded, pointed to me and said, "On'ria."

"What does that mean?" I asked. What followed was the most bizarre game of charades I'd ever played. It brought its two claws close together without touching, resembling the human hand sign for small. Then it took me by the arm and pointed back and forth until I said the difference out loud. *Small and scaleless.* It wasn't the most creative name, but the act of naming me alone provided some relief. It meant the dragon didn't plan on eating me for a while.

"Are you male or female?" If dragons were intelligent enough to have their own language, they certainly didn't deserve to be called "it." But I'd made a mistake, because apparently dragon culture has no modesty, and Serza had no issue showing me her female genitalia to demonstrate. "Okay!" I exclaimed, covering my eyes, "thank you for that!"

Serza gave me another puzzled look as she sat down. I couldn't help my laugh at the way she cocked her head like a curious kitten. She pointed to me, then to the leg, and mimed a trap opening. It wasn't a question.

"I thought you might be the baby dragon I helped all those years ago. You've grown a lot."

She gave me another smile, revealing teeth so sharp I had to force myself not to flinch from them, and pointed to me, herself, and then intertwined her claws.

"Are you saying saving your life bound me to you?" Another nod. The weight of it forced me to sit down. Serza wasn't just playing with her food. She had no intention of eating me, but, apparently, because I helped her, she was now indebted to me. So many questions swirled in my exhausted mind. How did she know English? Was I really the only person to help a baby dragon, or were there others also bound to the monsters I was taught would raze the earth and burn away the sinners? Did befriending this dragon put me on the side of Satan? Was I going to hell?

I barely registered falling to my knees and sagging against the wall over the hammering of my heart. I couldn't breathe and my vision blurred. I had to run, to get away, but only had the strength to curl into a ball, arms thrown protectively around my head. Something warm like a plate of cookies fresh out of the oven nudged me, and I whimpered, unable to make myself any smaller.

When I came back to myself—exhausted and with a throbbing headache—I was warmer than I had been since the night before and my pillow rose and fell in time with the sound of breathing. Serza had curled protectively around me during my panic attack, and I felt stuck between the prey desire to escape a predator cuddling me and the human desire to remain in the warm comfort of a living space heater. The decision was made for me. As I stirred, so too did Serza. "Sorry," I tried to say, but my throat was parched. I hadn't had anything to drink in likely more than a day. "Water?"

She got to her feet and led me to the underground river where the dragon pups played. They watched us with blatant curiosity as I knelt at the edge of the water and cupped my hands. The water was glacially cold and tasted of dirt, but it was the best drink I'd ever had. I splashed my face, the cool water relieving the puffiness under my burning eyes. And then I realized I was covered in dirt, soot, and God knows what else, so I waded into the freezing water, my skin erupting in goosebumps and my teeth chattering. One quick dip to submerge myself completely, and a rush into the heat of Serza's arms. She sat wrapped around me until everything, but my waist-length hair was dry. Uncle Barry didn't like me cutting my hair because it wasn't feminine enough, but for practicality's sake, I decided I needed to cut it before it became matted.

When we returned to the cave, I found the stick she had brought me before we got distracted by names and panic attacks and showed it to her. "What was this for?" She took it and drew a simple house in the dirt. I blinked. "A house?"

She pointed and nodded before pointing to herself again and saying, "Ahtl."

"Oh! You want to use drawings to teach me?"

She nodded and then drew a stick figure of a person. "Riag."

"Riag," I repeated, "Human."

The days—if you could call it that—passed slowly, filled with eating, sleeping, bathing in the icy water, playing with the pups, and learning the dragons' language. Without any sunlight, day and night blurred together, and I counted the months that passed by my menstrual cycle. During those days, I'd spend most of my time in her cell while she stood guard, nervous the smell of blood would attract a hungry clan member. By the sixth period, though, the rest were used to it enough they barely paid attention to us. Aside from the curious pups, the dragons were at best ambivalent to my presence. They called me On'ria, and I slowly learned the names of Serza's family. The giant red matriarch was called Neldr and the green patriarch was Jardl. Their pups were Ker, Loz, and Galde. They also had one named Yedr but he was too curious and ventured too far outside the cave. My uncle took his young life before his time.

I also learned Serza was unusual for a juvenile dragon. Most leave their caves to form their own clans by the time they'd reached her size, but, because of her stunted leg, she stayed back to help raise her younger siblings. Perhaps I should have tried to flee the nest as they did, but I had nowhere else to go. Mom and Dad were dead. Uncle Barry and the rest of the compound was probably dead. I didn't know anyone else, and Serza took good care of me.

About one year into living in their colony, Serza asked in Draconic, *"Would you like to go outside? Winter approaches and we should gather supplies for you."*

"Yes!" I replied without hesitation. It had been nearly a year since I saw sunlight and felt its warmth on my skin. I dreamed of the fiery autumn leaves adorning the trees and the fresh breeze in my burnt and matted shoulder length hair. Because nothing the dragons had was sharp enough to cut my hair, we devised a method of burning it short. It had started to grow out again, but without a hairbrush, it had already begun to mat.

I eagerly followed her out of the cave like Eurydice did to Orpheus. As soon as I saw the light at the entrance, I pushed past her and broke into a sprint. Ignoring the pain from my eyes suddenly adjusting to the autumn daylight, I laughed and threw myself onto the grass. I had spent so long in darkness that even the weak autumn sun filled me with a joy I had long forgotten. Serza made a sort of coughing sound I understood to be laughter.

"Let's go," she said, lifting me and placing me on her back. It wasn't the most comfortable position. I had lost weight while in their cave, but it was still a tight squeeze to sit between the purple spikes running down her spine. The sudden flap of her wings nearly unseated me, and, ignoring the spike digging into my stomach, I clung to her neck as we took off. Everything within me pitched and lurched as she soared above the trees and in the direction of a small town. She landed on the outskirts of the burnt out remains. *"I go no further. Get what you need,"* she said, *"I will find you if you are not back by sundown."*

I pressed a playful kiss to her snout and replied, *"Be right back."* I hadn't left the compound since I was a child, so it was a novelty to walk through a town, even if it was more like the burnt-out husk of one. Something terrible happened here and was likely done by dragons. I shivered and not from the cold. They had no qualms about eating humans—we were easy and bountiful prey—but it was one thing to know this and another to see the devastation they'd wrought. I caught a glimpse of myself in a broken store window and gasped in horror. I looked like a corpse and had the same pallor. Months in a cave made my skin a milky white and I hadn't just lost weight—I was gaunt. My cheekbones and collarbones strained against my skin. I had been eating whatever Serza caught me, but it clearly wasn't enough. I didn't recognize the face that stared back at me. Sofia had died the night a dragon took her and On'ria was the only thing left.

Unable to bear staring any longer, I hurried in the direction of a charred Walmart. In case anyone was hiding out inside, I slipped quietly into the store through a side entrance and grabbed a basket. First, see what they had in the way of clothes and blankets. Then, nonperishables so I could gain some of my weight back. And then books! God, I missed books! As entertaining as learning Draconic could be, I missed having other escapes.

I was so distracted by the prospect of creature comforts I didn't notice them sneak up until the double barrel of a rifle was pressed against my back. "Don't move," a man said. I'd grown so used to Draconic it took me a moment to recognize he spoke English.

"I'm not looking for trouble," I replied, putting my hands up, "I just need some supplies for winter."

The barrel nudged me forwards. "We'll let the prophet decide that." He led me to the back of the store where furniture and sleeping bags were piled near the entertainment section. People from the compound and faces I didn't recognize bustled about like worker bees. And seated on a La-Z-Boy® like a throne was Uncle Barry. When he saw me, he paled and got to his feet, tears spilling down his cheek. "Sofia," he said softly before turning to the man with the gun, "Get that damn thing away from her." I didn't see the man with the gun leap back like I was a rabid animal, but I certainly heard the weapon clatter to the ground. Uncle Barry swept me into a crushing hug. While I'd grown thinner and more brittle, he seemed to have grown larger than life itself. "My sweet little Sofia, I thought you were dead."

"I thought you were too, Uncle Barry," I replied, voice strained from his crushing hug and my own unshed tears. I didn't trust him, but he practically raised me, so it was a relief he and others in the compound were safe.

He stepped back, studying my pale, gaunt face. "How is this possible? How did you escape those demons?"

"They're not demons," I replied, and the people watching this display gasped and muttered among themselves, "They sort of... adopted me? I know it sounds crazy, but they're not evil. They're as intelligent as we are and just trying to survive." His smile tightened as I told him how I rescued Serza as a pup and my time with the dragon clan. His followers gaped at me with their mouths hanging open like dead fish.

When I finished, his grin was rictus. "That's quite the miraculous story." He clasped my shoulder just a little too hard. "I bet you're hungry for something other than cave rats and whatever else those monsters eat." He snapped his fingers and a female follower disappeared. Moments later, she reappeared with a can of peaches and a fork. I tried to eat it slowly, savoring the explosion of flavor on my tongue after months of foraged food. Too soon, though, the can was empty, and the juice all drunk. I eyed it mournfully until another woman appeared with a sweater and pair of thick sweatpants. She guided me to the changing room, and I took off the tattered pajamas I'd worn for months. The clothes were soft against my skin and for a moment, I luxuriated in feeling cleaner than I had since Serza carried me off.

Uncle Barry was waiting outside the dressing room for me. "You must be tired after your ordeal. Before you rest, though, can we talk in private?"

"Uh, sure," I said, not feeling in the least bit tired. Sleeping was one of the few activities available to me in the cave, so I was very well rested. He led me to what had once been the employee break room and sat at the table before gesturing for me to do the same. I felt like a child again, waiting to be chastised for committing a sin, either real or imagined.

He looked at me through steepled fingers. "I'm sure you've forgotten most of your Bible passages already. We'll have to resume our lessons as soon as possible so we can salvage this."

I blinked, not expecting the conversation to take a turn like this. "I—uh—you still want me to lead your flock."

He gave me one of his trademark pastor grins, turning on his indelible charm. "Well, who else is qualified to continue my teachings after my inevitable meeting with St. Peter?" I was too stunned to speak at first, so he took it as a chance to continue. "Of course, you'll have to show us that dragon's den so we can clear it out, but then——"

The thought of the dragons—my clan—coming to harm returned my voice to me. "Uncle Barry, I'm not staying with you."

It was his turned to look stunned. He sat back in his chair, eyes wide and face reddening. I imagined cartoon steam coming out of his ears. And then he laughed. A full minute of doubled over belly laughs. When he sat up again, he wiped a tear from his eyes. "That was funny, kid. You really had me going there."

"I wasn't kidding."

His face dropped, and with it, his genial façade. "I see. And who's gonna stop me from keeping you here?"

"The juvenile dragon with massive parents who have no compunctions about burning down the home of the man who killed their child?" I met his glare with my own.

"I think you should rest. You've been through so much and I'm worried you have Stockholm Syndrome." He got to his feet and left, locking the door behind him. I banged on the door, trying to get the attention of his little cultists, but they must have been under orders to ignore me, because they didn't so much as glance in my direction. Hours passed in that little room and the only way I knew it was nightfall was that they'd lit lanterns to navigate the aisles.

I dozed on the lumpy couch more out of boredom than anything else. A crash coming from the roof and the screams of the Walmart residents filled the air. *Serza.* I leapt to my feet and banged on the door. "In here," I shouted until she appeared in the tiny window. I stepped back as she tore open the door.

She sniffed me up and down. *"Did they hurt you, On'ria?"*

"No, but I'm glad you're here," I replied, throwing my arms around her neck. The pump of a rifle broke up our reunion. Uncle Barry stood flanked by armed men and women. "Whoa, hey! It's okay, she won't hurt anyone."

"No promises," she said, eyeing Uncle Barry. Her chest glowed, indicating she was about to set out a stream of fire.

"Let me handle this," I said in her language before switching to English, "Serza's friendly. If you let us go in peace, her clan won't bother you again."

"You speak the devil's tongue," Uncle Barry exclaimed, his eyes wide and horrified.

"Well, duh, I already told you that," I said, crossing my arms, "she taught me draconic."

"I see now. I know what you are. You're not my niece. I don't think you ever were." His eyes had that fanatical gleam to them that used to precede an especially exciting sermon.

"Then what am I?"

"Mystery. Mother of Prostitutes and Abominations. Rider of the seven-headed beast. The Whore of Babylon." He pointed his gun at me. "Sofia died a year ago. You're just the monster inhabiting her body."

I couldn't help my laughter. "Sorry, but really? You really think I've been body-jacked by a demon?"

"Admit it and let my poor niece rest, monster."

"I will if that means you'll let us go."

"Exodus 22:18. Suffer not a witch to live." He pulled back the safety on his gun.

"We should get out," I said to Serza, *"You may be mostly bullet proof, but I am not."*

Moving with a surprising speed for her size, she lifted me onto her back and took flight in the narrow hallway. Bullets ricocheted off her near impermeable skin and I made myself as small as I could to avoid getting shot. "You won't win this, Whore of Babylon," Uncle Barry said as we escaped through the hole she made in the roof, "there will come a day where you're cast into the lake of fire with the rest of your abominations."

Below me, Serza let out a deep, rumbling laugh. I joined in, ignoring the dull ache in my chest where I still held affection for my uncle. We were destined to clash again, but for that moment, it was just me, Serza, and the infinite expanse of stars.

~ * ~ * ~

Kay Hanifen is a recent graduate from Emerson College with a BFA in Creative Writing. Her articles have appeared in *Screen Rant*, *The Borgen Project*, and *Leatherneck* magazine, and her first short story is published in *Strangely Funny VIII* by Mystery and Horror LLC.

When she's not geeking out about superheroes or monsters, you can usually find her with her two black cats or on Twitter @TheUnicornComi1.

Knight-Time in Adelaide

Steven Streeter

The feeling was an eerie one.

Rundle Mall, Adelaide's premier shopping precinct, lay there, a red paved scar in a grid of bitumen, devoid of people. The heavy rains of the previous few days had finally stopped, but the years of old rubbish strewn across the ground still sat where it had been blown or had fallen, sodden into place by the moisture. The last few leaves on the scattered trees running down the center of the former road weighed heavily, water still dripping from their tips. Everything glistened with lingering drops, catching what little sunshine there was like a showcase of fake diamonds.

Only the hint of smoke on the air, not completely dissipated by the wet weather, sat uneasily on the scene.

A small flock of pigeons took off suddenly from atop the outdoor café in the middle of the eastern end of the mall, rising as one and moving across the cloudy sky like refuse on the wind. The unfamiliar sound of the car engine that frightened them grew louder, echoing down empty roads and alleys which made it seem like there was more than one. A solitary magpie let out a caw at its approach, but it refused to leave the remains of a disemboweled cat at the foot of an automatic teller machine. A second warning caw was answered by another bird, hidden somewhere, as the car grew closer.

Ignoring the dark traffic lights, the vehicle rounded the corner from North Terrace. It pulled to a halt across the intersection at the eastern end of the mall and the engine was killed.

The magpie cawed yet again, trying to scare off this new arrival, and then took to the air, alighting on nearby power lines, never taking its eyes from its meal.

A black crow landed near the dead feline. With an angry cry, the magpie swooped down and the two birds squawked at one another.

A low growl rolled down the length of the mall.

The birds flew away without so much as a backward glance.

The driver's side door of the car opened, and a man dressed in denim and leather stepped out. He gazed down Rundle Mall but could make out nothing out of the ordinary. He reached his hand into the car and pulled out a pair of binoculars. He lifted them to his eyes and scanned the long, brick-paved avenue. Still nothing to be seen; too many other structures blocked his view.

The passenger door opened, and a woman dressed in similar clothes to the man slowly climbed out. "See anything?" she whispered hoarsely, her eyes darting all about as she did so.

He shook his head. "But, I can hear it." His voice hardly rose above the breeze.

She closed her eyes and concentrated as well as she could.

The low growl rumbled across the empty shopfronts again, sounding like a distant train.

She shivered and hugged herself a little. "I don't like this," she muttered, her gaze now fixed before her, seeking something she could not see.

"Then why'd you come?" he asked emotionlessly.

"You said I had to," she muttered.

"You still could've said, 'No.'"

She shrugged and stayed where she was as he reached into the car and pulled the lever to pop the boot. He walked to the back and stood there, smiling, before lifting it up.

The woman groaned a little as he came to stand by her side. "Help me," he whispered. "It's why I wanted you to come along."

She sighed and followed him to the back of the car. He pulled off his leather jacket and flexed his arms, then allowed his companion to help slide a chain mail vest over his head. Leggings made of the same material were forced over his jeans, and the two pieces fastened together with U-bolts. He moved his arms and legs again. "Damn this is already heavy," he muttered.

The woman said nothing as she lifted the next object out of the boot.

The growling sound became louder. A thud came with it. All the remaining birds in the area took to the air. The clang of something striking a hollow, metal object echoed loudly and the growl became a brief roar.

The woman dropped what she held with a reverberating clank. The man hardly seemed to notice. His head jerked around in the direction of that distant noise and a slight grin touched his face for the first time since they arrived. "Yes!" he hissed under his breath.

"I really don't like this," the woman said as she bent to strap a metal leg piece over his thigh.

"We're going to kill one," he said.

"But with this?"

"Nothing else's worked! Bullets don't do anything against them, fire doesn't do anything, even artillery shells don't do anything. But in the past, there was something else people did, and that worked then, so it'll work now."

She shook her head sadly and adjusted the leather buckle on the back of the second thigh guard. The roar sounded again.

"Hurry up!" the man said. "It knows we're here. I want to confront it before it decides to seek us out!"

"It knows?" She fumbled with the final buckle as fear shook her body.

"Of course. Why do you think it's roaring like that?" He paused as she started to fit the metal codpiece about his waist. "They're smart creatures. They couldn't have taken over the entire city of Adelaide—not to mention the other ninety-nine cities—if they weren't."

She shook her head again, this time more emphatically, then stood up. "We have to stop this. We have to leave. Now."

He laughed. "Why?"

"Because if it knows we're here, then it's playing a game with us!"

He laughed a little louder and reached around to finish strapping the groin-protection himself. "But it probably thinks we're like all the others—come to Adelaide with a bigger and better gun, to see if that can do anything. It won't be ready for what it's going to face with me."

"You're insane."

"And you choose now, standing here, with me half-dressed, to tell me that's what you think? So, seriously, why'd you agree to come here with me, then, if you thought I was crazy? And don't give me that I forced you crap."

She offered a half-smile. "Because I didn't think you'd actually go through with it." She indicated the boot with a wave of her hand. "I thought we'd get to the freeway, and you'd realize this was totally crazy and it'd never work. I wanted you to get it all out of your system."

He glowered at her. "Well, you're here with me now. You're part of my plan. You need to keep this car away from them. There's enough petrol in the jerry-cans in the back seat to blow this car to pieces if one of them so much as breathes on it. And once I've done what I came here to do, I'm going to have to jump in the car however

I can and you're going to have to drive us back towards Melbourne as fast as you can. I need your help for this to succeed."

"But it's crazy!" she insisted. "How many others have tried something? All over the world? And failed?"

"But none of them have tried this." He strapped the forearm guard across his first arm.

"What if they did somewhere and it didn't work?"

"Look, they've given up on the so-called Hundred. No one's trying anything. While these things stay in the cities, the powers-that-be think it's worth sacrificing those one hundred cities all over the world just to keep them happy and out of their hair. Especially when the things in the oceans are a bigger threat, and it's been ages since anyone's heard what's going on in Northern Europe. They say people have been driven out of whole countries up there." He finished the first arm and offered his companion the second. "They were real all along, not just things from fairy-tales and mythology. And now they've come back to claim the world. Well, they're not going to keep this part of it." He looked at her. "Hurry up."

She obeyed wordlessly, strapping the guard over his long-sleeved top.

"I don't get why you have to be the hero," she eventually asked under her breath as she lifted the heavy torso protection out of the boot of the car.

His only response was a half-grin.

He let it slide down until the leather straps rested uncomfortably across his shoulders. The woman started to do up the side buckles as he reached in and grabbed a finely constructed steel helmet. He set it carefully over his head and dropped the visor as she finished the final buckle. She stepped back and looked at him. He merely held his hands up. She sighed yet again and grabbed two metal gauntlets, which she forced down over each hand.

He stepped back, hands on his hips and nodded at the reflection he could see in the window of the car. "Good," he said to himself, then turned and looked down at the empty mall. It was down there, waiting for him. But it would not know what hit it.

He opened the back door of the car and reached down in front of the cans of petrol before pulling out a finely decorated shield, with a coat of arms he had invented for just this occasion—a stylized dragon with a sword sticking out of its chest. He slipped his arm through the straps on its rear side and made sure its weight was balanced. Then, with his other hand, he stretched down to the floor of the car for a final time.

The woman watched as he pulled the object out: A sword, so new its blade caught what little light there was like a scabbard of illumination.

A solid, rhythmic thumping began, something hard striking something hollow and made of metal. *Boom...Boom...Boom...*

"It's waiting." The young man grinned. "It's time." He gazed at the woman; all she could see of him were his blue eyes, so full of eagerness and life. "Be ready. When I jump back in this car, we've got to be out of here before any of the others come."

"The others?" She looked around at the sky in panic; she had almost forgotten there was more than one of them. In each of one hundred cities in the world, ten had decided to make these places of human habitation their new homes. Exactly one thousand of them, spread all over the world. And for five years they had remained there, feeding on anything that moved. Quite orderly, especially when compared to the absolute carnage the trolls had inflicted in northern Europe. They had not become a menace beyond the confines of their chosen dwellings, unlike many of the other beings that still ravaged so many places in the world. And after the bombing of Dallas in the United States had proved futile in stopping them, it seemed like the governments of the world were prepared to just let them have a mere one hundred cities.

There were far more dangerous threats in the world nowadays, laying waste to whole countries. One hundred cities were nothing.

"The others," he said. He paused briefly then nodded. "Just be ready, okay?"

"O-Okay," she said.

He turned away from her and started off down Rundle Mall. *Boom...Boom...Boom...*

His every footfall made the metal he wore clank a little, echoing in the near stillness like a chiming bell. For three years he had been preparing for this day, maybe longer, maybe even since the day he had been forced to flee Adelaide, five years earlier. He had been eighteen when, like the million other inhabitants, he had been faced with a creature of myth and legend come to life. Along with his mother and sister, he had managed to escape. He did not know what happened to his father or older brother, but the chances were not good for their survival. Rumors spoke of enclaves of humans being hunted. Of those who stayed behind to loot the deserted shops being picked off like a shooting gallery. Stories designed to scare children were suddenly real. He had spent the next two years like so many others reading about them, in books of mythology. But unlike the rest, he had gone out and had armor crafted for himself. Had watched more movies with swordplay than was healthy, teaching himself skills and techniques. Taking lessons where he could. Going to gymnasia to build up his strength and stamina.

Now he was ready to face one, in the only way anyone had ever succeeded before.

Boom...Boom...Boom...

He moved to the southern side of the mall, beneath the canopies of locked and covered shopfronts.

Once past the central eatery, he could finally see the defining feature of Rundle Mall—the two metal spheres, each more than two meters in diameter, one on top of the other.

He stopped.

It was on top of the upper metal ball, its golden and red scales reflecting on the polished surface of the enormous artwork. Its long tail was thumping against the sphere, each blow creating the *Boom...* sounds he was hearing.

The dragon sat there, a king looking over its realm.

The crocodilian head was turned in his direction, smoke curling up from the enlarged nostrils on the end of a wide snout. The long claws on the end of its visible forelimbs shone like the metal blade he held in his hand.

A shudder ran through him. Apart from glimpses in the sky when his mother had taken him away from this city, he had never seen one in real life before. On television, in photographs, on the Internet, but not in real life.

It was magnificent. Glorious even...

It was a dragon. It was a killer.

He grit his teeth and resumed his slow, deliberate movement towards the large beast, towards the dragon that should not have existed, and yet not only did it exist, it now ruled his city. Well, if he was successful, then a whole army of knights could be dispatched, and just like in the days of yore, they could all be felled.

Boom...Boom...Boo...

The last thud was cut short as the monster raised itself up on its hind legs, stretching its pterodactyl-like wings out and lifting its head up high. It snorted like a bull. If it had been human, the young man was sure he would have interpreted that sound as one of derision.

He quickened his pace a little. Past Twin Street and down the southern edge of the mall he moved, not taking his eyes from the thing that regarded him so insignificantly. He only paused when he came to the old Renaissance Tower. Its two external glass elevator carriages lay shattered on the ground. Carefully he picked his way through the debris, trying hard not to take his eyes from the beast looming over the city like an unearthly tyrant.

He was sure the simple but ornate fountain outside the Adelaide Arcade—its third resting spot since it had been built in 1880—would provide him with what he thought would be adequate protection. The rains had even filled it with water, which he felt could help against the fire. He ducked quickly through the shattered entrance of the Adelaide Arcade, to gain some cover and catch his breath. The monster remained where it was. To the young man, it looked as though the creature was smiling a little. It was waiting for him. It was playing with him.

But it didn't know what he had planned.

He started to calm himself and looked around. The doors that closed the Arcade off had been blasted inwards. Traces of burn damage showed where at least one of the dragons had clearly entered. How long ago had that happened? The scorch marks had washed away a little with the weather and a number of spiders had established their own homes on the edges. For all he knew, that damage could well have happened in their first onslaught, when the dragons hunted and attacked everything they saw.

He shook his head to clear it. He had to focus. This was not the time to reminisce about the way the city once had been, or think about what might have happened. It was the now that mattered, and that now involved the risky protection afforded by a relatively small fountain.

He paused a brief moment, steeled himself, and then darted out and across the paved road. He only stopped when he was behind the tall water-feature, still watching his adversary as carefully as he knew he should. And now that he was still, and he had a chance to catch his breath, he finally took in the creature that loomed high above him.

Pictures and videos really had done nothing to prepare him for the sight of this monster. It was not just the fact it was a beautiful beast, with scales glittering like a living fire, nor its size, stretching easily as long as a bus with a wingspan even greater. It was the fact it was there. It was real. This was no CGI construct found in the movies, this was a living, breathing animal and it was looking right at him.

This was not a creature that, ten years earlier, all would have said simply could not exist—it was one of the beasts that had taken over his home city. They had killed his father and brother, his friends, and so many people he knew. They had turned Adelaide into a virtual ghost town. They had taken his life from him.

His anger was quickly rising. He became more focused on the beast before him. So, when it opened its mouth and craned its long neck forward, he dropped down as fast as he could into the water at his feet.

The explosion of flame that burst out struck the fountain. Paint peeled and smoldered, and the young man could feel the radiation heating his suit of armor like a cooking pot, steam rising from the surface of the water. Even through the clothing beneath the metal, his skin felt as though it was blistering.

He gripped his sword tighter and closed his eyes briefly, trying to summon the courage to act.

The heat stopped and he looked up.

The dragon had resumed its perch atop the metallic balls. The young man considered the expression on that reptilian face to be one of supreme smugness.

He climbed to his feet and moved out from behind the fountain. The animal regarded him with obvious disdain before leaping to the ground, landing barely two meters away. The young man took a slow step towards it, shield held before him, sword at the ready.

The dragon seemed to be waiting for him to make the first decisive move. The young man smiled behind the visor. And he lunged forward, striking with the weapon in his hand.

The tip easily pierced the skin on the monster's cheek, drawing bright crimson blood. The beast recoiled immediately and lifted its head and roared long and loud. The young man wanted to believe it was pain and shock. But he could not rest on his laurels, so he lunged forward again, aiming for the center of the broad, scaled chest.

Its forelimb swung in the path of his blow. The sword managed only a glancing blow just above the creature's wrist, drawing more blood and eliciting an even louder cry. The young man cursed under his breath and took another step closer.

A sudden high-pitched scream shattered the silence surrounding them. It was filled with terror and pain; then cut off just as suddenly as it had started.

The young man blocked that alien sound out of his mind. He could not afford to be distracted now.

However, the dragon's attention shifted to the source of that agonised cry and the young man took advantage. With a final thrust he stabbed at the beast's heart.

The blade slid in about two inches, drawing more blood. But then it stopped with a jarring halt, sending a shudder of pain through to his shoulder. He withdrew the weapon and stabbed again with the same result.

Smoke suddenly enveloped him, making his eyes water.

He looked up.

The dragon was staring down at him, fury now in its eyes, wisps of curled, brown vapor drifting from its nostrils.

He had wounded it. But why had he not managed to drive the sword in further? What was stopping...? It came to him in a flash of inspiration. He just had to time it and hold his nerve. He knew how the knights in the olden days had done it. The beast opened its mouth, and he held the shield before him, hoping beyond hope it would hold out long enough. The stream of flame came out and struck his shield with a force that made him stagger back a little, but then he jumped into it. The heat ran from the shield and up his arm. This time it was not just the feeling of burning, it was actual blistering was causing the discomfort, as his flesh bubbled and popped beneath his clothing.

But he had seen the pictures in the old books, had read all the myths. These had all portrayed dragon-slayers doing it one way and one way only. It was clearly why bullets did not work. Like whatever it was that had stopped his sword had done the same to all the projectiles. But the dragon-slayers of old had struck when the beast was breathing fire, and they had struck at the neck.

He swung his sword in a wide arc.

It sliced through flesh with an ease he had not been prepared for. He lost his balance as the weapon exited the gaping wound and the flame stopped. Red blood spurted onto him, the liquid warm and putrid. The monster rose up on its hind legs and this time its cry was a choked one. He looked at the animal and watched as it staggered backwards until it thumped against the two metal balls. It shook its head and tried to stem the flow of blood with its front claws.

He had done it!

"Yes!" he cried, throwing his arms up in triumph. "Yes!!" His voice echoed down the mall, scaring the few remaining birds into flight.

He had been right! He returned his attention to the dragon.

Its furious gaze was once more fixed upon him, the long teeth bared.

The young man paused. Why wasn't it dead? He had wounded it—why hadn't he killed it? Surely, he had sliced through arteries and veins. What had he done wrong?

Behind him, the explosion made him wince.

He spun quickly.

From the eastern end of the mall he saw a column of thick, black smoke rising into the air above the trees, buildings and everything else. A roar came from behind him, one he was sure was a laugh. He turned back to face his adversary.

It merely stared at him.

A loud growl filled the air, and it had not come from this beast.

He looked up in time to see a second dragon circling around overhead, its golden-red body catching the little light in the sky magnificently. He pointed his sword at the wounded monster and turned and sprinted away. He wondered if their wounds were self-healing, like the trolls that had beset northern Europe at the same time the dragons had struck the one hundred cities, and that apparently even now marched further south, headed towards the Mediterranean.

This was not the time to ponder such things. He did not care about trolls, or the sea serpents that now made shipping so hazardous, or even the Mokele-Mbembe, the dinosaur-like creatures laying claim to vast tracts of central Africa. There was even talk of something lurking in the River Murray, especially in Victoria. No. He only cared about Adelaide. He could do this. Maybe not on his own, but he could do this. A return to the old ways. The Knights of the Dragon, that's what he'd call his army. He'd get back to Melbourne and train up a group of warriors, and come back here and they would face them down and cut off their heads. He had not quite managed to do that, but he had come close. A longer sword, a sharper sword, maybe use a different metal. He would work it all out once he got…

"Oh, shit."

The remains of his car were burning at the end of the mall. The thick black smoke that rose like a signal into the air was barely dispersed by the breeze.

"Liza?" he muttered, not expecting an answer as he slowed down, coming closer to the burning vehicle.

The wet stain of red he noticed on the pavers answered his question.

He turned again, anger clouding his mind. He would return and finish the job; he would succeed this time.

The beast swooped out of the sky and landed on one side of mid-mall café. More gold in color than the one he had already attacked; this one was also much larger. A second landed on the opposite side of the empty building, its red scales holding a slightly purple tinge, its size about the same as the one he had already faced. Two of them. Well, he would be ready for them. He would not go down without a fight. He held the shield before him and lifted his sword.

Then, without thinking, he rushed forward, headed for the larger of the two, sword raised high, a war-cry on his lips.

The twin bursts of flame stopped him in his tracks, coming from two sides. His mind started to cloud over as the heat bore into him. His vision swam. The burning sensation bit into his core as his heart rate sped up. He stopped and slumped as his energy was drained. The sword fell from his hand, and he dropped to one knee.

The maw of the larger one engulfed his head. He looked up into a chasm of blackness and whimpered. Then, with a single snap, the jaws closed around him, piercing the metal he wore and slicing through skin, muscle and bone without a hint of resistance.

The two dragons exchanged glances. The wounded one joined them, the gash in its neck already pink with scar tissue.

This one had thought himself so smart, but he had not taken into account one simple thing—humans lied about their exploits. None had ever killed a dragon, they merely said they had. This one man, being so clever with his armor and shiny new sword had trusted his fellow humans.

He had been a fool, like so many before him.

They were going nowhere. Adelaide was their town now, and they were not giving it up for anything.

~ * ~ * ~

Steven Streeter is new to the world of publishing, with a number of short stories published and three books due for release from the end of 2021 to the middle of 2022. He is an Australian, at the upper end of middle age, the father of two teenagers, and is trying to make writing his career.

She, Being Born in the Body of a Maid

Taria Karillion

Even with her hair blackened by mourning ash, and dressed in her brothers' shabby britches, Rose was still pretty enough to be laughed out of the Elders' Council meeting—the scoffs and eye rolls and utter hubris provoking deep, burning nail prints in her tightly clenched fists. How *dare* they dismiss her offer, her bravery—after so many of their kinsmen had been lost to the cause? What the Councilmen failed to realize was shepherding an equally dim-witted flock from mountain lions and wildcats and their own blind ignorance had necessitated a degree of courage and agility that had seen her outlive all of her menfolk, God rest them. '*Headstrong, impulsive wench*' she might be, but she was a LIVE one!

Surely, one small ice dragon couldn't be much worse an adversary as beasts went.

With chin high and a brisk pace, Rose strode out to the Westward fields and began to search the evening skies for magpies. When she eventually lured one close with the silver buckles of her quiver, she lay down, feigning sleep. When the bird finally tired of waiting for a loosening of her grip, it gave a caw of what sounded like annoyance and flew off toward the hills. Rose immediately sprang up and followed it, for if, as legend claimed, Magpies were scavengers of dragon hoards, it was possible that, with patience, this one might lead her to the beast and the Assembly's handsome reward.

She caught her first glimpse of the dragon high on the Western Ridge, up beyond the snow line, nearly hidden from sight in a shroud of mist and gossamer flakes that twinkled like gems in the rays of the setting sun. So bright were they that, were it not for the ebony wings of her guide, the ghostly-pale creature would have gone entirely unseen.

Rose blew into her hands, regretting the angry haste of her departure—a person could perish in the mountains for want of a cloak. The air was already biting at her limbs as she began to scramble up the craggy, snowy slopes.

Perhaps the distraction of a plan would help. Her only option was to prevent its escape by firing an arrow deep between body and wing. That often worked on the eagles that preyed on her lambs. And—if her late brothers' stories were to be believed—dragons were so slow and lumbering on land as to be a manageable target for even her modest archery skills. But between the meagre number of arrows in her quiver and her shivering limbs, she would have to get far closer to her target than was safe in order to succeed. Speed and a sure footing would be her best allies.

Finally, cresting a vast, ice-laced boulder, she spied the beast— just over an arrow's reach away on a ridge between the fir trees. Having never seen an Ice Dragon up close before, its unexpected, iridescent beauty and shimmering white scales made Rose gasp. She stumbled, then ducked swiftly down out of its sight as it turned toward the sound of her boots on the frigid ground.

As quickly as frozen fingers allowed, she assembled the leather and lens of her spyglass, reckoned distance, noted the wind and measured her mark.

Steadying herself against the icy boulder, Rose raised her bow, stretched out fist and elbow, took a breath…and released. Once. Twice. The first glanced off, the second found a leg. The creature let out a growl and pulled the arrow free with its jaws as if it were nothing more than a briar.

One arrow left. One arrow to save her village.

With the faces of her fallen kinsmen framing her thoughts, she stepped clear of the boulder and stood straight and tall in the warmth of the vast, sinking sun. She took aim, her steaming breath almost dragon-like itself.

Breathe in…Breathe out…

Loose!

The flights whistled and an echoing roar rent the air. Just for a moment, Rose feared an avalanche, then snatched up the spyglass to see the dragon limp away toward a cave.

She sank down onto the snowy earth, trembling. What now?

Her blue-tipped fingers rested upon the scabbard of the dagger within her boot.

Maybe…

The spyglass revealed the magpie at the mouth of the dragon's cave, beside a strewing of bones and black and white feathers.

Not far. Don't think, just go.

As the light dimmed and muscles burned from the climb, the cave finally came into view. Within, the beast lay—stunned or sleeping—its juvenile proportions ranged across its glittering hoard. Rose arched a brow. Its head was huge, but its body was barely bigger than that of a plough horse. Reports of its size had no doubt been inflated by machismo, like the tall tales of fishermen on market day.

It was an oddly beautiful creature with full, fluid curves of flank, neck and wing, that—were it not a killer—would have invited a slow stroking. Its eyes were closed, and the protruding tips of its forked tongue trembled like that of a dreaming dog. The slow rise and fall of its chest and the rumbling sigh of its breath made it seem almost too benign and beautiful to put to sword.

Almost.

Slowly, silently, drawing her dagger, Rose glanced around for paths of escape before narrowing her eyes and scanning the creature's scales for any point of weakness. So focused was she that she failed to notice its nostrils flex and flicker. Nor did she notice a wetness at her feet as the dragon's tongue slowly circled them. As her blade rose and she took aim, the fleshy wetness tightened suddenly on her ankle, and she was flung upwards like a circle of dough. Enormous jaws sprang open then snapped shut around the falling mouthful.

~ * ~

The dragon gave an echoing belch and licked its scaly lips. *A modest morsel*, she thought to herself, but supremely satisfying another flock was now without its shepherd, according to the magpie's report. Easy pickings.

Stretching out one enormous claw she casually flicked the fallen, glinting scabbard at the bird, who cawed its thanks for the pay-off and shook another loose feather onto the floor.

~ * ~ * ~

As the daughter of an antiquarian book dealer, **Taria Karillion** grew up surrounded by far more books than is probably healthy for one person. A literature degree, a journalism course and some gratuitous vocabulary overuse later, her stories have appeared in a Hagrid-sized handful of magazines and anthologies, and have won enough literary prizes to fill his other hand. Despite this, she has no need as yet for larger millinery.

The Dragon's Curse

Ted Pennella

Henry sat behind a dilapidated farmhouse with his slender back against the half-rotted siding. He rubbed at small patches of cobalt blue scales on his slender, female hands, which made him hate his body even more. The morning sun brightened a dense fog, which covered the dry, dead prairie and left the house's nearby corner a fuzzy dark gray. He wrapped his arms around knees pulled up against his chest, his female breasts bound flat and covered in patchwork clothing. Sighing, he hung his head. As strands of midnight blue hair fell to cover a youthful feminine face, he thought to himself, *I'm human. I'm male.*

"You refuse the evidence of your own form, Henrik," a voice said from nearby.

A figure darkened the fog, which hid the voice's owner. Henry swallowed his anger and typical retort about the lies his body spoke. Pulling his gloves back on, he squinted in hopes of seeing some features. "Do I know you? Your voice seems familiar, friend."

"The God of Death," the overly tall figure said emerging from the fog, "is no one's friend. Especially to a dragon."

Henry stood to his five-and-a-half-foot height with dusty, lifeless soil clinging to cracked leather boots and green cloak. With a yawn, he arched backwards to stretch kinks out of his joints. A rip in an armpit of his makeshift clothing exposed a stretch of golden-tanned skin. Cobalt blue glittered off a partially hidden patch of scales before the green cloak closed. He glanced at the black cloak as it separated from the fog, wondering if this really was the god of death.

"You come for me here instead of one of my many battles?" Henry's voice slipped back to feminine as his anger grew.

The black cloak opened as an arm and hand, which appeared to be skin stretched taunt over bones, rose to point at Henry. "You have been chosen, Henrik, to be our next tool of punishment for the Guilty One."

"Guilty One?" Henry stepped close and gazed into the cowl. "Who in the Gods' Abyss is this Guilty One?"

Deep in the cowl, a pair of red eyes stared back at Henry.

Slowly, a lipless mouth smiled to reveal sun-bleached and gum-less teeth. With a chuckle resembling bones crunching, the stranger said, "Family reunions are so much fun."

"You really are the God of Death." Henry reached for the cowl, hoping for a better view of the god's face. "Any muscles between your bones and skin?"

"Your many millennia dead wife sends her love, Henrik," Death said derisively. The god shoved Henry away with a hand to his face. "She'll be so touched you wear her features."

"Damn it." Henry stumbled backwards. "Kill me, bastard."

A twig snapped out in the fog just before Tellos' voice called out. "Henry?"

An eighteen-year-old man in thread-bare clothing with short wavy brown hair and a scar stretching across his left cheek emerged from around the fog-enshrouded house. "Who you talking to? Ready to leave?"

"Tellos," Henry said, quickly pulling his own cowl up, "keep back."

"Why?" Tellos gave him a bemused look from his just over six-foot height.

"This guy is…" Henry looked over his shoulder to find Death gone. He sighed and muttered, "Let me gather my stuff."

Tellos chuckled, vanishing back into the fog.

Henry shifted clothes to again hide his femaleness. He hated this body and how people assumed he was a girl. After making sure his undesirable parts were concealed, Henry belted his sword back around his waist and picked up his small bundle of supplies.

"Henrik," Death whispered behind him.

Henry spun around with his sword half drawn. Despite his battle-sharpened reflexes, Henry found dealing with a god to be new territory. Standing there with that bony hand held out, Death lifted his hand to push his own cowl back. White, colorless skin clung to the skull beneath with no sign of muscles. No hair on the head nor eyebrows or even eyelashes. When the god blinked over empty eye sockets, Henry's skin crawled.

"Kill me or leave me alone, God of Death," Henry said with a hiss. He shoved his sword back into its sheath. "I've a life to restart in Havendell."

"Why are you female when human?" Death tilted his head slightly with a confused look. "You are male, after all."

"Female?" Henry turned after Tellos, as anger at his own personal curse rose to the surface. "You gods trapped my soul in a woman's body, so you tell me why."

"No, we didn't," Death said. In a blink of Henry's eyes, Death blocked Henry's path. He reached out and tapped a finger on Henry's forehead. "Maybe your memory didn't completely erase upon your rebirth. You remember her, if only subconsciously. Dragon memories are so tricky."

Henry knocked the hand away. "Stop the riddles. I am not a dragon and don't want to be one, despite who I love. Now, why won't you let me die?"

"Ask your king, Henrik," Death said, pulling his cowl back into place. "Your Dragon King."

"Dragon King?" Henry stepped toward the god, reaching for his sword menacingly. "Who is this Dragon King? Jacob?"

Only Death's toothy grin was visible as the cloak frayed into a dark smoke. As the god chuckled, his cloaked body merged with the fog encasing them until Death was once again just a vague shadow in the fog. "Brooding over his fate in the ruins on this date. Havendell Castle lays a half day's walk, as you fume and sulk."

"Damn your riddles!" Henry rushed the shadow. "Speak plain and clear."

Laughter echoed out of the fog, shrill and bone chilling. It faded slowly as Henry swung his arms through the spot the god had been. Giving up, Henry adjusted his pack and walked quickly around the house. Tellos leaned against the half-collapsed porch chewing on a bit of dried meat.

Henry strode hard and fast past the human, quickly eating distance despite his shorter stature. Anger at Death pushed him. Each step replayed one of Death's words until they all twisted into one long rambling riddle.

Tellos huffed as he came alongside Henry. For a mile, they walked in an uncomfortable silence. Finally, Tellos held out his hand as he spoke. "Here. Eat."

Henry spun around to block Tellos, forcing both to stop. "I told you to eat your fill last night. Can you not listen?"

"Like you do?" Tellos arched an eyebrow and smirked. "Running off and hiding behind the house?"

Henry stepped back and pulled his sword out. Pointing it at Tellos, he snarled, "I did not run off. I was tired and went to lay down."

"You done run off, Henry," Tellos said, not moving. "Whatever your reasons, it's the same thing. The first mention of the dragon and you done run away."

"Dragon? What in the abyss are you talking about?" Henry resisted the urged to cut the man down, telling himself he wasn't in battle. "A description?"

"Black with bright yellow-gold spots scattered about," Tellos said. "Why? You know him?"

"No," Henry said. Sheathing his sword, he stared at the taller man's half-bare chest. Long scars crossed Tellos' chest from the left shoulder down to the right of his belly. "The one I know is red with gold splotches. Jacob's my…well…friend. How far to Havenia?"

"You're in Havenia. Likely since yesterday morning," Tellos said. "Havendell's ruins are maybe a morning's walk south. A touch longer since we'll need to approach from the west."

"Ruins?" Henry jerked his head up to stare at Tellos. "You lie."

Tellos shook his head. "This barren landscape? It's what's left of Havenia. That dragon destroyed it."

"I don't believe you," Henry said. Tellos' words contrasted sharply with Henry's memories. Havenia and Havendell Castle always teemed with people and animals. Everyone grew wealthy from trade with neighboring kingdoms. "It's only been six years since Jacob and I left."

"My family has lived under that dragon for generations," Tellos said. "I'm the last human left here. Sometime soon, it'll finally eat me. Anyway, I know all of granddaddy's stories, and none tell of strangers like you. And he died a might longer than six years ago."

"How have you survived?" Henry gazed at the barren landscape around them, the fog slowly thinning out at ground level. "Not even grass can live."

"Squirrels and rabbits," Tellos said. "Those few edible plants I find. Most days, I'm just hungry. Not sure whether starving or being eaten would be better."

"Just leave," Henry said. "Why stay?"

"He won't let me," Tellos said. He clamped a hand to Henry's shoulder with a sad smile. "So, you here to get eaten by big, black, and ugly?"

"A fresh start without Jacob," Henry said. To say it in words hurt. His life until now had been centered around himself and Jacob. Pulling away from Tellos, in hopes of escaping his broken heart, he strode fast and hard, but found the memories still followed him. "I hoped to find a new path to happiness. You leave home, but all you really want is to return to those happier days. To see my fa...family. If I am a dragon, then I probably don't have any real family. No one who cares for me. Nothing, apparently, except fragments of a dead past. I must see Havendell for myself and what changes six years have wrought.

Worry and confusion contorted Tellos' face. He hurried after Henry. "Daddy got ate six years ago, and granddaddy three years before him. Momma got ate three weeks ago. I'm all that's left, and there ain't been no strangers here in my eighteen years."

"Lies," Henry whispered around the lump in his throat. "First my body lies about my gender. Then about my humanity. Now you claim it's lying abou—"

Tellos silenced Henry with a hand to his shoulder. "Grand-daddy would have had a story about you."

"I'm eighteen," Henry said as his confusion turned into anger. "I grew up with Prince Jacob as my best friend. We explored Havendell Castle together, and when we turned fourteen, left together. In six years, everyone can't be dead."

Tellos chuckled as he pushed Henry's cowl back. Holding up a hand with his fingers spread out, Tellos asked, "How many fingers you see up?"

"Four," Henry said. Unsure what Tellos was getting at, he knew it was insulting. "What does that have to do with anything?"

"That's the difference between fourteen and eighteen," Tellos said. Lightly pressing Henry's small nose, the man continued. "It's also how many centuries granddaddy claimed it'd been since the dragon had come. So, you must not worry your pretty, little head about days. I'll stick with you and keep track of the days, Henry. Heck, it don't bother me none that a dragon pretends to be human."

Henry struggled with conflicting emotions. Anger that yearned to beat Tellos bloody, and grief that wanted to be held. All the while, he felt confused about his own heart. Jacob's face kept coming to mind, yet that dragon was truly the last creature he wanted to ever see again. When Tellos reached out and wiped away his tears, Henry looked up at a hopeful face.

"Some company would be nice," Henry said, further confused.

A short time later, the otherwise still air shifted and ruffled the pair's cloaks. A deep roar broke the silence between the pair. Darkness moved through the fog as something huge passed overhead. Henry reached for his sword until another roar came from nearby. Tellos readied his bow with an arrow as he scanned the fog. Henry lifted his head and sniffed the air. As the wind shifted, Henry scrunched his nose in disgust and released his sword. Just hidden by the fog, wings beat quickly for a moment, and then stopped.

Stepping over to Tellos, Henry touched the arm gripping the arrow. "It's just Jacob. The lying bastard found me."

With eyes narrowed, Tellos relaxed the arrow in the bow, but stayed ready. "Is this the red and gold dragon you mentioned?"

"Yes," Henry said.

"Henry," a male voice shouted from the fog. "What in the Abyss are you doing out in this gods-forsaken fog so far from our home?"

"Our home, Jacob?" Henry stepped toward a growing shadow as he spoke. "You made it clear it was your home, you lying, two-timing, backstabbing, curdled-milk-blooded, overgrown skink!"

A twenty-year-old man emerged from the fog. Short red wet hair with blonde streaks topped the flush pale-skinned head. With narrow hips wrapped by a simple loincloth, the broad shoulders glistened with dew or sweat. The well-defined body stood just under six feet with no visible hair.

"You speared me, Henry," Jacob said with a sad look, which darkened at the sight of Tellos. "Is this boy my replacement?"

Tellos put his bow back onto a shoulder as he stood up. He pulled out his dagger, glancing from Jacob to Henry. "Let's move before the dragon's fire-breath finds us."

"This is the dragon we just heard," Henry growled. Hatred for Jacob competed with his desire to hold the red-haired dragon. Instead, he kept his eyes locked on Jacob. "Like all dragons, he can be human or lizard. This foul milksop is Jacob."

"Let's go." Ignoring Tellos, Jacob grabbed Henry's arm. "Since you lie and won't listen, I'll strip you naked and tie you up to ensure something new isn't shoved through my chest."

"You're the liar, Jacob." Henry jerked his arm free and grabbed one of Jacob's ears. With Jacob screaming, he pulled the redhead backwards. "I listened calmly to your lies and hate-filled words about me."

"Ow!" Jacob slapped Henry's arm. "Let go."

"Shush," Tellos whispered glancing around fearfully. "While you two argue like some old couple, the dragon hunts. Do you want to be eaten?"

"Old couple?" Both Henry and Jacob exclaimed in unison.

"Quiet." Tellos crouched, tilted his head, and then vanished into the fog.

"I'm done with you, Jacob," Henry said. He wanted to follow Tellos but didn't trust Jacob. "You've lied and insulted me for the last time."

"Fine." Jacob whimpered. Pain contorted his face, and tears rolled down his cheeks. With a strangled sob, Jacob ran east. With each step, Jacob morphed back into his dragon form. Red skin with large gold splotches covered a fifteen-foot-tall body which swelled to slightly wider. His body stretched more than thirty feet with a tail just as long. Jacob stretched his twenty-foot-long wings and leaped up to vanish into the fog. Henry couldn't see them but knew a pair of ridges ran from the head partway down the ten-foot-long neck. A whimpered cry floated down to Henry. Heartbeats later, another dragon roared to the south. Worried about Tellos, Henry took off at a run after the human.

~ * ~

As Henry and Tellos travelled uphill through a thick stand of trees around midday, Tellos broke the silence into which they'd fallen. "If dragons change their bodies, how do you know Jacob ain't the one from the ruins?"

A dragon roared in the distance. The fog had lifted and turned into a drizzle. Pulling his cowl down further, Henry said, "Jacob's a childhood friend. I know his roar and the one we've heard since leaving Jacob is not him. The human form Jacob took is how he always looks when human. The few other dragon's I've met all had one human form."

"So why ain't you a dragon right now?" Tellos pulled him to a stop. "Based on those scales I done seen, I bet you a real pretty blue."

Henry looked at Tellos, not sure what to say. "I'm not a dragon, Tellos."

"Yes, you are, Henry," Tellos said, shaking his head. "I've grown up in the shadow of a dragon. You think I can't tell a human from a dragon?"

"I could be a treasure hunter," Henry said. He thought of the many reasons humans hunted and imitated dragons. "Trophy seeker, mystic after blood or scales, or any of a dozen other idiots. Or maybe

I just want to see my sister again."

Pushing past Tellos, in hopes of escaping his pain, Henry stepped through the trees and brush to stand on the edge of a steep bluff. Below, a valley filled with trees stretched out nearly to the horizon. A break in the clouds let sunshine reflect off a river which meandered through the thick forest and around the ruins of a once mighty castle. On the near side of the river, bits of buildings, from roofs to partially collapsed walls, poked through the forest canopy to mark where a city once stood.

"Sis," Henry sobbed with a grief-strangled voice, tears filling his eyes. He focused on the ruined castle, with its walls mostly collapsed and the half-collapsed Keep soot stained. A lump rose into Henry's throat as faces, sights, sounds, and even smells of that long-ago time filled his head. His mother's scent lingered the longest.

"Big, black, and ugly done ate everyone," Tellos said with an arm wrapping Henry's shoulders.

Henry wiped tears out of his eyes. "This...this can't be true. They're all gone. Am I cursed?" Henry pulled off his gloves and stared at his hands. "I don't know what's real anymore. What do I do, Tellos?"

"Enjoy life." Tellos pulled Henry against him. "That's what Granddaddy always said."

"Easy for you to say," Henry muttered. Dejection weighed his heart down. Wanting to be alone, he shrugged off Tellos' arm. "Go. Get on with your life. Stick with me and you'll only get hurt."

"Or eaten," a familiar voice laughed behind them.

Henry spun around and stepped in front of Tellos while he drew his sword. He recognized the voice, which belonged to someone who should be long dead. Still, Henry called out, "Who's there?"

Bitter anger filled the man's words. "The stuff of nightmares, traitor. King of all Havenia. The one who will force you into rebirth."

A man in black robes stepped out of the trees' shadows. Black hair with golden blonde streaks hugged his head and hung down in a tail. A sharp nose and upturned brows accentuated the fiery orange, deep-set eyes. An aura of power floated about the six-and-half-foot-tall man.

"Theonaric?" Henry stared in shock, his sword-tip dropping. Memories of two lifetimes flooded his mind. First was growing up in Havendell Castle as a boy misplaced in a girl's body. Second were memories of growing up as a dragon surrounded by tall peaks. Both sets of memories centered around this man. Whether human or dragon, Theonaric was the source of Henry's cursed life.

Tellos fired an arrow. He stepped up beside Henry with another arrow already in his bow. "My mother's disease-ridden body didn't kill you? Let's fix that."

"You stupid human," Theonaric said with a snarl. Shifting to Henry, Theonaric added, "Did Jacob not tell you? I thought that's why you fled with him. Whatever. Time for you to bow to your king."

"You can't be Havenia's king," Henry shouted as memories of this man's hateful glares and physical abuse flashed through his head.

Theonaric swelled and lengthened. His robes crinkled and stretched with his body. Trees groaned and snapped as the man morphed into a dragon three times his human height. Long sleeves fluttered and grew into huge wings. The beating wings stripped branches off trees. Circular ridges formed on the head as the nose and mouth pushed out into a long thin muzzle. Splotches of gold-yellow scales lay scattered about the body, which now easily stretched forty-feet, with an equally long tail. "I am your Dragon King."

Tellos fired his few arrows. All stuck fast in the transforming dragon, but were quickly pushed out as Theonaric grew to full size. Henry yelled as he rushed forward and swung his sword at Theonaric's head, which sat at the end of a ten feet long neck. A clawed forefoot slammed into Henry's chest, who flew backwards into a tree.

"You couldn't defeat me then, Henrik." Theonaric snapped Henry's sword and shredded his clothing to expose a female body covered in patches of blue scales. "You won't defeat me this time."

Pain rippled down Henry's torso with each ragged gasp for breath. Every rib on one side felt broken along with dozens of other bones. His fingers and toes still moved, but they grasped no weapon nor had strength. Memories of Theonaric's broken and burning body popped into Henry's head. In a weak voice, he said, "The gods won, Theonaric. Not you."

Tellos backed away with his bow wielded like a club. When Theonaric focused on Henry, Tellos slipped down alongside the dragon. He slammed his dagger into the dragon with all of his strength. Theonaric jerked his head up, roaring in pain. A gust of air and blood knocked Tellos off his feet and his dagger beyond reach. A huge, claw-tipped wing slammed into the ground and pinned the human.

Theonaric grabbed Henry and threw him a dozen feet with a loud snarl. Henry rolled through brambles and broken tree limbs before he stopped. The ground shook with the turning of Theonaric, whose foul breath washed over Henry.

Smirking, the black dragon hissed. "You're as pitiful as your beloved humans. No one, not even your beloved human sister, believed their king was the dragon eating them."

Henry stared up at the gargantuan face. Like some surreal dream, the memory of having been pinned like this by Theonaric replayed in his head. As he did then, he asked, "Why did you do it?"

"Do it?" Theonaric growled. "Humans are nothing but food, Henrik. You wouldn't accept it before the gods cursed us, but someday you will."

"Not humanity. Not even Havendell," Henry said. His body healed, and scales formed faster than ever. The memories, though, came in random spurts. "You did something and pissed off the gods. You always were a greedy, pretentious bastard."

"I am king, Henry," Theonaric roared as he reared up. "What I say is law, yet you flaunted my edicts and did what you wanted anyway. It disgraced your colors before the entire Wyvern Council. What your sister and her babies got at the hands of Death was merciful compared to what I planned for you."

"King?" Snorting with disgust, Henry released his anger as his gut twisted into knots. "Of a dead race and a barren land. You're why the gods cursed dragons. I know it."

Theonaric speared Henry with a wingtip claw and lifted him off the ground. "Cursed? You're immortal, but you age and get reborn, forgetting each previous life. I'm the cursed one. I never age, never get reborn, and never forget anything. Not even your betrayal of your king and kind."

Blood filled Henry's mouth as all feeling left his extremities. His vision blurred as Theonaric brought him close to his huge head. "Come sundown, I swallow your little pet whole and alive. Are you dragon enough to stop me from enjoying his futile pounding from inside my stomach as he slowly digests?"

Theonaric jerked his wing and tossed Henry high into the air. Henry tumbled out past the edge of the bluff. In a blur of black and gold, Theonaric flew past him with a limp-bodied Tellos held in a foreclaw. Heartbeats later, Henry bounced off the bluff's sloping base before rolling into the trees. Like in the many battles he'd fought, muscles tore, and bones broke until he finally crashed into a thicket with long, needle-like thorns.

The numerous thorns and branches pierced every part of his body, including his head. As he lay there healing, Henry could only listen to the distant screams of that last battle as the memory echoed in his head. The dying screams of dragons surrounded him even as Jacob's roar joined in with those only he heard. This was the doing of the gods, and Death in particular. He just hoped Jacob was safe.

"Henry!" Jacob sobbed as the red and gold dragon's head filled Henry's vision. Pain encompassed his beaten and broken dragon body, though it paled to what his heart felt. "Theonaric did this, didn't he? I won't let father wi—"

A sharpened tree trunk burst through Jacob's chest. Grunting, the fifty-foot-tall God of Death leaned over Jacob and pushed the tree through Jacob and into Henry's left shoulder, pinning the best friends to the ground. "Never again will dragons betray their parents. Never!"

Henry jerked his head up off broken branches, which allowed his face to heal. "Dragons betrayed the gods? Theonaric's the Guilty One."

The words gurgled out with blood. An arm rose off more thorns. Wounds healed in heartbeats. Each breath hurt until his chest lifted off the broken branches piercing him. He stood and screamed as branches ripped flesh off his legs. Vegetation sizzled where his blood dripped. Cobalt blue with the occasional green streak covered his healing body.

Memories bubbled up and churned his anger. Everything was a lie, his humanity, his gender, and his very identity. Lies which cast Henry's future into a bottomless pit of despair.

"Henry?" Rocks and dirt tumbled down the bluff and pummeled him. Jacob morphed from dragon to human while sliding to a stop. "Are you okay? What happened?"

"Lies." Henry's voice gurgled as he finished healing. "He lied, and the gods slaughtered us."

"Who, Henry?" Jacob winced in pain when he wiped away the blood covering Henry's rapidly healing body. "What happened? Talk to me, my love."

Henry froze at Jacob's last words. For a heartbeat, he stared up at his wife clad in blood-splattered armor. She leaned over his half-conscious dragon head with fear etched on her face. *"Do you live, my love? Please, husband, don't die on me."*

Grasping Jacob's shoulders, Henry said with a shocked expression, "My wife. I look like my dead wife."

"What?" Jacob grimaced as Henry's clawed fingers sank into

his shoulders. "You're scaring me, Henry."

Henry quickly related his visions. "They're memories bubbling to the surface, Jacob. Theonaric lied to us dragons about something horrible he did. Something for which the gods blamed all dragons. It's so hazy, though."

"I don't," Jacob said, then paused. After a moment of staring at Henry, the red and gold dragon spun around and walked away. "This is payback for teasing you about being a man, isn't it? What do I have to do to prove to you I'm sorry? To prove I love you no matter your appearance, Henry?"

"I'm not talking about that, idiot." Henry strode after Jacob and grabbed an arm.

Jerking free, Jacob transformed into a buzzard-sized dragon. In a small voice, Jacob shouted through sobs, "You thrust a spear through my heart and left me for dead, Henry."

Henry heard the hurt and pain in Jacob's voice. The bravado he was so used to hearing was gone. "I...am sorry, Jacob. Where I speared you, I knew wouldn't kill you. But I'm not leaving Tellos to be eaten by Theonaric. I can't."

"You can't win against him," Jacob wailed, flying away.

Henry watched his friend and lover leave. Again. In a soft voice and with a lump rising into his throat, he whispered, "It's our fault, Jacob. Tellos deserves a chance at a future."

Striding through the trees alone, Henry couldn't stop the tears. The memories filling his head only made him feel worse. Theonaric's greed and jealousy of the gods were so apparent now, after so many millennia, but so too was Jacob's pattern of running away from commitment. Even as Henry found the woman who became his wife, Jacob stuck beside him. Hindsight showed him the love and affection which Jacob hid so thoroughly. Still, as mid-afternoon came, what stood out most was the image of his dragon self beside his human wife, who stood in ornate armor holding a double-headed pike. Theonaric and a majority of dragons stood arrayed on the far ridge of a narrow valley. An army of fifty thousand humans and barely a dozen dragons stood to either side of Henry and his wife. It was the moment before the start of the battle which ended the dragon race. During the peak of that battle the gods strode out of the surrounding mountains as giants and attacked dragons indiscriminately.

"Why must I remember?" Henry sobbed softly as he strode into a large clearing before the castle. "Our future stolen."

Wiping away tears, scales covered his hands and claws extended out of his fingertips. His dragon-hood could no longer be denied. Still, knowing he really was male now left a bitter taste.

"Come to save your pet?" Theonaric dropped from the top of the ruined castle's gatehouse as a dragon. The ground shook and stones fell. "Or to die early and be reborn anew?"

Henry backed up toward the trees as he reached for a sword he no longer had. When Theonaric lunged for him, Henry dove to the side. He tripped on a branch, so Theonaric snatched him up. Tossed high into the air, Henry struggled to transform into a dragon. Fear sucked the breath out of him and doubt kept him mostly human. As he peaked and began to fall, Theonaric slammed a wing into him. Shooting away with the speed of an arrow, Henry slammed into the Keep. Falling to the rubble-strewn castle yard like a sack of wet mud and rock, Henry heard the familiar roar of Jacob before losing consciousness.

~ * ~

"Stop," a giantess roared behind Henry. "Haven't they paid with enough blood and souls, Death?"

"I want every last one of these miserable cretins extinguished from all creation, Love," Death yelled. He held a huge oak tree with spiked roots over a pregnant dragon. "They stole immortality, but they won't enjoy it. Every one of them wanted to destroy us and take our places."

"That's not true," Henry's wife shouted, as she hugged his head.

Henry lay with the tree spiked through Jacob's unmoving back and into his shoulder. A second tree pinned his head and severed his neck a few vertebrae down. Unable to do more than move his eyes, Henry watched his wife. Her armor hung shredded and bent, revealing more of her body than he knew she liked. She leaned against him, and Henry wept when only one arm moved. Though she trembled, her voice boomed with that inner strength Henry loved. Every ounce of his being strove to be worthy of her love and devotion, to be deserving of the children they both wanted.

"Lies," War screamed, swinging Theonaric's broken and battered body over a hill to slam onto a still-burning stand of trees. "The humans sided with the dragons. We should destroy them all."

"Show me one dragon who would give up the immortality they stole," Death snarled, "and I might consider letting the survivors live. For a short time."

"Henry refused the immortality," Henry's wife said with a pat to his snout. "Walking the beach in our old age surrounded by children and grandchil-

dren is what we both want."

Henry tried to speak, tried to say he would gladly die now if it meant his beloved would walk away to live a long, happy life. Living forever sounded horrible and lonely. He gurgled blood whenever he breathed. Unable to speak against his king and those supporting Theonaric, Henry wept silent tears of despair for all he'd lose.

"She speaks the truth, Death," Love said running fingers along the tip of Henry's twisted wing. "Henrik does not crave the immortality forced onto him."

"You believe them over the facts of our children's betrayal?" Death slammed the tree down into the belly of Henry's sister, her death roar made all the worse by the convulsions of the unborn Death ripped out of her belly.

War stomped on Theonaric's neck and ground his heel, pulverizing several vertebrae. "We can't take back the immortality they've stolen. It could unhinge creation. What if we make them forget they have it?"

"Damn it," Death bellowed. "Why did Mother allow this?"

"Forget? Hmmm," Love said as she leaned over Henry, leering down at him. "Forget your wife and never know she carries your unborn children?"

~ * ~

"Henry?" Tellos knelt beside Henry, gently patting his cheek. "You done lived."

"Why couldn't I have died." Henry wept, sobs strangling his words.

"The gods done blessed you, I suppose," Tellos said. He checked Henry for injuries while helping him sit up. "Can you stand?"

"I'm alone. I've nothing and no one to return to," Henry sobbed. "I feel doubly cursed."

Tellos grabbed Henry's chin and urged him to look up. "What do you see, Mr. Blue Dragon? I see a certain red dragon fighting Theonaric. Does that mean you're still alone?"

"Jacob?" Henry watched the two dragons circle and dive at each other while breathing long streaks of fire. "He came back?"

"I don't know much about either of you," Tellos said pulling Henry up onto his feet, "but I think that's love."

"Theonaric is falling this way." Henry grabbed Tellos' wrist and pulled him along the Keep.

As they rounded the nearest corner, the ground shook and stones fell all around them. When they looked back, Theonaric climbed to the top of the gatehouse. A long gash on the neck bled freely but healed even as they watched. Jacob banked low overhead as he blasted Theonaric with a thick column of flame.

At the last moment, Theonaric slammed a wing into Jacob. When Jacob's head snapped to the side, Theonaric clamped his jaws onto the exposed neck. Panic squeezed Henry's chest as he pictured himself wandering the world alone after Jacob was forced into rebirth. Fearing that loneliness, Henry ran toward the gatehouse picturing himself as a dragon. His torso stretched fifty feet and his tail half again longer. At his shoulders, he stood a good thirty feet while his wings, if spread out, would be as wide as the castle. Streaks of green scattered about his cobalt blue body and wings. With each step he took, Henry morphed into being a full dragon. He screamed, "Jacob!"

Theonaric spun around using Jacob's momentum. Guiding the unconscious red and gold dragon with his wings, he sent Jacob into the courtyard to collide with Henry. Henry rolled his best friend over as Theonaric bathed them and the castle yard with flames. Using himself to protect Jacob, he clenched his jaws shut against the searing his wings and back got. At the same time, Henry felt the churning in his gut change. From his own body and restored memories, Henry knew his attack was acid, not fire.

Twisting his head around, Henry spat a quick series of three green globs at Theonaric. Jacob lifted his head and breathed a tight pillar of flames after Henry's attack. Forced back, Theonaric leaped into the air, beating his wings furiously to dislodge the viscous green acid. Henry moved so he shielded Jacob, having seen the nasty gash on the neck. Striding up the pile of stone which once were the castle walls, Henry roared his anger and hatred up at the hovering dragon. Theonaric roared his own challenge back at Henry.

"Your greed destroyed us," Henry yelled. With a surge of his now powerful legs, Henry leaped up toward Theonaric. He pumped his wings while spitting a jet of green goop at the black dragon.

"You betrayed your own kind," Theonaric screamed, diving at Henry.

The pair grappled; their wings entangling each other. Rolling as they fell, claws ripped into flesh and wings punched heads and sides. Striking the gatehouse, Henry screamed in pain even as he spat acid into Theonaric's face. Jacob slammed into the black dragon, dislodging him from his position on top of Henry. Knocked backward, Theonaric fell into the fetid moat below.

"You stole immortality from the gods," Henry said, sobbing. "I had a wife. A child on the way. The gods didn't curse us dragons, you did. You cursed our entire race."

"You weren't supposed to be immortal," Theonaric yelled, splashing about while turning over in the foul water. "No one but me and my chosen few were. You stole immortality. Your just as guilty as me, Henrik."

"You stole it from the gods, bastard," Henry snarled. "Death called you 'The Guilty One,' not me."

"Is that why there's so few dragons?" Jacob stepped up beside Henry to glare down at Theonaric. "We're feared, hated, and sterile thanks to you, Theonaric?"

"Me?" Theonaric jumped up, beating his wings to get airborne. "You turned your back on your own father! For who? Some food-loving excuse of a dragon."

Jacob spat a ball of flame at Theonaric. The black and gold dragon roared in pain, turned and circled back around toward the pair. Henry followed Jacob's attack with another large glob of green acid. Striking Theonaric's belly, flesh sizzled and melted. Pain-filled roars serenaded Henry and Jacob as Theonaric flew away.

Jacob turned to Henry in amazed horror. "That's worse than spearing me through the chest."

"I'm sorry, Jacob," Henry said leaning so their snouts touched. "Don't leave me alone."

"I love you, Henry," Jacob whispered, "be you boy or girl, dragon or human. I'll never leave you. Forgive me?"

Henry shifted his head and wrapped their long necks. Jacob pressed their hips together and entwined their tails. Henry flicked his tongue across the base of Jacob's neck before responding. "Always, my love."

Theonaric roared above them. Blood and muscles covered his belly, though scales already spread across the wound. He banked, heading in for another attack. Jacob and Henry separated.

"Let's finish this bastard off, Henry," Jacob said without taking his eyes off Theonaric. Glancing at Henry, Jacob smiled before he leaped into the air.

Fear stabbed Henry through the heart. Unwilling to lose Jacob, he crouched to also take flight. Tellos' panicked voice stopped him. Glancing back, flames and fallen stones pinned Tellos against the Keep's walls. All Henry heard was his wife echoing to him from his memories.

Henry leaped back into the courtyard muttering, "He's not

food. He deserves to live."

As he strode through the burning grass and brush in the castle-yard, Henry beat his wings to extinguish most of the flames. In pain, Henry knocked and pulled the rubble away from Tellos, which exposed the Keep's entrance.

"He's headed this way," Tellos said.

"Move," Henry yelled, spreading his wings. Tellos scrambled into the Keep.

When Theonaric slammed into him, pain lanced throughout Henry's body. The castle and courtyard shook. Forcing himself to move despite the pain, Henry craned his head as far around as he could, spitting another green glob onto Theonaric.

Jacob swooped in low and slammed into Theonaric, knocking him off Henry. Blood and acid splattered across the ground and rubble. The pair rolled with the blow, only to stop with Theonaric on Jacob. Jacob blasted Theonaric in the face. As the flames died down, Henry rushed in and jumped onto Theonaric's back.

Flames jetted from Theonaric's mouth. Clamping his jaws onto Theonaric's neck, Jacob wrapped his red-scaled legs around Theonaric to hold those black wings closed. Henry used himself to pin Theonaric against Jacob. Sinking his front claws into Theonaric's muzzle, Henry forced the snout open.

"I'm immortal," Theonaric said.

Henry answered by spitting a long jet of acid down the dragon's throat. As though on cue, Jacob released his jaws and pulled his head back. Theonaric's eyes bulged as his mouth and neck melted inside out. Green acid leaked from puncture wounds on the neck, which prompted both Jacob and Henry to skitter away.

"Melt as punishment for killing my wife and family," Henry hissed as a lump formed in his throat. His heart broke again as he remembered not his wife's torn and battered body, but rather her smile and laughter. Her scent returned, as did the feel of her in his arms. "And our life together."

Acid spurted out of a wound low on Theonaric's belly. Theonaric fell still as the acid overcame the dragon's rapid healing. Stumbling back, Henry roared his grief. He only vaguely noticed his surroundings enlarging. Collapsing to his knees, Henry morphed back to human, with his wife's looks once again encasing his tormented soul. Tears poured down his cheeks as he struggled against the sobs.

Jacob bathed Theonaric's melting body with flames, as though to completely destroy the black dragon. Through tear-filled eyes, Henry watched his best friend and lover morph back to human. Jacob wrapped his arms around Henry's neck and shoulders, so their foreheads touched. The embrace told Henry he wasn't alone. He understood now Jacob couldn't lose him. If not for Jacob, he would have died along with his sister and the majority of the dragon race. Silently, he begged for forgiveness from his long dead wife.

Crunching footsteps announced someone's approach. Death's bone-rattling voice said, "I so enjoy happy dragon reunions."

Henry forced his tired and sore body to stand. As Death stopped before him, Henry glared into the god's cowl. "I refused immortality, but here I am. It was Jacob's doing, wasn't it? And not all dragons received the stolen gift. Didn't you know that when you attacked?"

Death pushed back his hood to reveal that creepy smile and empty eye sockets. Looking past Henry to Theonaric's burning and melting form, Death spoke. "No, we didn't. Only when the souls were claimed was the horrifying truth revealed. Sadly, Theonaric's lies led us gods to commit genocide."

"My little sister? Her babies?" Henry struggled to speak around the lump blocking his throat as that memory replayed in his head.

"Were never immortal," Death said, his head hanging. "Never before, nor since, have I taken a soul in anger. My deepest apologies, Henrik."

"So, I lied to my wife." Henry felt his blood drain to his feet and his head spin. "I never was going to die. Never have children."

"Ah, but you did. Twins who were spoiled despite being raised by only their mother," Death said with a toothy grin. "Her love and devotion to you never wavered, even after her death many decades later."

"Decades?" Jacob stepped up to Henry's side. Fear etched his face, but Jacob squeezed Henry's hand tight. "So, his wife lived a long life surrounded by children and grandchildren?"

"A hard life made harder by protecting you both. She instilled in your descendants, Henry, the need to watch over both of your egg-encased bodies until your rebirth," Death said. Smirking, he added, "She cried when Love said you now wear her looks. Love is such a softy."

"Henry?" Tellos called from the darkening twilight. "You okay?"

Death smiled as he pulled up his cowl. As the god faded away, a dozen feet behind the god limped Tellos toward them. Like a whisper in the swirling smoke, Death said, "Your bloodline survived. He is the last."

Henry focused on the bloody and bruised teen. Tellos' hair lay plastered to his face and neck while his torn clothes hung off his hunched body. Jacob leaned in close to Henry and whispered, "Now I see the resemblance."

"You beat him." Tellos stumbled a few steps short of Henry and Jacob. Henry rushed forward to catch Tellos, whose green eyes smiled down at Henry.

"Yeah," Henry said as he wiped blood and dirt from Tellos' face. "He'll reform at some point, though."

"You done still cursed?" Tellos grasped Henry's hand and pulled it away from his face. "Still a dragon in human form? Or a man trapped as a woman?"

"I..." Henry paused. With a shy smile, he tried again. "Both. I'm finding my way to controlling my body. This look, let's say, is familiar."

"And comfortable," Jacob said as he wrapped his arms around Henry's waist. "Of course, I'll love you whatever form you take."

Henry's stomach growled loudly. Red-faced, Henry said, "Fly us out of here, Jacob. Tellos and I are starved."

"Of course, my love," Jacob said as he jogged away from the pair. "Be sure and hold on tight, Tellos."

"Hold on to what?" Tellos looked from Jacob to Henry in confusion.

"Before you answer, Jacob," Henry said with a stern glare, "look at Theonaric's state."

"I wasn't going to say anything rude," Jacob exclaimed defensively. Transforming back into his dragon form, Jacob leaned down to nuzzle Henry affectionately. "I'm a changed dragon, my love."

"I'll dissolve you into soup if you do, you big skink," Henry said, his stern face dissolving into a smile. Grabbing hold of Jacob's snout, Henry leaped onto his neck. "But you might like that."

"Dragons." Tellos smiled as he climbed up behind Henry.

~ * ~ * ~

Ted Pennella is an Oklahoma City based architect, writer, gamer, and pithy observer of the human condition. As an architect, he's keenly aware of layout, design, and spatial relations, which also benefits him as a storyteller. With short stories published in various anthologies, Ted fills his copious free time filled with woodworking, friends, family, and endeavoring to create the perfect cheesecake.

Nukes For Breakfast

Emily Martha Sorensen

[Public Comm]

To the United States:

We have intercepted the nuclear warhead you sent to North Korea. Please do not do that again.

Sincerely,
United Nations

[Public Comm]

To North Korea:

We have intercepted the nuclear warhead you sent to the United States. Please do not do that again.

Sincerely,
United Nations

[Public Comm]

To the United States:

We have intercepted the five additional nuclear warheads you sent to North Korea. Please do not do that again.

Sincerely,
United Nations

[Public Comm]

To the United States and North Korea:

You stupid idiots! We're just going to eat everything you launch! Stop trying to start World War III!

Sincerely,
United Nations Dragon Riders

[Group Comm]

Alexei, rider of Conflagration:

Great! Now China's sending one!

[Group Comm]

Samesh, rider of Ignition:

And Russia.

[Group Comm]

Kathe, rider of Incineration:

Told you all those mutual defense pacts were going to be a problem.

[Group Comm]

Ekon, rider of Combustion:

Guys, Britain just —

[Group Comm]

Wang Lei, rider of Cremation:
Samesh, rider of Ignition:
Kathe, rider of Incineration:

WE KNOW!

[Public Comm]

To all citizens of the world:

We now issue an official warning that World War III is attempting to begin. Please do not panic. The United Nations Dragon Riders have prepared for this day, and will prevent any damage.

Sincerely,
United Nations

[Group Comm]

Kathe, rider of Incineration:

Easy for them to say!

[Group Comm]

Samesh, rider of Ignition:

I think they're way overestimating what we can do with only five dragons.

[Group Comm]

Alexei, rider of Conflagration:

I've told them we needed more! Why didn't they demand more in the Dragon Defense Pact?!

[Group Comm]

Ekon, rider of Combustion:

The queen wouldn't budge any higher. I can't say I blame her, honestly. Volunteering five for permanent guard duty in our world was pretty generous. All the dragons get out of the deal is to eat our spent nuclear fuel rods, and they know it's toxic garbage we can't figure out how to store safely, anyway.

[Group Comm]

Kathe, rider of Incineration:

Speaking of eating, look at Cin's stomach monitor…

[Public Comm]

To all countries of the world:

Our dragons' stomach capacities are not unlimited. If too many nuclear warheads are released, we will have to allow our dragons to vomit up the contents of their stomachs so they can continue eating newly launched warheads. We assure you, you do not wish to have nuclear dragon vomit spewed across one of your major cities. Stop launching nukes.

Sincerely,
United Nations Dragon Riders

[Group Comm]

Alexei, rider of Conflagration:

Argh, two more got launched!

[Group Comm]

Kathe, rider of Incineration:

It's like they assume we're bluffing about the dragon vomit.

[Group Comm]

Wang Lei, rider of Cremation:

Aren't we? We're not going to cause the nuclear holocaust it's our job to prevent.

[Group Comm]

Kathe, rider of Incineration:

Guys, Cin's full now. Do I send him to Antarctica to vomit, or do I ground him?

[Group Comm]

Alexei, rider of Conflagration:

Ground him. We've still got the capacity for another twelve nukes between us.

[Group Comm]

Samesh, rider of Ignition:

Make that ten.

[Group Comm]

Wang Lei, rider of Cremation:

Nine.

[Group Comm]

Ekon, rider of Combustion:

Eight.

[Group Comm]

Wang Lei, rider of Cremation:

Why are we even trying to save these idiots from themselves?

[Group Comm]

Ekon, rider of Combustion:

We're not trying to save the world leaders from each other. They're all in protected bunkers. We're trying to save the common people from them.

[Group Comm]

Kathe, rider of Incineration:

I'm writing a scathing public comm right now.

[Group Comm]

Alexei, rider of Conflagration:

Don't. It won't help anything, and it might make things worse.

[Group Comm]

Wang Lei, rider of Cremation:

I'm not sure *we're* helping anything. I'm pretty sure the politicians with their fingers on the buttons keep assuming we'll eat anything they launch, so *not* launching nukes when everyone else is doing it makes them look weak.

[Group Comm]

Alexei, rider of Conflagration:

Well, what are we supposed to do? Stop?!

[Group Comm]

Samesh, rider of Ignition:

Yeah, about that…Ig's full.

[Group Comm]

Wang Lei, rider of Cremation:

So's Crem.

[Group Comm]

Alexei, rider of Conflagration:

Blast! So's Flag.

[Group Comm]

Kathe, rider of Incineration:

Want me to send Cin to vomit in Antarctica?

[Group Comm]

Alexei, rider of Conflagration:

Not yet! Ekon, how's Bust?

[Group Comm]

Ekon, rider of Combustion:

Getting pretty full.

[Private Comm]

Queen of the Dragons:

If you convince your leaders to open the portal, I will send more of my people to aid you.

[Private Comm]

Alexei, rider of Conflagration:

And what do you want in return?

[Private Comm]

Queen of the Dragons:

I merely want to help.

[Private Comm]

Alexei, rider of Conflagration:

Baloney!

[Private Comm]

Queen of the Dragons:

You realize we dragons have nothing to lose if your world becomes a nuclear wasteland? In fact, we would benefit, because we can feed off nuclear energy instead of prey if needed, and that is much more convenient than having to hunt down puny creatures, so it would be a net gain.

[Private Comm]

Alexei, rider of Conflagration:

Except you couldn't get here if we blew ourselves up, because we control the portal.

[Private Comm]

Queen of the Dragons:

I shall talk to your United Nations and see what they say.

[Public Comm]

To all countries of the world:

The next country to launch a nuclear warhead will receive a stomachful of nuclear dragon vomit upon their nation.

STOP LAUNCHING NUKES NOW.

Sincerely,
United Nations Dragon Riders

[Group Comm]

Samesh, rider of Ignition:

Good job, Kathe! They listened to you this time!

[Group Comm]

Kathe, rider of Incineration:

Told you a scathing public comm would help.

[Group Comm]

Ekon, rider of Combustion:

If it doesn't, follow through with your threat.

[Group Comm]

Kathe, rider of Incineration:

Oh, I will, believe me.

[Public Comm]

To all citizens of the world:

The Queen of the Dragons has offered us the protection of another four thousand additional dragons. She will explain what is needed to receive one stationed above your city.

Sincerely,
United Nations

[Group Comm]

Kathe, rider of Incineration:

Wait, what?

[Group Comm]

Wang Lei, rider of Cremation:

Four thousand?!

[Public Comm]

To all the people of Earth:

If you wish for permanent protection, you need only send up a firework or flare from your location. Any area that does so will receive the protection of one of my dragons immediately, and need never fear a nuclear holocaust again.

Sincerely,
Queen of the Dragons

[Group Comm]

Samesh, rider of Ignition:

Uh, guys…I'm starting to think the Dragon Defense Pact was never to our benefit in the first place. She knew having shields in place would make our leaders more willing to use swords. And she knew if the shields were insufficient, our only choice would be to capitulate.

[Public Comm]

To all citizens of the world:

The portal to the dragon world is opening now. There is no need to fear. We will all be protected.

Sincerely,
United Nations

[Group Comm]

Alexei, rider of Conflagration:

Get to the portal! We have one shot to close it!

[Private Comm]

Queen of the Dragons:

Your human partners have outlived their usefulness. Eat them.

[Private Comm]

Conflagration:
Incinerate:
Ignition:
Combustion:
Cremation:

Yes, Your Majesty.

[Public Comm]

To all my newest subjects:

I celebrate your wise decision, humans of Earth. We will now discuss the start of my reign.

Sincerely,
Queen of the Dragons and Sovereign of Earth

~ * ~ * ~

Emily Martha Sorensen writes clean fantasy adventures with clever characters, fun plots, and lots of humor. She thinks the world needs more happiness and laughter, so she goes out of her way to create stories about them.

Probably her best books to start with are Black Magic Academy, which is about a good witch who gets sent to a school for wicked witches; The Keeper and the Rulership, in which forbidden magic may be the key to building a new magic system; and Aquarius, about a married couple fighting a terrible curse.

She also has two webcomics: A Magical Roommate, which is complete, and To Prevent World Peace, which is currently updating.

Visit her online here: http://www.emilymarthasorensen.com

The Dragon Sword of Valenharel

Takayuki Ino

"Are thou Valenharel?"

The King of Woolruth, looked down on Valenharel from his throne. Brave and sturdy, well-known for his wise tactics, and well-liked; the civilized world's guardian was wounded and exhausted from the ongoing battle with the East's barbarians.

"Right. I am the mage swordsman, Valenharel."

If he were a subject of the king, he would have gone down on one knee and bowed his head, but Valenharel only nodded while maintaining an upright position. He stood with his legs shoulder-width apart and placed his hands on the hilt of a long black magic sword that was thrust straight to the floor. It was irreverent, to say the least.

"The barbarian army exceeds twenty thousand. Do thou really think thou can defeat them all by thyself?"

Valenharel hadn't come to this place willingly. It had only been six months since he had sunk the southern pirate fleet, and he had gotten a reward that would allow him to live and play for a few more years. He had had no intention of coming from the friendly climate South to the East, where the harsh winters were about to begin, and he demanded the key to the treasury as his reward only because he was unwilling to make the long journey. To his surprise, his demand had been agreed to; so he had come.

"What is the question now? The King of Woolruth asks for my help because he heard of my fame, did he?"

There was no doubt the kingdom was being driven into a corner. The capital, which had prospered as a keystone of eastern trade, was no longer as vibrant as it had been in the past, with only a small number of old men, women, and children passing by. The occasional men who were seen were wounded and useless as soldiers. Not a single one of the vassals present in the audience room was unharmed, either. Woolruth's army, which was considered the strongest in the ongoing battle against the East's barbarian tribes, appeared to have already been driven to the brink of collapse.

"The barbarian army's main body is only three days away from

~ 155 ~

the keystone of the capital's eastern defense, the SheWeton Pass fort. As per thine boost, thou can really drive the barbarian horde away, can't thou?"

Valenharel envisioned a map of the kingdom. If the king's words were correct, the barbarian army had already crossed the border. The only thing preventing the barbarian invasion now was the pass fort. If the pass fort fell, there would be no obstacle between it and the capital. It was evident the barbarians would overrun the capital of Woolruth.

"It is foolishness to doubt Valenharel. I'll have the barbarian horde defeated in just one night." Valenharel answered. Despite the confidence he put into his words he was still concerned as it had only been six months since the last battle.

"That's a lot of confidence. I wish I could believe in it."

After coming this far, it was easy to see why Valenharel's exorbitant demands were readily accepted. If the barbarians could not be turned away, the country would be destroyed. The reward of a key to the treasury, which was stocked with a pile of gold and silver accumulated from the east-west trade, would be cheap compared to the country's destruction.

"Be at peace and wait for good news." Valenharel held the jet-black sword on his shoulder, turned and left the audience chamber without making a bow.

~ * ~

Valenharel considered himself lucky. Born the third son of a peasant family, he left his homeland to become a soldier in the now-gone Duchy of Tebylonia. He was fifteen years old when he became the baggage bearer for the already elderly mage Gankel, thanks to his muscular body and the strength he had gained by working in the fields. At that time, the magical black sword was already so heavy the elderly Gankel could no longer carry it.

"Carry it carefully because one false move could endanger the lives of us and the people of this country."

The black sword, covered in multiple linen layers, was stored in a leather box specially made for it. It was Valenharel's job to carry the heavy, heavy case on his back to the battlefield.

Gankel rarely used the black sword. He fought and defended his country with lightning magic, storm magic, and hail magic. However, Valenharel remembered Gankel would occasionally open the leather box and weigh the sword to see how much it weighed.

The first time Gankel used the Black Sword in front of Valenharel was when the Duchy of Tebylonia was attacked by the overwhelmingly powerful armies of General Nephther of the Lefurian Empire. After being driven to his residence by the powerful northern general, the Duke of Tebylonia pressed Gankel to why he did not use the magic sword.

"It's not the time yet, my lord."

Gankel's words made the Duke of Tebylonia furious. His threat of beheading pushed Gankel to reluctantly use the black sword.

Under the cover of night, Valenharel carried the sword close to the enemy lines. And Gankel entrusted him with a message for the Duke of Tebylonia. The mage's message: 'Do not leave the castle until the battle is over.'

As soon as Valenharel returned to the castle, flames erupted in General Nephter's camp. Black shadows danced through the fire, and the darkness buzzed. Seeing the confusion in the enemy's camp, the bloodthirsty Lord Tebylonia ignored the mage's words and left the castle.

Valenharel, who did not step out of the castle that night, did not know what happened. He just remembered the next morning, he was out on the battlefield with the heaps of corpses all around. And Gankel was standing in the middle of it. Dead bodies of enemies and allies were all around.

The sword recovered from the battlefield was even heavier, so much so Valenharel, who was proud of his strength, found it hard to lift.

"Remember. The power of this black sword does not distinguish between friend and foe," the mage said.

The battlefield bodies were so damaged it was impossible to distinguish who the severed limbs belonged to. General Nephther and the Duke of Tebylonia could only be identified by the ornate armored torso of both, and their heads were, after all, never found.

With the death of Lord Tebylonia, his duchy was destroyed and divided by the surrounding countries. Nevertheless, many nations were willing to call on Gankel, who was an excellent mage, and Valenharel, the mage's sword-bearer, did not starve.

Gankel went from country to country, and Valenharel followed him around with his sword. Gankel used magic and sometimes the magic sword. Valenharel's role was to carry the black sword to the place the mage directed him to and retrieve it from among the countless corpses.

"That sword has an oriental dragon sealed inside it. If unleashed, the dragon will bring death without a second thought. If the dragon kills enough, the old magic will return, and the dragon will return to the sword. That's all there is to it."

Valenharel had never seen the dragon, if he had, he wouldn't have survived. The only thing he knew was the black sword, buried in the corpse, was clearly heavier than it was before it was used. Whether it was blood, flesh, or life itself, the sword would get heavier as the dragon ate.

~ * ~

It wasn't comparable to a horse's weight, but the black sword on his shoulders was heavy. In the presence of the king, he didn't drag the sword, but as soon as he left the audience chamber, Valenharel let his two attendants hold it. Both were strong young men, as strong as Valenharel had been in his youth, but the sword was still too heavy for one of them to carry.

The sword, which ate life and became heavy, would become lighter with time. Even so, only a man as great and strong as Valenharel would be able to carry it around.

From the capital to the fort at the pass, he made his way with two horses and a wagon. Valenharel himself and a Woolruth knight accompanying him rode the horses, while two squires rode in a carriage with a jet-black sword on board. He refused the king's offer to send a band of soldiers to escort him, partly because he didn't want them to see him fighting with the sword and partly because he didn't want them to be frightened by the sight of a dragon.

The wind that blew along the road to the fort was cold and cut through his skin. Winter was coming.

The barbarians had come across the deserts and great plains, through the deep woodlands. The king's view was that the barbarians intended to take Woolruth's capital and stay there because they were not prepared for the winter. It was evident if they crossed the pass, it would be a tough battle. He said the barbarians would not be satisfied with Woolruth alone, but that didn't matter to Valenharel. All he wanted to do was to finish his work quickly and return to the south.

"The fort is over there."

It looked like a rock from a distance, but it had the flag of

Woolruth flying from it. It was a solid-looking stone fort. Arriving at the pass fort, Valenharel climbed up to an overlook and looked at the east terrain.

"This certainly looks easy to defend…"

On either side of the narrow road were steep cliffs that limited the number of enemies who could attack it at a time.

"The fort has never been breached since it was built by the first King of Woolruth." the boyish-looking knight said proudly.

Valenharel sniffed, showing he wasn't impressed by the knight's words. "So, how many arrows do you have? What about the rocks for the slingshot? How many armed men do you have?"

The young knight was unable to answer when the lack of resources was pointed out.

"Oh well, it's too narrow here. It seems it would be better to proceed east and face the barbarians in a larger place. I won't ask you to follow me, though."

~ * ~

The power of the ancient magic was strong. The oriental dragon was in the depths of deep sleep and could not move, enclosed in the sword. It was only when something touched the dragon's wrath scale that it would awaken from its sleep.

Oriental dragons were gentle and did not harm humans by nature. However, they did not like to be touched on the wrath scales at their throats, and if they are touched, they become enraged and immediately kill everyone around them. Also on the jet-black sword, was a golden scale as big as the tip of a little finger. It was the dragon's wrath scale.

~ * ~

"But how do you get the unleashed dragon back into the sword?" Valenharel asked the old mage, who was lying on his sickbed from his battle wounds.

"I cannot bring it back. I only wait for it to calm down and return."

"The awakened dragon goes berserk and devours lives to satisfy its hunger. After devouring the lives at hand, the dragon becomes drowsy, just like a man. Unable to overcome the old magic, the drowsy dragon is once again captured and contained by the black sword." Even on his deathbed, that was all Gankel had to say to Valenharel.

After burying Gankel in the far north, Valenharel headed south with only the black sword, already too long, thick, and heavy to fit in the leather box. He sided in battle with those who paid more, and as a mage swordsman, he unleashed his dragon in the dark night. The dragon killed indiscriminately, and the sword was bigger and heavier than ever.

Alone, Valenharel headed down the valley road. He would not allow his squires, much less the young knight, to accompany him. Only Valenharel knew how to use the sword, and he had no intention of letting anyone else know how to use it, at this time. Though carefully wrapped in cloth and slung over his shoulder with a wide leather band, the heavy, long sword dragged on the tip of the blade. That, plus the spade for digging in the dirt, blanket, the earth-colored cloth that would hide his body, and the backpack with some water and food, almost made even the strong Valenharel run out of breath.

"Why do you care about the weight of the sword?"

Valenharel had asked such a question a long time ago.

"It takes time to digest the lives the dragon has devoured, you know." Gankel had replied. "If the digestion does not proceed, there will be no appetite. When thou wake the dragon up, if it remains full, it will only sleep again."

Valenharel was concerned the sword was still heavy.

The black sword had devoured the pirates and become so heavy it was impossible to lift. It was now light enough he could manage to carry it by himself, but the sword was still very heavy. Even if he invoked the dragon, it would be useless if it didn't have the appetite for life. However, it didn't matter if it was useless. The barbarians would quickly destroy Woolruth, so the contract wouldn't be a problem. All he had to do was retrieve the sword and somehow get back to the south.

The path became gentle, and when it opened a little, Valenharel left the trail. He started digging in the dirt at a slightly elevated spot overlooking the area. He dug just enough of a hole to allow him to lie down and laid a blanket on the bottom. He did his business in the shade and bit on some dried meat. Valenharel had thought the barbarians would set up camp in this place, which was a bit wider. It would not be until the sun came up the next morning that they would attack the pass fort. But before then, the dragon would clear everything away.

Valenharel chewed on his dried meat as he imagined corpses as far as the eye could see. It was an unremarkable sight for Valenharel, who was used to seeing to the bodies of those the dragon had killed.

It was dusk, and the earth rumbled in the distance. Valenharel untied the cloth that covered the black sword. There at the hilt center was the wrath scale, glowing as if it were gilded with gold leaf. An advance party of four horsemen passed right in front of Valenharel, but they did not see him in the shade of the trees.

A banner of the barbarian army could be seen at the end of the path. Valenharel's nails scratched at the golden scale, and the sword trembled. Placing the weapon on the trail, Valenharel ran back to the hollow where he had laid the blanket and covered himself with the earthen cloth.

Immediately Valenharel heard the dragon's roar. Under the thin cloth, he listened to horses' neighing, and the screaming of men. His body tensed as the smell of blood, burning flesh, iron, and gunpowder filled the air around him.

Valenharel knew the black dragon would not fall asleep; continuing to eat the lives of the barbarians, as long as they continued to fight. His only worry was the dragon would overeat. Knowing it was something that could be managed, Valenharel fell asleep in his narrow hole.

~ * ~

The next morning, amidst the carcasses of men and horses that filled the area, Valenharel found the black sword. He couldn't imagine how many lives the dragon had eaten. However, the sword had become so heavy and large it looked like a giant's sword.

Some of the bodies of the brave barbarian soldiers were still warm. The resistance must have continued until near dawn. Because the battle had been on going, the dragon must have kept eating, growing bigger and heavier before the old magic trapped it back in the sword. Valenharel tried to use one of the barbarians' horses, which had lost its master, to pull it with a rope, but the black sword wouldn't move an inch. It was too heavy for him to do anything about it.

The sun was up, and carrion birds were flying in the sky. In time, the area would be filled with the stench of decay. Valenharel left his black sword behind and made his way back to the fort with empty hands.

~ * ~

"Thank you for thy service."

In the fort Valenharel was met by the king and his army. They were at best, less than a thousand horsemen, with old men and very young-looking men standing out. They were probably expecting the barbarians to attack the fort at dawn, but that would no longer happen.

"The barbarians won't attack anymore. You should dispose of the corpses so there will be no plague," Valenharel said. He didn't know how many the dragon had killed. Still, it had been a fatal blow to the barbarian horde and would have instilled an unforgettable fear in them.

"I suppose we should," the King replied.

"About the reward, it is…," Valenharel didn't finish saying it.

The King shook his head. "It's an unreasonable request, but a promise is a promise. You can take all you want." The King laughed with the corners of his mouth twitching as he tossed the treasury keys at Valenharel's feet. "Well, those barbarians, I suppose we won't have to bury them. We can bury the entire valley."

Valenharel panicked at the king's words. The black sword was in the valley.

"What's the matter?" The King asked, seeing Valenharel's panicked look.

Once the valley was filled in, the terrain would change, and he wouldn't be able to locate the black sword. It would be difficult to dig out, and he would never be able to use it again.

Valenharel wondered how long would it be before the sword, which was so heavy and large, could be used again? A year or two probably wouldn't be long enough.

Besides, Valenharel was now aware of his mentor's lies. The dragon may not be hungry, but it would continue to eat lives if it was attacked. The dragon that ate more lives than it should, would become an even bigger and heavier sword. The dragon might have eaten the lives of 20,000 barbarians. It would be a tremendously strong dragon. Would Valenharel be able to use that sword?

Valenharel made up his mind. He already had plenty of reserves and would get rewards this time. It might be time to retire from being a mage swordsman.

"No, it's nothing."

With a bow, Valenharel left the king's presence and hurried with his two attendants on horseback to the capital of Woolruth.

Upon entering the royal palace, Valenharel opened the doors of the heavily locked treasury.

"My God!" Valenharel held his head as he collapsed to his knees, staring at the empty space in front of him.

After the prolonged war, Woolruth's treasury was utterly empty.

~ * ~

It was a construction site for a road through the mountains.

"What's this?"

A single long stick-like object was sticking out of the soil the excavator had dug up. One of the workers haphazardly pulled it out of the dirt.

"A fencing sword in a place like this?"

Brushing off the dirt clinging to the blade, he revealed a jet-black sword. It was slender, yet longer than a person's height.

"A giant's sword?"

"It's too thin for that," another worker said.

He held the long handle in both hands and lifted it up. "It's very light," he said.

"I wonder if it has something to do with the human bones?"

The construction work had been delayed. It appeared the site had been a battlefield, and a large amount of human and horse bones, as well as weapons, such as swords, spears, and shields, had been unearthed. Moreover, the unearthed bones were in pieces and had not been buried in an orderly fashion.

"It's a pain in the ass, but we'll have to report it."

Whenever there were artifacts unearthed, the rule was to notify an archaeological research team. Even more so when there were so many human relics and remains at the same location.

"It's not rusty, so it could be new."

Other workers at the site had gathered around. They placed it on the concrete and rinsed it off with water. The sword was made of something black, like a carbon material.

"What is that?" One of the workers pointed to a spot in the middle of the sword's hilt that was shining gold.

"Gold inlay?" The first worker to find the sword scratched at the spot with his nails.

"What?"

Suddenly, the blade trembled, and the worker stepped back. The black sword quickly transformed into a jet-black dragon on the concrete, twining around the worker's legs.

There was no time to scream. As the worker bent down to pull it away, the dragon's mouth, full of tiny teeth, bit off the worker's face. That was the first victim.

Buried and starved in the dirt for centuries, the dragon ate the lives of one worker after another. Still unable to satisfy its hunger, it took flight and headed for the city once known as Woolruth.

~ * ~ * ~

Takayuki Ino was born in Niigata prefecture, Japan. He graduated from the Chemistry Department, Faculty of Science, Science University of Tokyo. He worked as a government official of Japan for more than thirty years. During his career in the government, he lived in Washington DC and Bangkok. He was involved in international negotiations on various environmental conventions such as the Stockholm Convention on POPs and the Convention on Biological Diversity. He was also engaged in bilateral and multilateral cooperation.

He resigned from the Ministry of Economy, Trade, and Industry in 2017 and moved to Huahin, Thailand, with his wife and two cats. He published a guidebook of Japanese chemical regulations in English under his real name. He is now working as an advisor to a consulting company on a part-time basis.

He was a fan writer since his college days. His first novel was awarded the Nihon SF new writer award in 2009 by SF Writers Japan. The awarded novel "Oparlia, A Forest Planet" was published in 2010. Since then, he has published dozens of short stories. His latest works are "Honest mask" in an anthology "Post Corona SF" published by Hayakawa Publishing Corporation, "Distance under the Moon Shade" in a magazine "Night-land Quarterly" published by Atelier Third Ltd., and "Kazarov in a Powered Case" in an anthology "Memory of Resleave" also published by Atelier Third Ltd. (All in Japanese).

He translated his short story, "The Dragon Sword of Valenharel," into English himself.

Ophedities and the Dragon

J.F. Capps

"You're dying," the medicus said. Ophedities coughed again and waved him off, his hand covering his mouth to catch the blood that had flown from his frothing lips with the violent expulsion of air. He craned his head to the side and met the squat little man's gaze with one of his own.

"No one is to hear of this." Ophedities said, wiping the blood off the back of his hand with a rag. "I will make the Senate aware on my own time. Forget your services were ever needed in my quarters on this day."

The medicus paused as if unsure of what to do next, but Ophedities waved him off again before he rose to his feet and pulled his tunic back on. The grim realization he would be a victim to some fate other than combat nagged the edges of his mind, but he used his discipline to push it away. He didn't care what the diagnosis was. He only cared that he was dying, and it wasn't on his own terms or by the sword, and that was his greatest qualm with the entire ordeal. He pulled the golden circlet with the red ruby set in the center, the Eperikus, back down over the short hair of his head. It was a symbol of his position and power amongst both the Sarthaxian Army and the Senate, though no such symbol was really necessary. It was a formality, if anything.

He opened the door to his chamber and stepped out into the hot sun of the Ligonian summer and proceeded down the street. The urge to cough followed him the entire way. Red and gold banners waved from houses all along the roads, symbols of the citizens of the city-state who supported the war against Volkskeg. Ophedities smiled. He may not have been in complete control of Sarthax, but he felt as though it was his empire. The rank had been created for him; it was his pride to know he was the First Imperator. He held the envy and the admiration of both the Senate and the Legatus's, and the more he thought about it, the faster his pace. Sarthaxians waved to him and greeted him as he strolled by, and he forgot he was sick for a moment.

Until he laid his eyes upon the chamber doors of the Senate.

Ophedities pushed the doors open and entered, and the sound of debate entered his ears. The Senate was already in session for the day. Ophedities strolled down the corridor between the stadium seats, taking note of Lyphinius as he gave his speech on the proposed Sarthaxian invasion of Volkskeg.

"We will not win this war with the Draconians until we have the courage as a country to scale down the walls of the Bottomless and end them where they dwell!" Lyphinius said to the multitude of his peers and colleagues. "The Draconians lack the numbers to fight against our army, so they hide in the crevice! These small skirmishes we engage them in are simply not enough to ensure the security of Sarthax! Nay, all of Ligonia!"

"We shall scale the walls of Volkskeg in due time, Lyphinius," Ophedities said from between the seats as he came out onto the floor of the Senate. "Since we do not know what lurks with the Draconians in the crevice, we cannot chance our might and go down after them. We could play right into their trap."

"Hail, Imperator!" Lyphinius said with a fake smile and a show of empty hands. "A blessed day it is, since you have decided to join us!"

"A blessed day indeed, Lyphinius," Ophedities said. "We may have our enemy in numbers, but what they lack in numbers they make up in resolve and tactical advantages. Let us not forget, my friends; the dragons fight with the Draconians. Our detachment at Karsage even claims to have seen the Greatest Dragon flying to and from Volkskeg from the direction of the Unnamed. That gives them quite an advantage over us."

"Woe is the day the Imperator is a nay-sayer!" Lyphinius said. "What is it you would have your army do, Imperator Ophedities?"

"The Sarthaxian Army will wait to strike at the heart of the den of serpents until the time is right." Ophedities stepped further out onto the auditorium floor. His mind raced as his own conclusion to the problem began to formulate on the words of the medicus. He spat it out faster than he could think about it, but once it had exited his lips, he knew there was no turning back. He also knew he didn't want to. "As for the Imperator, I shall slay the Greatest Dragon before he can descend upon us here."

The Senate was in an uproar. Even Lyphinius' bravado was quelled. He stood jaws agape, looking at Ophedities in shock and disbelief as the Imperator pulled the Eperikus from his head.

"Should I not return, the Senate is to appoint a new Imperator in my place." He said as he handed the Eperikus to Lyphinius. "My immediate recommendation is Legatus Horus, as he is a man close to my own heart and a warrior of skill unsurpassed. Should the Senate feel he is not the man for the job, then they should pick on their own. Should I return, I expect the Eperikus returned to my head."

Silence fell over the congregation as Ophedities exited the auditorium. The people of Sarthax still greeted him with glee as he approached, but he could see their eyes turn up, missing the Eperikus they were so accustomed to seeing upon his head. Ophedities felt a strange relief wash over him. For the first time in nearly a decade he was not the Imperator. He was Ophedities the warrior. A man who had no need for a title, only his deeds.

~ * ~

The warrior returned home to his chamber and sent his servants to gather his horse, tack, and a month's worth of provisions while he had gone alone to his armory. He stripped away his tunic and replaced it with the leather bronze harness he wore over his upper body. A vast hoplon shield hung over his back, and two sickle swords were strapped across his lower back while a xiphos hung suspended on his right side. Grieves descended below his pteruges, and he held a massive longbow in one hand. He bid his servants farewell when they returned.

He set out. The reports from his men in Karsage were substantial. The Unnamed had been a favored resting ground for Kvahlenx for time-recorded, and the reports indicating the beast had been seen flying to and from that location was enough to send Ophedities questing after him. He was certain the monster wasn't going to break an ancient habit now, and the fact he was intelligent and felt the capture of the Unnamed was his greatest feat meant it probably occupied the city as his trophy home.

Ophedities found the weather pleasant the first few days of his ride. It stormed near the fifth day in the desert and soaked him and his kit. He pressed through the night, not daring to sleep in the rain, and rode on the next day, not resting again until the seventh night. He did happen upon the occasional village or outpost along his way, but it wasn't until the seventeenth day that he encountered his first hard look at what the Draconian hand had wrought since he had set out on his journey.

The Imperator spotted smoke from a distance as Argo drooped in the summer sky. A few miles later and he saw it was the remnants of a settlement. Almost all the buildings were burned to the ground, and of them some seemed to have been smashed or torn to pieces in some battle. Boards, bricks, and mortar were strewn in all directions. The bodies of the dead littered the street, and some of them had been partially eaten; the sure sign of a hungry Draconian warband. Ophedities dismounted his horse and had a look around, taking in the scene in the waning light of Argo, the waxing light of Acrea, and the glow of the fires. Smoke filled his lungs, and he began to cough.

The coughing became more and more intense, and Ophedities found himself brought to his hands and knees in the center of a dusty street. A spray of blood exited his mouth to bead in the regolith. He leaned forward on his elbows, trying to fight off the coughing and catch his breath, but he couldn't. He waited it out until he felt strong enough to push himself back to his feet. Then he had a seat on a pile of debris on the side of the road.

He waited there the rest of the night, and he rode on at sunrise.

Twenty-six days passed before Ophedities found himself on the border of the Unnamed, the grand city of the Meu. He had not seen it in his forty-six cycles of life until that moment and was impressed by its immensity. It sprawled for miles in all directions, a city of solid stone construction, of grays and tans and obsidian colors. Stone-step buildings built by ancient architects lined the streets and raised into the sky, some of them as high as seventy and eighty feet. A pit grew in his stomach as he thought of the thousands of Meu who had once lived here only to be wiped out in the first war in a battle not unlike the one he found his people engaged in now.

He was accompanied only by sounds; those of the winds howling through the streets and the clop of horse hooves. He reined his stallion about as he looked. He tried to discern the most likely location of the beast's lair. The buildings around him were of great size, but he didn't think they would be large enough or suitable for Kvahlenx to hide in. The Greatest Dragon was reported to be some sixty or seventy feet in length and of a powerful build. It would take something enormous for him to sleep in. And then he was sure he found it near the city center when he found the Meu oratory.

It was a pyramid nearly two hundred feet in height spread out over an area almost five hundred feet wide and stone stepped all the way from the bottom to the top. Ophedities urged his horse around the base of the structure, studying it as he went, but found no entrance for a dragon of the size he hunted. He dismounted when he had gone around the base of the pyramid and began his climb to the top, struggling for breath only once on his ascent. Then he found what he was looking for: The way in. The top of the pyramid had fallen inward at one corner. He knew he could scale the pile of rubble that led the way down.

The interior of the pyramid was dark, hollow, and full of debris. Wood and stone rattled beneath his feet. Ambient light permeated from the hole in the vast ceiling high overhead, giving Ophedities just enough light to see. He moved slowly through the crushed columns and furniture as he crept forward using his peripherals to puncture the darkness around him. There was no sign, that he could see, of the hulking shape he searched for.

"I know you are here, monster," he said, stalling in the darkness. He reached over his back and took the massive hoplon shield onto his left arm, and then drew his xiphos with his right hand. "Show yourself."

Something stirred ahead of him, and he felt the floor rumble beneath his feet. He kept his head down and to the side, letting the peripheral vision of his right eye scan for movement, but even the light that poured in from overhead was not enough to unmask his quarry.

"Mmm, dragonslayer," the great voice said from the darkness. "It must be a mighty purse that draws you to your doom this day."

"No purse," Ophedities said as he waited to see Kvahlenx. "I have come for my own reasons."

"And what might those reasons be, dragonslayer?"

"I am no dragonslayer," Ophedities said. "I am Ophedities. I hear you aid the Draconians in their campaign. I have come to put an end to that."

Laughter roared from the far end of the pyramid, but Ophedities remained steadfast and alert. The dragon seemed to be in no hurry to show himself.

"Mmm, Ophedities," the voice said. "Your name precedes you, but nay; I do not aid the Draconians. You must know your decision has cut your life short."

"My life ebbs regardless," Ophedities said. "Fear not, beast; I am still more than capable of besting you."

"Then let our songs be sung together, Ophedities!" The laugh came again, but this time Ophedities saw movement ahead of him. Something massive was pushing its way up out of the carpet of debris that littered the floor, coming to tower over him; at least twenty or thirty feet, by his impaired estimates. Then there was a blast of fire that traveled up to the ceiling from the mass and splashed against the stone in all directions, lighting the pyramid interior enough Ophedities could see the beast before him.

Kvahlenx was as big as he had heard. Ophedities guessed him to be seventy feet long and thirty feet at the shoulders, with powerful legs on the front and back of his body. He was a rusty-red hue all over, with thick scales and short spikes from his shoulders, neck, and face. The face itself was traditional; an elongated snout full of teeth, with green, cat like eyes that displayed unfathomable intelligence. The beast's neck craned down to allow him to look fully on Ophedities who stood ready for combat.

The roar that ushered up from within the chest of the beast was enough to ring the ears of the warrior and sail past him like the winds of a hurricane. Ophedities was steadfast, his gaze meeting that of the dragon.

"Mmm...what is it, Ophedities?" The great lips moved before him, an inhuman voice greeting him. "You have come to best me, and yet you stand watching as though seized with fear. Or is it reason that stops you, Imperator?"

"I did not come as the Imperator of Sarthax," Ophedities said, catching the dragon's slip of the tongue. "I am here as a free man of my own convictions. A man of no equal. It is not fear nor reason that gives me pause."

"Then explain." Kvahlenx stretched his neck forward, coming close enough to almost touch the man with his snout. "Or shall I just end this now?"

Ophedities maintained his position, his hoplon to his left side, the xiphos held in his right hand. The snout edged forward, the great plate-sized green eyes seeming to pierce into his soul. Ophedities didn't speak until the split second before Kvahlenx made physical contact with him.

"I wait...for opportunity," Ophedities said as the dragon's nose touched him. Kvahlenx was overwhelmed by the sudden storm of violence. The xiphos cut savagely across his face, spraying the man with the dragon's steaming ichor. Kvahlenx's head recoiled up and

Ophedities moved for the kill. He was under the dragon in one bound, the xiphos hacking and slicing great wounds in his target's neck. More blood was spilled. Hunks of flesh and scales clattered to the ground. Kvahlenx stomped and reeled, moving back while Ophedities took the advantage of intensity and violence of action to press the attack. Wings beat. Claws swiped, meeting nothing but air. Ophedities roared like a monster, his hoplon at the alert, his short sword connecting almost every swing, every thrust, rending his foe to shreds.

Then one of Kvahlenx's forelimbs made contact. Ophedities was thrown head over heels backwards, toppling through the debris of the pyramid as he did so. He rolled himself up as best as he could, forcing the xiphos against the inside of the shield and then sliding until he stopped. His foe thrashed under the orange glow of the fire he had lit on the ceiling ahead, and Ophedities considered pressing the attack again, but paused when part of the roof fell in between himself and Kvahlenx. The intense heat of the dragon's fire was enough to begin its collapse.

He decided to wait for his opponent to come to him again, though he knew he wouldn't be lucky enough to get in a second string of attacks like the first.

The monster recovered quickly, moving forward as it prepared another blast of fire. Ophedities crouched behind his hoplon shield while he began digging into his abilities, feeling the Veil of Shadow as it engulfed him. Before he could move, however, flames arched forward, spraying over a section of broken columns and stone carvings. Fire roiled past him, over his head and against the wall and in all directions. The sudden intense heat was like the very hub of Tarbos, but Ophedities held his position. He started moving as soon as the torrent of fire subsided, looking up only when he heard wings nearby.

That is when he saw Kvahlenx rocketing toward him like a battering ram of flesh, bone, and hatred.

Ophedities was almost clear before Kvahlenx passed his position but was still caught by the eruption of passing scales and mass as it cleared his location and crashed through the outside wall of the pyramid, carrying the two of them out into the streets of the Unnamed. The Veil of Shadow still cloaked him, so Ophedities scrambled to his feet and into cover, his movements becoming unnaturally quick and agile while also being cloaked in a swirling mass of darkness meant to hide his movements in a darker battlefield. He dodged away, from one covered position to another, while Kvahlenx whirled about roaring in the streets, seeking his prey.

"Mmm, a valiant attempt!" Kvahlenx's body crushed stone buildings to rubble in his effort to find Ophedities. "Now issue forward, warrior, that I may end this for you quickly!"

"Save your breath, beast!" Ophedities said, his voice carrying from a concealed area across from his true position. "You fight on my terms now! Come to me, that I may cease your suffering!"

The Greatest Dragon roared in fury. Flames lashed from his maw and incinerated the location Ophedities had thrown his voice to. Kvahlenx paused once the fire ceased and smelled the air for burning flesh.

Ophedities snuck around Kvahlenx, using the Veil of Shadow to cover his sounds and movement while flanking him. The warrior put his shield and xiphos away, replacing it with the long bow.

Ophedities struck Kvahlenx's armpit with an arrow when the monster exposed it.

The beast thrashed and turned to find Ophedities, but the warrior had already returned to the shadows. Fire poured out of Kvahlenx's mouth in a never-ending torrent, blazing over everything in sight as Ophedities hid, peppering his foe with arrows from a safe distance, moving with every shot. Arrows stuck in Kvahlenx's shoulders, face, and sides. Still the dragon fought. When he saw his blasts of fire were not working to stave Ophedities ranged attack he switched to a new tactic; surging forward and crushing buildings with his body to kill the warrior, or at least limit his hiding spots.

The sudden confusion of flying debris and falling buildings forced Ophedities into a retreat. He had to stop shooting and back-pedal to avoid getting crushed, and that is when his Veil of Shadow failed. Instantly Kvahlenx was upon him, his eyes wide and a sinister grin on his face. Flames gushed, and this time Ophedities was off guard. He dropped the bow as he brandished his shield. The flames licked up his right arm while he tried to duck behind the hoplon. Fire adhered to the front of the shield, and the Imperator howled in pain while he tried to extinguish the flames on his right arm.

It was the temporary victory Kvahlenx needed to gain the upper hand. The Greatest Dragon rushed forward, catching the flaming hoplon in his mouth and jerking it up and forward, pulling Ophedities with it. The man came loose and tumbled off to the side, hitting the ground back-first. The shield bent in half in Kvahlenx's maw before being spit out. The dragon capitalized on Ophedities temporary setback, striking down at him with his mouth full of razor-sharp teeth, but the warrior fought through the pain and was quick to regain his feet, the two sickle swords coming out in a frantic arc. He was once more at Kvahlenx's face and neck, rending new lacerations. Kvahlenx whirled about, caught off guard by the sudden loss of momentum, and his tail hit Ophedities full in the chest, tossing him backward into the ruins of a stone temple.

He used the toss to gain ground from the beast.

Ophedities was limping, his body battered from the number of throws he had been subjected to since the fight had begun. Something rattled in his chest. He could taste blood. Smell it. His heart thundered like an avalanche inside him.

He refused to die.

Instead, he moved through the columns of the temple, emerging into an open coliseum or like structure littered with broken bodies, armor, and weapons. It smelled of fresh rot. This was not something left over from times past; these people had been brought there to die by Kvahlenx. Ophedities faltered, startled by the discovery, and it didn't take him long to realize that most of the bodies had been partially or mostly eaten. He stepped forward, over and between bodies as he had done on a thousand battlefields a thousand times before…but this time it was different.

These men wore Sarthaxian armor. They had not come here to fight Kvahlenx. He had brought them here and eaten them. There had been no glorious death. Nothing deserving of a soldier. The beast simply used them as a food source.

Ophedities felt the crushing weight of Kvahlenx foot before he even heard the beating of his wings. He was bounced off the ground and found himself looking up into the face of the Greatest Dragon as his forepaw pinned him to the ground with only his head and right arm exposed. The sound of his own ribs popping and cracking echoed off of the walls of the coliseum a second before his scream of anguish did.

"Mmm, welcome to the end, Ophedities," Kvahlenx said. Blood poured down over Ophedities from the steaming wounds he had opened. Some of it even started to coagulate into a congealed acrid mess. Ophedities squirmed as pressure was applied down on him.

"You lied," Ophedities said through blood-stained teeth. "You said…you said you were not aligned with the Draconians…and yet the evidence lies all around us."

Kvahlenx laughed. "Mmm, Imperator! You are a *fool* to believe anything your foe tells you! The Draconians are a means to an end! They will rid the world of you weak hair-folk one city at a time…and I will gain the trophies of your once great civilizations for myself! A testament to the Child of Argo! And in the meantime, I shan't go hungry!"

Air was quickly escaping Ophedities lungs as he felt his chest being crushed. He tried to cough, but pain poured through him instead with a sick spastic wheeze. He mouthed something to Kvahlenx, and the dragon lowered his head.

"I would have…my last words," Ophedities said. Kvahlenx lowered his snout down, almost touching Ophedities face as he listened, his paw grinding down on his opponent.

"Speak, frail one. I grow impatient and hungry," Kvahlenx said.

"My name will be written in the stars!" Ophedities said with the air he had left. His wounded right hand closed around the hilt of a Sarthaxian xiphos lying near him. He wasn't sure if it was his or if it belonged to one of the warriors who had fallen before him. The swing was sloppy. Ophedities' wavering judgment caused him to miss his target, the jugular behind Kvahlenx jaw at the top of his neck, and instead brought the sword much farther forward in a sloppy blow that busted the monster's eye. Kvahlenx howled in agony. His foot came down full force on Ophedities, crushing the warrior flat below it.

He was dead before the dragon's maw closed around him.

~ * ~ * ~

J.F. Capps is the author of "Ophedities and the Dragon", "Eddie", "For the Love of the Wind", and "Winter's Orphans". He spent twelve years with the U.S. Marine Corps, both active duty and reserve components, and currently works as a professional woodsman.

He lives on a small farm in the hills of east Tennessee with his wife and four kids.

Of Stolen Crowns and Fricasseed Sheep

John Lance

"Hey! Wake up!" The knight pounded a mailed fist on the sleeping dragon's snout.

With a startled snort, the dragon reared back, almost smacking his head against the stalactites lining the roof of his cave. The golden glow of his scales illuminated the cavern and was reflected onto the walls through the prisms of a million diamonds. Piles of coins and gems filled the cavern in an ocean of treasure.

WHAT? WHO? The dragon roared, pawing at his muzzle and unfurling his leathery wings to keep his balance.

"My partner and I have some questions for you," the knight said.

The dragon glared at the human. YOU HAVE TEN SECONDS TO EXIT MY LAIR OR I'LL BURN YOU TO A CINDER.

The knight held up his shield which was emblazoned with three white crowns on a field of blue. "Do you know what this means?"

THAT YOU HAVE AN UNHEALTHY CROWN FETISH?

"It means I am a servant of the king and responsible for keeping law and order in his realm. A crime has been committed, and I have been charged with finding, and punishing, the guilty. Even an overgrown lizard like you must respect that authority."

YOUR TONE IS QUITE INSULTING. I DON'T RECALL EVER ENCOUNTERING SUCH A RUDE KNIGHT, EXCEPT, WAIT A MOMENT. The dragon snaked his head down so his snout was level with the knight. LIFT YOUR VISOR.

The knight snapped his visor open, revealing a large bulbous nose, bushy white beard, and piercing blue eyes.

LARRY? IS THAT YOU?

"My name is Sir Lawrence."

THE YEARS HAVE NOT BEEN KIND LARRY. NOT THAT YOU WERE MUCH TO LOOK AT BEFORE, BUT AT LEAST THEN YOUR BEARD WAS STILL BLACK. The dragon tsked. WHO'S YOUR TROLL FRIEND?

"This is my squire, Flint."

Flint stood two heads taller than Sir Lawrence. His skin was a mottled gray and blue; his long, matted hair was kelp green. Except for a strategically placed loin cloth the troll was completely naked. The dragon flared his nostrils as the troll's rusty, metallic smell wafted over him.

Flint waved a heavy, eight fingered hand at the dragon.

"Flint is an excellent squire."

ALSO FIREPROOF. The dragon observed.

"An added bonus."

I DIDN'T REALIZE THE KNIGHTHOOD WAS ACCEPTING TROLLS INTO THEIR RANKS.

"We're not."

OH? BUT YOU SAID HE WAS A SQUIRE. SQUIRES BECOME KNIGHTS.

"Human squires become knights."

BUT NOT TROLLS? HOW STRANGE. IS IT BECAUSE YOU THINK TROLLS ARE STUPID?

"What?"

A LOT OF HUMANS EXPRESS THAT OPINION. DON'T WORRY, I UNDERSTAND. I THINK HUMANS ARE STUPID.

"I don't think Flint is stupid, he's very smart. For a troll."

I SEE. VERY SMART. FOR A TROLL. GLAD YOU CLEARED THAT UP. JUST BE CERTAIN HE DOESN'T EAT ANY OF MY SAPPHIRES.

"Of course, he wouldn't..." Sir Lawrence frowned. "Damn it, Flint, spit it out right now."

With a deep sigh the troll spat a fist sized sapphire onto the ground.

IF YOU ARE DONE MASTICATING MY POSSESSIONS FEEL FREE TO SHOW YOURSELVES OUT. I WAS HAVING A LOVELY DREAM ABOUT DELICIOUS FRICASSEED MUTTON WHEN I WAS SO RUDELY AWAKENED.

Sir Lawrence shook his head. "Absolutely not. A crime has been committed and we're not going anywhere until justice is served."

The dragon rolled his eyes. FINE, LET'S GET THIS OVER WITH.

"Do you know the wizard Finigan the Magnificent?"

The dragon stroked his tusks thoughtfully. FINIGAN, FINIGAN, NO, DOESN'T RING A BELL.

"Really? He was the most powerful sorcerer in the land."

WAS HE A DRAGON?

"No."

THEN HOW POWERFUL COULD HE HAVE BEEN, REALLY?

Sir Lawrence ignored the slight. "Last night someone broke into his citadel and raided his vault. All his valuables were stolen."

The dragon shook his head disapprovingly. BURGLARY IS A TERRIBLE CRIME. THIEVES SHOULD BE BARBECUED.

"Funny, that's exactly what happened to Finigan."

The dragon's tail twitched.

"The bandits made off with his gold, silver, gems, the usual. Unfortunately, they also stole the crown jewels. You know, the crown, orb, scepter, all of it. The king gave them to the wizard for safe keeping since Finigan's vault was the most secure in the land."

CLEARLY AS ERROR IN JUDGEMENT.

"Indeed. The king wants the royal regalia back."

I CAN SYMPATHIZE.

"I'm certain he appreciates your sentiment. But what he, and I, would appreciate even more is if you turned the crown jewels over to me so I can return them to the king." The knight held out his palm.

ME? The dragon placed his paws on his breast and cocked his head to one side, giving him the appearance of an inquisitive crocodile. I DON'T HAVE THEM.

"That's what you said about the missing princess thirteen years ago."

The dragon shook his head. THAT WAS A TERRIBLE MISUNDERSTANDING THAT TAINTS MY REPUTATION TO THIS DAY. I WAS SIMPLY SHOWING THE YOUNG LADY A NICE TIME. SHE SPENT AN EVENING PLAYING WITH MY JEWELS. ISN'T THAT EVERY LITTLE GIRL'S DREAM COME TRUE?

"And the ransom demand you sent to the king?"

A MISCOMMUNICATION. GIFT GIVING IS A PART OF DRAGON CULTURE. I DON'T EXPECT YOU TO UNDERSTAND.

"So, you expect me to believe, all this, your entire hoard, was donated?" The knight waved his hands at the mountains of treasure surrounding them.

PEOPLE LIKE TO GIVE ME PRESENTS. IT MAKES THEM FEEL LIKE THEIR HOUSES ARE LESS LIKELY TO BURN DOWN.

"That's extortion."

AND THAT IS LIBEL. I MUST WARN YOU MY PATIENCE IS GROWING THIN.

"That's too bad because I've got a lot of questions for you."

AND IF I REFUSE TO ANSWER?

"You'll answer. Otherwise, I'll be forced to re-introduce you to Ol' Betsy here," Sir Lawrence patted the pommel of his sword. "Been a while since she had a taste of dragon and she's mighty hungry. Particularly for an old dragon with a few chinks in the belly armor, if you know what I mean."

The dragon absentmindedly ran the tip of a talon along the long scar that snaked across his belly and down his flank like a river twisting through a jungle. ASK YOUR QUESTIONS.

"Where were you last night?"

HERE.

"Can anyone corroborate your story?"

The dragon looked around the cave. THE BATS, I SUPPOSE.

"Is that a joke?" Sir Lawrence asked.

DO YOU NOT SPEAK BAT? THEY TELL SUCH WONDERFUL STO-RIES. MOSTLY ABOUT GUANO, BUT EVERY NOW AND THEN THEY DIS-COVER SOMETHING INTERESTING. LIKE A DEPRESSED TROLL HOWL-ING AT THE MOON BECAUSE HE CAN ONLY BE A SQUIRE AND NEVER A KNIGHT. OR...

"Fine!" Sir Lawrence interrupted. "If you're not going to cooperate, I'll just have to search your lair myself."

The dragon's heavy tail crashed down in front of the knight, blocking his path.

"You can either get out of my way voluntarily or I'll make you move," Sir Lawrence said through gritted teeth.

YOU AND WHAT ARMY?

"The king's. The generals are on standby, and they can have their troops here in the morning. And let me tell you, the army has gone through quite a transformation since the last time you and I tangled. They still have trebuchets and I'm sure you remember the ballista, those big, crossbow-looking things. But the royal engineers have outdone themselves and cooked up something new called a can-non. If you thought the ballista was scary, wait until you see one of their twelve pounders. A cannonball will drive your teeth right through the back of your skull."

The dragon blinked slowly, then grudgingly lifted his tail out of the knight's way.

"Come on Flint, let's have a look around."

The vast treasure reminded Sir Lawrence of desert dunes. Waves of coins, some taller than Flint, created valleys and mountains of wealth. For a moment, Sir Lawrence felt his resolve slip. It would take weeks, months, years, maybe centuries to comb through the treasure bit by bit. The crown could be anywhere.

Duty won out. Girding himself, the knight began his search.

With each step he sank ankle deep into coins. Flint closely followed, his lumbering gait causing small avalanches of treasure as he passed.

Despite the seeming chaos, Sir Lawrence began to see patterns. Diamonds and pearls were intermixed with silver coins, but never gold. Emeralds and jade were only amongst the platinum coins and always in clusters of three. All the gems were intermixed with copper.

Then there were the household items. Golden chalices, vases, plates, utensils, writing quills, gold, it seemed, could be used for any purpose. Sir Lawrence picked up a golden lute. "Am I supposed to believe you play music?"

PLEASE, BE CAREFUL. I HAVE EVERYTHING PERFECTLY ARRANGED.

"'But of course. I would never want to disturb any of your ill-gotten gains." Sir Lawrence casually tossed the lute away, scattering a pile of aquamarine in every direction.

"Whoops, sorry about that," Sir Lawrence said disingenuously.

YOU DID THAT ON PURPOSE. The dragon's eyes blazed blue-white, but the knight's attention was elsewhere.

"You're an art collector?" Sir Lawrence asked, pointing at a collection of paintings and sculptures tucked into an alcove. "And is that a portrait of the queen mother? Why would you want these things?"

WHY WOULDN'T I WANT THEM? THEY ARE UNIQUE AND VALUABLE.

"Like the crown jewels?"

The dragon didn't reply.

"Do you even care how much any of this is worth? Or do you just hide it away so others can't enjoy it?" Sir Lawrence picked up a diamond and tossed it back and forth from one hand to the other.

The dragon slithered up next to the knight. STOP. TOUCHING. MY. THINGS. The dragon hissed, flames flickering along his jaws.

"Ah, ah, careful." The knight waggled his finger at the dragon. "My shield and armor are enchanted to protect me from your fiery breath. Try to charbroil me and you'll just wind up burning your beloved paintings."

WAS YOUR ARMOR ENCHANTED BY FINIGAN THE CRISPY BY ANY CHANCE?

Sir Lawrence looked away uncomfortably. Then he squinted. "What's that?"

In a corner of the cave were suits of armor, a myriad of

shields, and stacks of swords.

JUST SOME TROPHI…I MEAN, COLLECTIBLES. I COLLECT ARMOR. IT'S SHINY. The dragon explained lamely.

Sir Lawrence picked up a shield black with soot. Wiping his hand across its face, the knight revealed three crowns on a field of blue. Then his gaze fell on a sword with a pommel shaped like a griffin.

"That sword is Sir Valor's. He was guarding Finigan's vault, but we haven't been able to find him since the attack."

HUH. TWO IDENTICAL SWORDS. WHAT ARE THE ODDS?

"Not very high," Sir Lawrence growled. Drawing his own sword, he shouted, "Enough lies! You are going to tell me the truth or so help me Ol' Betsy and I are going to carve you up like a dinner roast. I've done it before, or have you forgotten our first encounter?"

DRAGONS NEVER FORGET. The dragon hissed as he backed away, taking no notice as treasure scattered in every direction.

"Then return what you stole!" Sir Lawrence punctuated his demand with a flourish of his sword.

YOU'RE QUITE A DETECTIVE LARRY. I APPLAUD YOUR EFFORTS.

Sir Lawrence's face grew grim, and he leveled his sword at the dragon's heart. Flint stood behind the knight, licking an emerald and scratching his butt with equal vigor.

AHEM, the dragon cleared his throat. I SAID, I APPLAUD YOUR EFFORTS. The dragon looked pointedly at Flint.

The troll, finally noticed the dragon's gaze, frowned, as if working through a particularly difficult math problem, then nodded. Dropping the emerald, Flint placed his immense hands on either side of Sir Lawrence's helmet and clapped. There was a loud gong followed by a squish, like an overripe melon being dropped on a flagstone.

Ol' Betsy fell from Sir Lawrence's lifeless fingers, but the dragon caught the sword with his tail before it hit the ground.

THIS WILL MAKE A FINE ADDITION TO MY COLLECTION.

Flint grunted.

AH YES, AS AGREED, YOU MAY HAVE WHICHEVER THREE RUBIES YOU DESIRE.

The troll held up four fingers.

OH, DID WE SAY FOUR? MUST HAVE SLIPPED MY MIND. THAT HAPPENS WHEN YOU REACH FIVE HUNDRED YEARS OLD. YOU CAN HAVE YOUR FOUR AS A REWARD FOR A JOB WELL DONE. BUT FIRST, WHAT ARE YOU GOING TO TELL THE KING?

"Knight fall off mountain. Got smooshed," Flint said.

AND…

"And…," Flint's forehead furrowed, deep in thought. After a moment he continued, "And dragon okay. No steal."

PERFECT.

The troll seemed to take an inordinately long time to select his jewels, settling on the four largest he could find.

I HEAR TROLLS CAN GET ADDICTED TO RUBIES. PERHAPS I SHOULDN'T HAVE SHARED ANY WITH YOU WHEN WE FIRST MET. WHY DON'T YOU LEAVE THE GEMS WITH ME? YOU KNOW, KICK THE HABIT. GET A CLEAN START. ALL THAT.

Flint made an obscene gesture.

FAIR ENOUGH.

The troll bit into a ruby and shuddered as red sparks jumped and danced up and down his skin.

"Yummy," he slurred happily.

I'M GLAD YOU APPROVE. IF I NEED YOUR SERVICES AGAIN, I WILL SEND THE BATS TO GET IN TOUCH. IF YOU LIKE RUBIES, I CAN ONLY IMAGINE WHAT YOU'D DO FOR FIRE OPALS. NOW IF YOU DON'T MIND, IT HAS BEEN A LONG AND TRYING DAY. WHAT WITH THE FALSE ACCUSATIONS AND ALL.

Flint took a few moments to lick the ruby dust from his fingers, then hoisted Sir Lawrence's body over his shoulder and stumbled out of the cave. The dragon heard a glassy crunch as the troll bit into his second ruby.

The dragon settled down and waited, watching the cave entrance for any sign of Flint's return. The shadows lengthened and the sun set.

Only when the moon had risen did the dragon feel certain the troll was truly gone. He slithered to the rear of the cave. After once again examining his surroundings for any sight or smell of an intruder, the dragon rolled an immense boulder to one side to reveal a small chamber. Within were the dragon's most prized possessions. His five favorite rubies, the largest blue diamond in the world, handfuls of fire opals, rare gold coins from the earliest human kingdom, pearl jewelry from the queen of a far-off land, the very first diamond he ever stole, and his latest additions, a crown studded with diamonds and sapphires and its matching orb and scepter. Beside these the dragon placed Ol' Betsy.

He took a moment to admire his collection and then, with a furtive glance over his shoulder to be certain no one was watching, he rolled the boulder back into place.

The dragon considered the mess caused by the troll and knight. It would take days and months to organize and sort his treasure properly. He yawned. There would be plenty of time for that after a short five, or ten, year nap.

Climbing to the top of his largest hill of gold coins, the dragon spun around in a circle three times, then collapsed onto his bed.

Closing his eyes, the dragon slipped into happy dreams of roasted lamb and jewel encrusted crowns.

~ * ~ * ~

John Lance lives in New England with his lovely wife and daughters. He enjoys spending time with his family, reading, writing, and working in his garden. His stories have appeared in *Raygun Retro*, *Misunderstood*, and *Under a Dark Sign*.

Something the Cat Dragged In

Robert Wenson

A bell tolled in the tower. Poros hurried down the five flights of stone steps from his arcanium, shouting "I'm coming!" at every landing. Finally he reached the ground floor and opened the door to the street. "Gyrus!" he exclaimed. "I'm happy to see you. Welcome to my home."

"So this is your home now," Gyrus said. "A little grand for a sorcerer of the Second Rank, isn't it?"

The two sorcerers were both elderly and grey-haired. Gyrus was a trifle stouter, Poros's beard was a trifle longer, but otherwise they might have been brothers.

"Now, don't give way to envy, my old friend," Poros said.

"Envy? Certainly not," Gyrus said. "Why should I grudge you your good fortune?"

Poros looked about at the rugs and tapestries of the entrance hall. "Well," he said with a smile that was almost a smirk, "I have been lucky—I'll admit that."

"You needn't admit it," Gyrus said. "Everyone knows it already. It's not every sorcerer who lands a plum post fresh out of his apprenticeship."

"Spellcaster-in-Ordinary to His Majesty King Rethron II of Balium," Poros said. The words had never lost their relish for him.

"Who just happened to have been the wealthiest monarch of them all," Gyrus said.

"He was very generous to me," Poros said. "And I'm grateful to him for it."

"He was generous to a lot of people," Gyrus said. "Then, when he left nothing but debts to his successor Rethron III, you were booted out—"

"I was not booted out," Poros said stiffly. "The king and I agreed that I should retire."

"Retired, then. You came here to Pyrgopolis with a small fortune, just in time for Sothebo to die without an heir so you could buy *his* tower instead of building your own."

"As I said, I've been lucky," Poros said. "I didn't acquire just his tower—I have his library as well."

"Now I *am* envious. Pretty big, wasn't it?"

"The compendia of over *two hundred* sorcerers," Poros said. "I've only had a chance to look into a few of them, so far. Retired or not, I have to spend much of my time keeping in practice."

"'A sorcerer who grows rusty—'" Gyrus began, quoting the old saw.

"'—Might as well dig a hole—'" Poros added.

"'—And jump into it—'"

"'—For he's of no more use than a turnip,'" Poros concluded. "But enough chat. Let me show you about."

~ * ~

A week later, Poros returned Gyrus's visit.

"This is a *great* honor, sir," Gyrus said humbly, bowing low as Poros entered his tower.

"Oh, let it alone," Poros said. "We're the same age—we were apprentices together—and we're both sorcerers of the Second Rank."

"Only my joke, old friend," Gyrus said. "Come along to my study and we'll open a bottle of wine."

Seated in the study, the bottle of wine between them, Gyrus said to Poros, "So what have you found in Sothebo's library?"

"Not as much as I had hoped," Poros replied casually. "Open any compendium and you'll find most of the spells are the ordinary ones every sorcerer learns during his apprenticeship and writes down in *his* compendium. But towards the back you can *sometimes* find something."

"Such as?" Gyrus asked eagerly.

"Often it's more curious than useful," Poros said. "I can't see myself conjuring an elephant—for one thing, my arcanium is up five flights of stairs, and for another, there isn't a way to *un*-conjure it. Then there's turning wine into water—that's just a party trick."

"Talk about putting a damper on the party," Gyrus said. "But come on, I can read you like a book. You've found something better."

"Well, yes," Poros said. "I found it in Sothebo's own compendium—the last spell he worked on before his death. He discovered a way to store spells."

"Store spells?"

"Yes. You take an ordinary wooden wand, the kind we all use

to direct our magic, and store a spell *in* it. Then, when you want to cast it, all you have to do is say a trigger word; you don't have to go through the whole incantation."

"I'm impressed," said Gyrus. "How does it work?"

Poros grinned. "That's not the way, even between old friends. You must offer me something equally valuable in return. Do that and I'll give you the technique. I'll even throw in the elephant."

A young woman entered the study. "Oh," she said. "I didn't realize you had a guest, Grandfather." She turned to go.

"Stay," Gyrus said. "Poros, let me present you. Granddaughter, this is my friend Poros, a sorcerer of the Second Rank. Poros, the Lady Callista."

"Welcome, sir," the Lady Callista said.

"Your servant, my lady," Poros replied, stumbling over the words.

The Lady Callista was undoubtedly a beauty. Of middle height, her figure was slender where slenderness was called for and ample where amplitude was justifiable. Her eyes were large and a soft brown; her nose small and perfectly regular; her mouth perhaps a trifle wider than perfection would require, but capable of a most attractive smile which displayed her flawless white teeth. She moved with grace, spoke in a clear but slightly husky alto, and crowning all, literally as well as figuratively, was a waving abundance of the reddest of red hair.

Poros was a bachelor by chance, not choice; and sorcerers, for some reason, find red hair unusually beguiling. He fell in love with the Lady Callista at once. With admirable self-command he confined himself to polite commonplaces while she was present. As soon as she left, he spoke without reserve to Gyrus, begging his friend to recommend him to her and to facilitate his courtship.

Gyrus could not control his laughter.

"Why this unseemly mirth?" Poros asked after several minutes. "Do you think I'm joking? Or am I so unworthy as to be absurd?"

"No, *old* friend," Gyrus said when he could speak. "I can see that you're perfectly serious. But consider that she is young…and you …aren't."

"Old?" Poros scoffed. *"You're* one to call others old. Look at you—grey hair, wrinkles—compared to me you're decrepit!" He left, spluttering with indignation.

His dudgeon stayed with him all the way back to his tower.

"Perhaps it's true I'm not as young as I once was," he said. "I tire more easily—but I haven't been getting much exercise lately—I shall have to do something about that. I don't remember incantations as well as I used to—but there are so many to remember. I do have to confess that I nap most afternoons. And, come to think of it, I've developed a habit of talking to myself…" He repaired to his study to think.

Unbidden, a memory came to Poros. Somewhere, in one of the compendia, he had read of a conjuration of youth. In his mind's eye was an image of the spell—the color of the ink, the handwriting, the place it occupied on the page…Unfortunately, not the exact words—or the particular volume. "Why didn't you copy it, you idiot?" he asked himself.

Poros plunged into the long and tedious search with determination. Tedious, because each compendium bore a spell of TIME-LESSNESS, preserving it from fire, flood, and rot, which had to be removed before the book could be opened. Properly, the spell should have been renewed when Poros was done with the compendium, but he merely set the book aside and took another from the shelves.

He did not bother to read each volume carefully. He skimmed through the pages, confident he would find the page corresponding to the image in his memory.

There it was! *To regayne ye puissance & vigour of youth, First take iii minims antimonë & cast it into ye Cauldroun, Recite ye chant Baraganza Cropis Para Lamidorum Perfluentum & at ye thyrde word brake open ye Egge of ye Dragon—*

A dragon's egg. The conjuration required a *dragon's egg*. Poros leaned back in his chair and gave himself up to despair. A dragon's egg was as unobtainable as basilisk blood, or silphium from Lemuria.

A meal and a night's sleep renewed his resolution. "If I want a dragon's egg," he said, "the first step is to find a dragon." He ascended to his arcanium. First clearing his worktable of jars and bottles, he spread upon it a large sheet of blank parchment. He opened a new bottle of black ink and with an eagle's quill he placed in the exact center of the sheet a small black dot and labeled it "Pyrgopolis" in painstaking calligraphy. He picked up a wand. *"Quaere inveni depingeque dracones."* At each word he tapped the parchment with the wand, then poured out the rest of the ink over the dot. The pool of ink spread over the parchment. Behind the expanding edge it coalesced into lines and other dots representing roads and rivers, towns and villages, and into patterns of various sorts indicating hills, marshes, forests, and other terrain features; all forming an exact map of the region about the city.

The ink reached the edges of the parchment. The features shown on the map shrank inwards toward the center, while new ones appeared on the edges. Poros watched and waited patiently, knowing the answer would be a long time coming. If there were any dragons at all still in existence, they would be far, far away from Pyrgopolis.

The sea came to view in the upper right corner of the map. Next to it, as the map expanded, appeared the Mountains of Laughter, so called from the ogrish cachinnations that perpetually echoed from unknown throats. No one had ever found the source of the laughter; no one had ever wanted to. Not far inside the mountains appeared the words *"Hic dracones"* and the map stopped. Here Be Dragons.

Poros felt a sudden qualm within and realized he had been half hoping the search would fail.

He could stop where he was—abandon the idea and live out his life in peace. No one knew what he had been planning. But when he contemplated doing so, there came into his head the thought of the Lady Callista; the insatiable curiosity that lurked within every sorcerer and was so easily awakened; and anticipation of the applause and envy he would receive from his fellows. He placed a single drop of red ink on the black dot of Pyrgopolis, tapped the parchment with his wand, and commanded *"Viam."*

The drop transformed into a thin red line extending from the city toward the mountains, not directly, but following the roads the map had already drawn. When it reached a point near the mountains it left the road and wound its way along, avoiding lakes and swamps and going around hills. When it reached a river it turned right or left, following the path of the waterway until it reached a ford, where it crossed.

It arrived at the mountains, entered them, and slowly, with much hesitation, moved among them. Twice it seemed to take a wrong turn, for the tip stopped and drew back, then moved off in a different direction. Finally it stopped at the edge of the area inhabited by dragons.

~ * ~

Still without committing himself, Poros developed plans for an expedition. The dragons were a hundred leagues away and he had not walked so far as a single league in many years. He would journey to Anthorai, the furthest village on the way, and spend time there accustoming himself to long marches. As a blind, he would let it be known he had removed to the country to study spells too dangerous to cast in the city. When the time came to set out, he would hire a mule to carry provisions and gear. This would include his compendium, of course, and the map, and also a supply of wands to be charged with spells by Sothebo's method.

In a few days it would be his birthday. A birthday was always a day of good omen for starting a great task. He would decide then.

On the night before his birthday Poros prepared an augury. He took three small slips of parchment and on one wrote the rune "success," on another, the rune "peril," and on the third, the rune "disaster." Before going to sleep he placed them under his pillow.

The next morning Poros rose, breakfasted, bathed, and dressed before examining the augury. He took the slip with "success" upon it and turned it over. A rune had been inscribed in the night; he consulted the Book of Runes and found it was the rune for "egg." A good omen! On the reverse of "peril" was "dragon." *That* was hardly a surprise. And on the reverse of "disaster" was the rune for "cat." A mystery, there. Poros had no fear of cats, nor any great liking for them. They had little use in magic because of their inherent unpredictability. "All it means, perhaps," he said, "is that I should watch my step, lest I trip over one and break my neck."

Poros decided to go. He packed his tools of sorcery and left his tower, putting a spell of TIMELESSNESS on the door so it could not be unlocked or opened. He then went to the tower of Gyrus to take his leave and put over his blind.

"I'll be away for quite some time," he told his friend. "Perhaps several months. I've found a number of spells that should amply repay study, but they're quite tricky, and dangerous if you make a mistake."

"I can help you there," Gyrus said. "I have something to trade for Sothebo's technique."

"What is it?" Poros asked.

Gyrus handed him a small pouch. "Within this pouch are four small metal stakes, made of gold, silver, iron, and lead. They are called WARDS. Properly placed and activated—the instructions are in the pouch—they will create an impenetrable shield. Nothing material can pass through, and magic will dissolve when it touches the shield."

"How is that a help?"

"First you erect the shield. Then you step out and cast your spell. If anything goes awry, you jump back into the shielded area and you're perfectly safe."

"But you said nothing could go through the shield."

"I was getting to that. Anyone *inside* the shield when it is created can leave and return at will. It's a fortress, not a prison."

"What's the catch? Every spell has some kind of limitation."

"They can only shield a place: a house, say, or even a field or orchard, *if it is already known by a name*. You can't just walk out into the countryside and set it up."

"No problem there—I'm sure I can find a cottage to stay in. Here—in return I'm giving you Sothebo's method." Poros handed a scroll to Gyrus.

"You're sure it works?"

"Yes. I've tried it with several minor spells in my arcanium. According to Sothebo, the same method should work for major spells just as easily. I really must be going now."

"Do you wish to take leave of the Lady Callista?"

"Why, yes."

Gyrus left and returned with his granddaughter.

"I am going away for a time, my lady," Poros said to her. "Should I succeed in my task, I shall tell you of it upon my return."

"I should like that," the Lady Callista replied. "Farewell."

Poros kissed her hand and departed.

~ * ~

During his journey to Anthorai, Poros reviewed the dragon lore he had been able to find in his books. There was surprisingly little, suggesting few had taken an interest in the subject—or perhaps few had survived to pass on their knowledge—and what scraps of lore there were contradicted each other. Dragons could fly; or perhaps not. They breathed fire; except when they didn't. They hunted by sight; they hunted by scent. However, there was a consensus that dragons were intelligent and very, very dangerous.

Poros spent nine weeks in the village, taking longer and longer walks until he felt confident of being able to travel five or six leagues in a day. When he was ready to set out, he purchased provisions for three months, and hired a mule to carry them. He also took nine wands, leaving four spare ones, and selected major spells to charge them with. "STEALTH and HASTE, of course," he said to himself.

"TIMELESSNESS, to cast on the egg so it doesn't hatch before I can use it. THUNDERBOLT, to use against the dragon if it attacks. ILLUSION, to deceive it should it hunt by sight; STENCH to baffle it should it hunt by scent. That's six. There may be bandits, so FEAR would be useful. Two more; there's no telling what I may encounter, so I'll let Fate take a hand and pick two at random." He took his Cubes of Fortune and rolled them to select a page in his compendium and then a spell on that page. "CLOUDBURST? That sounds promising. Now one more... ELEPHANT? Why would I want that? Still, it's well to heed Fate; and I have four more wands, just in case."

Just before setting out, Poros used the minor RAINBOW spell to turn each charged wand a different color. As he walked along, he chanted to himself, "Red is for HASTE, blue is for STEALTH," and so on. He varied the order with each chant; otherwise, should he need the ninth spell he would have to run through the preceding eight in his head.

~ * ~

The road beyond Anthorai was little used. Of the ninety leagues from Anthorai to his destination, eighty were spent on the road. Poros found his calculation of the pace at which he could walk was in error, and it took him twenty days to cover them. If the last ten leagues off the road took him as many days—and nothing untoward happened—the entire journey there and back would take two months, and he had provisions for three.

~ * ~

Once he was off the road, Poros consulted his compendium each morning and cast DIVINATION to learn what might be ahead of him. He was therefore unsurprised, on the second day, to be challenged by a trio of bandits. "Your money or your life!" the leader demanded, using the time-honored formula.

"Of course," Poros said. "Just a moment." He opened his pouch and looked in. "Here it is." Out came the FEAR wand. He aimed it at the bandits and spoke the trigger word. They yelped and ran a hundred feet away. Then they stopped.

"Why are we fleeing?" the leader said. "It's only one old man and a mule."

Skeptical bandits, Poros thought. *Of all the luck. Well, I'll give them something to be afraid of.* He took out the pink wand, cast the spell, and a mighty elephant appeared. Poros caused it to trumpet loudly and charge the bandits. This time they ran away screaming, the elephant in chase, until bandits and beast went over a distant hill and were lost to sight.

I'd better recharge them at once, Poros thought. He bent to pick up the green FEAR wand he had dropped, only to have it crumble to dust. He shook the pink ELEPHANT wand and it crumbled likewise. *Does casting a major spell destroy a wand?* he wondered. *Sothebo said nothing about that. Why didn't I try it at home? And only four spare wands…two after I reload the spells I just used.*

~ * ~

Two days later, Poros did not need DIVINATION to sight a herd of camelopards between himself and the ford of a river he must cross. Camelopards were territorial and very temperamental; it would not do to attract their attention. Using the incantation from his compendium, Poros cast STEALTH upon himself and the mule and carefully (STEALTH was delicate and easily broken) began to circle around to the ford. He had almost reached it when a shift in the wind brought the scent of the herd to the mule, who brayed in alarm, shattering the spell. Poros, needing both hands to control the frightened mule, could not use a spell. He made his way toward the ford, hauling the animal by its bridle. Behind, the camelopards looked this way and that, searching for the cause of their disturbance. When Poros and the mule were halfway across they came charging down.

The leading camelopard was only a hundred yards away when Poros reached the far bank. He let go of the mule, which bolted up the bank and away. The sorcerer brought out a wand, pointed it upstream, and cast CLOUDBURST. The resulting downpour swelled the river. Poros scrambled up the bank ahead of the rising waters. The charging herd saw the flood, stopped, and milled about indecisively for several minutes before going back the way they came. After creating a new CLOUDBURST wand, Poros had only one spare left.

After these two hazardous encounters Poros proceeded even more carefully. He forced himself to memorize the incantation for STEALTH so he would not need to use his last wand. It took him another ten days to reach the edge of the Mountains of Laughter.

On the morning of the fifteenth day since leaving the road, Poros took out the map and studied it carefully to orient himself and take the correct path onwards. While he was doing this, the rumble of a distant chuckle came down and the mule trembled with fear. "No good taking you up there," the sorcerer said. He led the mule into an evergreen thicket where it could not easily be seen, took from it a pack containing the second month's provisions, and cast TIME-LESSNESS on the animal. "There. You'll stay here, safe, and be ready for me if—no, *when*—I get back."

~ * ~

Slowly Poros entered the mountains and traveled among them. He used STEALTH continually, not knowing how watchful dragons might be—did they post sentinels? Did they patrol? As he went he blazed a trail, chipping rocks or making marks with chalk. He made his way over high passes, groped through dark caverns, and crept along narrow ledges, forcing himself to overcome the terror of a thousand-foot drop just a few inches away. All the while, disturbing laughter sounded about him, sometimes at his side, other times far overhead or deep in the earth.

After five days of this he reached the top of a steep pile of boulders and found he had attained his goal. Here Be Dragons, indeed! Before and a few yards below him lay a plateau, several hundred acres in extent and occupied entirely by dragons.

They were not as large as he had imagined: the biggest was perhaps fifteen or twenty feet long, not counting the tail. Their scales were small and smooth as polished metal so they rippled bronze and green in the sunlight. They had wings, and used them, as Poros realized when one swooped low over his head from behind, then rose to a great height and circled over the plateau before coming down and joining its fellows. He did not see any sign they breathed fire, but whether this was because they could not, or chose not to amongst themselves, he could not tell.

For some reason the mountain laughter sounded only faintly in that place. The air instead was filled with draconic hisses and grunts, ranging in pitch from the bass of the largest adults to the treble of the little—calves? Kittens? What *was* the correct term for dragon young? Poros could not remember it, or whether he had ever known.

He collected himself and began to search for eggs. This did not take long; Fortune, or the map, had led him to exactly the right place. At the foot of the rocks, directly below, was a dragon and next to it a nest containing nine or ten eggs.

Poros considered. It was day, and the dragons were active; he could not see any sleeping. Therefore, they must sleep at night. The best time to steal an egg, he decided, would be at the first glimmer of daylight, so he would have the entire day to escape. He found a hollow among the boulders, concealed himself and went to sleep.

He woke well before dawn and waited patiently. There was enough of a moon for him to see the dragons were asleep, but not enough to venture down and take an egg and begin his return.

With nothing else to do, Poros thought about the egg. Would the mother miss it? Could dragons count? If he took two, the extra would be a good thing to have. If he made a mistake with the conjuration he could try again; if not, there were any number of aging sorcerers who would covet the egg—he could name his own price.

The waning moon passed overhead and the sky in the east grew lighter. Poros used the STEALTH wand on himself, to avoid using an incantation in the hearing of the dragons. Keeping an excruciating balance between caution and haste, he made his way down to the nest. He took one egg and put it in his pouch. Dragon eggs were large; there would not, after all, be room for a second. He clambered up and over the pile of boulders and fled. At the first turning he used a wand to cast TIMELESSNESS on the egg and another to cast HASTE upon himself.

~ * ~

It had taken five days for Poros to penetrate the mountains; speeded by HASTE (while it lasted), guided by the blazons, and driven by the need to get as far as he could before the theft was discovered, it took him one day to return. At sunset he reached the mule. Exhausted, he could go no farther.

At dawn he freed the mule and set off homeward. Every few minutes he looked back to see if he was being pursued; but it was not until mid-afternoon that he saw a black speck in the sky, coming from the mountains. He cast the FARSIGHT spell from his compendium. The speck was indeed a dragon. *Maybe it's only hunting,* he thought. *Maybe it's hungry.* He led the mule off the road and removed the last month's pack of provisions from its back. "Sorry, but this is where we part company," he said. He uttered the incantation for HASTE and ran back to the road and away.

Ten minutes later he was obliged to stop to catch his breath, but he had put nearly half a league between himself and the mule.

Looking back, Poros saw the dragon stoop to the mule but rise up again and continue its pursuit. He quickly concealed himself in a clump of bushes near the road, took out the wand charged with ILLUSION, and sent an image of himself running away from the road. With satisfaction he watched as the dragon swerved to follow it. Regaining his breath, he resumed his escape.

It was not long before he saw the dragon returning. It must have realized it was chasing a phantom. He could not use that trick again. However, he had confirmed dragons hunted by sight. He found another clump of bushes and hid himself again. The dragon circled overhead several times and then headed back, along the road. It swooped down; several seconds later Poros thought he could hear a faint bray of terror. *It's given up,* he thought with relief. *It can't find me and has decided to settle for a dinner of mule meat.* He returned to the road and once again began to run. He was not so confident, however, that he omitted to cast an occasional glance behind him.

Before long he noticed with alarm the pursuit was not over, though it was continuing oddly. The dragon, rather than flying directly after him, bobbed down to the road and rose again, over and over. Its up-and-down motions still brought it closer and closer, so Poros found another hiding place.

The dragon drew closer, and Poros realized what it was doing. When it came down to the road it lowered its head and moved it from side to side like a tracking dog. *They hunt by sight* and *scent,* he thought. *This will be tricky.*

The dragon closed the distance until Poros could hear it snuffling. Closer still; when it was only a few yards away he aimed the STENCH wand and triggered it. The dragon recoiled, eyes shut tightly, coughing and choking. It moved back until it was out of range of the smell and sat for a minute breathing heavily. Then it shook its head, put its nose to the road, and came forward gingerly. When it reached the fringe of the STENCH it jerked its head back, turned around, and flew off.

The sun is setting, Poros thought. *The dragon will likely go to sleep, especially just after having had a heavy meal. I'll go along as best I can by starlight and later by moonlight. But not with* HASTE; *I'm an old man and too much will kill me.*

A few miles farther the idea came to Poros that it might be well to have the THUNDERBOLT wand in his hand—just in case.

~ * ~

Poros stopped when the east had just begun to lighten. His nerves were tingling. "Something's wrong," he said to himself, turned about and looked up. Silhouetted again the thickly clustered stars, dimly lit by the thin sliver of the moon, the dragon was diving toward him. He raised the wand and at the last moment sent the THUNDER-BOLT. The spell hit the dragon squarely; the beast somersaulted backwards twice and crashed to the ground. Poros did not wait to see if it was dead or only stunned, but set off at once. Seeing little difference between death by HASTE and death by dragon, he used the spell again; by now he had the words of the incantation by heart.

I don't dare use my last wand, he thought. *And yet there's no guarantee the next time I'm attacked I'll have time for an incantation, even if I had one memorized. If only I had a chance to rest and think!*

The first few times he looked back he saw nothing. Then, when the sun was still below the horizon, he saw the dragon rise. High in the air, glowing in the orange light of dawn against the dark sky, it flew back toward the mountains until it was lost to view.

~ * ~

"What a story *this* will make," Poros said, giddy with relief. "Not only going deep into the Mountains of Laughter and stealing an egg from under the noses of a hundred dragons, but fighting one off every step of the way back!" For sorcerers, like anglers, were not above improving a tale. "But right now I need a rest." Near the road was a willow, its branches drooping to the ground; he lay down under them and fell asleep at once.

~ * ~

Poros woke at noon, much refreshed, and resumed his journey. As each backward glance showed him only an empty sky his confidence increased; so did the intervals between glances.

The sun was halfway down from its zenith when Poros looked back briefly, turned, and looked again. "Clotho, Lachesis, and Atropos," he whispered. Far off was a flock of black spots. He didn't need FARSIGHT to know that they were not birds. "Here we go again," he said, and cast HASTE. *Even now I can't outrun them,* he thought. *And it must be still sixty leagues to Anthorai; I certainly can't keep this up until I get there. Not to mention the thanks I'd get for bringing a dozen or so dragons down on them. But at least I'm buying myself some time. Somehow, somewhere, something* must *turn up, or I'm doomed.*

What was that near the road, far ahead? A farmhouse—a *place!* If he could get to it and use the WARDS.... Poros looked back. It would be a near-run thing unless he could think of a way to delay the dragons. He had three loaded wands and the spare, which he could not stop to charge. Remembering the bandits, he decided against FEAR. The dragons could easily dodge a CLOUDBURST. That left ELEPHANT. "It worked once, more or less. Maybe it will work twice. They've flown a long way—they're probably hungry." He turned and cast the spell, turned again and ran on.

Poros had halved the distance to the farmhouse when, far behind, he heard a trumpet of defiance. He turned and looked. The dragons were flying warily about the elephant, which stood its ground and fiercely lashed its trunk. One charged in from the flank, then another, and soon the elephant was down under a dozen dragons. One remained aloft, circling high overhead.

The HASTE spell dissipated when Poros was still a hundred yards short of the farmhouse. Gasping for breath, he forced his aged legs to carry him onward. Ten yards short of the remnants of the decaying fence that stood about the house, he fell, unable to move even one more step. He closed his eyes and prayed to the gods his death might be quick.

Time passed; Poros dared to look up. The dragon was still there, far above. "It doesn't want to tackle me alone!" he thought. "The THUNDERBOLT taught it to be cautious." He managed to drag himself to his feet and stagger inside the fence. In the distance the other dragons were still dining off the elephant. "By Hecate," he gasped, "I'll beat them yet!"

He took the WARDS from his pouch and placed them carefully, as Gyrus had instructed. Gold on the East, silver on the West, iron on the North, and lead on the South to anchor the others. Then he spoke the activating words. From each WARD rose a thread of light. The threads extended upwards and bent inwards, drawing together and joining over the roof of the farmhouse. Between them the air began to shimmer faintly. The shimmer strengthened until the house stood within a ghostly dome.

Poros lay down and slept like the dead for a night and a day and another night.

~ * ~

When he awoke he found his refuge surrounded by dragons. Although the sun was well above the horizon, most of them were asleep. Three were not and Poros could sense the vengeful attention with which they regarded him. One had a bloody snout; it must have run head-on into the shield. The fence, which had been outside the shield, was gone, and there was a wide belt of scorched and blackened ground surrounding the shield. Dragons, it appeared, *did* breathe fire, but the shield was proof against it.

He turned and looked at the farmhouse. Was it occupied? Almost certainly not. If it was, the occupants must be cowering in the cellar. They could have no reason to feel kindly toward him; alone, aged, tired, and virtually defenseless as he was, even one could easily slay him or give him to the dragons. He did still have the wand of FEAR, but it would be callous to use it. He had one empty wand. It was only then he realized he had started out with *thirteen* wands. No wonder things were turning out so badly!

Poros paged through his compendium and finally chose to charge the wand with FRIENDSHIP. He entered the house and found it, as he expected, empty; until he entered the kitchen and found a large but gaunt calico cat on the sill of the partly open kitchen window.

A cat! Poros remembered the augury—disaster would come from a cat. He thought of using the wand of FEAR, but who could tell what a cat maddened with fright might do? Instead he raised the wand he was carrying and cast FRIENDSHIP. At once the animal came to him and rubbed against his leg. He picked it up and scratched its head and was rewarded with a loud purr. Disaster averted!

Unfortunately, there were still the dragons. "I'm safe inside the shield," Poros said to the cat, "but I can't cast spells through it. I can go out and cast a spell from a wand and return, but all I have left is FEAR and I'm sure *that* won't work. They'll never give me time to complete an incantation.

"I could stay here and wait for help. The problem with that is that I'm far from settled parts—perhaps that's why the place was abandoned. Will anyone happen by before my provisions run out? Suppose someone does. Either he can defeat the dragons—very unlikely—or he'll go back to Anthorai, or even Pyrgopolis, and report the presence of a cluster of dragons…if the dragons don't get him first. And suppose I *am* rescued. I'll be forever known as the sorcerer who *foolishly* provoked the dragons and let himself be helplessly trapped by them. I'd rather die than face humiliation like that. We're in this for victory or defeat, Puss.

"Victory, defeat—or a draw. If I return the egg, will they go away?" Poros had not noticed the cat had left while he was thinking aloud; he was startled when it leaped through the open window and left a dead field mouse at his feet.

Poros thought for hours but could not find a way to escape. Finally he gave up and went outside. He walked up to the shield; the unblinking dragon sentinels watched his every move. He took the egg from his pouch, laid it on the ground, and gave it a gentle push so it rolled through the shield.

And they ignored it! One of the dragons lowered its head, pushed it forward to the shield, and stared unblinking into Poros's eyes; he realized it was not the egg that mattered to them, but the theft. They would not leave before executing vengeance upon the thief.

"Very well!" he shouted at the dragon. "Leave it there! When I've defeated you, I shall get it back! And by all the gods, when I'm young again I'll arm myself with a hundred spells of murder and mayhem—I'll return to your lair and destroy you all!" But Poros knew the dragons recognized his threat was empty.

~ * ~

Night came. Poros sat in the only chair in the house, at the only table, forcing himself to eat. *No wonder there are no stories of* anyone, *let alone a sorcerer, defeating a dragon,* he thought. *No wonder there is so little lore. There does not exist a single spell powerful enough.*

The cat, who had been sitting on the table next to him washing itself, looked at him and meowed. "Hungry, are you, Puss?" Poros asked. He gave it a bit of dried meat. The cat sniffed at it, gave Poros a look as if to say, "Is that all you have?" and jumped out the window, leaving the scrap untouched.

"There does not exist a single spell," Poros said out loud. "Not a single...Not a *single* spell! But what about a combination of spells?" In his mind's eye he saw himself leaping through the shield and battering the dragons with spell after spell, each one building upon and exploiting the effect of the one before. The image faded. "But I would need wands to do that, and I haven't any...Poros, you *idiot! There's wood all about you.* You can *make* wands!"

There was the table at which he was sitting, the chair in which he sat. He remembered that outside the farmhouse and inside the shield were a few old sticks of firewood and a rusty axe. He rushed out and returned with the axe and a piece of wood.

The axe was dull as well as rusty, Poros was inexperienced with tools and had not yet fully regained his strength. It took him many minutes to hack a number of splinters from the wood. He took one and with his knife began to whittle it into a wand. "Think of it, Puss," he said, forgetting the cat was not there. "The sorcerer who stole a dragon's egg and defeated a *horde* of dragons."

The cat returned with something wriggling in its mouth. It jumped down to the floor and began to play with its catch. Suddenly it yowled. Poros smelled burning fur. He looked down. The cat had not caught another mouse. It had caught a baby dragon.

"By the Furies!" Poros exclaimed. "Where did you get *that?*" The cat had retreated to the top of a cupboard and was looking down and hissing, its eyes wide with outrage. The pieces of the puzzle came together for him. "The egg—it must have been on the point of hatching when I took it. Passing it through the shield dissolved the spell of TIMELESSNESS The cat was inside the WARDS when the shield went up, so it could go out and come in again; and the egg was *also* inside, so the baby dragon could pass through with the cat." The little dragon puffed out a gout of flame. "Interesting," Poros said. "They can breathe fire almost as soon as they're out of the egg."

The little dragon puffed out another jet of flame. The pile of splinters on the floor caught fire. The wood was old and dry and blazed up in an instant. The little dragon squealed with excitement and ran about the floor, puffing out more flame, igniting the legs of the table, then the chair, then the remainder of the stick of firewood. It flapped its wings and rose into the air. It landed on the table and puffed, setting fire to Poros's pouch, in which were his remaining wands and the compendium.

Heedless of the flames, Poros seized the pouch and ran outside. He flung it to the ground and, heedless of the flames, beat it with his hands until it ceased to burn. With dread he investigated its contents. The compendium was half-destroyed; one of the wands was charred and useless, the other still intact. *Which spell was on it?* He turned to face the farmhouse, which was now an inferno, raised the wand and triggered the spell. He gave a sob of joy when CLOUD-BURST appeared over the house.

Rain poured down and the fire diminished. But the spell spread and spread and evaporated when it reached the shield. There was not enough left within to quench the blaze, which quickly regained its ferocity. When the roof caught fire Poros realized the farmhouse would soon be no more than a pile of ashes. It would no longer be a *place,* and the WARDS would no longer protect it.

"May the gods grant it's still there," Poros said as he leafed through the remains of the compendium. "It is!" And as the sun rose, the roof collapsed, and the shield faded, Poros chanted the words of the spell of TIMELESSNESS, casting it upon himself.

The little dragon wriggled out of the embers and flew to the others, one of which took it under her wing and nuzzled it. The others, seeing the shield was gone, played their fiery breath upon the motionless Poros, but to no effect, as time, and hence change, did not exist for him. At length they ceased, took to the air, and departed on their long journey back to the mountain.

Ere long one returned, accompanied by her offspring. She stooped low over Poros, grasped him in her claws, and flew after the others. But she did not return directly; instead, she took a wide detour, and dropped Poros into the sea.

~ * ~ * ~

After 20 years as a draftsman / structural designer / civil engineer and another 22 as a computer programmer, **Robert Wenson** retired in 2020 to concentrate on a new vocation as a writer of fiction. He has had pieces published in the *Jupiter* and *Neptune* volumes of the *Planetary Anthologies* from Tuscany Bay Books. He lives in Bethlehem, PA with his wife of 30 years and their two children.

The Dragon Lord

A.K. Stuntz

Armin gripped his sword tightly and took a deep breath. This was it, his time to shine and show the rest of the village he should be a knight. He swallowed down the bile burning at the back of his throat and took a tentative step forward.

Darkness surrounded him. An eerie silence filled the area. The only sound was the tapping of his feet on the hard stone floor. Weren't Dragons supposed to have excellent hearing and a great sense of smell? Why wasn't the dragon coming after him?

He stepped further into the cave, squinting his eyes as he tried to see in the darkness. A smart knight would have brought a lantern or at least a torch along. His hand found the wall, and he followed it deeper into the blackness. The coolness of the stone helped dry his sweaty hands as he searched for any sign of the horrid creature.

His heart pounded so hard he was sure the dragon could hear it—if there was a dragon. Maybe the stories weren't true. Maybe the dragon lord didn't live in this cave. Maybe it didn't terrorize the towns, light hay piles on fire, and steal sheep, cows, and people. Or maybe, it was waiting for him to get close enough so it could eat him.

The sword he carried felt heavy in his hand. The thought of taking a life had him pausing in his search. Would he be able to kill the dragon? He pushed the thought to the back of his mind. He would do what was necessary to become a knight.

His fingers continued to brush against the cold wall, sending particles of dirt drifting to the ground. The temperature was changing, becoming warmer the further he went. The texture changed too. It was no longer the hard rocks but a soft scale-like feel. His eyes went wide, and he froze as the wall moved. He was touching the dragon!

He yanked back his shaking hand and took a step back. The mighty beast uncoiled. Fire flew from its mouth, lighting the cave and giving Armin his first good look at the powerful creature. With wide eyes, he stared at the large dragon.

A roar erupted, echoing off the walls. Armin stumbled backward, tripped on a rock, and went crashing to the ground. His sword flew from his hand, landing somewhere off to the right, and his shield went to the left. He scrambled on hands and knees, desperate to find the lost weapon. He could make do without the protective gear, but he would surely die without the blade.

Frantically, he searched the area with his hands and once again chastised himself for not bringing something along to light his way. His hand touched the cold steel of the blade, and he nearly cried with joy. Now he just needed to find the dragon.

The ground shook as the monstrous creature stomped about the area. This dragon seemed to have the ability to see in the dark, something he wished he could do. Fire lit up the cave once more, giving the knight a clear view of the beast he was sent to kill. He clutched the sword in both hands and charged towards the fading figure, slashing and poking as darkness descended again. His hands shook as he jabbed into the blackness, making contact with something solid.

Armin let go of the weapon and backed up quickly, wiping his sweaty palms on his pants. An ear-splitting cry pierced the quiet night, and the creature crumbled to the ground, sending shockwaves reverberating under his feet.

He was having a hard time wrapping his head around the idea he had killed a dragon. He stared into the dark where he thought the dead monster lay, straining his eyes to get a look. His heart ached at the thought of its death. It was only protecting its home. It didn't deserve to die.

He sunk to the ground, covered his face with his hands, and sobbed. "What have I done? I…I killed…a living thing." He swiped at the snot and tears with the back of his hand as he sat there in the damp, dark cave.

"For goodness' sake. I've never heard anyone cry over a dead dragon before." A female voice rang through the cave.

Armin stood up and spun in a circle. Thanks to the darkness, it was impossible to see. "Who are you?"

A tiny burst of fire flew through the air, landing on a torch sticking out of the wall. The light cast a harsh glow over the red dragon, who wasn't dead at all.

The shock sent his heart racing and pounding so hard he thought it would bust. Armin scrambled backward, stopping when he reached solid stone. He slowly rose to his feet, keeping the winged creature in his sight the whole time.

"Stop staring at me. I haven't done anything wrong." She smacked her tail on the dirt.

"You...You..." He pointed his finger at the red-winged creature.

"Speak, boy." The dragon's voice boomed through the damp cave causing his heart to skip and jump.

"You can talk!" He finally spat out.

"I'm the dragon lord. Actually, I prefer lordess." She flapped her wings, sending a cloud of dust swirling in his direction.

"I stabbed you with my sword. You're supposed to be dead."

"Well, you didn't exactly get me. I just pretended so you would think I was dead, and people would leave me alone. It would have worked too. If you hadn't started bawling like a baby. There's nothing worse than a crying human." She spun around several times before laying down and wrapping her spiked tail around in front of her.

"I did not bawl like a baby." He crossed his arms over his chest. How dare she call him a baby. She should feel special that someone actually felt sorry for killing her, not making fun of them.

The dragon snorted. "Whatever. You can leave now so I can finish my nap." She laid her head down on her front legs and closed her eyes.

"Umm...Miss. Dragon Lordess, I was...I was wondering if maybe....Well you see, the village will never believe I killed you without proof." He wrung his hands together.

She popped open an eye. "You didn't kill me."

"I know, but..."

"You want the villagers to think you did."

"Something like that." He sat down on the cold ground. "I want to be a knight, but they say I'm not big enough, not strong enough, not brave enough. I thought I could prove myself by killing a dragon."

The red beast rolled her eyes. "Here." She flung a massive claw in his direction. "My claws fall out every so often. Take it and tell the village you slew the mighty beast that lives in the cave."

A toothy grin appeared on his dirt-smeared face. "Thanks." He swept it up and inspected it, pleased with his trophy. "What's your name anyway?"

"Why does it matter?"

"I just want to know. Do dragons even have names?"

"Of course we have names. I'm Chora. Now go before I

decide to eat you after all."

His smile disappeared, and he rushed to grab his sword and leave the cave. "Thank you."

Chora snorted. "Boy, do you even know the story of the dragon?"

Armin stopped and turned to face her. "The older dragons killed the people of the villages. To stop the massacre, the people pulled together and slew almost all of them."

"That's what they tell children now? What a bunch of hogwash."

He dropped his sword on the ground and sat down, the dragon claw still in his hand. "Fine. If that's not the true story, tell me what is."

"I don't have time to teach someone who doesn't really want to learn. Leave now." Chora blew a small puff of fire out one nostril, but Armin didn't move.

"I want to know."

With a heavy sigh, the dragon lifted her head and locked her eyes with his. "Dragons are noble creatures meant to protect the people, but the people turned their back on us. A plague came through the land, taking many human lives. The people begged us to help, so we used our powers and took the sickness from them, absorbing it into our own bodies. To ensure no one else would get the disease, we burned the villages.

"As you may have guessed, the people didn't like this. They deemed us evil and uncaring. We were weak from the sickness we took into ourselves. The people easily overtook us, killing any dragon they saw, even our young. We were not the monsters. Humans were.

"In the olden days, knights and dragons worked together to keep the kingdoms and villages safe. But after the massacre, all of my kind went into hiding. Not many of us are still alive."

Armin sat silently, trying to process what she said. It made more sense to him than the story the villagers told the children. He always wondered why after hundreds of years; the dragons would decide to start killing the villagers. But could he really trust a dragon?

His eyes stayed locked with Chora's, and his whole body tingled. Yet, he couldn't drag his eyes away from the beautiful creature before him. He couldn't speak or move. He was entranced and slightly helpless. Surely, she wouldn't eat him now, not like this?

Flashes of burning villages and screaming women entered his

mind. One image after another flashed before his eyes. Finally, his mind settled on a picture of a young dragon sitting on a rock playing with a yellow flower. The war cries of men rang in his ears as they charged up a hill. A sword sliced through the air, drawing blood, so much blood. It stained the grass, the boulder, and the flower. An overwhelming anguish overtook him as he watched the young dragon close his eyes as death took him.

Seconds later, he was back in the cave staring into Chora's eyes. His heart ached with her pain. "It was your child they killed."

Chora turned her head, but not before a tear slid down her face and dropped to the ground. Now he understood her hatred for humans. All those stories his mother told him were just to cover up what the villagers did.

With a determination he didn't even know he had, he stood and walked right up to Chora. "I'm sorry." His hand trembled as he touched the red beast before him. "I want to make it right. Let's make a pact with each other."

The dragon lifted her head, her eyes penetrating down to his very soul. "What kind of pact?"

He had her attention. That had to be a good sign. "We could work together like the knights and dragons of the old days."

A puff of smoke blew from her nose as she snorted. "The people would never stand for it."

"They won't have a choice. You are the powerful dragon lord. I mean lordess. Think about it, you and me, working to protect the villages. The people would look at you differently." He smiled at her hopefully.

She rolled her eyes. "You just want fame and recognition."

"Is that so bad? I want to be a knight, a good knight who helps the people."

"Fine." She held out a claw, and he hesitated slightly before taking hold of it and sealing their pact.

"This is going to be fun. I'll see you in the morning." With a bounce to his step, he grabbed the prize Chora gave him and headed out of the cave.

For the next several months, he spent every waking moment with Chora. She was a wealth of knowledge, and her stories were always exciting and funny. The villagers looked down on the fact he was with a dragon, and they hated it when they flew through the air over the village, but he didn't care. For six months, life was almost perfect.

Then it happened the day he waited for his whole life. He was going to become a knight. He raced to the cave. "Chora, Chora, you will never believe it. I'm going to be a knight." His excitement faded the moment he saw the angry look on her face. "Sorry, did I interrupt your sleep?"

"You betrayed me." Her voice echoed through the chamber, sending him scrambling backward. "I trusted you, and now everything is gone."

She unwrapped her tail and swung it in his direction. He ducked the first swing and barely avoided the second one. "I haven't betrayed you. We're a team."

"The villagers came here. I can smell them." Fire erupted from her mouth, filling the cave, forcing him back to the opening.

"Chora, stop, please. I can't control what other people do or where they go." He caught sight of her tail just as it was coming down and jumped backward. The tip scrapped his arm leaving behind a trail of blood. He drew his sword and backed further away.

"I knew I couldn't trust humans. You will pay for what the others have taken from me."

"What did they take? I'll make them bring it back. I can fix this."

Her nostrils flared. "You can't fix this. My eggs are all gone, smashed. All that's left is a broken mess." The ground shook as the great dragon lord stomped out of the cave, smoke billowing out around her.

"I don't want to hurt you." His mind scrambled to remember everything Chora taught him about fighting. He adjusted his stance, holding his blade out in front of him, ready for whatever she threw his way. The sword kept slipping through his sweaty hands, causing him to panic, which only made it harder to keep hold of it. He sucked in a deep breath and desperately tried to calm his pounding heart.

Like a monster from a bad dream, Chora emerged from the smoke. Her tail swung wildly in his direction. He ducked, then sidestepped, just narrowly avoiding the spikes on the tip. This is not what he expected. The next swing brought along with it a burst of fire. He dropped to the ground and rolled as spikes followed him.

Flames licked at his skin and scorched his hair. This time the swinging tail made contact, sending him toppling head over heels down the side of the mountain. The sword slipped from his hand, clanging and cluttering as it bounced its way down. His body collided with a solid oak tree, stopping his descent and creating a sickening crunching sound.

The air left his lungs, and no matter how he tried, he could barely take a breath. So this was it. This was how his knighthood would end. Without him ever actually being a knight. The dragon landed on a stoop to his right. The smoke and haze surrounding her made it difficult to see, but he knew she was there. Pain shot through his whole body, and he watched the dragon lordess.

'You will suffer as I have suffered." She narrowed her eyes and stared for a moment before spreading her wings and taking off into the sky.

Armin lay alone at the base of a tree. His life would end right here on the side of a cliff, with a beast circling overhead waiting for him to die. He closed his eyes against the pain that washed over him. At least he had done something meaningful for the last six months.

The dragon flew over the village, smoke puffing from her nose. Fire shot from her mouth as she descended upon the unsuspecting people. "If the dragons will not be allowed to live, neither will the humans."

A tear slid down his cheek as he lay there, powerless to stop her. Smoke filled his nostrils as he closed his eyes for the last time.

~ * ~ * ~

A.K. Stuntz is the author of the fantasy book World Of Magic. She grew up in Pennsylvania, where her love of reading and writing began. As a child, she would devour any book she could get her hands on, but anything with other worlds and magical creatures has always been her favorite.

Encouraged by her mother to follow her dreams and see where they took her, she started writing short stories. It turns out her dreams take her to magical places full of dragons, witches, and wizards, and she loves every minute of it. With each story she wrote, her passion grew, and in 2017 she finally wrote her first novel.

She now lives in Arkansas with her husband, son, and small animal farm. She is an avid horseback rider, and when she's not writing, you can find her in the barn or on the back of her horse, dreaming up new stories and new worlds.

The Dragon's Eye

Geoff Hart

"Still, you might have left some for me."

Freya smiled and rolled her shoulders before sheathing her sword, four feet of shining steel that seemed like a shortsword next to her imposing frame. "There were but six of the ruffians, and I left you the largest, as I know you prefer it that way." She patted the smaller woman on the head, knowing how much her friend hated that.

Mouse snapped her teeth at the larger woman's hand, but it was halfhearted. "Quality, not quantity...Yes. But still..."

"Never mind. Next time you can have them all, and I'll stand back and critique your technique."

"That seems only fair." Mouse paused a moment, then gave her friend a wicked smile. "But surely you must be thirsty from all that exertion?"

"*Me*? Pshaw! I hardly broke a sweat. But I concur: we should toast our fallen foes. At their expense." She tossed a small purse in the air and caught it; Mouse had already taken the others. One of the aforementioned men groaned at their feet; the others lay senseless, stretched at length upon the ground, showing various degrees of contusion and blood loss.

"The Boar?"

"It seems appropriate for these pigs." She kicked the groaning man once, and then again for good measure, but her heart wasn't really in it. The two women strode off in the direction of what had become their favorite drinking place in Losthaven.

As the spring weather was warm, Freya ordered a glass of chilled white wine; Mouse opted for a tankard of her usual brown ale. They raised their drinks to toast their fallen foes, but before they could bring the drinking vessels to their lips, the room blinked and they found themselves elsewhere; more alarmingly, their drinks had not accompanied them. Someone cleared his throat. They turned; hands gone to their swords.

After a moment, Freya lowered her hand. "I know you." The mage was cloaked in shifting shadows that made it hard to see his face, though every now and then a feature emerged, like the moon from behind clouds. "Shadowseeker! Given your reputation, it seems odd you'd summon *us*. There's said to be little that lies beyond your grasp."

"I'm he, but my grasp is perhaps shorter than rumor suggests." The wizard bowed.

The two women exchanged glances, and Mouse shrugged. Freya turned back to the wizard. "Without meaning to be blunt: *Why* have you summoned us?"

"There's something I need retrieved."

Freya snorted. "Wizards generally either retrieve their desires themselves or seek things mortals like us would be foolish to attempt. Why would we cooperate in such an endeavor?"

Shadowseeker chuckled. It wasn't a pleasant sound. "You've made a false assumption."

"And that would be?"

"That your cooperation is required."

Freya pursed her lips. "You placed a *geas* on us? *Seriously?*" Her hand returned to her sword.

The wizard waved his hand dismissively. "One works with the tools that come most easily to hand."

"And what if those tools *turn* in one's hand?" Mouse drew a handspan of her long dagger from its sheath.

The wizard frowned. "Pay attention, young lady. Have I not already made it clear you have no choice in this matter?"

"I beg to differ." Mouse closed the gap between them in the space between words, her dagger blurring towards the mage's throat. Before it could penetrate skin, it struck an invisible barrier and sprang from her hand, landing some distance away. The mage hadn't even blinked. Mouse glared at him, massaging her hand, then went to retrieve her weapon. The blade was bent at an inconvenient angle. Shaking her head, she returned to stand by her large companion.

"As I was saying, there's something I need retrieved."

Freya put a hand on Mouse's shoulder. "Forgive my friend. She's a barbarian, and therefore impulsive. Tell us what you want retrieved." Mouse tried to shrug off the hand, but Freya had a very heavy hand.

The mage nodded. "A gemstone known as *the dragon's eye*. It's currently being held by a dragon, appropriately enough."

Freya's throat tightened. "*A dragon*, you say."

"Yes. A rather *large* dragon. One with a reputation for *ad hoc* mayhem and slaughter."

Freya blanched. "You don't mean…the Beast of Belfor?"

Shadowseeker nodded.

"That would be suicide."

"Disobeying my geas would also be suicide, and let me assure you, you'd prefer to die at the hands of the dragon."

Freya nodded. "Very well. And what assistance will you provide?"

"Nothing of much use. Dragons are famously resistant to magic—else I'd retrieve the gem myself."

"Information, then."

Shadowseeker thought a moment. "There's little to be said. It's a dragon, thus essentially invulnerable. Magic won't work against it. But you have a reputation for cleverness your appearance belies, and that's likely to be better proof against a dragon than anything I could provide." He mused a moment longer. "I can transport you to the dragon's lair and retrieve you once you have the gem." A small, slender length of wood appeared in his hand. "When you have the gem, break this and you'll be returned to me instantly, before the dragon can harm you."

Mouse made to speak, but Freya had retained her grip on the smaller woman's shoulder and squeezed. "A promising start. What else?"

"Nothing of any use, I fear."

"And what shall be our reward?"

Shadowseeker smirked. "Is it not true you generally work in exchange for whatever you can carry away with you?"

Freya nodded.

"Then that's what I offer you."

"I'm sure we'll be grateful."

"I'm sure it would be wise if you were—and did not overreach."

Mouse made to open her mouth, and Freya's grip tightened. The smaller woman winced, but held her tongue. "Then we shall follow the path of wisdom." She sighed, took a deep breath, and visibly relaxed. "Very well. We'll need the day to equip ourselves. We'll return here on the morrow."

"Be sure you do, lest…"

"Yes, we know: the geas."

The wizard gestured impatiently, and the two adventurers found themselves back in the Knackered Boar, a fine crystal glass of white wine still rising towards Freya's mouth. She blinked and halted its progress before it could spill down the front of her jerkin. Mouse wasn't so lucky; her reflexive twitch caused her tankard of ale to cascade across the table, narrowly missing Freya.

"Wizards be damned!"

Freya sipped at her wine. "Undoubtedly. Yet not soon enough to be of any use to us."

"So, we'll beard the dragon in its lair and seize the gem."

"You say that like it's an easy thing. No man in living memory has defeated a dragon in hand-to-hand combat." She sipped again. "Nor any woman. Indeed, only one person is said to have done so, and he had the help of a god's enchanted weapon and armor. We have neither."

"And yet, haven't you defeated giants in combat?"

"It was but one...and no, not really. That's a story for another time. More importantly, giants don't vomit flames hot enough to turn the finest steel into a puddle of glowing iron."

Mouse looked ruefully at her bent dagger. "There's that."

"Aye, *there's that*. And while I'm bathing in that puddle, what will you be doing?"

"Seizing the gem and returning it to Shadowseeker. Perhaps he'll be so grateful he'll reanimate your smoldering corpse so we can resume our companionship."

Freya snorted and drained her wine. "That reassures me less than you might hope. I'll need time to think this through, and along with enchanted armor and weaponry, time's something we lack." She summoned the serving wench, and ordered three fingers of whisky, a sovereign remedy against sluggish thought.

Mouse attempted, unsuccessfully, to re-sheath her bent dagger. "And while you ponder, I'll replace this piece of crap." She flung it into the hearth—in hindsight, perhaps not the most auspicious omen. Seeing Freya's reaction, she shrugged. "Barbarian or not, I don't believe in omens. Neither should you."

~ * ~

The next morning, the two presented themselves at the wizard's home, Freya with a woven sack slung over her shoulder. The door opened before they could reach for the handle. Glowing sigils appeared along the hallway leading past several side chambers to another door. The two women exchanged glances.

"Don't even think of it."

Mouse raised an eyebrow. "You do me a grave injustice."

"I'm not sure you fully understand the meaning of that term. Nonetheless: *Don't!*"

Freya led the way to the door, which again opened before she could touch it. Shrugging, she passed through, followed by the smaller woman. They found themselves facing Shadowseeker across a low table. He inclined his head in a shallow nod. "Upon reflection, I thought of something that may help you." He gestured at two crystal flasks that rested on the table beside the small wand he'd shown them the previous day.

"And those are?"

"Potions that will make you proof against flame. Well, perhaps only for one blast of *dragon* flame, but better than nothing I expect." He snapped his fingers and two clay pots appeared beside the flasks. "And burn salve. In case the potion loses its effectiveness, and you need to restore yourselves afterwards."

"*Burn salve? Are you mad?*" Mouse's voice held a dangerous note, so Freya grasped her friend's shoulder, hard.

Mouse winced and glared at her friend. "Someday I'll have that hand for a souvenir."

"Perhaps today will be that day." She turned to the wizard. "What my friend *meant* to say is; we're grateful for any assistance you can provide." She sighed. "On to practicalities: How will we know the gem? A dragon's hoard should be full of such baubles."

"You'll know this one by its glow. Other gems may reflect or refract the light; this one will glow a warm amber even in the absence of light. There's nothing else like it in the dragon's hoard."

Freya nodded. "That seems clear enough. Then let's be about it while we still have the daylight ahead of us." She gathered the crystal vials, clay pots, and wooden wand and placed them carefully in her sack. They clinked against other mysterious objects.

Mouse looked a question at her friend, who ignored her, eyes still warily on Shadowseeker. "Get on with it."

"Very well."

The wizard spoke a word that echoed from the walls, and as the echoes faded the two found themselves standing on a hillside. A cavern mouth gaped before them, emitting puffs of sulfurous steam at random intervals. Around them, as far as the eye could see, desolate heathland stretched to the horizons.

"Welcome to Belfor, friend Mouse."

"It seems somewhat over-rated."

~ * ~

Freya lowered her sack to the ground, then squatted beside it. From the sack emerged a storm lantern, which she set about kindling with a lucifer. As she replaced the glass over the lantern's eye, Mouse grimaced.

"That's the best you were able to come up with? Fight fire with fire?"

"You have a better idea?"

"And I note you're not wearing dragon-proof armor."

"Indeed, your keen powers of observation have yet to fail you."

Mouse grimaced. "Enough. What *are* your plans?"

Freya smiled warmly at her friend. "To utilize my considerable charm to persuade the Beast to part with its gem."

"So long as you have *a plan*."

"Sarcasm suits you poorly. Just follow my lead. Have I failed you before?"

"Not so far. But there's always a first time." Abruptly serious, she held out a hand, and Freya used its support to clamber to her feet. The two women locked eyes.

"Mouse…"

"Yeah. Me too." She retrieved her hand from where it had disappeared into the larger woman's hand. "Let's be about this."

"First, the potions." She withdrew the crystal flasks from her bag and handed one to Mouse. The two clinked the flasks together, and they chimed. Then they downed the contents.

"Nice. I particularly like the honey aftertaste."

Mouse grimaced and spat the dregs onto the ground. "Tastes like that blasted honey wine my people drink. It's little wonder we're all so touchy."

The two stretched, Mouse so deeply her joints creaked. Then Mouse checked that her various weapons were loose in their sheaths, and made a sweeping bow, urging Freya to precede her into the cavern. Freya returned her bow, and strode to the cave mouth, where she paused.

"Hello the cave! My name's Freya, and my friend is Mouse. We come seeking the Beast of Belfor. Have we your permission to enter?"

There was a long silence. Then a deep, deceptively soft voice replied. "Enter."

The two exchanged glances and entered. The cave's floor was smooth, as if something large and heavy had flattened or crushed the rocks long ago. Stalactites descended from the ceiling, but had been snapped off well above head height; their fallen points had been pushed to the side, where they formed windrows, as if they'd been thrust there by a double-moldboard plow drawn by a giant. The cave angled downwards, flowstone glistening in the light of the lantern, water dripping occasionally onto the bare heads of the women. There was only one path, so they followed it.

Soon, the passage widened and a golden glow reflected lantern light from farther down the throat of the cave. Freya took a deep breath, masking Mouse's sharper inhalation, squared her shoulders, and stepped out into the open area. The walls gleamed with a pale luminescence, and the ceiling was dotted with pale blue sparks, like the constellations seen on a cloudless night far from a city's vapors. As far as the eye could see, gold lay heaped carelessly in piles and drifts and hills, with occasional sparkles of gemstones. But it was the dragon who drew the eye.

The dragon's body was as long as two oxcarts joined end to end, with neck and tail about the same length. Its black scales gleamed like polished obsidian in the light from Freya's lantern. With each breath, it emitted a faint but unmistakable brimstone scent, and its eyes glowed a warm amber.

Mouse grinned up at Freya. "Actually, I rather like the scent. Reminds me of using a lucifer to light a lamp."

Freya shushed her and eyed scales as thick as her fingers were long and talons as long as her dagger. She kept her hand resolutely away from the hilt of her sword and turned to meet the dragon's gaze. "My people name you the Beast of Belfor. Have you another name I should use?"

The dragon met her gaze a long moment and Freya forced herself not to look away. "You could not pronounce my name. Belfor will do."

"Belfor it is, then. We appreciate your making the time to speak with us."

The dragon snorted, flame shooting several feet from its nostrils. "At least you're polite. State your case."

"We're here under a geas, otherwise we'd never think to disturb your peace." She took a deep breath. We're here to obtain a gem known as *the dragon's eye*. If we can have it, we've no quarrel with you. You can keep your gold and everything else in this cavern."

"You're indeed a polite one. And yet you're both well-armed—your tiny friend perhaps overly so. This speaks of less polite motives."

Freya ducked her head, conceding the point. "I offer this small gift as proof of my honesty." Freya opened the sack, and from it, pulled a heavy golden chain that clanked as she laid it carefully on the floor before her and straightened. "Furthermore, I offer you this: the finest distillate of the grape known to my people." She pulled a magnum bottle from the sack. "I'm told it will burn well in your belly." She twisted free the cork and took a large sip and swallowed visibly. "You have my word, and my deed as proof, that it's not poisoned. As if *any* poison could harm you."

The dragon bowed his head, but without taking his eyes from them. "Your offers are generous. Allow me a moment to ponder." The dragon's golden eyes closed a moment, which stretched uncomfortably. "I've *considered*. I find I've no desire to exchange my gem for your gifts. Indeed, it seems I could keep both your gold *and* the gem, and dine at my leisure on your smoking flesh."

"Should you choose that option, we'd be forced to defend our lives. And though you've never been defeated in battle, one of us might get lucky. There's always that risk in any pass at arms."

Belfor snorted. "Yes, there's always that risk. I'm losing no equanimity over it."

Freya heard Mouse's teeth grinding together. Her small friend had been born to a tribe of northern barbarians, and even at her birth, she'd been scrawny. As Mouse told it, her mother, as was customary after the birth of a defective child, had left her for the wolves; her people knew the weak were unlikely to survive, or to thrive if they somehow survived. But the wolves returned the infant to the village and stood guard over her until her mother relented and reclaimed the unwanted child. With some justice, they considered it an omen. Being less than half the size of her peers, she'd learned that what she couldn't accomplish with brawn, she could accomplish with speed and skill.

Before the dragon's words had finished echoing, and before Freya could stop her, Mouse threw herself at the dragon. She feinted right, and as the dragon's head swung in that direction, flung herself left, onto its right foreleg. From that insecure perch, she bounded to the top of its head. A long fighting knife appeared in her hand, mid-air, and in an instant, she'd wrapped her short legs around the dragon's neck as if she were riding a horse and pressed the blade to the corner of the dragon's eye.

"And yet, there's that geas of which we spoke, and politeness can only take one so far. I must therefore leave my friend's social graces to her, and rudely insist that you choose which dragon eye you'd prefer to lose."

The dragon licked its lips with a long, snaking tongue. "You make a persuasive argument."

"Indeed, my argument is keenly argued."

"Very well. The gem shall be yours—in exchange for your gifts."

"And what guarantee have we you'll honor your side of the bargain and let us leave when I dismount?"

"You have my word. I swear on my name." And the dragon uttered a sound that swelled to fill the cavern, briefly causing the blue sparks on the ceiling to glow harder.

"Freya…the gem?"

Freya capped the lantern's eye, and in the darkness that gathered, looked left and right. Atop one of the side piles, a diamond the size of a goose egg glowed warmly amidst the shadows. She waded carefully through the shifting gold and seized it, then placed the gem carefully in her sack. At the same time, she palmed something from the sack.

"Mouse, I have it."

Mouse leapt nimbly to the floor, landing on her feet facing the dragon. "A pleasure meeting you. One I hope will never be repeated."

"Indeed, once was more than enough." Belfor's thick lips curved in a predatory smile, and flames flickered in its nostrils. The sound of snapping wood in Freya's hand was drowned by the roar of flame that lashed out and filled the cavern where the two women had been standing a moment earlier. Flame that washed over them even as they faded from view.

~ * ~

They reappeared in Shadowseeker's chamber, their clothing falling from them in smoking rags. Freya made an abortive movement to cover her nakedness, then relented and stood proud, chin thrust forward. Mouse, naked as the newborn pups of her namesake, made no move to hide her body, and defiantly met the wizard's eyes.

"The dragon lied," Mouse observed out the side of her mouth.

"Indeed. I've a notion to return and confront her on this issue."

"A very small notion, I hope."

The wizard cleared his throat. "Ladies? I trust you have the gem?"

Freya nodded. "You hadn't mentioned our clothing would be unprotected by your potions."

The wizard raised his eyebrows. "If you'd sampled the pleasures I've sampled, you'd understand why I've no interest in your bodies. But very well." His eyes lingered a moment on Freya's ample breasts and Mouse's slim hips before he snapped his fingers, and they were clad once more.

Freya nodded. "Our thanks. Now, if you'll indulge my curiosity, I have a question." Without awaiting his reply, she continued. "What's the purpose of this gem? What function does it serve?"

The wizard tried to look down the bridge of his nose at her in condescension, but as she stood a foot taller than him, failed. He harrumphed. "That's two questions. It's…something mystical that simple swordsmen…swords*women*…such as yourselves could not possibly comprehend."

Freya smiled, and his eyebrows furrowed. "Then it wouldn't, I suppose, be the vessel in which you've stored your soul to keep it safe while you work your magicks?"

Shadowseeker blanched, but didn't answer.

"I see," Freya said. "That changes the situation somewhat."

The wizard rallied. "What have I to fear? The gem's a diamond, and unbreakable. You couldn't possibly harm it. Nor have you the magical acumen to use it against me."

Freya opened her hand to reveal the diamond clasped in what appeared to be a nutcracker, dwarfed in the hand that held the diamond. "And yet, jewelers cut diamonds every day using tools such as this diamond cutter. I'm confident I could get in one good squeeze before you enspell me. That would presumably be unfortunate for your gem. And for you."

Mouse chuckled. "I need to buy you more whisky."

Freya bowed shallowly, without taking her eyes from the wizard. "It would be impolite to refuse such an offer."

Shadowseeker cleared his throat. "Very well. What do you want in exchange for the gem?"

Freya smiled. "I believe the traditional reward is three *favors*. It would seem unwise to presume upon your kindness and ask for more."

"*Unwise* is hardly the word." His glare would have blistered their skin had they not still been protected by his potion.

"Then I shall follow the path of wisdom and ask for only three. To be redeemed later, at a time of our choice."

Shadowseeker gritted his teeth. "Very well."

Mouse cleared her throat. "And one more thing: gold sufficient to replace the necklace we left with the dragon."

"Done." The wizard gestured, and a gold necklace fell to the floor at Mouse's feet.

Mouse bent to retrieve it, then her lips quirked. "And one further thing: as we learned from the dragon, the words of the powerful are rarely to be trusted."

Freya nodded. "Indeed. To seal our bargain, we shall require your oath upon the gem I hold."

The wizard glared his displeasure, but complied. "I so swear." And as he did, there was momentarily an invisible but heavy presence in the room. Freya nodded, and tossed him the gem, which he caught, juggled a moment, and then pocketed.

"If you've no further use of us?"

The wizard spat on the floor, then snapped his fingers, and they found themselves back in the Knackered Boar.

"That ended better than I'd anticipated."

"Indeed, particularly since *my* necklace was naught but gilded lead. And there's your offer of whisky that would further sweeten the ending."

"A deal's a deal," Mouse replied, and strode to the bar.

~ * ~ * ~

Geoff Hart has reputedly been telling tales (sometimes ending up in considerable trouble thereby) since he was 6, but took nearly 25 years to realize he could earn a living at this trade. Since 1987, he's worked as a technical writer and scientific editor for IBM, the Canadian Forest Service, and the Forest Engineering Research Institute of Canada.

Since 2004, he's been a freelancer, and only occasionally stops complaining about his boss. Geoff has worked primarily as a scientific and technical editor, specializing in authors who have English as a second language, but also does technical writing and French translation.

He claims to have survived at least two bouts of leading or managing publications groups with only a minor need for ongoing therapy. A Fellow of the Society for Technical Communication (STC, www.stc.org), he has published 400+ nonfiction articles on communication as well as the books *Effective Onscreen Editing* and *Writing for Science Journals*, and spends an altogether unreasonable amount of time mentoring colleagues. His training is in plant ecology and plant physiology, which continue to fascinate him. In his spare time, he has committed three SFnal novels and a short story collection and has sold 37 stories.

Visit him online at www.geoff-hart.com.

The Seventh Trap

Adam Knight

"Damned smart of you to send for me," Odkin said. He cocked his hips and rested his hands on his belt. "When it comes to dragonslaying, I know all the tricks." He was taller than most men, with piercing eyes and a hawkish nose. His dark hair was cut short by his own hand. A scar ran from his left earlobe to the bridge of his nose, pulling the skin around it into a slight, permanent sneer. He drummed his fingers.

The mayor of Haven remained seated behind his fortress of a desk. He pressed his twitchy, bureaucratic fingertips together. "Then you are cognizant of our problem," he said. It was not a question.

"Only what the boy told me. Missing livestock, some scorched fields. A drunk disappeared."

"That is correct. It was one of our local boys, Wilfrey, who we sent to Bailingport to seek you out. We've lost seven head of cattle, thirty-five sheep, twenty-one pigs, a burned field of millet and a missing citizen who, unfortunately, has a problem with drink. Your reputation is sterling, as I'm sure you know. Few have achieved the heights of success you have known."

"Sure." Odkin winced inside at the words "have known." It had been too long since the last job.

"Then tell me, please. Can the town of Haven look to you for protection? Can you rid us of this foul beast?"

Odkin leaned against the mayor's desk. "Can I? Sure. However, I don't do charity work, though."

The mayor laughed nervously. "Of course not, my good sir! We would never dream of imposing on your charity. We are prepared to compensate you fairly."

"Two thousand gold krins as a retainer. I hate when someone hires four dragonslayers and sends them all in, planning on paying the only one to survive. Been burned like that before. Then, eight thousand gold krins for killing the bastard, or an equivalent in land holdings, but I have to see the land first. Plus, I keep all rights to the dragon's hoard and to the body."

Odkin waited, his breath held. This was the point in the conversation when many clients balked. Ten years ago, there were plenty of dragonslaying jobs to go around, and he could pick and choose. But he needed this one.

"My, that is a steep cost."

Odkin shrugged. One thing about having a reputation, you had the leverage to bluff. "The cost is the cost. Maybe you can find another dragonslayer who will do it for less. But you might have to hire two, or three, or more, 'cause they'll most likely end up dead. Hire me, and I'm the only dragonslayer you'll need."

The mayor clasped his hands and looked up at Odkin. "Very well. I will speak to our treasurer about procuring the deposit. If there is anything I can do to aid you, please do not hesitate to ask. We will be in your debt forever."

At ten thousand gold krins you sure will, Odkin thought. Desperation and fear did wonders on tight purse strings, but the desperate and fearful were tricky to deal with, almost as tricky as the dragons themselves.

~ * ~

Most commoners thought dragonslaying was all slashing swords and battle cries. Odkin knew it began with research. Even before he could determine what type, size, or age dragon he was dealing with, he had to find out if there even was a dragon. Hoaxes ranged from the simplistic—a couple of local boys might steal some sheep or set fire to a field—to elaborate rackets involving dozens of people and sophisticated deceptions. Sometimes rival dragonslayers set them up to misdirect the competition. Odkin began with scholarly skepticism, but soon knew he was dealing with the real thing.

The next step was to assemble his team. Odkin hated working alone. Bringing along other warriors at least provided the dragon with a distraction while Odkin made the killing blow. The tavern was always the best place to start looking, and it was there he found Groth.

Sitting at the table with his iron stein, Groth looked like a grizzly bear holding a thimble. His musculature was like an animal pelt draped over his entire body. Long, black, shaggy hair sprouted from every follicle that could conceivably sprout hair. Despite Groth's odor—sweat, rotten food, feces, and alcohol—Odkin sat at the table with him. To his dismay, Groth spoke little of Odkin's language, and Odkin knew almost no words in Groth's barbaric tongue. They struggled through a short conversation, and Odkin convinced Groth to join him. Groth sought no compensation, something common among the barbarian tribes of the north. Some sort of test of mettle, Odkin knew, a kind of spiritual journey. Odkin thought it a stupid and wasteful rite of passage, but it suited his own mission just fine.

The next morning, in a weapons shop, Odkin found the perfect sucker. Sixteen-year-old Wilfrey—the same boy who had been sent to Bailingport to find him—was drooling at the swords and spears he wanted but could not afford.

Wilfrey begged to join him, and Odkin gave the idea some thought. Wilfrey's zeal would make him easy to command. His parents, who entered the shop knowing their son would be there instead of doing his errands, were not as enthusiastic. Of course it would be dangerous, Odkin told them, but their son would be in the service of the most skilled dragonslayer in five hundred leagues. His parents certainly couldn't disagree, and when Odkin offered them half the reward money, they consented. Odkin would have offered all of the reward money if he had to; there was no chance a boy who had never lifted a sword in his life would survive a battle with a dragon.

As Odkin procured the mountaineering gear, food, maps, and winter clothing for the job, he never walked from one shop to the next without being stopped and asked for a story. He never paid for a drink or a meal, and never had to open a door. He devoured the attention.

The morning of their departure, Odkin went to the dry goods shop for final provisions. As he returned to the tavern, a dozen locals had gathered in the town square. Dressed in colorful gowns, striking drums and ringing bells, they surrounded Odkin and began shouting.

"The Order of Myxo bo Ghirra will not wait idly as you threaten the dragon's life!" an old man shouted. "The might and grandeur of dragons is to be revered and feared, not challenged. Desist in your folly!"

Odkin rolled his eyes and pushed through the crowd. He forced his way to Groth and Wilfrey, donned his gear, and urged them to do the same. He ignored the hecklers, who began chanting in unison: "Minn os lom trava hritha ki mandonar."

"Who are they?" Wilfrey asked.

Odkin tried not to laugh at the boy, all elbows and Adam's apple. Groth was silent.

"Dragoncults, kid."

"What are those?"

"Well, in a word, they're nuts," Odkin said loudly. "Basically, in the old days, people lived in fear of dragons all the time. This was hundreds of years ago. Only a few dragonslayers existed, and their titles were handed down from their fathers. Well, then the monarchy collapsed and the kingdom fell apart, and anyone could call himself a dragonslayer. Soon there were fewer and fewer dragons. Well, nowadays there are hardly any, and these dragoncults started popping up, telling people dragons are superior to humans, and we should be worshipping them, not killing them."

The crowd pressed in. A young woman wearing a wooden dragon helmet jangled bells in Odkin's face.

"Ancient and mighty is dragon magic," she warned. "You darken the world with your violence. Shame on you!"

"Look, lady, I've been paid to do a job here. A job no one else can do. So why don't you bleeding hearts step aside, let us go up the mountain, and take care of your problem. Otherwise, the only warmth you'll get this winter will be from dragonflame."

The woman looked to the sky.

"Oh, let us pray that is the case. What glorious illumination and heat radiate from the fire of the dragon!"

"Maybe they're right," Wilfrey said. "I mean, dragons are so rare now—"

"Dragon worship is, in the words of our ancient ancestors, a steaming pile of dragon shit. Dragons are nasty, greedy beasts, and if you don't stop them, they just get bolder until the countryside is toast. Trust me, kid, we're doing a good thing."

A gob of spit hit Odkin in the face, and he wasn't waiting for things to get any more interesting. He hitched his pack up on his back, yanked his hood over his head, and shoved his way through the crowd. Behind him, the voices of the Order of Myxo bo Ghirra chanted together in unison: "Minn os lom trava hritha ki mandonar!" If he'd known he'd be harassed by the townsfolk this much, he reflected, he would've charged the mayor more.

~ * ~

The mountains above Haven were sheer and wind-ravaged, and the passes clogged with snow and ice. Odkin had hunted in nearly every climate—dragons in the hills, in deep forests, by the seaside, even one that had taken residence in the sewer system of an abandoned city. Dragons in mountain caves were nothing special.

As they ascended the mountain, Odkin was grateful for the pelts and gloves he had purchased in town. He kept his eyes on the mountainsides for any clue of the entrance to the lair. Dragons never lived in natural caves; they bored smooth tunnels out of solid rock. The deeper the cave, the older the dragon. Even massive dragons could fold their bodies down to fit in a tight space. Many dragons set up traps along the way to prevent anyone from even finding the entrance, but Odkin was the best, and had seen all the tricks, and was ready for them.

The first came along a sheer cliff side. Odkin noticed a hairline fracture along the grain of the rock ledge. On his hands and knees, he blew into the crack, and immediately called a halt. They set up the rappelling gear and scaled the mountainside to avoid the trail. When Wilfrey asked why, Odkin threw a rock at the ledge they had almost stepped on. With a roar, the rock gave way, and slabs of granite tumbled down into the valley below.

"If the three of us had stepped on that, we'd all be dead. Dragon rigged it up to catch us. Only six to go."

"Six what?" Wilfrey asked as they made their way up the rock face.

"Traps. Dragons, you see, are superstitious bastards. Especially about numbers. They love sevens. They'll live in caves with seven chambers, take seven mates, collect seven suits of armor from their victims, and set up seven traps. The dragons are almost as bad as their cults."

At this, Wilfrey laughed.

Odkin kept his eyes sharp. "That dragon did us a favor, though."

"Why?"

Odkin grinned. "Now we know we're on the right path."

It was in the late afternoon when Odkin saw the entrance to the dragon's cave. It would be a hard climb, but the entrance was poorly hidden. That meant one of two things—the dragon was too old and weak to bother with better protection, or it had grown arrogant. Either was a weakness Odkin could exploit.

They arrived at the entrance to the cave at nightfall, with the wind whipping around them and screaming over the rocks. Odkin's muscles ached from the exertion and the cold. He was about to tumble into the mouth of the cave when he paused. Stalactites hung from the cave ceiling, which Odkin thought strange. Stalactites only grew in limestone, and these mountains were all granite and shale. He tossed a coil of rope into the cave. The moment it passed over the threshold, the stalactites released and crashed to the floor. Odkin coughed as rock dust poured out. Trap number two.

After clearing out the rock debris, they set up camp for the night at the mouth of the cave. They would take turns keeping watch, but Odkin could see the caves would be extensive. There was little chance the dragon would find them there. The next day would be the day of battle, and they would need plenty of rest going in. So they built a decent fire and ate roast mutton and boiled peas. It was a lot of work, but Odkin wasn't saving the food. Besides, it would probably be Groth and Wilfrey's last meal, and he thought it should be a hearty one.

~ * ~

The past year had been the worst of Odkin's life. Reaching the heights of fame and success had taken hard work; but falling from those heights was harder. His lifestyle had been funded by dragon-slaying, and dragons had been all but wiped out in the civilized regions in the past decade. He began chopping wood and quarrying stone to pay for his luxuries, which one by one he had to abandon. He went from owning several estates to only one, to renting a room in Bailingport. His collection of swords, which served his vanity more than his trade, was sold off piece by piece. The wealth that once poured into Odkin's life now poured out.

And as the poverty worsened, so did his fear he was obsolete; that his success in slaying had merely hastened his downfall. So that morning, as he, Wilfrey, and Groth burrowed deeper into the mountain, he suppressed the lightning bolts of excitement that shot from his gut out to his fingertips. On the outside, he remained calm.

Wilfrey knew no such restraint. He chattered about bravery and adventure and what the local girls would think of him. Odkin let him. No sense in spending an awkward, boring hour in silence before battle.

"So…what do you want to be when you grow up?" Odkin asked, though he really didn't care.

"Whatever I do," Wilfrey said, "I don't want to work on my family's farm. I'm not cut out for manual labor, you know. What I'd really like to do is become an adventurer. A dragonslayer like you, Sir

Odkin. I know people say there are no more dragons left, but obviously that can't be true. And dragons can live so long and burrow so deep; surely there must be hundreds of them in the unexplored parts of the world. Maybe they've built whole cities. And when I grow up, I want to protect mankind from them. I want to learn everything about dragons."

"Ever use a weapon?"

"My mum won't let me. I only get this stupid sling." Wilfrey's face was glum as he swiped at the strip of leather dangling over his shoulder. "But I practice every day, and I can hit jays from a hundred yards. Everyone in my family says someday I'll be the hero of all the farmers, and I'll be called Jayslayer, and every bird in the sky will fear me."

Odkin nodded and smiled and put up with the boy's patter and hero worship, but always spoke to him respectfully, always treated him as a colleague. Odkin knew he needed Wilfrey. Scaring him off would ruin the day and possibly the entire quest. *No scary dragon stories*, he thought to himself. *Don't tell him about the time I had to carry Sir Ector from the dragon cave in a bushel.* The boy would serve some purpose on the mission, even if that purpose was to be dragon bait.

"Why don't you wear any armor, or even a helmet, Sir Odkin? Aren't you worried about the dragon hurting you?"

"Nah. I know everything a dragon's going to do, even before it knows. Besides, if the dragon hits you, a little leather or mail won't save you. I prefer to keep my arms free and my sight open. As for the big guy." Odkin pointed to the hulking Groth twenty feet ahead, "His stink is better armor than solid plate. But he'll be a great fighter. Just you wait and see."

Odkin considered switching places with Groth. As the experienced dragonslayer, he'd know the traps better. But the lead position was also the most dangerous, and he'd rather Groth be there than himself.

Though the sounds of howling wind and whipping snow had long faded, the air was still bitter cold. Odkin remained sensitive to any rise in temperature, as a dragon's body produced so much heat it could warm its chamber and the surrounding caverns. Unlike snakes, lizards, and other ordinary reptiles, dragons were warm-blooded, which is why they could live in frozen mountain caves or sweltering wetlands and even in the mouths of active volcanoes with equal ease.

Groth led the trio up a twisting, tight passage, and for a few moments disappeared from sight. Suddenly, Odkin felt a blast of hot air pour down the chute, and he shouted for Groth to stop. A gush of flame blasted up, enveloping the barbarian. Groth threw himself to the ground, bellowing and rolling left and right.

The sound and stench of crackling flesh and hair made Odkin queasy. Wilfrey trembled and quailed. They crawled ahead as fast as they could, but Groth had already extinguished the flames. All over his body, the skin was scorched red and black. Through it all, Groth uttered not a whimper of complaint. His face remained stoic, though Odkin saw underneath it, he masked excruciating pain.

"Flame spike," was all Odkin said. "Number three."

From then, Odkin took the lead, and insisted on silence. His senses heightened as he felt the air, inspected every inch of rock, and sniffed the drafty tunnels. Odkin soon recognized a familiar scent—a mix of carrion and sweat, of brimstone and rotting bones—the scent of a dragon.

Odkin reached behind his back and withdrew his sword, an unusually long and thick one specially designed for dragonslaying. He held it out before him, handing Wilfrey his torch to light the way. He was ready for anything in the passage ahead.

Well, almost anything. But not for another dragonslayer.

Dressed in the armor of a long-forgotten order, a towering knight faced the three intruders, his breastplate clanging, and a helmet with full visor concealing his face. In one hand, he raised his sword—one nearly the size of Odkin's, which required two hands—and in the other a steel shield. Odkin's mouth flapped open uselessly. Despite years of experience battling dragons, he knew little about fighting other men.

Wilfrey turned and ran. Groth could barely hold himself up. Odkin had no time to worry about either.

"Hey there!" he called out, but he received no reply. The strange knight strode towards him, first at a slow gait, then gaining speed until he was running full tilt ahead, with his sword raised, his armor making a thunderous racket.

Odkin lifted his sword to parry the first blow, but a knight with this much strength could chop him in half with one stroke. He braced for the impact.

He heard a whirring sound behind him, and a stone whipped by his ear. The stone struck the knight on the breastplate, and when it did, the pieces of armor suddenly fell apart, clattering to the ground. Odkin let go of his breath. Trap number four, an illusory knight, made only of discarded armor and dragon magic.

He looked behind him. Wilfrey hadn't run; he'd fallen back to take out his sling and loose a stone the size of a fist. The boy smiled.

"Did I do good, Sir Odkin?"

Odkin smiled back. Maybe the kid would be useful for more than bait.

Only a hundred feet beyond the fallen knight, the passageway opened into a wide chamber. Dim light pervaded the space. More dragon magic, Odkin knew.

Lying all about the chamber floor was the dragon's hoard, and as an experienced slayer, Odkin learned much about the dragon from a quick examination. Based on the quantity and age of the collection, it was an old dragon, probably four or five hundred years. While some dragons took great care in maintaining, organizing, and displaying the trophies of their kills, this dragon made a proud display of his carelessness. This dragon would be an old, arrogant son of a bitch, Odkin knew.

The dragon lurked out of the shadowy recesses of the cavern, and Odkin was delighted.

The jade-colored scales on the dragon's body were falling off in patches. The few teeth that remained in its mouth were rotted and dull. A white film covered the dragon's right eye. In its old age, the creature had grown slovenly; it could do little more than totter feebly as it dragged its bulging belly across the floor. Old, arrogant dragons could be dangerous, but Odkin would be doing this one a favor by killing it. He signaled wordlessly for Groth to shift to the right. Despite his burns, the giant warrior hefted his axe and skirted the back of the chamber. Wilfrey drew in a slow, awestruck gasp at sight of the dragon. Odkin called to him, snapping him out of his reverie.

"See those big rocks off to the left? I'm going there. The big guy is going to attack first on the right. When he charges, use your sling and take out the dragon's good eye. Think you can do it?"

"Definitely, Sir Odkin. I can hit jays from a hundred yards. Everyone in my family says—"

"Good. Now get ready for a battle, kid."

With that, Odkin slid to the left, making his way to the boulders. The dragon did not seem to notice him; it was too busy worrying about the hairy giant waving his axe.

Groth charged. Odkin marveled that a man covered in burns

could show so little discomfort, not even a whimper. He hefted his mighty double-bladed axe over his head. Odkin waited for Wilfrey to loose his stones.

Nothing.

Odkin looked over. Wilfrey had wandered over to a pile of golden coins. In paralyzed horror, Odkin watched as Groth attacked the dragon head-on. It was a marvelous show of bravery, but it was also suicide. The dragon whipped its tail out, smacking Groth to the ground. He dropped his axe, and before he could stagger to his feet, the dragon pinned him to the rocks with its spindly arms, then slammed its jaws onto him. Bones crunched and Groth was transformed into a gory heap. Whatever Groth's spiritual journey had been, it was over now. Odkin sprinted over to Wilfrey and grabbed him hard by the shoulder.

"Where the hell were you, kid?"

Wilfrey's eyes remained fixed to the heap of glowing gold coins. Odkin understood. He tried to pull Wilfrey away, but the boy squirmed and struggled to get back. Odkin reached down and grabbed an empty helm—well, empty after he dumped out the skull—and urged Wilfrey to use it to scoop up the coins. The boy did, and the instant the helm touched the gold, it became superheated, and Wilfrey dropped it with a yelp.

"Wh—what did I—"

"Cursed gold," Odkin said. "Trap number five. Would've burned your hands right off."

Wilfrey sighed. "You saved me, Sir Odkin!"

Odkin grimaced. "Yeah, well Groth wasn't so lucky. Come on—"

Wilfrey glanced at the messy heap of Groth under the dragon's claws. He doubled over, but Odkin yanked him back up. The dragon closed in.

"Sling! Stones! Do it!" Odkin yelled. Wilfrey trembled as he fumbled with a stone, dropped it, picked it up, then made a shot that was errant by twenty feet. Then he began crying. Odkin was about to return to the pile of boulders when he realized his dilemma. The warrior who fought for free was dead, and the boy who owned half the reward was still alive. He swore at himself for being so sloppy.

"Hey kid. This is your chance for glory. Take a big, deep breath, load another stone, and knock out that bastard's good eye. If you can hit a damned blue jay, you can do this."

But it was too late. Wilfrey turned and ran back out of the chamber. Odkin stopped worrying about the money dilemma. A push off a mountain pass, a sad story to his parents, and a token handful of gold would fix it. He turned to face the much more pressing dilemma behind him.

When he did, he dropped his sword from shock.

The dragon was no longer fat and tottering. It was muscled and sleek, with a perfect coat of scales and glistening, brutal claws. In its open maw were two rows of teeth, not one missing. Its eyes were free of the veil of blindness.

"False aging. Clever bastard," he murmured with awe. It was a complication—a big one—but this far in, he could not retreat. He grabbed his sword, shouted a stream of curses at the dragon, and felt the fire rise inside of him. He could do this.

When he heard the whirring sound of the sling behind him, he smiled. Wilfrey was back.

Then tremendous pain crashed in the back of his head, sending him sprawling. He tried to stagger to his hands and knees, but the dragon pounced. It flipped Odkin over onto his back. He waited as the dragon loomed over him, its fiery eyes boring into his. He waited for the killing blow.

Dimly, Odkin heard footsteps. Wilfrey stood over him, reaching out to stroke the dragon's forearm.

"Sir Odkin, thank you for bringing me to see the dragon. It's an even more wonderful creature than I'd been told."

Odkin tried to speak, but his words slurred out. The little brat's stone must've bruised his brain.

"Sir Odkin, you really ought to have more reverence for these creatures. They're beautiful, powerful, and wise. Mean men like you have forgotten, but now that the most famous dragonslayer got eaten, maybe people will respect dragons more."

Thoughts, questions, curses, and accusations swirled around Odkin's muddled head, but he concentrated all his effort into one word.

"Seven."

~ * ~

Wilfrey smiled.

"That's right, seven traps. The seventh one happened last week, in Bailingport. You listened to my story and walked into the mayor's office. The Order of Myxo bo Ghirra was in on it, the mayor was in on it, even the dragon was in on it. We knew how desperate you were; all you had to do was hear how desperate we were. I've had a wonderful time on our quest, Sir Odkin."

Odkin mumbled something unintelligible. Wilfrey couldn't tell if it was "Me, too" or "Screw you," but he just smiled.

"Minn os lom trava hritha ki mandonar. In the ancient language of the dragon-talkers, it means 'Small is man before the might of the dragon.'"

Odkin spat out a stream of curses at the boy.

"I only wish you had a little more respect," Wilfrey said. "Not just for dragons, but for me, and the Order. Our beliefs aren't dragon shit. Though I guess, after you've been eaten alive and digested over the next month, you will be."

Odkin moaned.

The dragon lowered its head to Wilfrey, who stroked it.

"You've been patient, Myxo bo Ghirra. The Order thanks you and sends its respects. You can eat the foolish warrior now."

And the dragon did.

~ * ~ * ~

Adam Knight is a writer and teacher living in northern New Jersey. His debut novel, *At the Trough,* was published in 2019 by NineStar Press. An educational dystopia, *At the Trough* explores a near future in which schools and teachers have been replaced with videos and games. An exceptional student, her wild-child girlfriend, and a bitter ex-teacher team up to take on the system. The novel is available in print and digital form through most major booksellers.

His short fiction and essays have been published in numerous magazines and anthologies. "Hoping for Red" was published in audio form on *Escape Pod* in 2018. "Little Me, Big Me," was a finalist in the *Arcturus Review* Fall 2017 Fiction contest. He is currently seeking representation for a cosmic horror novel about an old man in an insane asylum who must stop a secret society from summoning an undersea god—that sank the Titanic.

Outside of the writing life, Adam is a dedicated runner and a not-very-dedicated bass player. He enjoys reading, walking his dog, and catching up on TV shows that everyone else saw years ago.

Hoarders

Xauri'EL Zwaan

Topher was hired as an intern five years after the CEO of OmniCor Industries had turned into a dragon. He was the twelfth multi-billionaire so far to metamorphose into a giant fire-breathing lizard, and others had followed since; people were beginning to treat it as normal, something that just happened when one ascended to the ranks of the super-rich. There was no denying it had been good for business—at least, for the businesses run by dragons. The phrase 'hostile takeover' had acquired new meaning. Profits at OmniCor were soaring on leathery wings. The company's stock price was blazing. They were one of the most coveted employers in the business, and Topher had been very lucky to get an unpaid internship there. That was what he told himself on the late nights of crunch when the caffeine and the diet of ramen noodles were beginning to run him ragged, anyway. It was his dream job.

Topher had been there for six months when his supervisor, Dave, came by his desk and, concern and solicitude painting his eyes, handed him a stack of paper. "The CEO," he said mournfully, "has requested you personally deliver this to him. I'd just like to say you've been great to work with, Topher, and I've really valued the dedication you bring to the team. Good luck."

Topher had so many questions, far too many to actually ask. This was obviously a time sensitive task, so he nodded wordlessly. Dave shook his hand, squeezing it in that manly, companionate way of his, then shuffled off, shoulders drooping.

On the long elevator ride to the penthouse floor, Topher ran through everything he knew about dragons, first the few established facts, the spotty news reports, then the much more voluminous tales and fantasies. Dragons had been a hot topic when he was doing his undergrad; the Norse Mythology courses were packed to the hilt, with more sections opened every year, but still unable to fully absorb student interest. Topher had been lucky to get in. Topher had always been lucky; that was what he told himself as the elevator climbed. Surely if he was quick-witted and displayed a can-do attitude, he could get through this.

The elevator doors opened on a cavernous office, acres of deep blue carpet and miles of plate-glass windows, curtains drawn, shrouded in darkness, smelling of sulfur. A massive shape was curled in the middle, bigger than an elephant, with glints of red-gold scales twinkling here and there. Rising from the middle was a tower of computer servers, the control center of OmniCor's vast commercial empire; God alone knew how he used the things. As Topher stepped gingerly from the cab of the elevator, an eye opened and focused on him. The orb was the color of liquid fire with a slitted pupil at its center.

There was a rush of air that raised the humid heat of the office by at least a couple of degrees, and a throaty rumble which vibrated his bones in their sockets. "Ah," the CEO said, "This would be the quarterly earnings report. How nice of them to send me a copy in person. And what's your name?"

Topher arched an eyebrow quizzically. Had the CEO not requested him personally to bring it? "Topher Greene, sir," he said, putting the same false confidence into his voice he had affected during his interview with the VP of Sales.

"Topher Greene? Ah, yes, the new intern. I've been hoping to have a chance to meet you, Topher. May I call you Topher?" This was followed by a rumbling chuckle; as if Topher would object to anything the CEO wished to call him. "Just come over and hold it up to my eye, will you?"

Topher made himself walk closer, right up to the gently pulsating, heat-shedding hide, and held the report up. The CEO scanned the document with a gentle flick of his molten eye. "I see," he said in the deepest basso profundo. "Sales growth slower than expected. Tell me, Topher, are you a virgin?"

Topher gulped involuntarily. "No, sir," he whispered, his voice sticking in his dry, swollen throat.

"Pity," the CEO muttered. "So few young people wait until marriage these days. Myself, I think it shows a certain discipline that is much lacking in the new generation."

"Would that be all, sir?" Topher asked in his best customer service voice.

"Tell me, Topher," the CEO growled, "How is employee morale these days?"

Topher shuddered. "It's good, sir," he said in a near-squeak. He took a deep breath and tried to steady himself. "On my team, at least. Everyone's working hard to hit those goals."

"Really," the CEO said skeptically. "No dissatisfaction? No gripes about the workload, the office culture, the HR policies?"

Topher shook his head. It was well known by now that dragons could smell lies, but he tried to spin things as best he could. "Just the usual grumbling," he said, infusing his voice with every ounce of bravado he could muster. "Every team's got to let off steam now and then, you know? We're all pushing in the same direction."

The CEO sighed, raising the temperature another couple of degrees as he did so. "Topher, my boy," he said in a careworn voice, "I know there's been an effort under way to unionize the staff at HQ. Has anyone been talking to you about that?"

Topher's bowels clenched. So that was what this was all about. But of course it was. "Yes," he said helplessly. "A few."

"And what do you think, son? Should the sales staff form a union? Get together and demand better pay, shorter hours, a more generous leave policy? Would you join a union if they held a vote, Topher?"

Topher breathed deep and slow, then felt a kind of meditative calm descend on him. There wasn't much he could do now to save himself, so maybe candor was the best tactic. "This is one of the ten most profitable companies in the world, sir," he said, trying his best to sound reasonable. "Surely it wouldn't hurt the bottom line too much to hire a few more staff. The hours we work on urgent projects are pretty harsh. The burnout rate is high."

"I hear you, Topher," the CEO said, his voice dripping with sincerity, "but you must see, my hands are tied. I have to answer to the shareholders." As if he couldn't roast any errant shareholders where they stood. "Profit is the name of the game, kid. I didn't get where I am by cutting hours and raising pay."

"Of course, sir," Topher replied, his heart sinking. He was losing hope he would get out alive.

"Now, Topher," the CEO said conversationally, "what would you say if I asked you just who it is that's been talking about this union thing?"

Topher straightened, his chin tipping up. If he could not save his life, he could at least hold on to his dignity. "No," he said forcefully. "I'm not going to name names."

"You disappoint me, lad," the CEO crooned. "And here I thought you wanted to look out for what's best for the company. The company looks out for what's best for you, after all."

"Are you going to eat me?" Topher asked in a small voice.

"Oh, no, no," the CEO laughed. "You're quite an asset to this company, Topher. I've heard nothing but good things about you. A man on his way up. It would be a real shame to lose you. But consider this for a second, my friend," he said jauntily. "There's a neighborhood on the South Side that's ripe for redevelopment. Prime real estate, covered in public housing and low-rent apartments. There's a fellow that's been after me to clean it out for months, but there's not enough in it for the company to make it worth my while. Just think of all those people, Topher. Families. Children. The poorest of the poor. Now think of how good you have it here. People like that would kill to be in your position. You have to look out for number one, first and foremost."

Topher's heart nearly seized up. *Clean it out?* He was just talking about evicting people and leveling their homes, wasn't he? Topher had the distinct feeling he was not.

"Think it over, boy," the CEO growled, "and give me a call when you've made a final decision. But don't wait too long. A deal like this doesn't come along every day. That will be all."

Indecision poured through him like the dizziness of a shot of hard liquor. Was supporting the union worth people's lives? But if people didn't strive to make things better, people like him, how would anything ever change? Lives were being ruined already by the way the staff were treated at OmniCor. *His* life was being ruined. He could feel himself burning out, working himself to the bone just to make this leathery thing another dollar. And the CEO didn't care one bit.

In the depth of his despair, Topher suddenly found a little bit of steel buried in the center of his heart. He took a deep breath. "I don't need to think it over, sir," he said in a hesitant but rapidly strengthening voice. "I resign."

The CEO's burning eye widened. "You *what?*" he growled.

"Resign, sir," he said, his heart beating like a timpani. "Effective immediately."

The CEO's head reared toward the ceiling, foot-thick neck arching. Night-black wings unfurled and eclipsed the trickle of light shining through the curtains. "You ungrateful little shit!" he roared. "I'm giving you the kind of opportunity people wait their whole careers for! And you're going to throw it in my face?"

"You're a monster," Topher shouted back. "People like you

don't deserve to exist! You crush anyone who crosses you beneath your goddamn foot. Well, I'm not going to be crushed!"

There was a howling hiss as the CEO drew in a deep breath. Topher backed up until his shoulders hit the elevator doors, and his hand somehow found the open button. He stumbled through the doors and hammered on the door-close. Just as the doors slid together, there was a terrible whoosh, a rush of intense heat, and a tiny flicker of flame through the gap.

The next day, sitting at his computer, Topher brought up a job search site and typed in "nonprofit". His degree was in Business, but it was a transportable skill, after all. Maybe he could find work with some kind of organization that fought for tenants' rights. If anyone had any rights anymore. Dragonfire was no respecter of persons or property.

But in a world in which there are dragons, he thought with a slowly widening smile, *perhaps there can also be dragonslayers.*

~ * ~ * ~

Xauri'EL Zwaan is a mendicant artist in search of meaning, fame and fortune, or pie (where available); a Genderqueer Bisexual, a Socialist Solarpunk, and a Satanist Goth. Zie lives and writes in a little hobbit hole in Saskatoon, Canada on Treaty 6 territory with zir life partner and a multitude of cats.

The Bala Worm

James Dorr

"Right, sir," the barmaid said—Janie, her name was—when I came home to my own the first time. The lord of her bed, too, soon enough after. And others of the unmarried women. The village, off the normal tourist routes, was old-fashioned in many ways, including a respect for *Droit du Seigneur*.

Of course, I had had an American education, which made me somewhat of an exotic, as well as being the titular lord. And I did have gold too, or its modern equivalent, money and credit. Possibly not so much as I wanted, but....

Then I met Sylvia.

Every so often a rock band came down from the town of Bala, at the lake's far end, to play in the pub here. No one knew quite why they did—for experience, maybe—since Janie's pub's owner could scarcely pay them anything worthwhile. But with the bands came the normal entourage of young people. Groupies. Contrasting vibrantly with the village folk, even the younger ones like Janie.

But it was something for people to do on a Saturday evening, and so the villagers filled the pub along with the groupies, even if few of them actually danced. And as Earl, I got in free—one of my perquisites.

One among many. I winked at Janie, and several more of the Llangower women, as I pushed my way into the taproom. I thought I might have a few pints first, then join the dancers after I'd watched them for a bit. But, as I turned to go back to the main room, its tables and chairs lined against the walls to leave its center free, I caught a flash of long, jet black hair, glistening in the lights from the band-stand, milk white legs underneath a shimmering, lizard-scale mini, a face like—an angel? No. More than an angel, at least to my interest. You have to remember I am a young man. Rather, a face like a *fallen* angel.

I caught her eye. I nodded to Janie as she approached me, but continued my way through the crowd. "Do you dance?" I asked this new woman, no doubt one of the ones who had come in with the musicians.

"Try me," she answered. She tossed her head.

The crowd parted enough to give us room and, when that dance ended, we stayed together for another. At length I invited her back to the taproom, where it would be quieter and, finding a table, I asked her name.

"Sylvia," she answered.

"My name's Bram. Bram Llangower." I saw her eyes widen at the name. "Yes," I added, "the 'lord' of the village. The twenty-third Earl."

She laughed. "Should I call you 'your grace' then?" Then she kissed me quickly and, before I quite knew how to react, she'd gotten up and already disappeared into the crowd.

~ * ~

That was a Saturday. Sunday I had to busy myself about the manor house I was trying to get back into livable condition. I wrote checks—I had credit, as I have mentioned, and it was no problem to order materials for the repairs against future income—and, speaking of income, wrote my solicitors in London about an advance on the next quarter's interest. Monday I went back into the village and stopped at the pub to enquire about Janie. I had this notion she might be angry about my having ignored her Saturday, so I was hoping to make amends to her.

But she wasn't there.

"I haven't seen her all afternoon, sir," the publican said. "I called her parents to see if perhaps she was feeling ill, but they said they hadn't seen her either. Still, a young girl—and at an age when they're sometimes wild—I shouldn't worry too much about her."

"What do you mean?" I asked.

The publican shrugged. "Sometimes, you know, they take it in mind to go off to the city. Like Swansea or Cardiff...."

"You mean you think she might have left with the band the other night? But she'll be back in maybe a few days?"

The publican shrugged again. "I can't say I know about that, sir. She won't be the first girl to just disappear. To go off—who knows? Perhaps to Liverpool, if it was the musicians she followed."

I ordered a stout and sat at the bar, but the publican had no more to tell me. I took his advice, though, and didn't worry. I knew what he meant—at the college I went to, there were certainly young birds enough who weren't really students, but just hung around.

Girls—and blokes, too—who'd left their homes, but really had no place else to go to.

Still, it *was* a bother. I am a young man and even a few days without a woman was, for me, annoying. But then when I went to find one of the others I had courted—courted and coupled with—to my chagrin she was missing as well.

But a third, well, she was still present and ready and so, by the week's end, I had all but forgotten Janie. Or, like the publican, at least resolved not to worry about her.

But then, the next Monday, I'd gone to the market to fetch a few things and, as I was driving back to the manor, who should I see in the road but Sylvia?

"Hullo!" I shouted. I stopped the car.

"Hello," she called back. "Your grace," she added, with a smile. She was dressed the same as she had been that Saturday: black, scale-covered minidress—in the sunlight, I saw the material looked like vinyl—with boots to mid-thigh, thick red waist-cinch the color of dark flame, hair unbound and as black as a raven's wing.

"Want a ride?" I asked. After she'd gotten in, I asked her if the band had come back to town, but she shook her head.

"No," she said. "Actually, I've taken a house here. Or at least near here, in Parc, across the water."

"Ah," I said. "But then you didn't walk here. I mean, Bala Lake is narrow enough, but it's nearly twelve kilometers long...."

She laughed. "Oh, no. I've hired a motorboat for the lake, and then it's only a short hike up on the other side. It's close enough to still be a part of your late ancestor's domain, I'd imagine. I mean the first Earl—you know, the one who slew the Worm?"

"I beg your pardon?"

"The Bala Worm. Don't you know? The local dragon. That's how he got his land and his title...."

I started to laugh. "Look," I said, "let me invite you to *my* house for dinner. It's on the lake, so we can bring your boat right up to it. Then you can tell me more about the first Earl of Llangower. I mean, I know there is a sort of family legend, but how do *you* know so much about it?"

She started to laugh too, a silvery laugh like bells in the dawn wind that blows up the lake through the Cambrian Mountains. "Actually," she finally said, "I'm a sort of a student."

~ * ~

I did not get her to bed that night, although it wasn't for want of trying. We left on good terms and, a few nights later, she came down again from her mountain fastness to join me for dinner, though at the pub this time.

"Say," she asked, when we'd finished eating and were sipping the wine I'd bought us, "where's that blonde waitress? You know, the plump one you waved to that night with the band, just before you approached me to dance?"

"You mean Janie?" I asked. I turned red then. I knew what she thought. "She, uh, kind of disappeared," I finally said. "I mean, I came in the pub the next Monday, after I'd met you, and she wasn't working. The publican told me something about how she'd gone with the band to Liverpool or somewhere."

Sylvia's eyes held mine. "Was he sure about that?" she asked. "I mean about Liverpool. Did she write her folks after she got there?"

"I don't think he said she did," I answered. "But I can ask him." A few minutes later, after I'd ordered us more wine as well, I told her the publican said she had not written. And that another village girl had disappeared too, just this past weekend, making it three in all.

I thought about this third disappearance. Her name had been Meg, a freckle-faced brunette with deep blue eyes, though not so spellbinding as Sylvia's eyes were. I thought I had satisfied her well enough she might stay, but then Sylvia's voice broke in on my thoughts.

"Bram," she said. "These were all young girls? Maybe my age. Or the age of your waitress?"

I blushed again. "Uh, yes," I answered.

She looked in my eyes again. "Bram," she said, "remember what we were talking about the other day, about the first Earl and the Bala Worm? Dragons are long-lived—five hundred, six hundred years, more than that sometimes—and it's well known that, as they become old, they fly down from their caves in the mountains and prey on young people."

"Now wait a minute," I protested. "You mean you're saying these girls might have been eaten by a *dragon*? And it's connected with that story about my ancestor? I don't believe you—and anyway, don't dragons only eat virgins? I know for a fact...."

My voice trailed off as Sylvia glared at me. "Oh?" she said. She stared at me that way for several seconds, as if to demand of me through her silence how I was so certain about who were virgins and who might not have been. Then she said, "You know, I'm a virgin."

This time *I* said "Oh! Uh, no, I didn't know. But...," I thought fast, to find some way I might take advantage. "...but if, I mean, you think you're in danger...."

She laughed. "More from you, maybe, than from the Bala Worm. Still, don't you see? If the dragon your ancestor slew was an old one, a fully mature male, and if it had time to have had issue before it was killed...."

I nodded, playing along for the moment. "Then what you're saying is the timing would be right for this dragon's son to be getting an appetite?" Somehow, I thought then about my own issue—or lack of any, unlike with my ancestors, what with even village girls these days knowing all about how to prevent such things. Then about Sylvia. How I should settle down some day and start having my own sons, to carry the line on. But then, I couldn't help it, I added with a leer, "I mean, for the birdies—even if not virgins."

"Look, this is serious," Sylvia answered. "They will eat ordinary people, of either sex, though they *do* have a special thing about virgins. I don't know why—maybe it has to do with the smell of man. Or trust or something. But what's important is people won't stop disappearing until it's been satisfied."

She paused a moment to sip her wine, then caught my eye again as she added, "Of course, there's also the gold to consider."

"*Gold?*" I spluttered. I'd just taken a drink of my wine too. I may as well confess it now—she was speaking my language. While I did have a modest income, my success with the women often required my buying them trinkets. And even village girls these days seemed to have a certain sophistication.

"Yes," she said. "Don't you know the ballad they wrote about your ancestor? I've only seen parts of it in translation, but it makes clear the dragon he slew had a hoard of gold somewhere in the mountains. At least *he* believed that. He managed to get some too, some that had stuck to the dragon's body, although he died before he was able to find its lair. He was wounded, you see, in the course of combat...."

"But still," I said, "there *aren't* any dragons. They're mythical creatures. That is, there may be some hidden treasure up in the mountains. Perhaps my ancestor's fight was with robbers—I understand there were quite a few back then, who preyed on travelers—and maybe it was *their* gold he got some of. Maybe later someone exaggerated the story...."

"Maybe," she said. "Look, I want you to come to my house tonight." She suddenly laughed, as if she had virtually read my thoughts. "No, not for *that*, Bram. As far as that goes, I do have a guest room for overnight visitors. But, as I told you before when you asked how I knew about your family, I am a student. A student of dragons."

She finished her wine, then started to get up.

"Bram," she said, "I have some things there I think I should show you."

~ * ~

"So there it is," she said, after we had arrived at her home and she'd shown me into her library. All around us were shelves of books, some musty with age, and boxes and cases of rolled up maps and even manuscripts—God knew how old *they* were. In the center was a long table, piled by now with books and papers. And the one big map of Wales and England.

"You see," she pointed, "in County Clwyd, this was where the Denbigh Worm was finally destroyed. Some say its bones are still in the church crypt there. And here," her finger moved east, to Anglesey, "peasants are said to have managed to trick the Worm of Penmynydd into fighting its own reflection. Dragons aren't very smart, or so they say. And then here," she moved south now, into County Powys, "the Llandeilo-graban Worm lay waste the length of the River Wye. While here," her finger moved back north, in almost a straight line back toward Denbigh, except that it stopped scarcely twenty-five kilometers southeast of where we now sat, "the Llanrhaidr-ym-Mochnant Worm was sighted on many occasions and some say wounded, again through trickery. Or so the tales go."

"But what is your point?" I asked. "I mean, do you think these might have all been the same dragon? That is, if there *were* dragons."

"Bram," she said with a laugh. "You're so bullheaded. My point is this. With so many reports, whether some were of the same dragon, or they were all different ones, it stands to reason there's *some* truth behind them. And that's just here in Wales." She leaned over the map again and this time she pointed east, across the border. "Here, for instance, still not that far away, were the Bromfield Worm and the Brinsop Worm. The latter one, incidentally, said to have been destroyed by none other than the famous Saint George. And here," she pointed south, and then southeast. "At Mordiford there were several dragons, and at Deerhurst and Chipping Norton, and here, the Uffington Worm, another of Saint George's victims. I could go on. In Cornwall, for instance...."

"Okay," I said. "I'll go along that far. At least a lot of people at one time *claimed* they saw dragons. And maybe killed them—we may as well add the Bala Worm and my own ancestor. Yet these things all happened in the Middle Ages, and here it's already the twenty-first century. If they're as big as the stories say, and they fly around breathing fire and killing people, how come there haven't been any noticed in the time since then?"

"First of all," she said, "they usually stay in their caves in daytime." She'd gotten up and was fumbling with a vellum manuscript, which she now brought, still rolled up, to our table. "And when they do come out at night, since people nowadays don't believe in them, if they see them they usually find other explanations. The fiery breath is a meteor, for instance. Or maybe the whole thing's a UFO. But also, remember, dragons only achieve their full growth in their final years. At birth they're worm-like and very tiny—almost too small to see. Then, as they grow, they shed their skins like snakes, taking different forms with each molting...."

"Now wait a minute. You mean they disguise themselves? That they don't even look like real dragons until they're almost ready to die?"

"Yes," she said. "At one point, for instance, they almost look human. One of the older legends in England, the Laidly Worm of Spindleston Heugh, even describes a person being turned into a dragon, although the story claims it was by sorcery. And other stories say dragons will sometimes take human wives." She saw the look on my face, I think, because she laughed then. "Of course, fact *does* sometimes get mixed up with fancy."

"I dare say," I said. "But then, how do you know? I mean, how do you separate what you call 'facts' out?"

She smiled. "By comparing common elements in all the legends. You toss out the spurious. As for young dragons appearing human, there is other evidence. In the poem *Beowulf* for example, the monsters there are also described as being human-like, walking on two legs, although at the end of the epic, when Beowulf—or perhaps a descendant—slays one of the old ones for its treasure hoard, it's perfectly clear what he fights then is a full-grown bull dragon."

She paused and looked at me, her hands still on the rolled-up parchment. "Now hear me out, Bram," she said. "Most of these stages of growth take decades—sometimes centuries—and during much of the time they stay hidden. A sort of a hibernation, you might say. Yet, when they are active, they have been spotted although, again, people have tried to find other explanations. Their next transformation, when they first grow wings, may well have given rise to the vampire legends, for instance. Such as the one your own namesake, Bram Stoker, wrote only at the end of the nineteenth century. And here's what's important. Don't you see how these things only come at certain times? All the dragon legends in England, taking place in the Middle Ages, probably within a hundred years or so of each other—unless, like *Beowulf*, what's being recalled took place as long ago before then as the Middle Ages were before our time. Then vampires, practically unknown in literature up until then, suddenly begin to crop up in the eighteen hundreds, so fully described you'd almost think Stoker had actually seen one...."

"Then you think he, and others around his time, really did see one?" I had to admit, she *sounded* convincing, but what she was saying....

"Possibly, yes," she said. "Or they heard stories—again there's a lot of fancy mixed in. About digging up graves, for instance, when even young dragons actually nest in caves, although perhaps sometimes old mausoleums or other manmade cave-like structures might have been meant. In any event, once it's able to fly, there's not that much left to its evolution. Filled with blood—for dragons that's like concentrated food—a dragon's next step is to find a place where it can be sure it won't be disturbed, like up in the mountains. There it will sleep for maybe nearly another century, growing slowly, painfully almost, into its final stage. That's when it mates, Bram. When it starts the cycle over, craving human flesh to maintain its enormous energy. That's where it is now."

"The Bala Worm," I said. "The *new* Bala Worm. You mean it's full grown. Or actually very old, since that's the last stage of its development. All from a—what? An almost microscopic egg that was laid somewhere just before my ancestor supposedly killed the first one?"

She nodded. "Yes." Then she started to unroll the parchment she'd brought to the table. "This is rather rare," she said. "It's on loan, actually, from the collection at Cymmer Abbey, down near

Barmouth. The monks there believe in dragons. In fact they believe some of the treasure the first Worm hoarded, which your ancestor spent what was left of his life trying to find, was originally theirs. I promised them when we kill the new dragon...."

"Hold it! What do you mean, when *we* kill it? I...."

"Look," she said. The parchment was flat now, gnawed with holes where mice apparently had gotten to it at one time or another, but there was enough left for me to tell it was the ballad about the first Earl. A "first edition," as one might call it.

"It's in Welsh," I said. That was the first thing that struck me about it. But then I started to look at the picture that illuminated the top of the scroll—a dragon coiling up from the margin, half coiled around a man in armor, and, so faded as to be almost forgotten, next to a rock to the left of the dragon....

"The Old Tongue, yes," she said. "Medieval Welsh. Can you read it?"

"A little," I said. My grandmother had insisted, when I was small, that I learn it. "But who's the lady?" I asked, pointing toward the faded figure.

Sylvia giggled. "That's the virgin. Your ancestor wasn't all that noble. He used her as bait. But the thing is, *he* was able to kill it—you see his sword there, sticking into its belly? That's the one place the scales are soft enough to stab through."

I nodded. "Sure. Like I'd be fool enough to face something as big as that thing. I...."

Sylvia suddenly kissed me again. Quickly. Like she had done at the public house, when we had first met.

"Bram," she said. "About the virgin. I'd help you, you know. And, traditionally, there are rewards for dragon slayers beyond just getting to find its treasure."

I must have sighed then. "Sure," I said. "But Sylvia, don't you understand? Despite all your theories. Despite the monks, even, at Cymmer Abbey. The fact remains, there *aren't* any dragons."

"Then look there," she said. "Do you realize it's almost morning?"

I looked at my watch, then out the window where she was pointing. Below us, through the trees, was the lake. The sun was just starting to rise on the other side.

"Look," she whispered. "Above the sun."

Then I saw it. A sudden redness, far in the distance. The color of flame.

"Keep looking," she said. "They move rather quickly."

I saw it again. A definite flame. Much nearer this time. And then a shape, as if it were descending to catch an updraft from the lake, a form of a bat with a sinuous neck, a tail trailing behind it. Flying right toward us.

"Look in its talons," Sylvia whispered. I tried to, but suddenly it was right over us, making the roof shake with the wind it stirred in its passage. I ran out the library, into the hallway, trying to find a room with a window on the other side of the house I might look out of. But when I had found one, the—the *thing*—was gone.

I went back to where Sylvia was waiting for me, the manuscript with its illustration still flat on the table.

"People will say it's just wind," she said. "Some kind of storm, maybe, those that were even up to see it. Some kind of freak lightning."

"It wasn't," I said.

"No, it wasn't," she echoed. "And, when you get back to Llangower this morning, I think you'll find another young girl will be missing."

~ * ~

I was no hero. Not then at least. And for killing a dragon, I'd never even been able to have much luck shooting a gun, not and hit anything I tried to aim at. I had fenced in college, but somehow an epee—even if, theoretically, its blade would be thin enough to penetrate a dragon's armor—seemed so inadequate as to be silly. And armor itself, well, even though that seemed to be the traditional costume one wore for such ventures, this was, after all, the beginning of the twenty-first century.

Yet, as Sylvia had predicted, another village girl was missing—this time for all I knew one who might actually have been a virgin, although I'll admit I had had my eye on her. And somehow, hero or not, I found myself being drawn back to Sylvia's library.

Something had clicked in my mind that morning. Some kind of pattern. And something about the Earl's ballad too. The illustration.

I brought a Welsh dictionary with me, to help with obscure terms, and started translating it line by line. Although great parts of the poem were missing, it began to become apparent some kind of trick was involved in his victory. The problem was what, though. And where he had fought it—the illustration suggested he'd found the dragon's cave and attacked it as soon as it came outside, unable to fly with its wings still folded. But, as the text pointed out, he had been wounded and had to go home because he'd lost too much blood, and, once recovered, when he'd tried to find the cave again he couldn't.

But, on that second score, we at least had maps. And I had an idea. I looked, again and again, at the topographical chart where Sylvia had marked the locations of the medieval legends. With her permission, I took a pencil, connecting the dots with a network of lines.

"What are you doing?" Sylvia asked.

"Eliminating the spurious," I said. "Like you say you do with the legends themselves. Look here, for instance." I pointed to a line I'd just highlighted. "This was a dragon you say had been killed, but suppose the legends exaggerated and it had only been chased away. It went to its lair, one might presume, then reappeared here."

I drew another line. "Also here and here. Let's suppose these were all the same dragon. While this one wasn't." I scratched an earlier line I'd drawn out. "But rather was connected with these sightings over in England."

"So?" Sylvia asked.

"So, now I draw perpendiculars to them. Here. And here." The new lines began to converge over Bala Lake—no, not quite over. Somewhere over the Cambrian Mountains that rose to the west beyond Sylvia's cottage. Yet not converge perfectly. Not to a single point.

Shrugging, I put my pencil down.

"So nothing," I sighed. "I'd hoped that, maybe, I could pinpoint the Bala Worm's lair. But all we know thus far is it's in the mountains. And that much we could have guessed anyway, when it flew over your house that morning...."

"Bram, what is it?"

I'd started to laugh.

"I've forgotten the obvious," I finally gasped. "Our own sighting." I leaned over the map and drew another line, this time between Llangower and Parc, where Sylvia's house was, extending it farther on into the mountains. I marked a series of dots on this new line where it crossed the others I'd already drawn. But still no convergence.

I put my pencil down again. I may as well say it here and now, that while another girl had disappeared from the village—so much for the notion that even a possible virgin might have appeased the thing's hunger—that wasn't why I'd hoped to pinpoint the cave's location. Rather, my ancestor *had* found it too, even if he had lost it afterwards, and, from what I could translate of the ballad, the treasure he'd seen in it hadn't just been a few trinkets of gold, but rather a fortune. And I needed money. Not just needed it, I *desired* money—even more than I desired Sylvia.

Sylvia, whose perfume filled my nostrils as she leaned closer to look at the lines I'd drawn.

"Wasn't the sun over here?" she asked. She picked up the pencil.

"What?" I asked.

"We saw the dragon above the sun. Directly above it." She marked a dot to the right of Llangower, then another in Bala Lake the same distance right of the line I'd drawn. "I'd say about here."

"Then it flew in a curve?" I asked.

"Maybe," she said. She drew a shallow arc. "Perhaps the wind...."

Of course! I thought. The wind in the valley, up from the coast at Barmouth Bay, just as the sun starts to heat the mountain air. Something as big as what we'd seen couldn't avoid being blown off course. Couldn't avoid having to make corrections.

I took the pencil, then asked for a ruler and a calculator. When Sylvia brought them, I started changing my other lines, some to a greater extent, some a lesser. I thought about curves. Of course it was still guesswork, but, as I continued, the new lines I drew began coming together.

I thought about curves. Lines that bent instead of straight ones.

"*Arenig Fawr!*" Sylvia suddenly whispered.

"What?" I asked. My mind was wandering—the illustration on the manuscript, still unrolled at the end of the table. I knew about fencing.

"The cave," she said. "If you've drawn these lines correctly, it's on the south slope of Arenig Fawr. You've seen the mountain."

A swordsman's arm sticks straight out when he's attacking—that's what gives it leverage—yet the first Earl's was bent in at his side. And the spikes on his armor—the strangely extended shoulder protectors, the points at his elbows. The dragon, too close to breathe fire at the end without burning itself too. Instead attempting to coil around him, like some great constrictor.

"Bram, are you listening?" Suddenly Sylvia kissed me, hard. "I know where the cave is—at least I think I do. It's in a valley, a sort of hollow, only one or two kilometers away. I've *been* there, Bram. But the cave must be hidden, probably covered by shrubs or bushes. That's why the first Earl couldn't find it again when he looked for it—they'd had a chance to grow back to conceal it."

I heard her. I kissed her back. But I was thinking—my ancestor never attacked the dragon, not with his arm bent, at least not directly. The ballad suggested there'd been a trick.

And I knew what that trick was.

~ * ~

The next day I called a firm in Glasgow that made reproduction armor. I gave them special specifications, including that it be made of the lightest weight, yet strongest metal, and that it and its accompanying shield be lined with asbestos—my ancestor's wounds had included burns, from what I'd been able to read of the ballad. I borrowed heavily against my income—I had to argue with London about that—and further ordered knives and a sword of the sharpest steel, arranging to have it all completed within the week and air-shipped to a field at Barmouth, and thence by truck up the valley to Parc and Sylvia's cottage.

We made that our base of operations. I slept in the guest room and fitted it up as a sort of gym, bringing in weights and other equipment to build my stamina. Once the fight started, well, that would be something else, but simply getting to where we expected to find the cave, even though not very far on the map, would take enough out of me.

And we went on field trips, while we awaited the armor's arrival. To Cymmer Abbey and Castle Carn Dochan, the latter on foot since it was a local ruin and one legend said it had, at one time, been damaged by dragons.

We read, ate, and slept dragons. Talked only of dragons. We'd both agreed calling in the civic authorities would do no good. Who would believe us? Even the parents of the missing girls, two more of whom disappeared within that long week, only clucked and blamed the rock bands that still came through every fortnight or so.

Which left it up to us, I in my armor, she as my helper. The Earl and his squire, the former of whom, to be sure, was aware that if we were successful his desire for gold—for other things gold can buy—would be quite sated.

For other things also. I may as well say it. I'd come to love Sylvia, love the way she moved. Love the way she called my name when the crate from Glasgow finally arrived. How she helped me unpack it.

How, in the lamplight of her library, she helped me lay the full plate armor out on the floor, the spikes and blades of its metal shell gleaming. The knife blades I'd had them weld, points out, onto it, porcupine-like to improve on my ancestor's trickery.

I tried it on right then, that evening. I exercised in it, learning its feel. The next day I rested, conserving my strength, and then, the next morning, we set off into the Cambrian Mountains, to Arenig Fawr, to find the Worm's lair.

The going was rough, as you might well imagine. There was no safe way to carry the armor, so I had to wear it, though Sylvia helped with my shield and sword, my gauntlets and helmet. We rested frequently, I often making sketches of the terrain around us, using a notebook and pencils I'd packed in a sort of *sporran* looped to my waist, so, unlike the first Earl, we'd have no trouble retracing our journey should need arise. While Sylvia, more lightly dressed in a hiking skirt and blouse, made tea on a small stove she had insisted she take along with us, despite the burdens she already carried.

"We must be civilized, Bram," she had said. I loved her for that. I lusted for her—though not at the moment. But after, I thought, as I'd watch her spring up, clean the stove and repack it, take up the other equipment as handily as any squire and lead on, ever upward.

But after. The dragon killed, then the reward. The thought kept me going until mid-afternoon when, having turned at a standing rock, we passed through a small grove of overgrown bushes and into a bare rock, bowl-like depression.

Sylvia stopped short. She looked about her—another standing rock, a slope upward. Another rock, behind it a shadow.

"Bram," she whispered. She waited until I had caught up to her. "Bram," she said again, still in a low voice. "I think we've found it."

I nodded. I wiped the sweat from my face. I moved to the side to look into the shadow, saw how it opened up into a kind of cave.

"Bram, are you frightened?"

I shook my head. No. Truth to tell, I was too tired by then to be frightened. But I was rewarded—a smile and a kiss.

"Very well, then, Bram," she said. "Are you ready? You'll stand where you are now, where it can see you when it emerges. While I take the standing stone." She smiled again. "The virgin's part, you know. Where I can cower and hide behind it."

I nodded. "Yes," I said. I held my hands out while she pushed on my gauntlets, then helped me strap the shield on my left arm. She handed my sword to me, then kissed me once more.

"It will be sleeping," she said. "I didn't want to tell you, but last night, while you were asleep too, it took another victim. I heard from the village. At least, though, it won't be hungry when it wakes."

I nodded again, then held my head straight while she placed on my helmet, strapping it down to the hooks on my armor. *How had she known?* I thought. We'd both been up at dawn. But then I shrugged, as best I could in the armor's stiffness—of course, if she'd been up slightly before me, she might have *seen* its flight back from the village.

"I'll wake it," she whispered. I watched as she took up her post by the standing stone, ready to duck in an instant behind it.

"Okay," I whispered.

I pulled down my visor.

And then I heard her cry. Shrill. Ululating. I heard an answering call from inside the cave.

The cry of dragons.

Sylvia was a student of dragons—of course, I realized. She knew how to call them. I watched, as best I could, through the eye slits of my helmet while, for a long moment, nothing happened.

Then, all of a sudden, the cave's inside was lit with flame. And I saw the treasure! Heaps and heaps of gold. Glinting with its own fire. Jewels and silver.

Then darkness again, for a moment only.

And then it appeared—head first, then the neck—faster than I had thought something so big *could* move. Snake-like it rushed at me, wings still folded. I thrust at it—once only. Swinging my sword at it. All I had time for.

Then I remembered—I needn't attack it. I put my shield up instead, warding its flame off, and let it rush to me.

That was the plan. To let it attack me from the start, as the earlier Worm had attacked my ancestor, finally impaling itself on the sword he had purposely braced against his side. Except I had sword points studded all over me.

I let it hit me, holding my ground. Staggering slightly as, too close to use its flame anymore, it arched up its body and whipped it around me.

I felt it coil—harder. Trying to crush me. Hearing the creak as my armor withstood its force. Sank to my knees beneath its weight, but my armor still holding.

And then I heard the Bala Worm's shriek as the knife blades sank into its sides and its belly. Louder, deeper, each time it coiled tighter.

And now I shrieked too, but my whoops were of triumph as the great creature's convulsions slowed. As the Bala Worm slumped down, pulling me with it, onto my own side. That didn't matter.

The Worm was dying.

"Sylvia!" I shouted. Where had she gone to? I struggled to free my arm from the dragon's coils and pushed up my visor.

My other arm still trapped, my legs pinned beneath me, my armor nailed firmly—with me still inside it—within its great bulk, but that didn't matter.

And then I saw Sylvia mounting the back of the still twitching dragon, hiking her skirt up above her knees. I couldn't see everything she was doing, except that her legs became stained with its blood. I saw her climb down its other side, as if dancing, sliding a circle around me. Saw her sit, finally, in front of the dragon and take its huge head into her lap.

She stroked the head silently for a moment. I saw she was crying.

Then she looked up at me.

"Their breath impregnates us," she said. "I don't know how. But in that sense I lied to you—about being a virgin. I just haven't coupled with other humans. In return, though, we receive long life and, after we've laid our eggs successfully, we, too, undergo transformations."

She stood up then, laying the Bala Worm's head gently on the ground. "It's their life cycle. I don't understand it." She started slowly to take off her clothing. "For its completion, we must lay our eggs in our lovers' corpses. To nourish the grubs, you see. So they'll grow quickly."

She laughed then. I shivered. I couldn't help it. "Sylvia," I shouted. "I can't move! Don't you see? I don't care about you and the dragon. Just help me get the weight of it off me so I at least can get out of this armor!"

She had her blouse off now and, as she turned to lay it over the Bala Worm's lifeless head, I caught a glimpse of something…not human.

"You don't understand yet, do you Bram?" she said, reaching down now to loosen her skirt. "Why the old dragons get hungry for human flesh—you do deserve to know. Young women, tender, virgins or not, provide the best nourishment for the young ones after their father's own flesh has absorbed it. But any human flesh will do, especially if it's preserved, undigested." She paused and smiled, then bent to untie her shoes. "Perhaps, especially, if it's cased in metal armor to hold it safely, like meat in a can, until his...*my* children are ready to eat it."

That's when I screamed. Not at what she said, but, when she turned and tossed her hair and I saw, beneath it, the nubs of wings growing. I saw them sprout quickly, spread out before my eyes, black and bat-like, as black and scale-shimmering as the dress she'd worn when I first met her.

This—that I thought I'd loved?

Lusted for, anyway. That and the dragon's gold.

"Sylvia," I said. I suddenly realized, lust or no lust, I *had* been a hero. "The dragons' life cycle. If your...if *its* grubs are just hatching out now, at least it will be another five hundred years before they've reached their full growth—before they've grown up enough to start killing people again. So at least it's over. At least for now."

She laughed again, louder. An inhuman sound. She turned to the wind, naked, letting her wings billow.

"Yes, Bram," she said. "*My* grubs will take that long. As for the others...."

"The others?" I asked.

"Yes," she said. "I'm afraid I lied a second time when I let you believe the medieval dragon legends might all have been reports of the same Worm. As if they'd all come from a single sire whose mate laid just one egg. Actually, though, we lay many more than one."

She caught the wind's current then, launching herself in it, laughing and shouting back down to where I lay trapped.

"And I do have sisters."

~ * ~ * ~

James Dorr is an Indiana-based short story writer and poet specializing in dark fantasy and horror, with forays into mystery and science fiction. His The Tears of Isis was a 2013 Bram Stoker Award® finalist for Superior Achievement in a Fiction Collection, while other books include Strange Mistresses: Tales of Wonder and Romance, Darker Loves: Tales of Mystery and Regret, and his all poetry Vamps (A Retrospective), along with his latest, Tombs: A Chronicle of Latter-Day Times of Earth, a novel-in-stories from Elder Signs Press. Dorr has been a technical writer, an editor on a regional magazine, a full-time non-fiction freelancer, and a semi-professional musician. He currently harbors a Goth cat named Triana, and counts among his major influences Ray Bradbury, Edgar Allan Poe, Allen Ginsberg, and Bertolt Brecht.

For more information, Dorr invites readers to visit his blog at http://jamesdorrwriter.wordpress.com.

He can also be found on FaceBook at https://www.facebook.com/james.dorr.9.

His Amazon Author Page can be reached at http://www.amazon.com/James-Dorr

Unmasking the Dragon

Matt Bille

"This is the dumbest TV show idea ever," Stan said. He hacked at the rain forest in front of him with a machete, cutting a swath in a way that reminded him oddly of hacking through pop-up ads every time he went to his favorite website. Not that he was going to get www.girlswholovecameramen.com out here.

Mac snorted and chopped some vines across their non-existent trail. "Ah, you're just bellyachin' because that girl in La Paz didn't faint at your sheer manliness."

Stan had already noticed the further they got from civilization, the more their leader forgot to do his Scots accent. "No, I'm belly-aching because we've walked for three days looking for that little cleft in the Andes Jose claims leads to a land of dragons."

"Not dragons," Barb said. "*Continuar.*"

"Which means dragons. And there are no dragons. And we're going to get killed or maybe starve to death. I haven't had a real meal since that monkey grabbed my last fried chicken bucket and all my Snickers bars melted."

"This is paradise," Mac insisted, crushing a bug the size of his boot with his boot. "Fame and fortune! We needed a cameraman, and I know you're the best."

Stan let himself be mollified.

Barb shaded her eyes looking to where the setting sun shone directly into her eyes through a cleft in the Andes mountains. Three days looking for a cleft in the Andes Mountains. No luck.

"Camping spot up there, guys," she pointed. "Good flat spot."

"Probably a drilling ground for army ants," Stan said. He watched Barb take charge and start clearing out some branches. A tarantula that could have eaten most dogs scuttled toward her and received a kick that sent it into Earth orbit.

"Wow," Stan said.

"Hey, before I was a supermodel, I taught kindergarten for rich kids," Barb said. "I don't take much crap."

Amazing woman, Stan thought. He hadn't even known Oscar de la Renta made hiking clothes, let alone jungle boots.

"Let's camp," Jose Lagado, who'd been quiet, said. Their guide and assistant porter had latched onto them in La Paz and claimed to know every tree in this cloud forest, and had taken to bringing up the rear. In the first place, he liked to look at Mac's blonde girlfriend slash communications expert from that angle, and in the second place, he had shown himself only slightly more knowledgeable of the area than a sloth. Since he'd talked his way into a well-paying job, paid by people who now hated him, he kept mostly out of sight.

They made camp, and Stan sighed, picked up the camera, and asked Jose to tell the story again.

Jose wiped sweat from his face with a cloth and smiled. "Si. Five or six times when I was a child, men didn't come back from El Hueco—the gap. Still they went there, because the treasure was there. Treasure hidden by the last Incas, who marched all the way from Machu Piccu to a secret hideaway so far from their roads the conquistadores would never even look for it. My grandfather brought back gold rings and bracelets; enough to buy us a house. But he told also of the dragons. He said he would never go back there, and he never did. It's been twenty years now since the last fools tried their luck. The last local fools, I mean. Gringos still show up."

"Tell us about the dragons," Mac said.

"He didn't say much. But he said the *continuar* was the most terrifying thing in all the world, and he had escaped it only by his own cunning and his skill at rock climbing. A giant, scaly lizard thing. He said it looked like the beast in an old movie he saw. *Dragon Stomper? Dragon Smoocher? Dragonslayer,* that's it!" Jose had long ago gotten his patter down: the right mix of good English, pidgin English, and Spanish to sound exotic and macho. He wondered where Barb had gotten to. He wondered if her *galan,* Mac, might meet with a horrible accident.

"So like a dinosaur with wings?"

"Yes. like one of the dinosaurs they have in the museum in La Paz. And with *mucho grande* teeth. He said it was so fantastic we could not imagine it. The movie was the closest he could come. He saw it breathe fire, and it had horrible claws. I told you gringos don't know enough to stay away. Three times hunters from the United States have gone in to kill a dragon trophy. We only found burned-out boots from the last one."

Mac motioned for Stan to turn the camera to him. "There's always been strange wildlife in these forests. Some people say the dregs from little silver and iron mines have been flowing down the Jacarta into the valley for hundreds of years. Some people say a meteor landed here long ago and turned the sky red and poisoned the ground. I've even heard a helicopter looking for the meteor crater detected radiation before it crashed for mysterious, but I'm sure perfectly explainable, reasons. So this is a place where even the weirdest nightmare creatures might have become reality."

"We're getting paid by History Channel, not SyFy," Stan grumbled.

"The key word, lad, is 'paid,'" Mac said. "Now where was I? People have come out of this forest with everything from three-legged birds to an iguana with two heads, or maybe it was the other way around." He chuckled at his own laugh line. "Anyway, we won't really know what's through that cleft until we find it." He glared at Jose.

"Hey guys, look at this," Barb called from the other side of the little clearing. She was disentangling something from a bush.

"Mist net," Mac said. "Used to trap birds for study. Some ornithologist came through here once."

"And left his stuff," Barb said. She hauled out a rotting canvas bag, a Barney metal lunchbox inscribed with "EMERGENCY FLARES—DO NOT EAT," and a mostly-still-wrapped Twinkie. "My God," she said, "This thing looks fresh. And not even the bugs would eat it."

"There goes our Hostess sponsorship," Stan said. "What the hell, gimme the Twinkie. I'll have it for breakfast."

"It could be swarming with microbes you never even heard of."

"At least then we'd make a discovery," Stan growled. He considered it a moment, opened the Twinkie, and devoured it.

A spectacular burst of color and sound erupted over their heads as a flight of scarlet macaws passed.

"Damn, I wish you had the camera on them!" Mac said.

"Damn, I wish I had some birdshot and some ranch sauce," Stan said. "And that I'd saved the Twinkie for dessert." He wondered what was really in that Barney lunchbox.

They stayed in the camp for two days, waiting to see if Stan survived the Twinkie. It was a near thing. Mac a half-dozen times reached for the satellite phone to call for help, and a half-dozen times put it away since there wasn't any help out here.

Stan lost about thirty pounds, but came back to the living, By the third morning, he felt almost himself. He'd taken everything in the medical kit, whether it had anything do with explosive diarrhea and vomiting or not, and he'd drunk every ounce of water in camp.

He looked west again as Barb, nearby, slurped dew off a book-sized leaf. Stan started to make a hilarious comment and remembered Mac had the shotgun. Oh, well.

"Hey," he said. "Now that I can look through that cleft without the sun in my eyes, it looks like a cleft."

Everyone stared.

Barb did a facepalm.

Mac whacked himself on the head with the shotgun barrel.

Jose said nothing. He was being paid by the day and had seen no reason to point out anything that might actually get them to their destination.

Mac hit himself again, and Barb ripped the shotgun away from him.

"Right. Let's go see the dragons," he said, rubbing his forehead.

Another day of strenuous effort and they started into the cleft itself. The ground was rockier here, but it was better than struggling through the jungle or rain forest or whatever where alleged ants too big to be genuine ants (or hamsters, for that matter) were going for their ankles every waking moment.

"I remember the story now," Jose said. "For the gold, we follow the left side, down where that creek goes."

"Where do we find the dragon?" Stan asked, eyeing the cliffs on either side of their entry point.

"No need to look for the dragons," Jose said. "Dragons are always looking for a free meal."

"You're safe, then. You weren't free, you were bloody damned expensive," Mac said to him.

"Can't be many places a critter like that can hide," Stan said. "I mean, did you SEE that movie? *Dragonslayer?*"

"Long time ago," Mac said. "All I remember was the girl was going to be sacrificed because she was a virgin, and the boyfriend went off to slay the dragon and I was yelling at the screen he could actually solve this problem without getting barbecued. Moron."

The shadow of great wings passed over. Everyone stopped and looked up, but the sun was high, and for a moment they couldn't make it out. A chill, or maybe a poisonous centipede, ran down Mac's spine.

Then the beast landed twenty paces in front of them. Its huge black eyes stared at them. Its enormous batlike wings slowed, then stopped their flapping. Its front paws came up, sporting claws the size folded umbrellas would be if they were curved a little and sharpened a lot.

"You have GOT to be kidding me," Stan said.

"Mutant wildlife…I guess it can mutant a lot of different ways," Mac said.

"Mutant isn't a verb," Barb mumbled. "It's 'mutate'…"

"SOMEONE has to say it," Stan said.

The beast roared. Barb thought that, if it wasn't for the sheer volume of air being moved, the roar would sound more like a squeak.

"SOMEONE has to say it," Stan said.

Mac turned to Barb. "If he says that again, shoot him."

"But he's right, someone does—"

"All right, all right!" Mac said. "Let's get this out of the way. On the count of three, everybody say it. One, two, three!"

"It's a *(&$^&%$% MOUSE," they all chorused.

The eighty-foot flying mouse curled its wings and daintily licked its front paws. A small cloud of steam emerged from its nostrils, as if it was just making sure the fire-breathing parts were all working.

"This is gonna knock the bottom out of Godzilla movies," Stan said. "We found the biggest monster in the world, and it's…" he turned to Jose. "What about the giant scaly lizard thing."

"Oh," Jose said. "I should have added my grandfather was lying the whole time. He never got a mile from town in his whole life."

The dragon nodded as if in understanding.

"Anyone have some cheese?" Stan asked, then remembered he'd eaten it.

Mac went to whack his forehead with the gun again, remembered too late he didn't have it, and punched himself in the mouth.

"Wait," Stan said. "That thing could kill us in one second, and its reputation says it should have by now. What's stopping it?"

The dragon looked at Barb and made a mewing sound.

"Oh, come on,' Stan said. "Beauty and the beast?"

"I don't care if it's a cliché, beauty and the beast makes money," Mac said. "Get to it!"

Moments later, Stan had the camera out and was filming as Barb held out a leaf to the terrifying monster. The thing took it gently from her hand with its claws.

Stan moved around to capture the scene from all angles. Perfect. Beauty and the beast…well, the sort-of beast…well…it had all the weapons to be a murderous fire-breathing dragon. As with Mac, its one weakness was ex-cheerleaders.

"Now can we go home?" he asked.

The world premiere of *Mouse Dragons of the Andes* was the lowest-rated show the History Channel had ever broadcast. Lower than reruns of *Ancient Aliens*. Lower than the ridiculous *MonsterQuest* episode about giant bears with the writer from Colorado, for readers of this story old enough to remember 2008. No one could believe this supposed team of dedicated scientific explorers had picked a mouse to use as their obviously CGI fake monster. No one believed there had ever been a dragon, or the story about the gold, or that Mac had ever had a supermodel girlfriend. Also, after History Channel ran four weeks of ads hyping the world's most incredible, famous, and amazing mouse, Disney had started filing lawsuits, plus someone belatedly realized R.L. Stine had already used their title. The studio that did Mighty Mouse wasn't happy, either.

After the premiere, what was left of the exploration team tried valiantly to knock off the entire liquor supply of the city of Hollywood.

"Can't believe Barb ran off with Jose," Mac muttered.

"Might not have if you hadn't tried to murder him. Girls always fall in love tending men with gunshot wounds."

"I don't think that makes sense," Mac said.

"Nothing makes sense," Stan said. "We labored mightily and brought forth…well, you know."

"You say the 'm' word, I'll strangle you with my bare hands."

"You would, but I'm not sure I'd mind it right now. So have another drink."

~ * ~ * ~

Matt Bille is an author in Colorado Springs, Colorado. He is a novelist whose first two books, *The Dolmen* and *Raven's Quest*, have garnered excellent reviews. He is also a naturalist, historian, science writer, and defense consultant. A former Air Force officer, he is the author of over 20 technical publications and articles on space- and zoology-related topics. He is the lead author of the NASA-published history *The First Space Race: Launching the World's First Satellites* (2004), a groundbreaking account of the early Space Age.

Matt wrote two books on the world's rarest and least-known animals, *Rumors of Existence* (1995) and *Shadows of Existence* (2006) and is working on his third. He has been a freelance contributor to reference books including *Grzimek's Animal Life Encyclopedia* and the *Nature Yearbook of Science & Technology.*

He is a member of the National Association of Science Writers and an Associate Fellow of the American Institute of Aeronautics and Astronautics. He appeared on two television programs on mystery animals and blogs on the latest science and technology news at Matt's Sci/Tech Blog at http://mattbille.blogspot.com.

If all that still sounds boring, he is a leading amateur expert on the giant armored fish *Dunkleosteus terrelli* and is frequently seen at comic conventions as his favorite literary character, wizard Harry Dresden.

Wormslayer

DJ Tyrer

You're the slayer of dragons?" the knight in the black tabard with a white cross upon it asked of the man who had just walked up to him across the dusty ground.

The sun beat fiercely down upon the steep-sided, scrub-scattered Levantine valley.

"They call me Wormslayer."

The second knight wore no tabard, the spikes projecting from the rust-streaked cuirass of his armor precluded such a covering. The Hospitaller looked him up and down with an arched eyebrow.

Tapping a spike with a mail-gloved finger, the knight said, "You suspect a jest? Out here in the East, you must have seen many an outlandish sight. Surely, my armor is not that strange?"

"True enough, but whilst I've seen many a spiked shield in my time, mounted with a steel dagger or a spike of antelope horn, I have seen no armor quite like yours."

There was a distant rumble, a shudder beneath their feet. Loose stones skittered down the sides of the valley.

"The dragon wakens," the knight murmured, casting his gaze along the length of the valley to where a dark cave, large enough for a cart and horses to pass through with ease, gaped.

He turned back to the Knight of the Hospital. "This armour has seen me through several battles. I've slain five of the dragons known as worms thanks to it—they entwine about you and squeeze …killing themselves, impaled upon the spikes."

The Hospitaller nodded in understanding.

"I've also slain a wyvern and a fiery drake. Without wishing to risk invoking the sin of pride, I believe I am the greatest living slayer of dragons in all of Christendom. Have no doubt, brother, I am the man whom you seek."

The ground shuddered again.

"Tell me about your dragon."

The Hospitaller spat dust from his lips, then crossed himself, as if the mere mention of the beast were a curse to be warded off.

"We call it the Abomination of the Desolation." He waved his leather-gauntleted hand about them, indicating their arid surroundings. "It appears like a serpent of great length, the veritable spawn of Satan out of Eden."

He coughed, the air was thick with dust, then continued, "It rose from the earth here three years ago. A party of knights from my order and that of the Temple had paused to rest from the worst of the heat of the day, whilst hunting down a raiding party of Saracens. The dragon devoured all but one, a squire who managed to leap upon a horse and escape from its snapping jaws." He shrugged. "Of course, nobody believed him, at first. Not until half the party that came to investigate the massacre only narrowly avoided being devoured, too."

Wormslayer looked about at the valley. "They chose to pause here? Even without a lurking dragon, this valley invites slaughter." He craned his head back. "The heathens could lurk up there and send down darts and arrows and stones with impunity, or they could plug the mouth of the valley with warriors and wait for your people to die of thirst—there's no spring here."

The Hospitaller shook his head. "You misunderstand my words, Wormslayer. This place *wasn't* a valley when they camped here. It was the Abomination that ploughed it out of the ground."

Wormslayer gave a whistle. "That big?"

"That big," the Hospitaller said with a nod, crossing himself once more. "We've sent our best men, the Templars and my order, to slay the Abomination, and all have failed. All manner of would-be champions have come for the reward and none survived to collect it. Even a contingent of two-dozen brave warriors failed to defeat it." He sighed. "You are the last. If you fail, the only option left to us will be to summon the entire army of the Kingdom of Jerusalem to battle it. Perhaps, with the Holy Rood at its head, that will be enough— but, if too many die it could leave our realm defenseless. Yet, not to do so risks it stirring forth to ravage the country."

Wormslayer sniffed. "Size makes no difference."

"So, you'll slay it?"

"I have no doubt I can slay it, even if it be as long as the Euphrates. Consider it already dead."

The Hospitaller fixed him with a look that said he'd heard many wild promises out here in the Levant on crusade and put little store in such words.

"I'll restrain my urge to celebrate until I actually see its corpse before me."

"Well," Wormslayer said, "you'll see it soon enough."

The ground shuddered once more. "Very soon."

"This is where I leave you." The Hospitaller started to turn. "Oh, here…." He paused to produce a dagger, which he handed to Wormslayer.

"It may not seem much, but, within the blade, there's a single thorn from the Crown of Christ. May its holiness protect you from the Devil's spawn."

The knight nodded and slipped it into his belt. "Thank you."

The Hospitaller turned once more and headed back down the valley to its entrance, where their horses were waiting, bridles tied to a stunted thorn tree.

"God be with you, Wormslayer," he called over his shoulder.

Wormslayer drew his sword from its sheath.

"I'm shriven and have fasted. I am as ready as I ever shall be— whether to win a victory over this devil or to meet my Maker."

He held the sword inverted before him, like a cross.

"By God and my strength, I shall prevail."

"I pray it's so," the Hospitaller called back to him, mounting his horse. "I pray it's so," he murmured in self-echo, riding away.

Wormslayer turned his gaze away from him and looked towards the cave entrance, knelt, and prayed as he waited. He could feel vibrations through the earth, growing stronger, juddering up through his knees and along his spine, that told him the great worm was nearing the surface.

He stood and readied his sword.

With a roar like thunder and an explosion of dirt and stones, the Abomination burst from the cave mouth like floodwaters over-whelming a dam.

The Knight didn't flinch. No matter a single one of its fangs was the length and thickness of his forearm, he had no doubt he would prevail as he had done so many times before.

The dragon surged towards him along the length of the valley, a huge limbless snake with a heavy head, the eyes of which were fixed upon him as if they were boring deep into his soul, uncovering his every sin. He could practically feel the hunger and the hatred, the very taint of Hell.

He cried out to God and swung his sword in a mighty two-handed blow as it reached him, the blade scoring a bloody line across its broad snout.

It smashed into him with the force of a battering ram, sending him flying backwards, his sword spinning from his hand.

Wormslayer felt ribs crack from the blow and landed heavily, the air driven from his lungs. He gasped a curse, then chuckled to see the blood dribbling from the wounds the dragon had inflicted upon itself by striking against his spiked armor.

The knight pushed himself up from the dusty ground and retrieved his sword from where it landed.

The huge serpent bore down on him again, so long it hadn't even drawn its tail free of the cave yet.

He dodged and slashed, scoring a bloody mark along its scaly flank.

It turned and snapped at him, a fang striking his arm. Wormslayer heard the sound of rivets popping and chain links shearing apart, then felt a shaft of flame pierce his limb. A cry of pain burst past his lips as the fang tore deep into his flesh.

"Enfold me," he shouted. "Crush me, you fiend."

Failing to oblige, it snapped towards him again. He barely managed to dodge out the way, slashing wildly with his sword as he did.

Their battle continued to surge wildly up and down the length of the valley, the great serpent twisting this way and that with surprising alacrity to try and seize him in its enormous jaws, whilst he fruitlessly sought to strike a telling blow, perhaps against the beast's wagon-wheel-sized soulless eyes.

"Damn you, fiend," he gasped, his breath ragged. He was tiring fast, yet the dragon slowed no signs of slowing, nor even of pulling its full length free of the cave that was the entrance to its home.

He swung his sword again, then threw himself bodily out of the way of its jaws, landing in a crouch.

Wormslayer gazed up into the vast maw that gaped above him.

An idea struck him.

He thrust himself forwards as it lunged towards him, roaring as he went.

The jaws snapped shut, closing upon him, then tore open again as the serpent gave a roar of pain that sent him flying from its mouth like a bolt from a crossbow.

He flew through a rain of blood, then everything went black for a moment as he smashed into the wall of the valley.

Wormslayer barely managed to stand on shaking legs before it lunged at him again.

His drove his sword arm upwards, thrusting the blade of his weapon with as much force as he could muster, the tip penetrating through the roof of the dragon's mouth.

A killing blow.

The great worm pulled back, dragging the sword from his hand, arching and twisting, as if it might somehow extract the blade through its desperate thrashing motions.

It shuddered and pulled back, withdrawing partway into its cave before collapsing limply onto the dusty ground.

Wormslayer fell to his knees with a laugh, then let out a grateful cry to God for bringing him victory.

Then, the ground shook and broke apart.

~ * ~

The Hospitaller watched the battle from a distant hill. Whilst he couldn't make out much detail, he could see the knight and serpent conduct their deadly dance and prayed aloud for the man's soul, certain he would fall before it, certain he had when the great jaws enveloped him.

He cheered as Wormslayer drove his sword home and the dragon died.

Then, cried out in horror as the ground buckled and cracked, throwing the knight to the earth, to vanish in a thick cloud of billowing dust, as he himself fought to keep his footing as the hill undulated beneath him, like the deck of a ship.

The earth broke apart, revealing a wide black pit.

The Hospitaller lost his balance and fell to the ground, looking up in horror, certain Wormslayer must have plunged down into the depths of the pit, and watching as six enormous heads rose from it, each atop a long and sinuous neck that extended, in turn, from a body he felt certain was the size of the Holy City, a vision from the *Revelation* brought to life before him. The seventh head hung limp and lifeless from its shoulder.

The Hospitaller crossed himself.

Not a worm, but a hydra, the dragon was no mere serpent but a seven-headed demon from the depths of Hell.

They had been so wrong...

Then, he saw movement amongst the still-billowing dust, a dark mote beside the vast bulk of the creature. Wormslayer.

Unseen by the Hospitaller, the knight had retrieved his blade from the head he'd slain and now, held it ready once more as he charged the dragon.

The Hospitaller almost laughed at the reckless action.

~ * ~

The beast loomed over Wormslayer like a mountain. Yet, for all its mass, he felt a certain confidence; having slain one head, he might yet slay them all.

A huge, clawed foot rose and plunged towards him, but Wormslayer threw himself out the way and slashed at its heel.

The dragon roared again and multiple heads lunged at him.

Wormslayer dodged, barely evading the snapping jaws, and slashed left and right with his blade.

He needed for it to try and swallow him again, but it seemed to have learnt its lesson from the death of its first head and, when he set himself ready for it to seize him, it merely snapped at his limbs, gouging deep and painful wounds.

Were its fangs poisoned? With its size, it hardly seemed it would need venom, but his sluggishness was growing and he could feel a burning pain spreading through his limbs.

If he were to win this struggle and send his soul to Heaven victorious, he needed to bring it to an end soon.

It struck him again, a fang tearing through the mail of his left leg as if it were little more than cloth. He stumbled backwards and landed on his backside, his sword flying away to disappear into the darkness of the pit.

He'd allowed himself to be distracted, his mind wandering, growing misty with pain.

He needed to do something. But, what?

The dagger…

He reached for the dagger the Hospitaller had handed him. It was still in his belt.

Wormslayer said a silent prayer of thanks to God for preserving it upon him.

Now, if only the holiness of the thorn within it was enough to defeat the dragon…

Somehow, he got back onto his feet, avoiding the next slash of its fang, and the next, and then he stabbed at its eye with the dagger. The blow missed its mark, but drove deep between scales with a dark spray of blood.

The dragon roared with pain and the head whipped away, tearing the dagger from his hand.

Wormslayer cursed.

Then, he swore again as the head he had been so certain he had slain twitched and lifted back up into the air with a mighty roar.

He stared up at it in horror.

The dragon's tail lashed and caught him, sweeping him almost to the edge of the pit.

He felt his ribs crack and a sharp pain in his side as one snapped and dug deep into his organs. His cuirass had buckled, and the spikes were dented or broken off. Even if the dragon chose to swallow him now, Wormslayer doubted they would achieve anything.

It had thwarted him.

Or his hubris had.

He was defeated, he knew it. But, he would not go quietly…

Wormslayer had a dagger of his own, one with a nicked blade that had been his father's, neither blessed nor ensorcelled. It was all he had, and he drew it now to make his final stand against the dragon.

He held it before him as he called upon the Name of God for strength.

Weary as anything, it took all his effort to throw himself aside as one of the seven heads dropped towards him, fangs bared, then drive the dagger blade sideways at its eye.

The point of the dagger struck home, and the blade drove deep into the glassy eye, which popped wetly, splashing him with its vitreous humor.

The dragon roared as its neck arched skyward, head thrashing from side to side.

But even as he felt his spirits buoy, another head flashed towards him.

Too late, he raised his dagger.

~ * ~

The Hospitaller watched as the great jaws closed upon Wormslayer, the knight vanishing from sight.

He waited, praying Wormslayer would burst free of its belly, the spikes of his cuirass puncturing its unholy flesh, but no such thing happened.

The Abomination gave a seven-throated roar the Hospitaller

was certain was a cry of victory.

Wormslayer had failed. The man who had boasted, with justi-fication, of being the greatest dragonslayer in Christendom had failed, had met his match on the desert fringe of Outremer. If he couldn't stand against the Abomination, it seemed no man could.

The dragon shifted and looked towards the Hospitaller.

He didn't wait any longer, and rode with speed towards the nearest castle, bearing news of Wormslayer's fate.

He would return with an army.

Not that he felt much confidence it could prevail where great heroes had failed.

Behind him, the dragon took its first steps away from the pit.

~ * ~ * ~

DJ Tyrer dwells upon the northern shore of the Thames Estuary, close to the world's longest pleasure pier, in Southend-on-Sea. They studied history at the University of Wales at Aberystwyth, worked in education, and have a particular fascination with language, spending any free time working on conlangs. DJ is the person behind *Atlantean Publishing*, which has been going for more than two decades, and has been widely published in anthologies and magazines around the world, such as *Winter's Grasp* (Fantasia Divinity), *Tales of the Black Arts* (Hazardous Press), *Pagan* (Zimbell House), *Misunderstood* (Wolfsinger), and *Sorcery & Sanctity: A Homage to Arthur Machen* (Hieroglyphics Press), and issues of *Fantasia Divinity*, *Broadswords and Blasters*, and *BFS Horizons*, and in addition, has a novella available in paperback and on the Kindle, *The Yellow House* (Dunhams Manor).

DJ Tyrer's website is at https://djtyrer.blogspot.co.uk/

The Atlantean Publishing website is at https://atlante-anpublishing.wordpress.com/

Don't Mess with Dragons

Craig Crawford

Iqrii towered over the corpse, his full form filling much of the cavern. Sorrow and disgust slipped through him as he ran his eyes over the body.

The young dragon had been decapitated—no doubt a trophy being paraded and displayed somewhere. Iqrii spied other wounds including bruises from magical strikes. Blood trails on the ground showed six missing claws on the front limbs.

More trophies.

Iqrii warned Margota to be careful multiple times. Several bands of "dragon hunters" roamed the lands of Cy looking for targets. Margota, only a couple hundred years old, hadn't soaked in enough magical strength yet to warrant a tough hide, and he'd done a little strutting too. He'd bragged about dropping on a roving band of mercenaries and cutting them to shreds three moon cycles back.

Iqrii warned him then not to underestimate the humanoid races because they multiplied like rats and worked in teams like ants.

Iqrii reshaped to his favorite human form: a thin young man looking just past the age of adulthood. Stepping carefully, he looked for clues. Shifting his vision, he saw no heat signatures remained. Margota's corpse smelled a few days old. Iqrii wouldn't have contacted him again for months if it hadn't been for their earlier conversation and Iqrii wanting to impart a couple of extra defensive measures to his young friend.

Nothing remained of Margota's wealth—the assassins picked everything clean. The debris from two magical protections lay in disarray near the entrance. Someone dismantled them—a savvy wizard too. Iqrii passed along the instructions for a snare and a defensive field and whoever snuck in took them both apart.

Iqrii quietly scanned the inside of Margota's entire cavern. He let his eyesight slide back and forth between infrared and different color spectrums looking for information. He happened to look up and spied an extremely faint aura near the cavern ceiling.

Iqrii levitated himself upwards.

Forty feet up, he discovered a gem set into the underside of an outcropping. Clever—Margota hid a multifaceted gemstone into the rock. The invaders probably hadn't looked upwards, especially with Margota's wealth all around him. Even an experienced wizard would have been thoroughly tested to sense it this far up.

Iqrii dug it out. Margota had listened to at least some of Iqrii's suggestions after all. He pulled out the Eye Stone and wrapped his hand around it. Coalescing with the energies, he saw through the stone. It showed the chamber below and it took no time for Iqrii to rewind to the attack.

Six of them invaded, a woman leading the way. Iqrii watched as she slipped in first, dismantling the protection grid Margota set up. And she did it without stirring the young dragon—impressive for a human. She was a real threat not to be underestimated.

As she stepped through and then dismantled the magical snare, a monstrous man—one of the mountain folk from the southern steppes, muscled and wielding a huge axe, stomped in landing the first blow. Two others spread out shouldering bows. One of the archers belonged to the race of shadow people who lived on the northern edge of Cy. Just like their name, their dark skin and a form of magic allowed them to blend into their surroundings. Another danger in Iqrii's eyes. A second wizard—a younger man, kept to the woman's side. He prepared defensive spells for his friends, but he didn't possess the same caliber of power as the woman. Their leader, a tall, gaunt man shouted out to the others, directing the onslaught.

Iqrii watched as Margota's eyes snapped open after the first blow, groggy and unawares. The axe cut deep into his neck and arrows peppered him about the face, distracting him. The female countered Margota's one attempt at an offensive magical counterstrike and the battle barely lasted two minutes.

Iqrii wasn't convinced Margota would have survived the axe strike even if he had managed to kill everyone.

Iqrii replayed the sequence a dozen times, taking in the actions of each person in the cave. He noted details as to how they struck, the weapons they brandished, and the tactics used. He replayed it over and over until satisfied.

Pocketing the Eye Stone, Iqrii laid his own magic upon Margota's corpse. Returning to his original form, stretching far larger than Margota, he coughed up a huge chunk of spittle and doused Margota's body. The slime oozed across Margota's corpse, covering and dripping down the sides.

As the outer layer dissolved, the air mixed with the contents of Iqrii's incendiary sac and Margota's body erupted into a pillar of fire.

Iqrii watched the remains burn, making plans behind his eyes. "No one else is defiling this corpse." He stayed until the body was only ash, then shrunk back to his human form. He exited and followed Margota's killer's most likely path.

~ * ~

Geffrey snuck out the window well after dark and ran to the home of Rambert, the taxidermist. His place sat further out along the edge of Amberton, but the heroes brought in the dragon's head and Geffrey wanted to see it. His buddy Cord saw it when they returned from raiding the dragon's cave, but Geffrey had been stuck in the fields with Da. They wouldn't let him come out later either.

A fire lit the inside of Rambert's house, meaning he or his wife was awake. Rambert's work shed sat behind their house so he might be able to get a look inside. Sneaking along the road and alert for other people still wandering about, he crept his way past their house.

The half-moon offered some light, and it was late enough Geffrey guessed most people lay in their beds. He could slip in, take a peek and get home before anyone noticed. Geffrey slid around the side of the house, keeping below the windows and worked his way to the shed.

He abruptly halted.

No light shown inside the shed, but the door hung open. Geffrey crouched down into the shadows and watched. Had Rambert come back out or not stopped working for the night? No way he left the door unlocked, let alone open—not that anyone in town would steal the dragon's head. From what Cord said it was bigger than either of them and took two men to carry it.

Something thumped from inside the shed. Not loud, but Geffrey heard the shuffle of a boot on flooring. He tensed. Rambert must have come back out, though without a torch or lantern. Had he forgotten something?

Geffrey held his spot, hoping the man would leave and head to his house. He didn't want to go home without getting a look at the head. He'd never seen a dragon, living or dead, but he listened to the stories from the mercenary bands when they rode through town.

Faint noises continued from inside the shed and Geffrey almost turned around. If Rambert came back out, he might get caught and that meant a whupping the next day.

A dark shadow emerged and stood in the doorway. It looked Rambert's size in the gloom and Geffrey froze, afraid to even shift his position. The man stood still, neither leaving nor reentering the work shed. His head turned slowly, settling in Geffrey's direction.

Geffrey held his breath.

A blue glow erupted from the man's eyes, lighting up his face. It wasn't Rambert. This man looked years younger; dark haired. From the glowing eyes, Geffrey knew he was a wizard of some kind.

"Come here child," the man said.

Geffrey prepared to run, but his arms and legs didn't respond. Suddenly he stiffened, those blue eyes boring into his own. Helpless, he stood and walked forward. He tried to halt his legs with each step, but they worked against him. He stopped directly in front of the man. "Follow me," he said, spinning on his foot and walked back inside the shed.

Geffrey entered and panic reared. In the faint light from the man's glowing eyes, he saw a body on the floor. It looked like Rambert.

"You'll do nicely," the man told Geffrey. "I need a messenger and I've a task for you before you return home. I've learned much but tell me what you know of Amberton and the tavern where the dragon killers are holed up."

~ * ~

Geffrey walked up to Haffrey's Pub, hanging just outside the front door. He peeked in through the window as ordered. He saw everything, but it felt distanced, like his consciousness watched from the back end. The other wizard sat behind his eyes, taking everything in. Except Geffrey didn't feel like this wizard was a person. He couldn't explain it, but as he caught words and thoughts, they felt different than human—alien.

Geffrey felt himself pushed further back and he felt the sensations of falling asleep.

The place jostled even as the hour closed upon midnight. Partying continued from the previous few evenings and anyone who was anyone stayed late. The locals hung on every word and reveled in the presence of these travelers.

Iqrii spied the mountain folk plopped onto a bench, the frame sagging with his girth. He flirted with one of the townswomen. A short, thin man recounted their deeds, relaying how they'd gone head-to-head with the beast only to kill it.

Iqrii soured.

The female sorcerer sat at a big table listening to the others, but he doubted she drank very much. She didn't appear the partying type and her eyes still flashed with alertness. Their leader and the other wizard, though, they looked like they'd tossed back several drinks. It was the shadow person—a female who looked ill at ease. Probably the well-lit tavern—they didn't like bright lights or being out in the open.

Watching for several minutes, gauging each of them in turn, Iqrii finally sent his will through the child and ordered him in.

Geffrey burst through the door, working up panting breaths. Some of the conversation died and frowns slid over several faces wondering why a boy so young wandered so late.

"What is it, Geff?" The pub owner called. "Jerrick will have your hide for slipping out this late."

"It's...Rambert."

The beefy pub owner shook his head. "What of him?"

"I snuck to his place to get a look at the dragon's head, but he was arguing with someone."

More frowns. "Who was he arguing with, son?" the leader of the dragon killers asked.

"I don't know, but he was mad. He slapped Rambert and knocked him down. I turned to run, but he caught me. He hurt Rambert and sent me directly here."

Everyone shut up, all eyes on the boy.

"This other person—was it one of our people?" The pub owner asked. "Or a stranger?"

Geffrey shook his head back and forth. "No one I know. He threw Rambert on the back of his horse and brought him here. Told me to get the dragon killers."

As much booze as the mountain man had probably consumed during the evening, he sobered almost instantly and grabbed his axe like it weighed nothing. "Boy," he growled in a deep baritone bark. "Describe him."

"Tall, but younger; maybe ten years on me."

"And he knocked Rambert around?" The pub owner asked, disbelieving.

"Like he was nothing. He's outside and he told me if you didn't come out, Rambert is as good as dead."

"Delhi, Faerd," the leader said. "Out the back and around to the front on either side. Maarit. Gurdin, Padraig and I are going out front. You cover our backs and prepare for a fight."

The woman nodded. "Aris, you sure you don't want me around the side with Delhi?"

"Keep behind Gurdin to give you cover until we know what's going on. Let's go people."

Everyone else in the pub backed out of the way, the shuffling of chairs and the clunking of mugs setting down on tables the only other sounds. Delhi, the shadow woman, slipped out of the light and out the back without creating a sound. Faerd followed her lead, ducking left. Aris strapped on his blade and led the way out the door.

Out in the middle of the street a man sat slumped and tied to a barrel. He faced sideways, his head down and his arms limp. No one else walked the street in either direction.

Aris carefully stepped off the porch of the pub and into the street. The mountain man gripped his axe in both hands, his eyes sliding up the street and then down the other side. The younger wizard, Padraig, produced a small metal rod, holding it in front of him crossways.

No one approached the man tied to the barrel.

"I don't see anyone," Padraig whispered.

A young man casually stepped out of the darkness, seemingly from nowhere.

"You're the one who tied Rambert?" Aris called.

"Yep."

"Why? What is this all about?"

"My first thought was to ambush you. I thought about sending the boy in with an incendiary and taking one of you out while picking off the rest one at a time. It would have worked easily enough. From the look of things you've been carousing for a good amount of time. I'm guessing you're not at your best."

"What do you want?" Gurdin barked.

"A layered series of sneak attacks wouldn't have been difficult at all. But those are the tactics of assassins. Which, after all, is all you are."

"Did we do something to you, friend?" Aris asked.

"I've heard bragging about facing the dragon in the caves, strutting in and taking him steel to claw. It's what you told everyone in town. You didn't tell them what really happened—how you snuck in like cowards."

Gurdin slapped his axe haft against his meaty hand. "Anyone calls me a coward is looking to die."

"Call a tree a tree and a rock a rock."

Gurdin took a step forward, but Aris stopped him with an arm. "You haven't told us who you are or why you're here. Why did you attack Rambert? He had no part in this."

"He has the dragon's head. He's fashioning it into a trophy. In my book that qualifies as being involved."

"You better not have hurt him badly," Aris said.

"Oh, he's dead. No doubt about that."

"Aris," Maarit hissed. "He's radiating magic. He's literally shining like a bonfire."

"Who are you?" Aris asked.

"I could have employed multi-layered attacks and taken all of you out one after the other, but I realized it would only be seen as the same base tactics employed by humans. It wouldn't invoke any real fear. The fact is, it would only place me alongside you, sneaking up on someone from behind."

"That's enough!" Gurdin roared. "I'll not be taunted and slandered by a whelp. You apologize here and now or by Rord, I'll strike you down and they'll tell stories about the stain in the road."

"Oh, I'm no whelp. Not like the one you skulked in and killed unawares. No, I decided the best way was to show you and everyone in town you don't mess with dragons. Even the young ones sometimes have friends. Much older, more powerful friends."

The young man slapped his hands together and light strobed, momentarily blinding all of them. Blinking out the lights behind their eyes, they watched as the young man's form flowed like water, expanding in all directions. It grew to a height well beyond the mountain man. The entire body radiated a glowing blue aura. Two sets of tapered wings spread out on either side of its body, rounded and reminding them of a dragonfly. A long indigo tail wound out from behind ending in a crystalline barb.

This dragon raised up on two legs, and two more sets of arms stretched along the length of its body. A long neck swayed above them ending in a slim head. Bony crystalline horns jutted from the back of its skull and it looked down on them with large metallic blue eyes like an insect. "Let's see how you stand up against a real dragon."

Maarit fired a crackling beam of white energy Iqrii's way.

He raised two of his clawed limbs and spread his talons like a fan. The beam's trajectory bent and fired harmlessly skyward. His other two sets of talons closed into fists and knocked together.

A shockwave fired forth slamming three of the four in front of him to the ground. Aris, Padraig and Maarit bowled over backwards, slapping against the street.

Only Gurdin withstood the onslaught. Mountain folk outweighed the other races holding almost four times the girth, their bodies several times denser. They were also notorious for shrugging off magic and spells. Gurdin bellowed at the top of his lungs and rushed forward cocking his axe high in the air.

Iqrii's tale whipped around like a long blue streamer. It struck in a blur and the crystalline spine sunk into Gurdin's side just under the armpit. He grunted, but it knocked him off step and he stumbled forward. Losing his momentum, Gurdin got an arm out and flipped sideways, skidding across the ground. He missed Rambert and the barrel he was tied to, but he flopped into the street.

Iqrii rose to his full height and slammed his back leg over Gurdin, smashing him to the ground.

Arrows fired up into Iqrii's face from two different directions. One glanced off the top of his head missing his eye, but another stuck into the side of his cheek. Ducking his head, Iqrii snapped his head around and spat a viscous goo, spraying it from one side of the pub to the other.

Aris got his feet under him and grabbed Padraig by the arm, scooting him backwards. "Get to cover!" He yelled.

Maarit used her own magic and created billows of thick smoke. They poured out from her hands, and she spread it out above them, creating an opaque cloud.

The front of the pub exploded in fire. Flames shot to the sky twice the height of the building. Fire and light flashed spreading to the buildings on either side of the pub.

Gurdin struggled from underneath, but Iqrii leaned his full weight on the big man. He gasped and growled. "Let me up and I'll show you the bite of my axe, dragon!"

"Gladly." Iqrii's twin sets of wings beat together creating a staccato hum. He raised upwards off the ground, one of his feet clamping around Gurdin's back. He dug his talons into the man's sides and the reverberating wings lifted them both off the ground. Iqrii swung his foot and tossed Gurdin into the front wall of the pub.

Aris, Padraig and Maarit ran up the block, getting beyond the burning pub front and the building next to it. The arrows quit for the moment, and Iqrii scanned the sides of the building, shifting through different visual spectrums. He spied the shorter archer ducking around the back corner of the pub but saw no sign of the shadow woman.

Gurdin flopped out of the flames from the front of the pub, rolling and slapping at the fire on him. He panted and winced. One of his meaty hands looked charred and black. He managed to get to his feet, looking for his axe. Iqrii spied it too and flicking one of his talons, sent the great axe skittering across the dirt toward the mountain man.

Gurdin staggered and picked up his axe. He winced, flinching toward the side where Iqrii punctured him with his tail.

"You're about done, mountain born. The tail isn't just for skewering." Iqrii slid sideways through the air as his four wings carried him up the block. His eyes stayed on Gurdin for a moment longer, watching the giant man shudder. He swayed as the poison took effect. Gurdin teetered on his feet but managed a step. He grunted again, overbalanced and dropped to the ground.

Iqrii spied the other three ducking into a storefront, two buildings up the block. His wings shifted in tandem vibrating loudly and he swung over the top of the building. Hovering, both sets of Iqrii's front limbs gesticulated, creating shapes and patterns.

A barrel of blue light fired downward and smashed through the roof of the building. Ozone hit his nostrils and through the hole, crackling flashes of cerulean light danced around inside.

Immediately a line of crimson erupted from the other two limbs and the backside of the building was doused in fire. It burned through the wood lighting everything it struck.

An arrow ricocheted off of the side of Iqrii's neck. Another followed it, but it snapped as it struck Iqrii's magic hardened skin. Continuing to hover above the burning building, Iqrii swung his head around.

On the backside of the pub another arrow fired from the shadows. It ricocheted off one of his horns, barely missing his eye.

Iqrii shifted his wings and his bulk swerved around toward the area. He saw no one, but his front limbs summoned more energies. Clapping his talons together, a violent spray of white light bathed everything on the ground.

Nearby people cried out. So did the shadow woman, nestled up against the side of a building. She wavered on her feet, her arms covering her eyes and Iqrii swung in from above. He fired his tail stinger and caught her just below the ribs. She shrieked and slammed into the wall.

Iqrii pivoted and flew back to the street, positioning himself three stories above the ground. He watched the front entrance of the burning building the dragon killers had ducked into. Flipping through visual spectrums again. He spotted people from Amberton watching from the shadows, but they only watched from the shadows.

Seconds ticked by and then Maarit and Aris exited the building. Maarit fired purple light in his direction and Iqrii took the hit on his left side. He didn't quite understand the spell, but it burned. Both sets of arms churned again, the first set creating a siphon to draw off whatever the woman struck him with, and the other two sent an attack Maarit's way.

No light show preceded Iqrii's manifestation. One of his talons gestured upward and Maarit suddenly shot straight up in the air. She rocketed skyward several hundred feet.

Iqrii focused on the wizard while his tail feinted strikes against Aris. The man deflected the crystalline barb with his blade retreating with each strike.

Iqrii's talon darted downward and Maarit dropped the entire distance to the ground. She cried out and almost managed a spell, but the ground came up fast and she smashed into the dirt with a loud thud.

Aris watched her hit and his arms slumped. He lowered his blade. "You've got us. We can't win."

Iqrii lowered himself to the ground. "You shouldn't have killed my friend."

"Your friend assassinated a group from Batterdam. We were hired to look into it."

"People always assume dragons are solitary creatures and we never talk to one another unless mating. They certainly never entertain the idea we might welcome each other's company."

"It still killed our people," Aris said.

"There's plenty of you."

"You know our kind takes affront to other creatures killing our own."

From his peripheral vision, Iqrii spotted a lone heat signature crossing two blocks down the street working itself behind a building. Iqrii snorted. "Your kind is a funny lot. You have no problem killing your own but take it personally when something else dares to do so."

"You can kill me, but others will come."

"Like ants," Iqrii said. "And I suppose by letting you go; you can broker some peace."

"No. My employer will send others, and more each time. Sooner or later we'll get a group big enough to take you down."

"Your kind is also very short sighted. Dragons are not physical creatures by nature," Iqrii said. He landed, his buzzing wings silencing. His great body immediately melted in size, shrinking back into the form of the young man. "We walk among you every day and most of you never know it. Even your friend, the sorceress. She sensed my magical ability, but she didn't pick out my control of the boy. We come and go as we please."

"We can still hunt you down. There are great wizards on Cy."

Iqrii laughed. "And some of them are friends with our kind. Most of them aren't stupid enough to challenge us. Whom do you work for?"

"Telling you will only lead to their demise and despite the threat of death I won't talk."

"I can grab you and ream your mind for the information, but I promise you if I have to go that route, I'll make it uncomfortable."

"Be that as it may. I won't bend. I have my integrity."

"Well spoken," Iqrii said. "I respect that. Your honorable in that at least, even if you are an assassin. You've still one member of your cohort alive. I'll kill you quick."

In a blur, Iqrii produced a spear with his magic and fired it. Aris deflected the spear, but the spear exploded on impact instead of glancing harmlessly away. Aris flew backward, losing his sword and collapsed in a heap. Magically taking hold of Aris's blade, he arced it up and pinned Aris to the street.

Spinning, Iqrii crossed the road, looking into the infrared spectrum. Several people milled about, but they didn't have the correct heat signature. Iqrii slipped around corners and people backed away from him. Iqrii ducked around buildings and through other streets before he found the last of the dragon killers.

The man saw him and took off at a sprint, but Iqrii used his magic to trip him into the dirt. Catching up quickly, he magically took hold of the man and levitated him into the air. "You are the one called Faerd. Yes, I sent your companions to Morana's lair in the realm of the dead. They can sit alongside my dragon friend. I require information which you will supply one way or another. Do you prefer to answer questions, or shall I take a magical route?"

"Will you let me live if I tell you what you want?"

"Agreed. It will help for you to tell of the night a dragon exacted revenge for killing one of its own."

Iqrii spent the next several minutes questioning Faerd as he floated in the air. No one in town got close, let alone tried to interfere. After a multitude of questions, Iqrii finally let him down. "You have a task before I agree to let you live. Two tasks actually."

Fear crept into Faerd's eyes. "What is it you want?"

"Everything you stole from the dragon's lair will be returned. Any money you paid from the dragon's coffers will be returned, and I mean all of it. I have ways of finding out if you did or not," Iqrii lied.

"Okay. I...I don't know if I can convince the people we've paid to give it back, but I'll try."

"If you don't, I'll come back. Tell them that. You and they are responsible for returning his provisions."

"What's the second thing?"

"You will return my friend's head to his cavern. And the claws you cut from his fore limbs. Then I want you to post notice that any who defile the lair will be subject to punishment. Tell all the tales you need to, but I will be watching. Anyone who violates his tomb lives on borrowed time. Do we have an understanding?"

Faerd silently nodded.

"Good. It's a small atonement for the deviltry you and yours have committed, but it serves a fitting punishment."

"What of my friends?"

"Do with them what you will, but their souls are meeting Morana. I didn't tally the male wizard, but I doubt he survived the hell I rained down on him inside the second building. They paid their price for killing my friend and defiling his lair. I suggest you find another line of work from here on out. I'm spreading the word among my kind. I'll have an accounting with your employers and my kind is going to set some new standards for coexistence. We're tired of this treatment."

Faerd only stared.

"Go," Iqrii ordered. "Spread word of my demands and don't

forget to tell them the penalty for ignoring me."

Faerd skittered back through the street toward the pub.

Iqrii watched him disappear. The people he named would be harder to kill, but then again, even if Faerd somehow warned them, they wouldn't be prepared.

They were only human.

~ * ~ * ~

Growing up, **Craig Crawford** read all the time. After being wowed by so many great novels, he got to wondering about these people who created all of these awesome stories and wondered if he could do it to. He's spent many years writing novels and short stories with a few, minor successes along the way. In the last two years, he's published eight short stories with five more due out in 2021 including a novella. He writes in fantasy, sci-fi, YA, horror, humor—whatever his imagination gives him.

You can check out his publications and other stories at his website if you have the curiosity: craiglcrawfordbooks.com.

Do Not Disturb

Gregg Chamberlain

A fireball roared past overhead just as Berens stumbled, almost falling to his knees. The hair on top of his head curled and crisped in the brief, blast-furnace heat.

The fireball exploded far down the mountain path. The brief glare ahead outlined Kasparov in silhouette, the fluorescent letters IFAR big and bright on the back of his windbreaker. Berens struggled to his feet and resumed running after his companion and fellow member of the Institute for Advanced Research.

"Let's go...to the Hörst Mountains...you said," Berens gasped, pulling up alongside Kasparov. "It'll be...an adventure...you said."

"Shut...up," Kasparov retorted, wheezing like a set of bellows.

Together, they hurdled a fallen pine tree blocking the mountain path. Behind them, loud and close, thundered the crash of other trees as they splintered and toppled to the ground.

"Folklore research...what could go wrong?...you said..." Berens was panting. "Check out...legend of...Sleeping Dragon... you said."

"Will...you...shut up!" Kasparov hissed.

They stumbled, almost tumbling, as they raced down the narrow mountain path. Stones loosened from the scree slid treacherously beneath the soles of their hiking boots. The ground beneath their feet trembled as they skipped and slipped along.

"Scientific...curiosity...you said." Berens' breath whistled as he sucked in air. "F-f-f-find...the truth!...behind the legend...you said."

"Jussst...sssshut...up!" Kasparov was gagging for breath.

Both felt a sudden wave of heat behind them. Berens dodged right; Kasparov left. Another fireball exploded on the path in the space they'd both occupied a moment before.

Berens, coughing and choking, crept out from behind a tamarack's blackened trunk. Looking across the cratered path, he saw Kasparov struggling free from the charred clutches of the underbrush.

"Mix business…with pleasure…you said." Berens panted, leaning against the hot trunk of the tree for support. "Fresh air…nice scenery…local beer…It'll be…fun!…you said."

Kasparov glared back at his co-worker. He took a deep breath. "Shut." Another deep breath. "Up!"

Their heads both snapped around at a rumbling roar from back up the mountain. As one they began running again, away down the path. The ground shook, sending them both flying through the air before the earth rose up again to smack them in the face as they landed.

"So tell me!" Berens shouted, levering himself up, spitting out dirt and pine needles. "Are we having fun yet?"

Before his partner could reply, a gigantic shadow loomed over the two, eclipsing the daylight.

A re-energized Kasparov leaped to his feet and streaked down the path, arms pumping. A frantic Berens followed, struggling to close the wide gap between them.

"Just. Shut the hell. Up!" Kasparov screamed back over his shoulder at Berens. "Shut up and run!"

Angry roaring chased after them down the mountain.

~ * ~ * ~

Gregg Chamberlain lives in rural Ontario, Canada, with his missus, Anne, and their two cats, who consider dragons to be wusses. He writes speculative fiction for fun and has several dozen published examples of the fun he has in various magazines and anthologies. Some day he hopes to see a dragon, but maybe not up close.

More Great Anthologies from WolfSinger Publications

Cat Tails: War Zone – edited by Rebecca McFarland Kyle and Dana Bell

Cats have been our companions since long before they graced the temples of Ancient Egypt. In addition to being members of our families, they have also stood with us through difficult times. From keeping pests and vermin away from our food stores to providing a comforting paw when we have been wounded; cats have been our sidekicks and friends in many different battles.

Cat Tails—War Zone contains twenty-five stories from Ancient Egypt to the far-flung future, about some amazing cats who have served as compatriots during war times. But beware, for they can also be tricksters sent to teach lessons.

The real heroes are the volunteers of SHADOW CATS, an Austin, Texas-based rescue that has saved the lives of 9,000-plus cats since 1997. Trappers, veterinarians, nurses, and adoption social workers volunteer to trap, neuter and return ferals, provide care for ill, injured and behaviorally-challenged cats, find perfect adoptive parents, educate on proper feline care, and advocate for real change in communities.

Proceeds from this book will continue their efforts.

Unintended Consequences – edited by Carol Hightshoe

For every action there is an equal and opposite reaction –
Newton's Third Law of Motion.

While Newton was talking about motion when he developed the above law, it can also be said that for every action or decision there is a consequence: sometimes good, sometimes bad.

Many times consequences can be foreseen and planned for. But there are times they are never seen. It is these unforeseen or Unintended Consequences that can have the biggest impact on individual lives.

An android working to pass as human.

A woman who loses her pre-destined 'soul mate' on world where they were marked at birth.

A Queen who uses magic to make her subjects more cooperative and helpful to each other.

A wife who authorizes a radical treatment for dementia to be performed on her husband.

And 16 more who will learn about the unintended consequences that will affect their lives.

Just Desserts – edited by Rebecca McFarland Kyle and J.A. Campbell

Whether you like your revenge with the molten fire of a fine old Scotch or the cool sweetness of a tasty meringue, the nineteen tales within these covers should offer something to assuage you.

Narcissistic co-workers, thieves of affection, and bad neighbors are given their due in ways imaginative and sublime.

Love 'em, Shoot 'em – edited by Dana Bell

One should never be afraid to love or shoot the one they care about. A famed markswoman once said that. Or so it's claimed.

Imagine a town with a dog sheriff from another planet.
A zombie attack clean-up woman.
An attractive alien who likes to play love goddess.
A magical concert with dead musicians that gets out of hand.
Or those of the old west who meet aliens.
Those from the far future hunted for not volunteering to die.
A woman who learns a lesson with a twist during war time.
And more…

Come along with our writers and travel the diverse trails of their tales, of loving and sometimes shooting, in these pages of Love 'em, Shoot 'em.

Extinct – edited by Dana Bell

What if those ancient creatures so beloved in fiction, myth, and science had not disappeared? What if they were real? What might have been developed to handle them, and how might man have felt about the thundering giants in yesterday's, today's, or tomorrow's worlds.

Imagine a sanctuary established for dinosaurs that displaces humans.

What if Raptors were used on a distance planet as scouts for the new colony?

Could Dodo birds have left a record about what happened to them? Dragons helping settlers? Inconceivable!

A conqueror learns a hard lesson from a goddess and two children create their own 'monster'.

Lovely, unique, tales of lumbering giants of old, ancient rulers of the skies, and many others once thought to be myth or legend appear here in Extinct?

Tales From the Fluffy Bunny – edited by Carol Hightshoe

Welcome to the Fluffy Bunny

We welcome everyone—especially those with a story to tell. Adventurers, mercenaries, guardsmen, merchants, noble and peasant. Whoever. If you have a tale to share, then come in and have a seat. First drink and a hot meal are on the house.

What's a tale without an audience to appreciate it? So, even if you don't have a tale to share, come in, pull up a seat and enjoy these 17 tales of how a warrior or their weapon earned their name.

Visit us at www.wolfsingerpubs.com for more information

www.ingramcontent.com/pod-product-compliance
Lightning Source LLC
Chambersburg PA
CBHW051102030726
47504CB00006B/1749